About the Author

Alan Gillespie is a writer and teacher from Fife, Scotland. He has studied at the Universities of Stirling, Glasgow and Strathclyde. His articles and stories have appeared in *The New York Times*, *The Guardian*, *The Herald*, *Northwords Now* and *New Writing Scotland*, and elsewhere. In 2011 he was awarded the Scottish Emerging Writer's residency at Cove Park. *The Mash House* is his first novel.

D1385667

The Mash House

Alan Gillespie

unbound

This edition first published in 2021

Unbound

TC Group, Level 1, Devonshire House, One Mayfair Place, London W1J
8AJ

www.unbound.com

ISBN (eBook): 978-1-78965-120-1
ISBN (Paperback): 978-1-78965-119-5

Cover design by Mecob

Printed and bound in Great Britain by Clays Ltd, Elcograf S.p.A.

For Chloe

Super Patrons

Geoff Adams
Jürgen Albers
Jason Ballinger
Lynne Barclay
Helen Bell
Tommy Bell
Sandy Benson
Samuel Best
David Beveridge
Layla Blackwell
Nicola Booth
Thomas Booth
Karen Brand
Georgina Buggie
Ian Buxton
Chloe Cannon
Colin Cannon
Kerry Cannon
Alberta Capasso
Paul Carlyle
James Carson

Jason & Laura Clark
Jason Cobley
Alex Cox
G Craig
Chris Crooks
Barry Crookston
Alan Crossan
Ross Cunningham
Stef D'Andrea
Elaine and Mark Dalloway
Hannah Davenport
Felicity Devanney
Marie Devanney
Michael Devine
Gloria Dhandapani
Rachel J Docherty
Ian Donnelly
Mark Donnelly
Lorraine & John Drew
Dennis Duncan
Justine Dunn
Alexis Elliott
Brooke Elliott
Brendan Farrelly
Kirsten Ferrol
Matthew Francis
Kerry Fraser
Lorna Friel
Craig Gallacher
Mary Frances Gallacher
Anna Gillespie
Carole Gillespie
Graham Gillespie

Iain Gillespie
James Gillespie
Jimmy Gillespie
Joseph Gillespie
May Gillespie
Pam Gillespie
Sofia Grace Gillespie
Peter Glen
Umer Goraya
Emma Grae
Chris Graf
Kathy Higgins
Robert Higgins
Michaela Hinchin
David Hodge
Peggy Hughes
Steven Hughes
Monique Huston
Barry Hutchison
David Irvine
Clifford Jaine
Troels Vang Jensen
Graeme Kane
Susan and Allan Kerr
Bryan Laing
Erik Lankman
Chris Lavelle
Ewan Lawrie
Laura Macdonald
John MacInnes
Iain Maloney
Scott Manson
Chiara Marini

A M McAllister
Susan McArdle
Alan McClure
Bob McDevitt
Ann McGinnis
John McGinnis
Alan McGowan
Cara McGuigan
Alistair McHugh
Graham Mcilduff
Erin McQuillan
Naomi Mitchell
Caitlin Murphy
Laura Murphy
Nicola Murray
Stuart Murray
Calum O'Neil
Susan O'Reilly
Susan O'Donnell
Jonathan Parkes
Simon Ray
Cheryl Anne Rennie
Holly Robertson
Mark Ross
Olivia Ryan Cairns
Harris Simpson
Julie Ann Simpson
Riley Simpson
Keith Sleight
Amanda Smith
Denise Smith
Raymond Soltysek
Siobhan Staples

Helen Steele
Gillian Stern
Gillian Stockley
Fiona Strang
Kirsty Strang-Roy
Kerry Tait
Sophie Tierney
Trish Tougher
Natalie Trotter-King
Jacqui Trowsdale
B van der Meulen
Leanne Welsh
Matthew Wilson
Sandra Wilson
Erin Wood
Michael Woods

1

The cat's brains were pink and glistening in the glow of the clear, high moon. Rivulets of blood puddled on the concrete. The dead thing's limbs were folded, and its face looked away from the road, towards the loch. The night was silent.

Alice had been driving with the windows open, and when she hit the cat the sound of its bell tinkled noisily until it landed, but now the road was silent. The blood formed a jammy shadow around the cat's body.

Alice pulled her car onto the verge. The Shore Road that ran parallel to the loch was wide with a good surface and quiet at this time of night. She sat on the bonnet and lit a cigarette. She always smoked when she was alone. Innes would take them from her mouth and stub them out.

There were a few houses nearby, but Alice had not lived in Cullrothes for long enough to know who the cat's owner might be. The creature had a red collar around its neck and a white love heart on its flank. The road was dark with no street lights, and the water on the surface of the huge loch moved softly.

Alice slipped her sandals off and stretched her toes on the cold concrete as she finished the cigarette. Smoking here,

1

polluting this clean, crisp air, felt subversive. Although it was dark and silent, she thought someone could be watching her. She pushed her hair behind her ears. It was blonde but needed a cut and a fresh bit of colour. She took a step towards the cat and looked at it again. If she had a signal she could call someone, but her phone was useless in the village. You had to get to higher ground before getting anything. She squatted and focused on the cat's side to see if its lungs were still expanding, to see if its paws or tail might still twitch.

Nothing. She stood and looked out to the water, smoking the cigarette down to the filter, until she caught a burn on her lower lip. The loch here was endless, small ripples rising like hackles and falling against the pebbled bank. People went out onto this water in canoes at the weekend. There were fish farms out there somewhere, further along the coast, hiring up all the kids who left school without good enough grades to move away for university. When she first moved up here there had been men standing out in the loch, the water up to their chests, casting fishing lines. The tourist information kiosk sold postcards to campers and tourists of the loch glowing as the sun went down behind it. This was the village's key attraction, along with the Cullrothes Distillery that put on tours and sold expensive bottles in the visitor centre.

Alice turned back and looked up and down the dark road. She bent and sunk the burning, fizzing cigarette butt into the dead cat's flank, right in the middle of that white patch shaped like a love heart. She rotated the filter as it smouldered then expired, the smell of singed hair reaching her. The cat's brains looked as though they were already drying out, the pink turning to grey, the blood congealing and settling. She gripped the cat's hind paws and held them together in her right hand, lifting the thing up and away from her. A drooling slobber fell from the wound in the cat's head and dangled in a thin strand to the road. Alice swung once, twice, keeping the corpse away from her dress and then released, following through onto her tiptoes, and the cat soared, rotated, twisted a little, visible only in the moonlight, and landed lightly in the loch. There was barely a splash.

When Alice was wee, a neighbour's cat had jumped on her head and got its claws caught in her hair and pulled her crying to the ground. She had always hated cats.

Alice stepped into her sandals and returned to the car. She turned the key and the interior light came on with the engine. On the passenger seat was her teacher planner, emblazoned on the front in gold font: Cullrothes Community School. Her breath tasted of smoke. Innes hated when she smoked. Said he could taste it way back down in his throat. She rummaged in her bag until she found some mints, shifted into gear and pulled back out into the road.

2

The phone box felt small with the door closed. Its glass sides sealed Sandy in from the fresh air and it was hot and muggy. He stood with his hand resting on the receiver so that he could pick up on the first ring, knowing how loud that sudden noise would feel in the quiet of the night. He had used this phone for years when he was a child, making hundreds of phone calls to his father asking for lifts home and extra pocket money when he had ventured too far and spent everything he had on sweets. His breathing was just returning to normal after the long, difficult hike through the heather-quilted glen, his heart rate settling. His feet were sodden from losing his bearings and skirting a marsh. But driving or walking east along the A861 would raise suspicion at this time of night, long after the ferry's last timetabled crossing to the mainland, when the roads were almost entirely empty.

The ferry was moored a little way out from the shore, its engines dead, with a few lights at the highest point of the mast twinkling. This ferry took only seven minutes to shuttle people back and forth to the mainland; after its last crossing at 8 p.m., the only way to escape the peninsula was to drive for three hours around the loch. The ferry took commuters to and tourists from the mainland, hikers and campers and caravanners turning up in their thousands every summer to ruin the beauty of Sandy's childhood home. You felt comfort knowing that nobody else was likely to turn up in the village once the ferry was finished for the night; a sense of isolation too.

The phone rang.

Sandy snapped it up, the noise echoing around the small chamber. He glanced up and down the road, one direction leading to the ferry terminal a little way up the lochside, the other winding through the glen for some miles, back to Cullrothes. He saw nothing. Heard silence.

He lifted the receiver to his face. Hello?

Hi.

Thanks for calling.

Half past eight. Just like your message asked. This is the number for the phone box at the ferry port isn't it?

Yes.

Who am I talking to?

I want you to buy a story from me. You do that sort of thing, right?

Depends on the story. What have you got?

I need money for it.

If the story's good, we'll pay. But it depends.

Sandy glanced up and down the road again. The anchored ferry had drifted a little closer to the shore, its white paintwork reflecting like a ghost on the water.

It's about the Distillery. There's stuff going on there. Things that shouldn't happen. I think you could make quite a big story out of it.

Are you an employee?

I don't want to say.

Listen, if we publish a story, we need to have proof to back ourselves up. Without photographs or other hard evidence a story's too risky to run. It's just something a guy's overheard or made up. So, if you've got a good story about the Distillery I'm interested, but I need more information.

It's drugs. The place is full of them. I don't know what kind it is. Brown powder, green buds, little pale pills. I haven't worked out how they get in. Might be by boat. Then they're kept at the warehouse until they get picked up by the delivery lorries. Going out all over the country. I don't know where he gets them from or where he sends them, but there's millions of the stuff. I've got photographs.

He?

Donald Fleck. The boss.

Have you gone to the police?

No. I wanted to see how much it was worth. I need money for it. I'm not bothered about it, he can do what he likes. Doesn't affect me. But I thought you could help.

And you've got photographs already? Hard proof?

Yes.

You work there?

Okay, I do.

I'll need to talk to my editor. I might be able to get you a couple hundred for it. I know it's not a lot, but I'll need to see the pictures and clear up some details. Ask the managing director for a statement. Do you live on site? One of the cottages at Distillery Lane?

The managing director?

Yes, Mr Fleck. We'll need to ask him to comment before we run it. Out of courtesy.

I'm not sure that's the best thing to do.

It's got to be done. Legal thing.

Can't you just run the story without that? A public interest thing? You'll sell a bunch of papers with it.

The voice on the other end of the phone began to laugh gently. Sandy tightened his grip on the receiver.

We already sell plenty of papers.

Yes, but this story, it's a scandal. It's huge for this area. Can't you just run it and make your money? You don't need to go asking Donald questions. Leave that to the police, if they think it's worth doing.

Are you scared of him? the voice asked. Does he frighten you, Sandy boy?

He battered the receiver into its cradle, slipped out of the booth and into the blackness of the forest by the side of the road. Sandy's heart butted against his chest and his ears roared. He turned back to the trees, which he knew so well from childhood games, and ran, his feet slapping into the mud, ran back to the village, to the Distillery, to the cottage in the lane where he should have been all night.

3

Alice scraped her hair back into a ponytail as the school bell rang. The children in the playground quietened as they lined up, and slowly the junior class came into the classroom, shrugging their schoolbags from their shoulders and dropping them to the floor. Cullrothes had an all-through school for pupils of all ages, streamed into junior and senior classes.

Good morning children, said Alice once they were all in. It was a bright and well-lit room with pictures of the children's work on the wall with their names underneath. Colourful display boards with punctuation guidelines and the classroom rules.

Good morning Miss Green, they chanted back in unison.

Alice walked around the tables as the children settled, pulling their pencil cases from their bags and hanging their little blazers on the hooks on the wall.

A chubby boy with messy hair was still standing near the doorway, rubbing his nose.

Derek, hurry up and get your stuff out.

The chubby boy's eyes were red, his lips chapped.

Derek, she said again, moving closer to him, and the boy struggled out of his blazer.

Settle down, boys and girls, called Alice. Come on, we don't have all day.

The children turned and faced a statue of Christ on the cross which hung over the chalkboard. Mary our mother, said Alice, crossing herself.

Guide everyone at Cullrothes School with your kindness and understanding. Teach us to be responsible and to always help others. Lead us when we are lost, and comfort us when we are lonely. Amen.

The children all copied Alice in crossing their chests, and then turned as a crowd to face Derek. His pink cheeks were wet with tears and his hands gripped at his dirty brown hair.

Derek, said Alice. Sweetie, what's wrong? She walked to him in quick steps and knelt down to his height.

Nothing, the boy whispered. Some of the children began to laugh.

Alice stood up. Does anyone know what is wrong with Derek?

A little girl with blonde hair put her hand up.

Yes, Ellie?

I live next door to Derek, said Ellie. He's upset because his cat has ran away in the night.

He has not, snapped Derek.

The cat didn't come back last night, continued Ellie. It was out all night. Him and his dad were out in the street shouting for it all morning. I heard them when I was getting my cereal.

Well, said Alice. I can see why that would upset you. But listen, sweetheart. Cats are resourceful. Sometimes a cat may stay away for days or weeks at a time before they come home. What's your cat's name?

Derek turned his head away from the teacher.

It's called Hercules, said Ellie. And it's black and white with a patch on its side shaped like a heart.

The rest of the children broke into loud whispers. Alice felt a ripple deep in her stomach and her face grew warm.

Class, called Alice. I need you to stay quiet. One voice at a time. Yes, Oliver?

The little boy called Oliver had a closely shaven head and his ears stuck out when he smiled. He pushed his glasses up his nose and said: Miss, can we make posters to try and get Hercules back?

Do you know, I think that's a brilliant idea. We can make posters. And we'll put them up in the village. Let's get Derek's cat home safely! Who can think of where the posters could go?

The children's hands shot up.

The shop, said one boy.

At the Distillery, said Ellie. Put them up in the visitor centre.

Oliver suggested the bus stop, and then the noise in the class bubbled over until Alice called them once again to attention.

You're quite right. The village will rally round to find Hercules. Would you like that, Derek? Would you like your classmates and your neighbours to help find your cat?

His chubby face was bright red, but he nodded, and there was a little smile forming on his dry, broken lips. The teacher smiled at him, enjoying herself, happy with the chance to bring some real-world context into this morning's lesson. Having never imagined how well this would turn out.

Alice organised the children into tables of four and gave each group coloured sugar paper, blunt scissors, glue sticks and some colouring pencils.

I have my own pens, said Ellie. Can I use them?

Only if you share them with your group, said Alice. Derek, come and sit here.

The chubby boy sat next to Alice at her teacher's desk. She wrote on a blank sheet of paper. When did you last see Hercules?

Yesterday afternoon.

Did you let him out?

No. It was Mum.

Was Dad at home?

Derek shook his head.

Alice lowered her voice to a whisper. Is everything okay at home, sweetie?

Derek pursed his lips and nodded.

Did you have a bath this morning?

I slept in too late.

It's very important for you to get up in time to have a bath and eat breakfast and get to school on time. You're not a wee boy anymore. We need you to be here fresh and ready to learn in the morning. Do you understand, sweetie? She wrote a few notes about their conversation on a piece of paper. Go back and join your group now, Derek.

The boy wiped his nose on the back of his shirt sleeve and sat back down with his classmates.

Children, shouted Alice. You have twenty minutes left to finish your posters. They need to be bright and colourful if we're going to get Hercules back. Make sure you put the words MISSING and CAT onto them. They need to have a drawing of Hercules as well. Does everyone know what to do?

Some of the children nodded and said Yes, Miss Green, while the rest of them carried on working. Ellie looked at Derek, but the boy was staring out the window, to the grey sky and the distant mountains, and the dark loch that lay a quarter mile away from the school grounds.

4

The old manse was on a low hill and from here you could take a footpath through woodland to the church, and then there was also a road leading down to the A861 a half mile west of the village. The Flecks had bought it from the church in the 1950s and now the priest lived in a little rented cottage down near the loch. The villagers had quickly accepted the new hierarchy.

Donald was in the fine tiled kitchen where he ran the tap and let the water grow hot, holding the back of his hand underneath the flow until it was too hot to touch. He lifted the light plastic basin up to the sink and held it there. Squeezed in some soap and let the hot water fill the basin halfway. Then he opened the cold tap on full and held the basin as it grew heavy with the water and the foam expanded.

What's this? said Margo. She was sitting in the living room reading a magazine and Donald came through struggling with the weight of the basin. Foam near spilling over the top where his hands gripped the rim.

I thought you might like a foot bath.

You're so nice, she said. Donald manoeuvred the basin gently to the floor in front of her. His knees crunched as he bent them and he groaned with the pressure.

Are you alright? That didn't sound good.

Fine. A bit stiff.

Margo bent down to pick off her socks and roll up the legs of her trousers.

Ready?

Ready.

She sat back and Donald took a foot in each of his hands and guided them gently into the foam and into the water. Margo stretched her neck and put her head back and moaned when her feet went under the warm water.

That's so nice, she said. That is lovely.

Donald held both of her feet there and firmly ran his thumb across her heels and up to the toes and massaged the gaps in between them.

I spoke to the accountant today, said Donald.

How did that go?

He stopped rubbing and looked up at her. Last year was not a good year.

We thought that.

Now we know it. We need to find new ways to get legitimate money coming in. Sales are down. People just aren't buying whisky like they used to; it's not our fault, it's happening across the board. It's all there on the balance sheet.

But we're okay?

We're fine. With the other money coming in that the accountants don't know about, we're fine.

Our hidden portfolio.

Yes, laughed Donald. He held one of Margo's feet in both of his hands and ran his fingers between her little toes, bending them back and rubbing them.

We could open the bedrooms up for guests again?

Donald shook his head. By the time you've paid for staff and for heating the place we'd just end up losing more money.

13

Well maybe it's time we started looking for some investment, she said. Make the books look a little better.

I'm not taking out a loan.

I don't mean that. I mean an investor, a backer.

Some Billy big baws to come in with a saviour complex. Thinking they'll swoop in and rescue us? No thanks. My father ran the Distillery on his own. He didn't pass it on to me just so I could sell it off when things got hard. He'd come bursting out his grave if he thought I was getting someone else in to help. He hated asking for help.

They heard the front door open and close. Young Bobby was back from work at the Distillery. He came into the living room and stopped still when he saw them. What's going on here, he said.

I'm giving your mother a foot rub.

Nice one. You can do me next, said the boy. He touched his father on the shoulder then sat on the couch and gave his mother a kiss on the cheek.

How was work? Margo said.

Fine.

Did you get the rota finished? Donald said.

Aye.

Did you remember about Sandy's holidays?

I said aye, didn't I?

Make sure of it. He's on holiday next month. No shifts.

You can trust me. I'm a big boy now. Young Bobby turned to his mother. What's for dinner?

Chicken and potatoes.

Mash?

Roast.

Sounds good. I'm meeting someone at the pub later. Can I borrow twenty quid?

Young Bobby looked at his mother, but his father answered: Do we not pay you already?

I'm running low this month. You can take the twenty back out of my wages if you want.

Then you'll be running even lower next month.

For God's sake, Dad. It's only twenty pounds we're talking about here.

Just so you can go and piss it up against the wall? Or is there a game on, is that it? Or horses? Or cards? Who you planning on giving my money away to tonight?

Young Bobby was balding already and his eyelids had begun to grow dark. It was clear that before long he would look similar enough that people would mistake him and his father for brothers.

It's fine, said Margo. I'll give you the twenty. It's only twenty! Call it an early Christmas present. Get me my purse.

Which one? asked Young Bobby.

The purple one.

Where is it?

In the kitchen.

Young Bobby left the room, and Donald opened his mouth to speak. But Margo interrupted him.

Just you keep on rubbing, she said, patting him on his bald head. That feels good. That feels really good.

5

Here came the girl Jessie in her grey school blazer with the shapeless pleated skirt and there was rainwater creeping in the toes of her shoes. A small-built girl going on sixteen with a bit of pink dyed into her hair and a smile that showed her diastema. The bag over her shoulder was weighed down with ring binders and textbooks to help with her exams and its bulk dragged at her collarbone. It had been a short walk through the village to get here. She sheltered beneath the awning of the low white building and pressed buzzer number 15.

Then she waited.

It was getting dark out. She had finished her shift cleaning at the hotel after school and her fingers still stank of bleach and old beer. A pile of discarded cigarette butts had blown into a corner next to the security door and she kicked at these with one foot, clearing the doorway for the residents to get in and out without slipping.

There was a quiet buzz from the telecom. A crackling little static. Then the door unlocked itself and she knew to push it open even though no voice had spoken.

In the hallway a strip light flickered. The air smelled like bad breath and chemicals. Newsletters about doctors' surgeries

16

and delivery services clung to a noticeboard. There was a handwritten sign too, which hadn't been there on her last visit. Sadie's Funeral, it said, Will Be Held This Thursday For Those Of You Who Are Interested In Attending.

The schoolgirl took the stairs two at a time and when she got to the first-floor landing, she looked up, smiling already, because Grandpa would be standing there in the doorway of his little flat, smiling back at her.

She walked quickly down the corridor to him and they kept on smiling at each other until she was close enough.

Hiya Grandpa, she said.

Hiya toots, he whispered, and showed her inside.

Grandpa's flat was roasting hot and she took off her blazer and kicked off her shoes before sitting on the little couch for visitors. Grandpa followed her in, leaning on his stick, his free hand stroking the wallpaper in case he needed it for support. He finally dropped into his armchair. Jessie waited while he cleared his throat.

So, he whispered, how are you?

I'm fine, she said. I've just finished at work. Remember I told you I was starting at the hotel? Just doing a bit of cleaning, washing the bedsheets, mopping the floors, that sort of thing.

Oh yes.

Just a couple of hours after school. It's cash in hand.

Grandpa held his hands out wide. Nice to make a bit of money, he said.

I'm sure it will be, she said. I'll let you know how it feels when I actually get my wages.

Oh, he laughed, that will be good.

I'll take you out for lunch, she said. A wee treat.

Oh, he said. His voice was serious now. That would be wonderful. He picked up a napkin and wiped his mouth and his nose with it. I always think, he said, it is so important to

17

earn your way. And never to get yourself into debt. He leaned forwards in his chair and spat the last word out.

Well, she said, that's why I took the job.

Good for you, toots. How's your mum?

Jessie's mind went back to the dark room with the thin carpet and the curtains drawn always to block out the sun. She's the same.

Ach, he whispered. Is she getting out and about?

No. She won't go out.

You would think she would want to. Staying in like that is not good for any of us. She just has to get herself outside.

She doesn't think it's as easy as that.

Well.

Never mind. How are you feeling Grandpa?

He sat back and cleared his throat. I've just had to make a doctor's appointment, he said. Have to wait a couple of weeks for it. So we'll see what they say.

For a check-up?

Grandpa pointed at this throat. I've been struggling to swallow, he said. Going to see about that.

Struggling to swallow? she asked.

Struggling with solids, he said. Liquids are okay. Tea, coffee, soup. Porridge. Fine. Anything else is getting harder and harder.

That doesn't sound very good.

Grandpa picked at a loose thread at the cuff of his shirt. He reached into a cabinet next to his armchair and got two shot glasses and a bottle of Cullrothes whisky. I can still just about manage a wee goldie, he said.

Jessie got up and held the two glasses steady while he wrestled the cork out and poured the drinks.

This one's my favourite, she said.

Mine too, he said. Well, here's to your first job. And he clinked his glass against hers.

And here's to you being able to swallow again, she said, and poured the drink down her throat in one. Grandpa took another mouthful, started laughing, and spat his whisky out into a napkin.

Jessie shivered as the whisky hit her stomach then she went to Grandpa's kitchen. Underneath the sink was a basin with sponges, bleaches and furniture polish. She took these out and sprayed down the kitchen surfaces. Squeezed a ring of bleach around the toilet cistern and wiped the seat. Grandpa had a lot of family photographs on the walls and she sprayed these with polish and then wiped the frames. One of her grandmother, long gone now. One of her cousin, a blonde wee boy, who lived in Australia. One of herself as a little girl, wearing dungarees, raking up leaves in somebody's garden. One of her father wearing a white shirt and a black tie at his graduation from the police college at Tulliallan. One of her mother, in a summer dress, laughing as the wind blew her hair on a foreign beach. Grandpa kept that one up even after her parents' divorce. He had never blamed her for it.

In the living room, she tidied Grandpa's envelopes and appointment cards into a neat pile next to his armchair. She took a few dirty mugs away and stacked them in the sink. Grandpa's bed was at the back of the living room, and she shook the covers and fanned them out and tucked them in neatly for him.

There we are, she said. Good as new.

Order is restored, he whispered, and smiled.

The carpets look okay, she said. Maybe I'll leave the hoovering until next time.

Oh, forget them, he said. He gripped the whisky bottle and poured out two more big nips.

How are you going to get to the doctors?

Bus.

It'll take you all day to get there and back. Can you not get a lift from somebody?

I'm happy looking out the window. And besides I've nothing to rush back for.

They drank these whiskies and then one more. At some point, Jessie put a record on. Old jazz music. Grandpa conducted the band with his thick hands and mouthed the lyrics, his eyes shining wet whenever the words brought some sad old memory back to him.

When Jessie was leaving, he lifted himself from his armchair and put his hands on her shoulders. Thank you for coming, he said.

No problem. I'll see you soon.

Oh, he whispered, I hope so.

I'll get you out for your lunch once these wages come in.

I'll look forward to that.

Okay, Grandpa.

Tell your mum I was asking for her.

I will.

Bring her round with you, next time.

That would be good. She's always asking after you.

Okay, he said. Bye, Jessie.

Okay. Bye for now.

6

Two men stood on the doorstep, their faces hidden by the peaks on their hats. Standing in the doorway, Sandy squinted at one and then the other, and looked down the long gravel driveway, to the wide gate which remained closed, and beyond that the cluster of low, white buildings of the Distillery. One of the men stepped forwards into the light, a smiling face with a heavy beard.

Oh, said Sandy. Moodie. It's yourself.

It's me and the boss, said Moodie. Come over for a chat.

Sandy nodded and stepped inside, opening the cottage door wider. Moodie came in, wiping his feet and rubbing his hands together. After him came Donald, the boss, who said nothing but thrust a full bottle of whisky towards Sandy's chest.

I'll get some glasses, then.

Moodie took off his hat and admired a framed picture hanging in the hallway: a landscape scene, stags grazing in the foreground, armed men surveying from a nearby hill.

Right, Moodie, said Donald. You know what's what.

The two men stepped into the lounge, slipping their short coats off. Dull flames burned in the hearth. A warm night outside but in the old cottage it was bone cold. A dirty plate sat on the arm of the chair positioned next to the fireplace.

Donald placed the bottle of whisky on top of a newspaper which lay open on the table. It was the Cullrothes 18-year-old, turned golden amber after its long marriage with the Spanish Oloroso sherry cask. Okay, he said to Moodie, and both men sat at the table after dropping their coats and hats onto the armchair.

Sandy came back with three glasses. He carried them with one hand, and in the other he held a small dish of crystallised ginger. Donald thumbed the cork from the bottle and poured three large measures. He tossed the cork into the fire.

Slainte, said Moodie, holding his drink out.

Sandy nosed the glass and sipped, holding the whisky in his mouth, swirling it around his tongue. He nodded, satisfied. What can I do for you this evening, gentlemen?

Moodie raised his eyebrows and glanced towards Donald, who had not yet drunk. The boss held his glass delicately, swirling it in slow circles. His eyes met cleanly with Sandy's and he drank the whisky in one quick mouthful. I'll have another, he said. Sandy and Moodie finished their own drinks before the glasses were filled again.

I got a phone call today, said Donald, from our friendly Officer Galloway. Our old pal. Seems that someone in our employ has been letting secrets slip.

Right, said Sandy, taking a long sip. Christ.

Finish that drink, said Donald, picking up the bottle again.

I'm fine the now.

Finish it, said Moodie, leaning into the table. With his coat off you could see the Celtic tattoos running up his big arms.

Sandy scratched the back of his head and downed the whisky. Donald filled the tumbler up halfway.

22

How long have you lived here, Sandy? Lived rent free, in my cottage, on my land?

Twenty-six years, said Sandy, and laughed. Christ, twenty-six years it's been. And I'm grateful for them, boss. Always will be.

Do you remember the state you were in when I hired you? Living at your mother's, relying on the dole for money, and drinking all the money you did get. We got you out of there, set you up here. You've become a man here, Sandy. Got yourself sorted out.

Sandy was about to object but Moodie nudged the tumbler across the table with his fingers. There was half a glass and Sandy opened his throat, pouring it across the top of his tongue. He slammed the glass down and swallowed, feeling his eyes water. That's enough for me, boss.

Donald pinched his nose and filled Sandy's glass back up.

I was telling you, Galloway phoned me up. Says he's come across information about illegal activity up at the Distillery. Specifically, the distribution of drugs. Pills. Powders. All over the Highlands. Lucrative, is what he hears. A complex and well-established infrastructure. Suggests he might have to come up and inspect the site. Access the warehouse. The barrels.

He can't do that. Not without paperwork. A warrant.

True, said Donald. He filled up Sandy's glass again. The bottle was only half full now. Galloway couldn't come on site without a warrant. But he doesn't need one. Galloway's an old friend. I've been topping up his pension for years now.

Sandy reached out for the whisky, rescinded his hand, then went back for it. Took a sip. Galloway's in your pocket? I never knew.

Wasn't in my interests to tell you. I like to keep myself to myself. Galloway's a good company man.

Moodie poured a half measure into his own glass and tilted the bottleneck forwards in Sandy's direction. Drink up, man.

Sandy's eyes were pink, and he poured the whisky into his body more slowly this time, savouring the taste. I didn't mean to hurt you, Donald, he said. It's money, man, I'm drowning; it's gambling and loans and I didn't know what to do. Galloway comes to me, says he can help. Just needs a wee bit of information, something from the inside. I never told him anything they could pin directly on you Don, I promise.

Moodie filled all three glasses again. Sandy held his with both hands, swaying on his chair. Donald swirled his, took a sip. He threw a piece of ginger into his mouth, chewed. Took another sip. Moodie read an article from the open newspaper.

I'll let your boy keep the cottage, if he wants it. And keep him on.

Sandy looked up. That's good. Thank you, Donald.

Drink your whisky.

Sandy did. His cheeks were red and when he breathed out the smell of alcohol was strong.

You're a stupid man, Sandy. You never did grow up, even when I thought you had. All the chances you got here. Every benefit. You're still that pathetic wee boy you were when I first met you.

Sandy could no longer speak. He hung his head. Donald nodded to Moodie. Moodie reached out and squeezed Sandy's shoulder. Go and run yourself a bath, man.

A bath?

Fill it up.

Sandy was pleased for an excuse to leave the room. He pushed the chair in and walked into the hall, using his hands on the wall to keep himself straight. The telephone sat on a low table, the cord tangled around itself and the cream handset stained. He thought of phoning Galloway but knew that he couldn't. What could he say?

The hallway led on to the bathroom and also the kitchen. Sandy paused between the doors; he could hear Moodie and Donald muttering to one another. In the kitchen, he opened the cutlery drawer and lifted out a bread knife. He ran his finger along the corrugated teeth and put it back down, swaying heavily against the worktop. A cup of tea would be good. The kettle was already full, and he flicked on the switch at the socket with a loud click.

Sandy, called Moodie's voice. Can't hear any water running in there, pal.

The whisky pulsed in Sandy's head; his cheeks ached from it. He stumbled to the bathroom and turned on the hot and cold taps at the same time, dropping the plug into place and squashing it down with his thumb. The roar of heavy water rattled off the tiles.

No bubbles, called Donald. Moodie laughed loud and quick then stopped.

Sandy looked at the waterline creeping steadily along to the end of the tub. The bathroom door was still open, and he retreated from there, into the hallway, over to the cottage door. He opened this and it swung to without a sound. Sandy stepped over the mat, onto the path, and the night's sharp wind caught in his throat like flesh. The gardens were dark, and the white ghost of the Distillery seemed to crouch below the mountains in the distance.

Closing the door behind him, Sandy came back into the cottage. The kettle rattled and struggled with the boiling water and then ceased. The bathroom doorway held a curtain of light steam. He went in there and looked into the half-filled tub.

Sandy had always been a slim man, thin as a pick when he was young. Now his body was looser, with a soft belly hanging delicately below his smooth sparrow's chest. He lifted his shirt over his head without undoing the buttons, folded the sleeves behind the collar and placed the wee parcel on the toilet seat. Donald and Moodie came into the bathroom behind him, blocking the doorway. Sandy unbuttoned his denims and dropped them to the floor, kicking them to the wall. Moodie had a full glass of whisky again, and he reached over Sandy's shoulder and put it in his hand.

Okay, Sandy. He took the drink and finished it fast and held the empty glass to his chest, swallowing with his head tilted upwards and his eyes closed.

That's enough, said Donald. Moodie stepped forwards and closed off the taps. The tiles fell silent as the water settled to a smooth surface. Their bodies pressed against Sandy's back and he shuffled forwards.

I've boiled the kettle, said Sandy. Can I have a tea?

Neither man answered, then after a moment Moodie left and went to the kitchen.

In you get, said Donald. Sandy hooked his socks off with his toes and kicked them to the skirting board where his trousers lay. He stood in his underwear with Donald behind him. In the harsh bathroom light Sandy's skin was jaundiced and scarred with dark shadows that shifted as he moved his weight from one foot to the other and stepped out from his faded and threadbare underwear.

Listen, Don. The whisky had smudged Sandy's voice, but he spoke with sincerity. You are like a father to me, and I am sorry. I should have come to you when I needed help. I owed money, a lot of money, and you could have helped, but I wanted to sort it out on my own, I didn't want to let you down. I've humiliated myself. Ruined my name. Court summons through the post. Debt collection men ringing me up. This is not the kind of man I am. It is not who I want to be. It's Galloway's fault. He made me trust him. He is a snake, Don. You shouldn't keep it going with him. He betrayed me and he'll do the same with you as well if he gets the chance. He knew I needed that money. He's smart. Knows how to get what he wants out of people. It's a terrible thing to be desperate like that. It's all paid back now – I'm back on terms and out of debt and I'll never do it again. I'm finished with all that.

Sandy cried a little, his cheeks turning red and his mouth wet at the edges. He bent and unwrapped a few sheets of toilet paper from the roll, wiped the corners of his eyes dry, his lips, and then blew his nose, clearing the nostrils.

Donald blocked the doorway and said: Get in the water, Sandy. Hurry up.

The bath was too hot and it burned Sandy's foot but he got in, hands gripping the sides of the bath as he lowered his body into the scalding heat. Sweat formed on his forehead. The water was still shallow, and he slipped as he settled into the steaming water.

Loyalty, Sandy. Loyalty is important to me. I've been loyal to you for your whole life. You are correct. I would've helped you, but you never asked, did you? Without loyalty this business is finished. There's plenty of men that've worked at this Distillery that I never trusted. I never let them in any further than they needed to be. But not you. You're living in my mother's own cottage for Christ's sake. You're calling Galloway a snake? At least he knows it. You're a worm, a sly wee worm hiding your secrets in the dirt. You'll take another whisky?

Donald stepped away from the bath and stood in the doorway. In here, Moodie. Another whisky for our pal Sandy.

Moodie came from the kitchen and handed Sandy a full measure of the Cullrothes. Sandy shook his head and stared at his own body, so Moodie dropped the glass into the bath, the tumbler rolling off Sandy's belly, the stench of the drink mixing with the steam from the hot water. In his other hand, Moodie held the toaster from Sandy's kitchen, and it was connected to an extension lead that ran into the hallway, where it was plugged into the electrics. Moodie perched the toaster on the towel rack next to the bath so that it was level with Sandy's head. He depressed the button and the empty toaster began to buzz and glow.

Donald nodded. Then he turned and left the kitchen, through the short hallway, opened the cottage door and was out into the night air before Sandy had managed to articulate his screams into cogent words. Pleading and cursing like a child.

He closed the door and walked slowly down the path, stopping to take a piss in the vegetable patch where Sandy had been growing rhubarb. Donald reached the gate at the bottom of the garden, then turned and looked back at the low cottage, the one his mother had lived in when she was dying. The kitchen window was opaque and misted from the boiled kettle, and the living room was softly lit by Sandy's lamp and the fading embers from his fireplace.

It was only when the lightbulbs flashed and scorched his retinas, then extinguished to black, that Donald closed the gate and walked away from the dark cottage.

7

The bell above the shop door tinkled when Alice went in with a bundle of papers under her arm. It was a dark shop, with a low ceiling and no windows, but it was the only place in the village to buy newspapers and essentials and it had a licence to sell alcohol. In the corner there was a small stand with merchandise for the tourists. Postcards, tartan hats, ornaments. Along one wall was the pick and mix range of sweeties. Where children queued up at lunchtime and filled the little paper bags with flying saucers and cola bottles. And in the back corner a freezer chest with boxes of frozen food for anyone who couldn't get a big shop from the mainland. They could come in here and buy a frozen pie or a frozen curry for the microwave or a tub of ice cream.

Alice stood at the counter. The woman behind it moved slowly from her chair next to the gas heater.

What can I get you? she asked.

Can I put one of these posters up in your window, said Alice. It's for one of my pupils. A wee boy whose cat's gone missing.

The woman took the poster. You're the new teacher, she said. At the school.

Yes. Alice Green. Nice to meet you.

Mmm, said the woman. She turned her eyes to the poster. I know this cat, she said. Smelly wee bugger. Stinks of tuna fish.

I'm putting posters up all around the village, said Alice. I thought your window would be a good place.

Oh yes, said the woman. But there's not much point, is there? If the wee fella's not home by now, he'll be dead. Hit by a truck or picked up by a hawk. Jumped by a fox. Something or other'll have got him. Don't you agree?

Well, said Alice, the kids have made up these posters anyway. I said I'd put them up.

You're welcome to it. But we don't supply the adhesive.

Alice took the poster back. She had some Blu Tack in her bag and she stuck it at the four corners to the window.

The old woman watched from behind the desk, then spoke: This new manager they've got at the hotel, he's your man, isn't he?

He is.

Are the pair of you settling into the village alright? And you're up here from Glasgow, is that it?

Yes. We like it so far. The scenery's beautiful.

The shopkeeper stared at the closed door as though she might see the view of the loch through it. True, she said. But you can't eat the scenery, can you?

The bell above the door chimed again and a weathered man came in wearing waterproof overalls. Alice recognised him. One of the ferrymen who helped load and unload cars on the Corran Ferry for those coming to and from the mainland. There were always two of them at work, whatever the weather. With their walnut faces and hunched shoulders.

Packet of cigarettes, Brian? asked the shopkeeper. Alice picked up a newspaper and flicked through it. There was a story about someone dying of a drugs overdose over on the mainland.

Brian leaned on the counter with hands that were as wide and pink as crabs.

Superkings, he said. Then: did you hear about Sandy?

Sandy Bell?

Aye, Sandy Bell.

What about him?

Found. Dead. Done himself in. Up at the Distillery.

The shopkeeper raised her hand and ran her thumb and middle finger against her temples, guarding her eyes.

A suicide?

Aye. Found him in the bath. Had a live toaster in there with him. The wiring in the whole place is shot. He never came in for work so big Gav Moodie went up there and that's how they found him.

What a sin, said the shopkeeper. A suicide. Can you imagine it?

The ferryman thumped his hands gently on the counter. Aye.

Just the cigarettes is it, Brian?

No, he said, I'm taking a box of this beer as well. He went to the side of the counter where the alcohol was and picked up a box of twelve bottles. I'll drink these tonight. Have a toast to Sandy.

It's a sin, said the shopkeeper. She started punching at the heavy buttons on the till so the man could pay for his cigarettes and his beer.

Alice put the newspaper down and opened the shop door to leave. Before she went out, she turned around. Excuse me, do you work on the ferry?

Aye.

She pulled one of the missing cat posters from her bundle. Could you put one of these up for me? You've got a sort of noticeboard on there, don't you?

31

Brian stared at it.

It's for a missing cat.

I can see that. We're no exactly going to find it swimming across the loch now are we.

No, she said, but could you put it up for me just the same? She put her hand to her throat and touched at her windpipe. Please?

Brian folded it up and the poster disappeared inside his overalls. Aye, he said. No bother.

Alice left the shop and walked down the Shore Road, enjoying the early September breeze around her bare legs. The loch was big and blue and gulls hung high in the air. After half a mile she opened the gate to the little cottage where the priest lived. She had not met with him yet but knew that he was familiar with the school and the children. He was down in the calendar to come and give mass in the assembly hall before the end of the month.

She knocked on the cottage door but nobody answered. The windows were obscured from the inside by net curtains. She slipped one of the posters from her bundle, folded it twice and balanced it in the priest's letterbox.

Alice stepped back and admired the cottage. It was built from strong blocks and whitewashed, with well-tended flower baskets hanging on each side of the door and an ornate crucifix pinned to the middle of it. It was the kind of cottage you might see in a magazine, and the small garden was green and flat with clipped trees along the fence to give the priest privacy from the traffic on the road.

Alice sucked in her cheeks and started to salivate. She let her mouth water then pouted her lips. Pushing outwards with her tongue she spat, quietly and without great heft, onto the door of the priest's cottage.

At the bottom of the garden path she latched the gate carefully once again behind her.

8

Donald woke with the alarm ripping him from sleep. The bedroom pitch black. He threw his hand at the clock and shut it off. But he was awake now.

He stretched and felt the sinews in his knees and elbows crunch. His pillow was damp with sweat. There was the smell of cooking food. He swung from the bed and opened the thick blackout curtains. Gorgeous sunshine flooded the room. Donald could only sleep when the room was in total blackout.

He went downstairs and Margo was in the kitchen listening to the quiet radio. She was barefoot with a short dressing gown wrapped around her. Morning darling, he said, and kissed his wife on the cheek.

She drew a line of butter across some hot toast. How did you sleep?

Better.

Is your shoulder still hurting?

Yes. I keep rolling over onto it when I sleep.

Have you taken any painkillers?

No.

You should.

Donald grunted and sat down at the table. It was wide and

dark oak with ornate legs. He sat on a high-backed leather chair. Directly across from him was the oil painting of the racehorse he'd bought on his last visit to the auction house.

Margo wiped the crumbs from her dressing gown and stacked the breakfast plates together. You never told me how it went last night, she said, when you went to speak with Sandy.

Well, said Donald. He admitted the whole thing. About leaking the story.

Stupid man, she said. Sandy, Sandy, Sandy.

It's dealt with now.

How did it go?

Couldn't have gone better.

And your hands are clean of it?

My hands are squeaky clean.

Let me know once you've spoken to Father Jaine, said Margo, about a date for the funeral. I'll do the flowers. From the garden. I've got some nice pots coming in.

You don't need to do that.

I want to.

That's nice, said Donald. That'll look good.

Donald showered while Margo cleaned up the breakfast dishes. He took a coffee out into the garden and settled on a wooden bench. As he bent his knees to sit there was the familiar grinding crepitus in the joints. It did not hurt at this time. Margo did have the flowers looking well this year. The lawn was neatly trimmed. Donald's father had purchased the Old Manse years ago. Donald wondered how much he would get for the manse now if he was to sell it. If he ended up deciding that he had to sell it.

From here Donald could see all of Cullrothes and all that he controlled. The sandstone hotel at the edge of the village, plump on the Shore Road for everyone who came in and out to see. The low white buildings across to the left towards the glen where the Distillery and its tied cottages stood. Where Sandy's body would soon be planted. The rambling wee houses and bed and breakfasts where the villagers and the tourists stayed. The pebbled beach and the choppy waters of the loch, and beyond that the mountains and the distant forest and the sky which was brilliant blue this morning. He drank his coffee and felt that this was a happy day.

9

The headteacher's office was bright, with floor-to-ceiling windows that looked out over the playground. Concrete surfaces with coloured lines and smudged chalks. In the corner was a standing lamp and on a corkboard there were pinned handwritten letters and colourful cards that said 'thank you' and 'good luck' and 'best teacher'.

Alice waited for Mrs Hughes to take her seat before sitting opposite. She put her teacher's planner on the desk, ran her fingers through her blonde hair and sighed. I love your dress, she said. It looks great on you.

Oh, said Mrs Hughes. Thank you. She was a short woman with a tight brown bob and a flat stomach.

Very flattering. I love the colour.

The headteacher put her palms flat on the desk and smiled. So, she began. I like to catch up with new staff after a few weeks. See how you're settling in, get your impressions of the school, find out if there's any problems. Anything I can fix? Nothing out of the ordinary?

Great.

How do you think you're settling in?

I think it's going well, said Alice.

What do you think is going well?

Alice sat back in her chair and looked to the ceiling. Good question, she said. I suppose I'm happy with the classes so far. The pupils are well behaved. Obedient. Keen to do well.

And what does that mean? Keen to do well.

I think it means that they're very compliant. They do as they're asked and they pay good attention.

We try to discourage the children from being passive learners here. Sometimes maybe it's a good thing if they're not compliant. If they're creative and take risks. Don't you think?

That's a philosophy I definitely share. I will bear that in mind.

My big thing is aspiration. You'll push our children as much as you can?

I promise that I will do that.

Excellent. That is what I like to hear. And you're settling well into the wider village life?

Yes. It's beautiful.

Thank you. We like it. That's good. Have you been to see the lighthouse yet?

Not yet.

You must.

We will.

What else is there? Lots of lovely walks. You could take a drive up to the Cat's Back. That's a sort of viewpoint. A tour of the Distillery, if that's your kind of thing. Although I hear they might be going bust.

Really?

That's what I hear.

There was a moment's silence. A clock ticking quietly. Birdsong from the other side of the glass window. The sound of children talking to other children down the corridor somewhere.

But I am glad to hear you feel you've settled in quickly, said Mrs Hughes. She unfolded a sheet of paper and glanced at it and then met Alice's eyes. But I'm afraid to have to tell you there's been a complaint.

About me?

Yes. A very minor complaint, I have to stress.

From a pupil?

From a parent. I received a phone call last night after school.

Alice straightened up in her seat and felt the skin on her neck start to blotch. She thought about the dead cat on the road and the splash in the water. She thought that someone had recognised her. Someone had seen the posters going up.

Before I go into the details, said Mrs Hughes, I want you to know that I am always supportive of my staff. I know this is a stressful circumstance. Especially with you having been with us for, what is it, just under a month? And you have my backing. One hundred percent.

Thank you. But I need to ask, what is it they've complained about? What've they said about me?

It is alleged that you have been using swear words, in front of pupils, during your lessons.

Swear words?

That's the claim.

Alice felt a wave of relief and unlocked her knuckles. The memory of the cat's dead eyes flirted in her mind. She thought about the smell of its fur on her fingertips. A sense of euphoria rushed through her skin making her forearms bristle.

It's ridiculous. I don't swear. Whose parent phoned in to tell you this?

I've decided not to tell you that. I don't think there's any benefit from you knowing which pupil has been at the root of the complaint.

I deny it. It's not true. I don't swear and certainly not in front of the children.

Mrs Hughes folded up the sheet of paper and added it to a tray of documents on her desk. That's what I hoped to hear, she said. Look: sometimes these things can slip out by mistake. I've done it myself before. The children here are very sensitive to things like this. It's a bit of a bubble they're living in away out here. They're not used to certain ways of speaking. Perhaps, unintentionally, you have let something inappropriate slip.

Alice began to protest but the headteacher held out her hand. I'm not going to take this any further, Alice. But please be careful with your interactions.

I always am. Of course.

Mrs Hughes stood up and patted down her dress. Good. Well, that's that.

Alice stood up and they shook hands. Turn around? she asked.

Excuse me?

Give me a little spin. Let me see the back. Does it fasten with a hook?

Oh, laughed Mrs Hughes. She put her hands on her hips and rotated 360 degrees to show Alice the dress. Well?

Gorgeous, said Alice. She picked up her planner and smiled with her teeth at the headteacher and went out the door and walked down the corridor.

At the end of the school day Alice stayed back in her classroom long after the bell. She untucked her blouse from her skirt and opened the windows to let the stuffy air out with its teenage stink and she put the radio on loud. The room was a mess. She went around and straightened the tables and chairs. She gathered all the abandoned colouring pens and put them in the correct containers. She knelt next to the bin and picked up all the pencil shavings that the children had dropped on the floor throughout the day. The pile of textbooks and essays and reports on her desk was so high that sheets were almost slipping to the floor. She went through these and organised them into neat piles, with the most important at the top.

By the time she went to the staffroom to get her handbag, most of the other teachers had left for the day. The cleaners floated about, with quick little steps, spraying and cleaning tabletops as they passed them. Alice stood at the wide double window here and looked out at the empty car park and chewed on an apple someone had left on the table. When she was finished she washed her hands and threw the apple core onto the carpet and stepped on it heavily so that its flesh mashed into the fibres.

Then she was down the stairs and almost out the school's main door before she stopped, looking around at her empty hands, and went back inside. She knocked and entered the office. Patricia was there, organising the outgoing mail.

Is that you away? asked Patricia.

Just about. I think I've lost my umbrella. Anyone handed it in?

No, sorry dear.

Where could I have left it? said Alice. It's not in the staffroom. I definitely had it with me this morning.

Have you checked with the janitor?

I'll do that. She half-closed the door. Then said: Actually, I was in with Mrs Hughes earlier. In her office. Maybe I left it there. Is it okay to check?

Sure. She's already gone so go straight on in.

Thanks. Goodnight.

Goodnight.

Alice walked across the hall and into the headteacher's office again. The blinds were drawn and the room was dark and warm. Mrs Hughes's desk was left neat. Alice lifted some sheets of paper from the tray until she found the document relating to her allegation.

She stood behind the headteacher's desk reading the handwritten notes. She read them again. Folded the paper and returned it to the tray, with the information memorised. About which parent had phoned and which specific child had complained about her. The allegations were lies and it was a relief to know who was behind them.

Dirty little bastards, she said, and let herself out of the office, clicking the door closed quietly behind her.

10

It was late when Jessie got home and the lights were all off. She unlocked the door and dumped her schoolbag in the dark hallway and kicked her shoes into the corner with the rest of them. She heard a light thumping noise from behind the closed living room door. Like someone stamping their feet. As she approached the thumping grew faster. She flicked the light switch in the hallway and her own reflection appeared in the mirror in front of her. Her hair was pulled out from its high bun and straggled each side of her face. The make-up from this morning had faded during the day and she looked pale, tired. Blemishes around her chin. Her school blouse was wrinkled. Her skirt needed a stitch at the hem.

She opened the door and the thumping intensified. Louder, faster, more urgent. She pressed her foot down on the switch of the floor lamp and fell into the couch, one leg curled beneath her, turned to the side. Murphy was up on the couch already and he crawled towards her, shifting his weight and yawning and pawing at her skirt with his big paws. His tail thumped the couch a little quieter now, his enthusiasm sated.

Hello big boy, said Jessie. Hello.

Murphy stared at her. Brown eyes framed in a golden face.

43

He was a five-year-old retriever and he wore a red leather collar.

Hello, she said again, oh, hello. She reached under his chin and scratched. He lifted his head. She cupped her other hand around his ears and rubbed the sinew there roughly. He angled his head to give her a better purchase.

Who's a good boy? she asked, and the thumping tail picked up speed. Who's a good boy?

Jessie unbuttoned the top of her blouse and reached for the remote control. She turned the television on and watched the news. A story about the stock market getting hit. Then a story about drug misuse in small communities. She grabbed Murphy under his armpits and pulled him closer to her, so that his head was in her lap with his forearms stretched right across her. His bony elbows dug into her thighs a little but she was happy with that.

The girl and the retriever watched the news and held one another. A politician was being outed for sleaze. A missing child's body had been found after a manhunt across on the other coast of Scotland. Here, there was a storm coming over the Atlantic.

After the news Jessie went to the kitchen and put the kettle on to boil. While the water heated she cleared her mother's dirty plates and cutlery into the sink and steeped them in hot soapy water. She sprayed the dirty hob with bleach and wiped that down. She stood eating a biscuit, Murphy sitting staring up at her, and looked through the window to the dark garden. Again all she could really see was her own reflection. She had light beer stains on her blouse from spraying out the drip trays. She wondered if she could get away with wearing the same one to school tomorrow.

When the kettle boiled she made a cup of tea and put this on a tray, with a clean ashtray and foil of painkillers. She took this upstairs and Murphy followed, his nose bumping her ankles. Quietly Jessie tapped her knuckles against her mother's bedroom door.

She entered. Inside was an intense smell of smoke and dust. The curtains were drawn tight and the room was only lit from the bulb in the hallway. In this faint glow she could see her mother's shape underneath the bedsheets.

Hello Mum. She smiled. Murphy stayed out in the hall and watched as Jessie approached the bed.

Keep that dog out of here, said her mother.

I will. I brought you some things.

There was an empty dirty mug on the bedside table and an ashtray full of smoked-down filters. Jessie put the new mug and the clean ashtray down and put the painkillers next to them. She put the dirty mug and the full ashtray on the tray next to her mother's cigarettes. There were three boxes of twenty neatly stacked within arm's reach, and one box already opened with the tan coloured filters sticking out.

Can I get you anything else? asked Jessie. She sat on the bed next to her mother. Anything to eat?

No.

How are you feeling?

Awful. Her mother rolled over and looked up at Jessie. I've not been able to get up all day. My head is killing me. You're home late.

I was working after school, remember? Then I went to see Grandpa.

You could have called me to let me know. Why didn't you call me?

I never have a phone signal in this bloody place, do I? What a waste of money that was.

Thanks for rushing back, said her mother. I could have done with you here you know.

I had to give Grandpa's place a clean.

The sheets on the bed felt greasy. Jessie's mother turned her head. Just leave me alone, she said. Like you always do. Go and look after someone else like you always do.

Jessie stood up. I need to take Murphy out. Has he been out today?

Her mother said nothing. Jessie picked up the tray with the dirty mug and the full ashtray and walked towards the door.

You'll never know what it's like to be me, said her mother, just as Jessie was closing the bedroom door. What it's like in my head. What it's like for me.

It was nearly midnight when Jessie got Murphy out for his run along the water's edge. They walked together through the small scheme of council housing with its yellow grit bins and flaking-fronted garages. She had changed into leggings and wore a warm fleece as it was always cold so close to the loch. The moon was high and bright and it caught the silver flickers and black stillness of the water. They walked along the shingles adjacent to the Shore Road that became the winding A871 that led eventually to the ferry and the mainland. But the road was deserted this late at night.

She unhooked Murphy's collar from the lead and he bounced away, a blonde ghost rooting around in the pebbles and straggles of seaweed. He would run so far and then come halfway back to her and stop and wag his tail and then venture further away again. On hot days he would be in the water already, but not at night.

They followed the water's edge around the coastline until the lights from the village were almost all hidden. There was a bench here and Jessie sat down, huddling her arms and legs together for warmth. Up on the road, she heard a car. It slowed and the tyres crunched on the mussel shells that littered the road and then the car sped up again and drove off towards Cullrothes proper.

Murphy, called Jessie, keeping her voice low. Murphy, come on now. The retriever bounded over and stood politely while she reattached the lead to his collar. Come on then, she said, there's a good boy. Who's my best boy?

11

The telephone was ringing in the other room and Innes could hear it from the shower. He stepped out and wiped his feet on the mat and rubbed a towel over his head then wrapped it around his waist. A tall thin body with a hairless chest and a good stomach. The telephone was still ringing when he got there dripping water onto the carpet.

Hello, he said.

This call originates from a Scottish prison, said an automated recording. It will be logged and monitored and maybe recorded. If you do not wish to accept this call, please hang up.

Innes rubbed himself through the towel and pushed the receiver closer to his ear. There was a moment of static silence as the call transferred and then he could hear an echoing background noise of voices and chairs scraping on concrete.

Hello, he said again.

Hello, said a man's voice. Good evening. Thank you for accepting the call.

Who is this?

Can I speak to Alice? I'm looking for Alice.

Alice?

Alice Green.

Innes looked out the window where he could see down the long shingly driveway to the country road that wound down an incline to the loch and the village. You've got the wrong number, he said. There is no Alice Green living here.

The man began to speak again but Innes had hung up before making any more of it out. He lifted the towel to his head and rubbed at his hair with it. Alice came into the living room.

Innes, she laughed. The curtains aren't even closed and you're standing here naked.

Who's going to see me? A pigeon? A sheep?

Just me, she said, and looked him up and down. Did I hear the phone ring?

Yes.

Who was it?

Wrong number.

That's weird.

I know. Maybe we need to get the number unlisted. Or just disconnect the damn thing.

Then we could never be in touch with anyone.

I don't want to be in touch with anyone except you, said Innes. He put his arms around Alice and she squirmed against his wet skin.

When do you need to leave?

Soon. About twenty minutes.

Why don't you phone in sick and just come to bed with me instead?

Oh, laughed Innes. Wouldn't that be nice? I'm sure my boss would love that. He's not the kind of guy you'd want to get on the wrong side of. Did you iron my shirt?

It's hanging up.

What are you going to do tonight?

I might go for a walk. Read a book. Drink some wine. Relax.

Sounds good.

When will you be home?

Just depends. Don't wait up. I'll see you in bed.

Wake me up when you get in, said Alice, so I at least get to see you.

12

Jessie was out in the garden one day, unpegging the washing that had been soaked in the autumn rain from the line, when the telephone rang. She dropped the wet clothes into the basket and ran inside. She didn't want the noise to wake her mother.

She answered the telephone and recognised her father's voice: It's me, it's your dad.

Hiya.

Just thought I'd give you a call to see how you're doing.

I'm fine. How are you?

Sorry I've not been over to see you. You know how it is with work. These shifts are a nightmare. Can't catch a minute to myself.

That's alright. You're busy. Work's busy. Can't be easy being Officer Galloway of the Northern Constabulary.

How's your wee job at the hotel going? How's that new teacher that moved up the road?

Miss Green? She's good. She's young and she's cool. I like her classes.

That's good.

Jessie untangled the telephone cord and wiped dust from around the buttons.

I'm going to see Grandpa later, she said.

That's good of you. He loves when you visit.

No bother to me. I'm happy to do it.

Listen, about that, said her father. You know Grandpa was in for some tests about his throat? How he couldn't swallow?

He told me.

The results are back.

Okay.

He's got cancer in his throat. That's what's giving him problems. There's a tumour halfway down.

Jessie sat on the arm of the couch. Murphy the golden retriever looked up at her from his bed, the brown eyes staring.

Right, she said.

They're not going to treat it. Say he wouldn't survive an operation. Too invasive.

Christ.

I know. Grandpa knows all this too.

Do they say how long he's got?

The doctor didn't want to put a timeframe on it. He's an old man. He could go very quickly or he could go on for a while. He's old but he is strong.

Can he eat anything?

Nothing solid. Soup, porridge, that kind of thing. Would you take him a bag of shopping?

Okay.

Are you okay to cover it? I'll transfer some money into your account later.

It's fine. Are you coming over at all? To see him.

I will. Work's so busy. Maybe next week.

I'll go and see him tonight.

Listen, don't tell him that I told you this. Let him tell you for himself. I just wanted to prepare you.

Okay. I'm glad you did.

And you'll take him some bits and pieces.

I'll take him some bits and pieces.

You're some girl.

Right, then.

Right, then. I'll speak to you later, Jessie.

Speak to you later, Dad.

Okay, bye bye.

Bye bye.

Up at the top of the scheme was a low square block of flats with a warden's office and decent flowerbeds and all the residents here wore an emergency button on a cord around their necks. In Flat 15, an old movie was playing on Grandpa's television. The volume was turned up too loud to chat but Jessie sat and sipped her whisky and watched. John Wayne swaggering across a dusty avenue. A woman with thick red lips and a handspan waist. Crashing fistfights and screaming horses and a big band soundtrack. Grandpa watched it with his fists clenched, sitting forward in his armchair, eyes wide and wet.

When it was finished, he turned the television off and sat back and touched at his face with a paper napkin.

That was a good film, said Jessie.

Marvellous, said Grandpa. Terrific.

Have you seen that one before?

Are you kidding? laughed the old man. A thousand times.

How are you feeling? she asked.

Grandpa swallowed heavily and squeezed his windpipe, then said: Can't complain. How is your school work going? Your assignments?

School's fine. I've got a lot of homework. We've got a new teacher. Keeps making us write essays.

Grandpa made a face.

You were going to tell me how you got on at the hospital, she said.

Grandpa nodded, finished the glass of whisky in his hand and picked up the bottle. It was a Cullrothes twelve-year-old, and there were plenty more of them in the cupboard. Jessie finished her glass and held it out empty and Grandpa poured more of the burnt gold out for each of them. He took a sip and then spoke.

Well, I've been having difficulty swallowing solids.

Can you swallow liquids okay?

Oh yes, he said. No bother. As if to prove it he drank some more whisky. But it's been taking a long time to eat a meal. I get halfway through and I'm exhausted. Keep falling asleep with my dinner on my knee.

That's no good.

So, I went over into town on the bus – he wiggled his hand to mimic the journey the long way around the loch – to the hospital. Took some blood. Kept me in overnight. Put a tiny wee camera down my throat. He pointed at it.

Right.

Grandpa put his whisky down and sat back in the armchair with his hands gripping the armrests. Got the results back a couple of days ago. He scratched at the armrests with his long fingernails.

Okay?

It's cancer, he said. He leaned forward and pointed at his throat and looked into Jessie's face.

Grandpa had an old clock mounted on the wall and it chimed now, seven times. Jessie stared at the floor while the hammer struck.

So, he said once the clock had fallen silent again, we'll just have to see how it goes. One day at a time.

Oh Grandpa, said Jessie.

Aye.

They sat in silence for a while, sipping their whisky. Jessie's toes curled into the soft carpet and Grandpa stared up at the ceiling and at the photographs on the wall opposite his armchair. The heating was on and it was warm and comfortable in the room.

See that photograph, he said, and pointed at a black and white print in a wooden frame on the windowsill.

That one? She got up and looked at the picture and handed it to him. Grandpa was there in it and so was her gran but the others were unfamiliar.

That's me, he pointed, and your gran. These were all our neighbours in Glasgow when we lived there. See him? That was my best pal. He was terrific. We all used to have parties on Saturdays. Visit each other at New Year's. Look after each other's children. Help each other with the gardening. Went on holidays together.

Jessie looked more closely at the young faces in the picture.

And now I'm the only person in this photograph that's still alive, spat Grandpa. The only one that's still here. His face was red and he pointed a thick finger at his own chest. Why?

I don't know, said Jessie.

Why did I get so much more time?

I don't know, Grandpa. But I'm glad you did.

He smiled and reached over and grabbed Jessie's hand. Me too, he said, and shook his head. But it's a mystery.

She got up and reached down around his neck and cuddled him and kissed his hot face and he squeezed her round the stomach.

So, he said, letting go. This. He pointed again at his throat. Cancer. We'll just have to see how it goes. One day at a time.

That's the best thing to do, she said. It's the only thing we can do isn't it?

13

Brian Ballater and his only boy, Craig, met in the morning at the end of the street at the red postbox, walking quickly with their hands jammed in their pockets to keep out the early cold. The sky was clear and the stars were endless, the closer ones throbbing with light and the farther away ones merging into a glittering tapestry against the black.

You're late, said Brian. His hair was combed neatly and he had a habit of tugging up the belt on his trousers.

You said to meet at five-thirty, said Craig. It's five-thirty now.

You should've been here early, said the father. I was here early.

Craig looked back up the road he'd walked down. It was a ten-minute walk up to the small cul-de-sac of houses. He looked over his father's shoulder to the street lights bouncing off the car windscreens.

You're only here early because your house is closer.

I'm at work the same time every day. I will not be late because of you. Okay?

Okay.

Aye, aye, aye. Let's go.

Father and son walked out onto the A871 heading east towards the water's edge. They did not speak until they were clear of the sleeping houses.

Did you bring your lunch? asked Brian.

Aye. Sandwiches.

No soup? It's a cold one today.

No.

Brian snorted and looked up at the sky which was at once the closest and furthest thing away from them.

It's going to be damn cold out on that water today. You can have some of my soup.

They walked along the road, in the middle of the road where there would be no traffic at this time in the morning, because the pavement was so narrow. Ahead they could see the flat blackness of the loch and out on it the dull red light blinking on the ferry's bridge. There was no sound except their footsteps and their breathing.

From the sky a small dark object came spinning down and Brian put his hand on Craig's chest as they both halted. The thing smashed at their feet and left gunk on the pavement.

Bloody seagulls, said Brian. They both looked up to the sky and there was a big gull circling wide, waiting for the men to move on so it could swoop and eat the insides of the mussel it had dropped from up high.

I love when they do that, said Craig. Dead smart aren't they?

Dead annoying, said Brian.

The pair of them carried on down the path towards the ferry and soon the gull fluttered down and landed, where it pecked and scratched at the broken mussel's flesh with its beak.

You know they're only hiring you on my recommendation, said Brian.

I know.

I've worked the ferry for thirty-six years.

You think I don't know that?

If you mess this up it's me that looks like an idiot.

I'm not going to mess it up.

You couldn't hold down your last job though, could you?

Craig blew out his cheeks. He was a tall boy with a freckled face and a scrag of brown hair. He opened a packet of strong mints he had in his pocket.

Want a mint?

Brian put out his hand and Craig put a chalky mint on his father's palm and they both walked along the road towards the ferry, sucking on their mints.

I mean it, said Brian after a minute. You listen to what you're told. You do what people tell you. No moaning, no nothing.

Aye aye, captain.

As they walked the road towards the ferry the sun began to come up behind them. It warmed their backs and cast long shadows on the tarmac in front of them and by the time they had reached the ferry port the first cars had already begun to queue up ready to cross over to the mainland.

They stood side by side, waiting for the ramp to lower.

You'll probably need to get a health and safety briefing, said Brian.

Oh aye.

Evacuation procedures.

Yeah.

I can't treat you special on here, said Brian. Just the same as any other colleague.

Sure.

So long as you know.

Just one question, Dad.

Aye?

What kind of soup is it we're having?

14

Moodie sat in the small office in the Distillery with rows of banknotes laid out on the desk. The brown hundred-pound notes with their pictures of Balmoral, the greenish fifties and the plastic castle at Inverness. Piles of purple, green and brown. The scabby little one-pound notes torn at the edges with cashiers' pen marks and the smell of other men's pockets.

The money had been brought in by the lorry drivers who picked it up from villages all over the country and the money was the proceeds from the bags of dried green buds and brown toxic powder that the Distillery sent out with its barrels of whisky every month.

This second life of the Distillery was a Cullrothes' best-kept secret. Margo was behind more of the operations than anyone liked to admit. Moodie was the messenger, liaising with the drivers and arranging the pick-ups and the distribution. Young Bobby knew bits here and there. Sandy had ended up knowing too much about it than was good for him.

Moodie ran the notes through his fingers, counting the denominations in his head and banding them up in piles. Sometimes he had got Sandy to sit with him at night like this when he was counting the money and the two of them had blethered. Moodie had liked Sandy. He had even told Sandy about the Americans and their investment plans. That had been a mistake. As soon as Moodie had let this slip, Sandy was a dead man.

He sat back in his chair and folded his big arms and thought back to the night Sandy had died naked and drunk in his bathtub. Margo had planned the whole thing, and Donald always made sure that Margo got what she wanted.

I've boiled the kettle, Sandy had said. Can I have a tea?

Donald said nothing but nodded, then after a moment Moodie left and went to the kitchen. It was a small room, with postcards and magnets from foreign countries pinning bills to the fridge. Late notices. Final demands. Letters from debt collection firms. The linoleum on the floor was pulling away at the edges and the hob was caked with grease. A dirty pot from Sandy's dinner was sitting unfilled in the sink. There was a calendar hanging on the wall but it was three years old.

Moodie unplugged the kettle from its socket and replaced it with the extension cord. There were crumbs to shake loose before he connected the toaster as well. He took a slice of white bread from the half-finished loaf on the board and spread some salted butter on it, scraping the knife close to the edges, aligned neatly with the crusts. The bread was tough, close to stale, but the butter was rich and creamy. Moodie leaned against the worktop and chewed the bread, then wiped his mouth with his sleeve.

Through the wall he could hear Donald spitting fire and brimstone at Sandy. A rehearsed speech. Donald was good at making speeches but not so clever when it came to pulling the trigger.

The cottage door had crashed shut as Donald left. Returning

to the safety of his manse with its security cameras and underfloor heating. Alone together, Sandy and Moodie held eye contact.

Well done Sandy, said Moodie. The media picked up the story. The village is full of the whispers. Donald's reputation's never been doubted like this before.

Sandy smiled and braced both fists on the edges of the bath to lever himself up and out of there. Moodie picked up the humming toaster and Sandy froze.

The leak, he managed, his tongue thick and pickled. I leaked the story just like you asked.

Our pal from America sends his regards, said Moodie. He centred his body weight and elevated his arms, the toaster clear and away from his torso.

Sandy saw what was coming and opened his dry lips to shout. The noise was a desperate animal whine. Pleading and cursing. Moodie pitched the toaster towards the pink man in the hot bath.

When the machine hit the water's surface Sandy snapped into a rictus and the back of his skull hit the side of the bath with a soft pop. Moodie stepped quickly back and watched from the doorway. Sandy's fingers splayed and the muscles under his skin began to crawl with the spasms. His face no longer recognisable. His eyes bulged and lockjaw gripped his mouth, sealing it. Overhead, the lightbulb dimmed then shone, flickering, sputtering. It took longer than Moodie expected. The toaster had sunk to the bottom and then floated again to the top, its plastic hull rocking back and forth between Sandy's twitching legs. Finally the lightbulb overhead flashed, its memory burning onto Moodie's retina, then extinguished to black. Moodie turned and left. Crumbs from the toaster forming a skin on the surface of the bathwater.

Moodie remembered that night only too well. He couldn't get rid of the images when he closed his eyes at night. He swung back on his chair and took a mouthful of whisky from his hip flask and scratched the tattooed insignia on his forearm.

15

When Old Jim appeared at a quarter past eight, Innes took an upturned pint glass from the shelf and began to pour. The beer came out in a slow thin trickle, foaming around the edges of the glass. When it was half full, Innes looked up. Old Jim was getting there, approaching the stool, walking slowly. He had only one leg now. Still he would come in at a quarter past eight to drink beer and work on his crossword puzzles. Innes straightened the glass and lowered it a couple of inches to build up a foamy head.

Pint of lager, son, said Old Jim. Innes put the glass down in front of him, frothing a little down the sides and onto the beermat. The old man slapped his newspaper down on the wooden bar top and began levering himself onto the stool. Innes watched. The old man never wanted anyone to help and it was pointless to ask.

The public bar at the Cullrothes Hotel was small and had not been decorated for years. A log fire puttered in the grate alongside old photographs of the loch and the mountains, pictures of men in kilts who were all dead long ago. There was a dartboard in the corner and a door in the back that led out to the beer garden. They put tables out there when it was warm enough. A stag's head, a big twelve-pointer, was mounted on another wall at eye level. It stared out at the empty tables with fierce dry eyes.

Quiet, said Old Jim. There was a European football game playing on the large television in the corner but nobody in the place to watch it. The commentary buzzing low in the background.

Always quiet this time of year, said Innes. So I hear. Busier when the tourists are about.

You can get closed early then.

Hopefully.

Old Jim took a yellow pouch from his jacket pocket, stuffed some tobacco into a paper, licked the gum and rolled it up.

They're talking about making that illegal, said Innes.

Rolling your own smokes?

Smoking inside. They're wanting to ban it in pubs, restaurants. They're saying it's bad for people to inhale. Passive smoking.

Old Jim looked around the empty bar. Only me and you here, son.

True.

Do you mind it? He held the roll-up in front of him.

Innes shook his head. Go for it.

The old man struck a match, lit the tip and sucked in, coughing weakly. His moustache was flecked yellow at the edges.

Innes turned to the optics. The dark rum was low and he replaced this with another bottle stored in the cupboard. He licked a sticky splash from the back of his hand.

I'll have a nip, son, said Old Jim. While you're there.

Innes took a tumbler and pushed it up into the optic. The glass filled with whisky, an eight-year-old, his cheapest one. The hotel was only permitted to stock Cullrothes whiskies.

The old man took the drink and splashed in cold water and dug a wallet out from his back pocket.

Who's going to stop us anyway, he said, staring at the lit end of his cigarette. They can make it illegal, pfft. Who would put a stop to it? Galloway? Is he going to come in here and say we can't smoke?

Innes pushed an ashtray towards him and he stubbed out the cigarette.

Now you're not going to be the one to say anything about it, son, I know that. And Donald. Owns this whole place and he smokes like a chimney himself. Who's going to tell him he can't smoke in his own pub?

Innes tossed the ash and the dead filter into the bin and wiped out the ashtray.

All I'm saying is, he said, they're saying in the papers that they're wanting to ban it.

Who?

Protesters.

Old Jim shook his head and picked up his newspaper and drained his beer and went back to his crossword. Innes filled up another pint for him, and made a note in a pad that the old man still owed him for three drinks.

The Cullrothes Hotel had gone out of business years ago and then had been bought by the Distillery. Renovated all the bedrooms and the bar and the lounge. Donald was the owner, but he got different managers to keep on top of the stocktaking and the reservations. This was where he brought clients to sample new malts and rare vintages. It lost money every month but nobody seemed to notice. Donald had hired Innes to manage the bar and the rooms but they took no overnights in the off season, between October and April, because there was such little demand for it. This was when Innes needed to get away from his old life in the city and start somewhere new, where nobody knew him or what he'd been accused of.

At a five to ten the door swung open and a tall, thin man came into the pub. He had heavy eyes and the hair on his head was receding. He came straight to the bar and slapped Old Jim on the back.

How are we doing, old man?

No bad, how's yourself?

Brand new, he slurred. The newcomer was Young Bobby, and Innes recognised him as the owner's son.

Evening, said Innes. He looked at his watch.

Large whisky, said Young Bobby. The good stuff, the eighteen-year you've got up on the top shelf there. Same for my old pal. He wrapped his arm around Old Jim and squeezed. Did you see the game? Did you see it?

It was on, said Old Jim. Wasn't really watching.

I had a coupon on for it, said Young Bobby. With a bookie over the water. Four hundred to one. First goal scorer and correct result. Bang on.

Much did you put on it?

A tenner.

Old Jim clicked his tongue and nodded approvingly.

Young Bobby pointed at Innes: This wee prick thought he was getting home early the night. Didn't he? Look at him. Look at his face. He's raging.

Innes poured the two whisky doubles out and brought them to the bar.

Slainte, said Young Bobby. He drank half the whisky in a mouthful.

Slainte, said Old Jim. I'll just have this one. He looked at

Innes. If I'm not up the road by half past she'll send out mountain rescue.

You been paying your way tonight? said Young Bobby. Has this wee prick been charging you full price for your beers?

Old Jim splashed a little water into this whisky and took a sip. Sorry son, how much do I owe you?

Put your money away, said Young Bobby. This wee prick's not going to charge you.

How much?

Your money's no good here, said Young Bobby again.

It's twelve sixty, said Innes.

You, Young Bobby leaned over and pointed at Innes. Don't you dare tell him he owes you money. Coming in here from God only knows where and making out you're in charge. See him? He nodded towards Old Jim. I've known him since I was...

Young Bobby looked at the old man then back at Innes and held his hand perpendicular to his waist.

...about this height.

Innes held up the palms of his hands and took a small step away from the bar. Old Jim stared into his drink.

You can give us two more large whiskies, but. Young Bobby turned and went to the toilet, bumping his shoulder off the door frame as he passed. And leave the bottle out.

Old Jim sank the remaining whisky in his glass and took a note and some coins from his wallet. Don't mind him, son.

That you off?

That's me off. He left the exact change that he owed on the bar. Bin this for me, will you. He pushed the unfinished crossword across the polished wood.

Better luck tomorrow.

The old man struggled from his stool and wrapped a scarf around his neck. He turned, finding the balance between his stick and the stiff leg, and made his way towards the door. Tomorrow will be a better day, he said, when he was halfway there. Innes turned to pour the other two whiskies Young Bobby had ordered. By the time he was finished, the old man was gone.

16

Flames gurned in the fireplace and the living room was warm. Donald sitting in his pyjamas with bare feet on the rug and holding a glass of good red wine. Margo was watching a soap opera on the television and she had a glass as well but it was empty.

Who's he? asked Donald. A man with a moustache had come into shot on the screen.

That's Pete. He's the one Linda's having an affair with.

Oh.

Linda's meant to be marrying Gerry.

Right.

But Gerry's not stupid. He knows something's going on.

Good.

Gerry and Pete used to be best friends when they were at school together, but they fell out over something.

What was it?

That's what we're trying to find out.

When the adverts came on, Donald took the remote control and switched channels. The football game was finished and the pundits were talking about which team had won. Donald drank the last of his wine and he took Margo's empty glass to

the kitchen and got them both a refill. Limping for the first
few steps as his kneecap crunched under his weight and then
settled. He put the glasses on a tray along with a dish of peanuts
and an ashtray and a cigar.

You're not smoking that in here, are you? asked Margo.

You don't want me to?

I'd rather you didn't.

Donald pointed to Margo's cigarette packet sitting on the
arm of the couch and said: What about those?

They don't stink the place out for days on end, do they?

Okay, okay. Donald put the tray on the coffee table and sat
on the couch with his arm around Margo's shoulders.

What time do you suppose Young Bobby will be in tonight?
It's getting later and later, said Margo.

Boys will be boys.

But he's not a boy anymore is he? If you keep treating him
like that he's never going to grow up.

He's probably just spending time with his pals.

You know you were asking about him gambling?

Aye.

Is it bad?

No. A few quid here and there. Makes the game more
interesting. He's just being one of the boys.

Has he got another girlfriend yet?

How should I know?

It's the kind of thing you would hear about. He certainly
doesn't talk about things like that me. I mean, I'm only his
mother.

I've got no idea.

Margo switched channels. The soap opera had started again
but they kept on talking over the top of it.

Do you not think it's about time he met somebody nice?

The problem is, his standards are too high. You've got it into his head that no girl from around here's ever going to be good enough for Bonnie Prince Bobby.

How could you say that about me? I tried my best to raise that boy properly.

I know.

If anything, you're the one that's spoiled him.

You're right.

So don't go talking about me like that, making out that I'm something to do with it.

To do with what?

He's turned into an arrogant person.

I don't know about that. He's got confidence in himself.

He's got a big head. He's full of it. I don't like to see it. When are we ever supposed to trust him to take over at work? How could he run the Distillery?

It'll be a long time before I'm ready to pack it in.

It'll come round sooner than you think.

Well then. But you're missing your show.

I am, quiet now and let me watch it.

Donald took his arm away from Margo's shoulder and she tucked her feet underneath her. He leaned forwards and drank his wine and lit them both a cigarette, balancing the ashtray on his knee so they could both use it. The clock on the wall chimed.

He'll be home any minute now, said Donald. He looked at his watch.

I'm past caring. He can stay out as long as he likes. Margo drank her wine. When this is finished, I'm going to my bed.

17

With Old Jim gone it was only Innes and Young Bobby in the bar. The two whiskies sat untouched.

One for you then, prick, said Young Bobby.

I won't, said Innes. I'm working.

Don't make me drink alone.

Innes picked up the glass and nodded. He was not a whisky drinker but it was the expected thing in Cullrothes. The villagers had whisky in the blood.

Slainte, they both said, and Innes drank half the measure. The heat rushed into his face and he swallowed a cough.

That new girl you hired, said Young Bobby. What days is she coming in?

It's just weekdays. An hour after she's done at school.

She's a good-looking girl, isn't she?

She's still at school.

You would know about that, wouldn't you?

Innes said nothing. Young Bobby pulled a stool underneath him and leaned both elbows on the bar. Wouldn't you? he said again.

Aye, said Innes quietly. He opened the dishwasher and started emptying the drip trays from underneath the beer taps.

The warm old beer washed down the sink with hot water and the rancid smell hit the barman's nostrils for a second then vanished.

Hey, said Young Bobby, don't start closing up just yet. You've got customers to serve still.

Just getting a head start, said Innes. He flipped all the beermats off the bar and threw the sodden ones in the bin.

Young Bobby drank the rest of the whisky and ran his tongue across his top lip. And he picked up the half-finished whisky that Innes had drunk from. He finished that as well. From his trouser pocket he took out his coupon from the bookie and held it up to the light. Just a little green slip of paper with handwritten scribbles.

Four grand, he said to Innes. For a ten-pound punt. Not bad at all. Look at it. Isn't it beautiful?

Innes glanced at the paper and lifted his eyebrows.

How much you making tonight? What are you going to get for this shift?

Twenty-five pounds, said Innes.

Twenty-five pounds, smiled Young Bobby. Two more whiskies! He held the same number of fingers out in front of him.

None for me, said Innes. He was spraying the bar top and the shelves with bleach.

God damn, shouted Young Bobby. He smashed the side of his fist onto the bar. Take another whisky, man! Trying to have a bit of fun. Celebrating my big win at the bookies. It's not going to kill you is it?

I've got the car with me.

There's no police for miles. The ferry finished hours ago.

I just, said Innes. I don't like it so much.

Jesus Christ, said Young Bobby. You don't like it so much. Well, learn to. He stood up off his stool. Pour two more.

Alright, said Innes. But I won't have one. I'm just saying. I don't want it to go to waste. I'll pour two but I won't be drinking it. He turned back to the optics and fixed the whiskies.

Bring them round here, said Young Bobby. Have a drink with me. Remember who runs this place. Remember who's in charge.

Innes put the drinks on the bar and came out from behind it. He stood next to Young Bobby, who was half a foot taller. I just don't like the taste of it, said Innes. I don't mean anything by it.

Young Bobby reached into his pocket and his fingertips pursed around a pinch of brown powder and he snorted it and then licked his fingers.

Okay, he said, and held the whisky out. Slainte!

Slainte, said Innes, but when he went to clink glasses, Young Bobby put his hand underneath the drink and tipped it up and towards Innes. The whisky poured onto his face and soaked his shirt. The glass fell from his grip. Shattered on the stone tiles.

Ha! shouted Young Bobby. You like it now, don't you? He was bright red, mouth stretched open in laughter, tears quickly appearing at the corners of his eyes, holding his own whisky low by his side, the drink spilling out over his hands and onto the floor.

Innes looked down at his shirt and wiped the whisky from his nostrils and pushed Young Bobby hard in the chest with both hands.

You idiot, said Innes, already beginning to smile a little, to see the funny side of it, but he had caught Young Bobby off guard. He took two quick uneasy steps backwards and tried to hold the whisky tumbler level so it wouldn't spill. He reached out to grab at the empty air in front of him and then his heel caught the edge of the rug in front of the fireplace. He spun around as he fell, slowly, as though it was a mime, so that he ended up turning his back completely on Innes. Then gasped as his fall was interrupted by that big twelve-point stag mounted on the wall. The tall man's throat met flush with the blunted edge of an old antler. He seemed to pause for a second, and then his weight bore down and the beast's crown punctured the neck with a soft, fleshy pop.

Young Bobby's whisky glass dropped from his hand and hit the stone tiles with a tinkle, a shatter.

Watch it, shouted Innes, but he did not move from the bar. The malt was still dripping from his own chin. Jesus! He looked at the tall man's back, stooped towards the stag's head as though dancing with it. The animal's lifeless eyes caught the light from the low fire which was nearly extinguished.

After a second, Young Bobby's legs braced beneath him, and his hands moved towards the antler, to dislodge himself from it. As he lifted himself a half inch, a trail of blood clotted and then fell to the floor, where the rest of it followed like water from a tap. Young Bobby's body went limp and the stag's head was torn from its wall fixings under the man's weight, scraping down the wall and bouncing onto its side, face to face with the man, who was now dead, like a couple of lovers lying in bed.

Bobby, said Innes. Hey. Hey. He ran his hand across his face and licked the whisky from his fingers. The blood was gathering thickly around the body. Getting close to the rug. Innes stepped forward and folded this over so it would not get stained. Underneath, the stone tiles were a lighter colour altogether.

Innes took his phone from his pocket and looked at it, but it was registering no signal. The ferry was off until the morning. The hospital a four-hour drive around the loch through the black night. And Young Bobby was already dead. Innes had pushed him and now the man was dead.

As though there might be another person there, a witness he hadn't counted on, Innes turned and looked into every corner of the pub. He looked behind the bar to check there wasn't someone crouching down there. He put his hands out to steady himself and put his head on the bar's cool surface to allow himself to think for a minute. Then he saw there in front of him the coupon with the bookie's handwriting. The mint green scrap worth four thousand pounds. And he thought about it for half a second before folding it back across its middle and tucking it into his shirt pocket.

He moved slowly around the bar and got the keys from the hook. It was normal for him to lock up early during the week. Especially when there were no customers left to serve. He stepped quickly across the room to the heavy main door, and quietly turned the key so the place was closed. It was normal.

18

Alice stretched out on the rug with her head down and the weight of her body on her palms and her bare feet. Straight arms and straight legs planted at shoulder width apart. She pushed her hips towards the ceiling and on her inward breath felt the hamstrings and calf muscles stretch, and then as she breathed out she thought about how good it would feel to drown Mrs Hughes in a puddle.

The knock at the door was a surprise. It was late and dark out and nobody from the village had visited before. Alice held the pose for seven more breaths and then there was another knock and she bounced up to her feet and sipped a glass of ice water.

There was a man at the door. She could see his shadow through the frosted glass. She kept a few steps back and put her palms on her bare stomach and called out: Yes, who is there?

Sorry to barge in, said the man. It's about the missing cat.

The missing cat?

Hercules. I saw the posters in the village. Are you Alice Green?

What is it you want?

I can help you find him.

Alice opened the door quickly and the man stepped back a

little and smiled. He was tall with wide shoulders and a tweed blazer. A little older than she was with some grey in his beard.

Are you saying you know where Hercules is?

Not exactly. He held out a business card. My name's Grant Valentine and I'm a journalist for the Courier. I thought I'd write a story about it and see if we can't get the wee guy home.

You want to put a story in the paper about a missing cat?

It's a slow news week. But no, it's not just that. It's a story about the campaign, about the kids making the posters, about this mysterious new teacher at the school.

Alice crossed her arms across her chest. How did you know where I live?

Everyone knows where you live. Everyone knows where everyone lives.

I don't know where you live.

No, probably not. I've got a place out of the village. Up on the road heading to the Cat's Back.

Alice scraped her thumbnail across her front teeth and said nothing.

Valentine said: I was down in the village visiting a friend and I thought I'd pop by and see if you wanted to help with this.

You could have got in touch with me at the school.

I could have. More fun this way though, isn't it? Besides, I wanted to see if the rumours were true. About the hot new teacher. He raised an eyebrow.

Pardon me?

I've come at a bad time. Have you got a cycling machine in there or something?

Alice felt his eyes move down her sports bra and her bare stomach and her shorts.

I was doing yoga.

Oh Christ. And I've barged in and interrupted your quest for inner peace?

Trust me, that's a long way off.

Look, I'll drop by at the school tomorrow. Do this properly. Bring a notepad and everything.

You're here now. Might as well come in.

You sure?

Why not? I was just about to have a glass of wine and don't much fancy drinking alone.

Sounds great.

Valentine hung his blazer over the back of a chair and took a seat on the couch next to Alice. He asked a few questions and wrote a few notes down on a sheet of paper. At some point he lit a cigarette and took a draw from it and then passed it to Alice and she smoked that one then he lit another for himself and they blew the smoke up towards the ceiling.

But there wasn't much to the story and by the time the bottle was finished Alice was straddling the journalist with her hands in his hair and her mouth on his. Feeling the benefit of the yoga in her hamstrings and her calf muscles as she kept her breathing at a steady and controlled rhythm.

19

Innes wiped down the bar surfaces and sprayed the tables with wood polish and cashed up the till and when he came back to Young Bobby's slumped body squatting next to the wall, the blood had stopped dripping and spreading across the tiles. It was nearly midnight now and outside there was a clear sky with a bright full moon.

Innes went out the back door into the beer garden. It was quiet. The water in the burn at the end of the garden babbled softly. This was the water that came down from the mountains and fed into the stream they used to feed the mash house in the Distillery. It was deeper further upstream but shallow enough here at the back of the hotel to paddle in.

The beer garden had picnic tables and benches that faced the sun during good weather. The views over the loch made this spot famous with tourists. Innes looked at the loch now. It was dark and vast. But it was too far to drag the body and there was always the risk of traffic on the Shore Road.

There were some old upturned whisky barrels lined up against the wall. When the beer garden's tables were full men would stand here and use the barrels as shelves for their elbows and their beers. Innes squatted down next to one. He tried to imagine how Young Bobby's long, bony body could fit into it. He moved the heavy barrel out from the wall, rotating it on the rim of its base. The top and the bottom were still sealed. He squatted next to it again. He sat on the ground with his back to the barrel and drew his knees up in imitation of a foetus to see if Young Bobby could maybe be folded up into one of the barrels, then scratched his scalp.

Innes thought back to what had brought him here to this village. The decisions he had made without thinking them through. In Glasgow he had been a teacher in an inner-city school. Still young and doing a good job some days and then making mistakes now and then. He had made it a core part of his profession to make children reflect on their actions and take accountability for their behaviour. And when it turned out that Innes couldn't reflect on his own actions or take accountability for the things he'd done wrong, that made him feel pretty stupid.

It wasn't even that bad. Not as bad as everyone assumed. He had been under pressure to produce exam results and so let his pupils see a secure assessment paper before they sat it. They all passed with full marks and then the suspicions started. In the staffroom and in verification meetings. The teaching council made Innes sign a non-disclosure agreement so he couldn't talk to anyone about it. Couldn't defend himself against the gossip and the speculation that came out of it. Being a teacher who got struck off the register came with all sorts of labels.

Telling Alice about it was tough. He hid it for as long as he could. She didn't know about the professional conduct meetings or the statements he had to write up. She even thought he was still going to school and taking classes for a while. Instead of hiding at home. She was a teacher too. Much better at it than he ever was. A natural. Eventually he had to tell her before someone else did.

Telling his mother the truth was even worse. She had been so proud of his teaching qualification. Told everyone about her wonderful son, the educator. When he got suspended she convinced herself that the system was corrupt. That it was a conspiracy. Wrote to the local authorities to tell them how baseless their accusations were. All this did was make Innes want to run to somewhere far away.

Now he managed this small hotel and had changed his whole life. Alice had come with him, so he was lucky for that. Lucky to have her. And Young Bobby's body was still waiting there slumped over on the stag's blunt antler for someone to do something about it.

Innes had ruined everything again. Maybe this was what he deserved. He wondered if Alice could forgive him, this time. He wondered if he could tell her, this time.

He put a hand into his pocket and pulled out the coupon and read the winnings again. He would have to find some excuse to go over the ferry to the mainland to collect. The thought of it set tingles up the back of his skull.

He picked himself up from the ground. Wiped the grit from his hands down the front of his trousers. There was a small maintenance shed and he went there to get a spade. Down at the bottom of the beer garden, away from the picnic tables and under the shade of an old, overhanging tree, he started to dig a hole in the soft earth.

20

Innes got home in the middle of the night. It was a short drive from the hotel along the A871 and then up a rutted track to the rented cottage. Alice was in bed. It was dark in the bedroom. He stood in the hallway and spoke to her through the open door.

There you are, she said. What happened? I was worried.

You have no idea, he said. It's been an absolute nightmare tonight.

Was it busy?

No, not that. I'll tell you about it but let me take a shower first.

Innes took off his clothes and rolled them into a ball and tucked them into the washing basket. He ran the hot water and got under. His fingernails were thick with dirt and ash. His forearms were splattered with filth and blood and there was ash there too, all specked with clean upward flicks where the bleach had sprayed his skin.

He got into bed without drying his hair and stretched and his elbows cracked.

So tell me about your night, said Alice. She was lying on her side with her head facing Innes and her hair was scraped back from her face.

You know that big stag's head on the wall in the bar? I noticed a funny smell coming from it tonight. I thought maybe it needed cleaning.

Probably hasn't been cleaned in years.

I took it down and pulled the head away from the mounting board a little. I thought the smell might be something to do with the adhesive, or whatever it is they use to mount these things. When I did that, all these maggots came pouring out.

Are you serious?

Hundreds of them. They must have built some sort of nest inside. Big fat maggots, all over my hand, falling onto the floor. It was awful.

Alice shoogled closer to Innes. He raised his arm and she rested her head on his chest.

What did you do?

I was so freaked out. I just took the stag's head outside, said Innes, to the beer garden, and burned it.

Oh my God.

You can still smell the smoke on my fingers. I tried to wash them with bleach. I had to scrub the floor tiles as well where the maggots had fallen.

Can you even burn a stag's head?

Not very well. I think I burned it long enough to kill the maggots. Then I buried it.

Where?

At the bottom of the beer garden – near the stream. Away from the tables.

What will Donald say? Aren't those mounted head things expensive?

It was rotten. Full of maggots. What was I meant to do? He'll probably have a spare one lying around in that big house of his anyway.

Alice cosied in tighter and lifted her leg onto Innes so that her thigh hugged his waist.

It's been a terrible night, said, Innes, kissing her on the top of the head. Anyway. How was your day at school?

Oh it went fine, she said. The kids were great.

Are you making better friends with the other teachers yet?

The other teachers are nice, she said. But most of them are older.

Well, he said, I'm sure you will make friends. He reached down with his spare hand and cupped Alice under the knee, pulling her leg up a little towards him.

What did you do tonight?

Stayed in. Had a bath.

Lovely, he said, and kissed her forehead again.

I wish, she said, you didn't come to bed with wet hair. The pillow's going to be soaked. She pulled her leg back and rolled away onto her own side. I've told you about that before.

21

Margo brought a teapot and a plate of buttered toast and jars of jam and marmalade. She sat next to Donald and poured the tea and took a piece of toast and scraped a thin layer of jam on it.

Want me to do yours?

No, he said, and bit into a corner of the toast where the butter had not melted in.

I didn't hear Young Bobby coming in last night, said Margo. Did you hear him?

Donald shook his head and chewed.

I would normally wake when he comes up the stairs.

Maybe he stayed over with someone. Wouldn't be the first time.

Just where else would he have stayed?

He's some boy.

I want you to have a word with him. It's not right the way he's carrying on. Why does he have to get so drunk all the time? Have you heard what people are saying about it?

He's just young. Donald refilled the cups of tea and passed the jam to Margo for her next slice.

It's not right. This is a small place. I don't want everyone seeing him as just a drunk. You shouldn't make excuses for it.

Maybe he just stayed the night somewhere else. We don't know that he was drinking.

Ha, said Margo. What else would he be doing? And who's he staying over with. That's what I want to know. There's a perfectly good bedroom here.

He's a young man. Sometimes young men find more interesting things to do at night.

I want you to have a word with him about it.

I will.

And don't make me out to be the bad guy here. I don't want him thinking of me as some old nag that's always getting on his case.

Sure, darling. Whatever you want, Donald said.

He helped Margo put the clean dishes back into the cupboards and sat with her in the living room. He groaned as he sat down.

Are you going to see the doctor about that shoulder?

He rotated his arm and it was sore. Is there any point?

What if it's something serious?

It's just old age.

You're not that old. I'm not married to an old man just yet.

I'll wait a while and see.

One week, she said, and then you're going to the doctor.

Okay. What would I do without you organising my life?

You wouldn't have one. Get moving. You're going to be late for work.

I suppose. Donald grabbed Margo's leg and kissed her. I'll see you later.

Before you go, she said, go and check Young Bobby's room. Just in case. Maybe he snuck in quietly last night and is lying up there sleeping.

Donald went upstairs with his kneecap crunching at every step and knocked lightly on his son's bedroom door before opening it. The bed was still made up and the blinds were drawn and it was cool and smelled fresh with the window open and a breeze drifting in with the earthy smell of the autumn morning.

No sign of him, shouted Donald at the top of the stairs.

Typical, said Margo. She was standing at the front door holding Donald's jacket.

He'll turn up at some point, said Donald, halfway down.

In God only knows what state.

He'll be here, said Donald, by lunchtime at the latest. He'll be home when he's needing fed. Don't you worry about that.

Margo stretched up onto her tiptoes and Donald kissed her forehead. Remember to let me know, she said, about Sandy's funeral arrangements. I'll need time to get the flowers cut and organised.

I will, said Donald. He's still with the pathologist for the exam.

They're not suspicious, are they?

All they're going to find is a burnt-out body. With a bellyful of the finest whisky. As soon as the body gets released, I'll get the ball rolling. I'll hear it first from the undertaker. Could take a couple of weeks.

Are you feeling happy that Sandy's out the way now?

I wouldn't say happy. I feel relieved. We can start shifting the bags again without worrying who knows about it. I didn't wish the guy any harm really.

He was just getting in the way, wasn't he?

He got too involved. Probably Moodie's fault.

You'll need to keep an eye on Moodie then.

Moodie's fine.

Moodie's a risk.

You let me decide who's a risk and who isn't. So I'll see you tonight then.

See you tonight, then.

Donald closed the door behind him and Margo looked up the staircase. I wonder where that boy could be? she said to herself.

22

Innes lay in bed until the pressure on his bladder grew too strong. He got up and went to the bathroom and rubbed the grime from his eyes. It had been four days since he killed Young Bobby. There were still moments when he could viscerally smell the damp soil and the smoke beneath his fingernails. The stag's singed hide had cast a putrid smoke that still clung to his skin. But the grave had sunk down with the heavy rain and there had been no drinkers using the beer garden so things were working out as well as he dared to hope.

He squeezed out a weak, amber stream of urine and went back to bed without washing his hands or wiping down the toilet seat. He wanted more sleep. It was already clear that he could never sleep all through the night again; not with the memory of Young Bobby's twisted face invading his eyelids.

He lay back and wrapped the duvet around him. Alice had already gone out to school earlier than she had to. She'd had the television on loudly in the other room and sang loudly in the shower and she'd slammed the door loudly and he knew there would be a pile of breakfast dishes left for him to clean up.

For the past few days he had lain awake while she got ready in the morning with his eyes closed, pretending to sleep.

The telephone rang in the hallway. He got up and answered it and stood in the dark damp hallway in his underwear.

Hello?

Hiya! It's me.

Hi, Mum.

I phoned last night but nobody answered.

I was at work.

Do they still have you doing the late shifts?

Yes.

I thought I might have caught Alice.

She was in last night. Maybe she was in the bath when you phoned.

Are you doing okay up there?

Fine.

You don't sound fine.

I am.

What's the matter?

Nothing's the matter Mum, I only just woke up, that's all.

You would tell me if there was something wrong.

Yes.

Innes leaned back against the wallpaper and wrapped the phone cord around his finger.

How is work?

It's fine, Innes sighed. It's easy. Pour the drinks, change the kegs, wipe the tables, lock the door. Piece of cake.

Not the fast pace of what you're used to.

Not quite.

Not as stimulating.

You can say that again.

Have you looked into appealing against the Teaching Council's decision?

No.

You should look into it.

I've been taken off the register, mum. They're not in the habit of changing their minds about these things. I fiddled exam papers. I did it, it wasn't some elaborate thing they made up.

The woman sighed. He could picture her sitting there in the conservatory with a strong cup of black tea. I just hate the thought of you wasting your mind.

I don't have much choice right now.

You're so clever. It makes me so angry.

Mum.

I know, I know. Well, how's the house?

Cottage.

How's the cottage?

He looked down at the worn carpet and the dark mouldy wallpaper. The dusty lightshade and the stained Artex ceiling that the landlord had said could have asbestos.

It's great, he said. Small but perfectly formed. And the rent's cheap.

What about the village? Are you making friends there?

They're nice enough, he said. Some of them are a bit weird.

How are they weird?

They just are.

In what way?

Christ, I don't know. They're weird people. But how are you? What's happening at home?

Your sister's still getting a hard time.

Why?

Everyone still talks about what happened to you. About what you're supposed to have done. And why you're not teaching anymore. You know what they're like, these gossips.

Why would they give Evie a hard time?

Because you're not here, Innes.

Right. Mum, I need to go.

Okay. But how's Alice getting on? Enjoying her new school?

Loves it. She's doing great. We've been invited to a ceilidh with some of her colleagues.

Oh brilliant.

She's fitting in really well. Seems to have met lots of new people.

Good. You should ask that girl to marry you one of these days.

Oh for God's sake.

I'm serious. She's given up her whole life, moved job, moved house, to go up there with you. To live among all the weirdos, as you would put it. It would have been much easier for her to just chuck it.

It would have been easier.

You don't have to get married straight away. But I think it would be nice for her to know you want to. That you appreciate what she's done. Show her that you're committed.

Of course I appreciate it.

I can lend you the money for a ring. I think it would be good for you both. Something to look forward to and plan for. Something positive in your lives.

I already have positives in my life.

You know what I mean.

Yes.

Think about it.

I've got to go.

Okay. Say hi to Alice for me.

Say hi to Evie.

I will.

I'll speak to you later.

Speak to you later. Love you.

I love you too.

Innes replaced the phone and went into the small living room. He ate four strong painkillers and swallowed them dry then switched on the television and closed the curtains and lay on the couch. Daytime shows came on loud and bright. He watched a man cooking a roast dinner. An actress came on and talked about a new drama series. Young men and women walked up and down the studio wearing new fashion styles for the winter. Adverts came on for life insurance and children's toys and garden furniture. The rain tapped against the window and Innes pulled a blanket around himself and down at the bottom of the beer garden Young Bobby's body had lain for four days now in that shallow grave, next to the burnt-out scraps of the big stag's head.

23

It rained all the following week and into the middle of October. Hard, fat rain that swelled the loch and left deep sheets of water on the road. The stream at the bottom of the hotel's beer garden got fast and heavy, pulling itself over the rocks and fallen branches. Derek's missing cat posters fell in the ditch and got picked apart by gulls to make nests. There was no sign of Hercules. Grandpa spent another night in the hospital, getting more tests, more implements slid down his dry throat. In the Distillery warehouse, the barrels sat with the whisky slowly colouring as it drank the grain from the wood.

Sandy's funeral was set for a Monday. Father Jaine insisted that the service was to be brief. Margo worked on the flower arrangements all Saturday and all Sunday and Sandy was getting a huge spray of lilies and iris teardrops that stretched from one end of the coffin to the other.

Before the funeral Donald and Moodie went to see Sandy's body. The post mortem had gone as well as anyone could have hoped. He was resting there in the cold back room of the church, in a small coffin that fit snugly around him. They'd dressed him in a cheap suit that looked too big for the thin body inside. His mouth was glued shut and the skin over his eyelids was as thin as cigarette paper. Sandy had always had a big nose, and there it was still. They'd used a lot of make-up to get the complexion just right.

Oh, Sandy, said Donald. Look at the state of you.

Moodie rapped his knuckle on the side of the coffin as though assessing its quality.

Waste of a good suit, Donald said.

Waste of a good tree, Moodie said.

The two men stood side by side and looked down at the dead man's face. What more was there to say? Father Jaine had set out a box of tissues and there was a hook for hanging coats on. The room was cold. Finally Donald made a dismissive noise with his throat and turned and Moodie turned as well and the pair of them left Sandy to it.

Father Jaine's service was brief in the church and afterwards the congregation left the building and walked down the Shore Road that ran along the coast. The rain was still coming in sideways from the Atlantic. And there were not many there. Donald and Margo. Moodie and the rest of the men that worked in the Distillery in their black jackets. Old Jim was limping along on his one leg. Grandpa had come out for it as well and he stood braced in the rain with a tweed hat pulled down low on his forehead and a thick coat that covered him up to the bridge of his nose.

The pall bearers brought Sandy's coffin out from the church and slid him into the back of the hearse. The white and purple spray on top. Then the hearse engine strummed and the long black thing moved slowly out into the road, heading straight for the water until it turned, and the congregation moved to the side, and then they followed along behind on foot. The wind and the rain tore into them. One woman tried an umbrella but it was almost ripped from her hands.

The black car followed the shoreline and the men and

women in their black suits and jackets walked on behind, heads hunched so their faces would be spared the worst of it. The hearse turned to the left and climbed a short hill to a vantage point above the village where there was an old cemetery. This was where the sons and daughters of Cullrothes came to be planted.

Old Jim struggled up the hill and Margo gripped onto Donald's arm and Grandpa was some way back although a few of the men from the Distillery had slowed their pace, and lingered so that the old man was not entirely alone here. And he was coming, he was coming.

At the cemetery a couple of young men from the council in hi-vis vests stood to the side leaning on their spades. Sandy's grave was there and freshly dug, just a gash in the earth as thin as a runrig. The heavy rainwater had made the walls of the hole smooth and condensed. The grass was short and slippery here so the mourners padded around in their brogues and their fat heels, minding their balance, and the wind up here in the cemetery was fiercely whipping in. Rolling down off the mountains and across the loch and soaring up to this spot, into their faces.

It had taken longer than usual to get the body back. In the end, the pathologist could find nothing to confirm his initial suspicions.

As the coffin was lowered into the wet mud Father Jaine offered another prayer whose words were ripped away by the wind and then Sandy was gone. The two boys from the council in the hi-vis vests started shovelling the drenched mud back on top of the coffin, the first few scoops hitting with a hard thud, and by the time the congregation was halfway back down to the Shore Road, the grave was full again.

In the hotel bar, Innes was waiting for the mourners. The fire was crisply burning and a long table underneath the window had plates of sandwiches and sausage rolls and scones. As the people arrived he gave them a complimentary whisky or white wine or red wine. The tables filled up with people you didn't usually see in here. Old women with thick ankles and old men wearing suits that drowned them.

Some day for it, said Old Jim. He struggled onto his usual stool and sat looking at the whisky in his glass, swirling the burnt liquid up and down the sides and watching the trails forming.

Donald came to the bar. Only one drink each, remember, he said to Innes.

I'll make sure of it.

There's not that many of them.

It's some day out there.

A hell of a day.

Young Bobby's not been about?

Haven't seen him.

Donald sighed and grabbed his nose between his wet fingers. I wish that boy would let us know where the hell he is.

Gone walkabouts? asked Old Jim.

Aye. Hasn't been back at the house for a week. Haven't heard a damn thing.

He'll have found a nice girl on the mainland, said Innes. He'll be back.

His mother's worried sick.

Old Jim started rolling a cigarette from his pouch. It must be about a week since I last saw him. That was in here, wasn't it?

A week ago?

About that. It was just me and Innes and Young Bobby came in and had a few whiskies. Remember that?

I don't think that was last week, said Innes. It was longer ago than that.

Well did he say anything about going anywhere? asked Donald. Was he alright?

He was half cut, said Innes.

He was more than half cut, said Old Jim. He'd been on the goldies and he threw back a few more in here with me. Then I went up the road.

And? said Donald.

He left just after Jim did, said Innes. I had a drink with him and then he left.

Gentlemen, said Father Jaine, rubbing the rainwater from his hair. I'll have a brandy.

Innes poured the drink into a wide glass and gave it to the priest.

A nice spread, said Father Jaine. He had pastry crumbs flaked down his black pullover and there was the smell of egg mayonnaise on his breath.

Help yourself, said Donald.

I will do. Thanks. So what's this I hear about you getting an investor?

An investor?

I heard there's some American property guy looking to put some money into the business.

Where would you have been hearing something like that, Father?

From another priest. On the mainland. Just parish gossiping.

That's all it is then. Gossip. There's nobody going to interfere with my business.

I'm sorry I brought it up.

No need to apologise. We appreciate you doing the service.

It was a tricky one. Not ideal circumstances. I wish I could have said more.

Well it's over now.

Thank God for that.

Some day for it.

Hell of a day, said the priest. He held the brandy glass in the palm of his hand and swirled it round and round then brought the rim to his pink lips and poured the whole measure down, nice and slow, then sighed. A hell of a day.

Donald rolled his neck around his shoulders and felt the muscles tighten and contract. He stared at the empty spot on the wall where the stag's head used to hang. Need to get that replaced, he said.

I can help you put up the new one, said Innes.

I could do with having a look at the wall fixings on the old one.

I remember what they were like.

I wish you hadn't buried the damn thing without letting me see it. Do you know what those cost?

What happened to it, asked Father Jaine.

The boy genius here set it on fire, said Donald. Then buried it out the back. Says it was full of maggots.

Thousands of them, said Innes.

That's no end for a majestic thing like that, said the priest. Are you going to leave it there?

It's fine, said Innes sharply. It's buried good and deep and it's just fine where it is.

Maybe I should have a look at where you've put it, said Donald.

Honestly, said Innes, there's no need. It's well out the way. You wouldn't even know it was there.

Hasn't there been enough holes dug today, said Old Jim.

Probably, said Donald. Aye, there probably has.

24

The police car pulled slowly into the residential street. Here there were neat lawns and colourful flower arrangements and solid iron gates. He parked next to the yellow grit bin and got out. Stretched. This had been his home for a long time a long time ago.

It was howling wind. You could hear whistling down from the mountainsides and frothing up the loch and rattling in the forest. A wind so powerful you wouldn't be surprised to look down and see a fish lying at your feet.

Galloway walked up the short garden path to the pebble-dashed house. The building looked faded, or dimmer today than in his memory. Maybe it was the grey weather.

Smart in his white ironed shirt and the black tie of the Northern Constabulary. A wiry man who was not very tall but still had a six pack and struggled to grow any facial hair. Short hair that had been red and now was greying. He looked up and down the street, not sure how many of the neighbours remained the same.

Weeds grew full around the plants in the bedding. The grass had been cut this year but not for a few months now. The bench next to the front door was chipped and scarred after the years it had sat out. He remembered building this bench from its flat-pack box. Remembered sitting on it in the evening sun and drinking white wine and laughing.

The upstairs curtains were pulled shut in the bedroom window at the front of the house. He lifted the knocker and chapped three times. A dog growled, barked three hard barks. This was the blonde puppy he had seen photographs of. Jessie was always talking about her dog.

He could hear no footsteps coming down the stairs. No doors opening or closing inside the house. No voices or television in the background. Just the quiet street and his own heart beating hard in his chest outside his old house and the dog growling in the hallway behind the door.

Galloway wrote a note in his pad: *Just popped by to see if you were in – from Dad.* He turned quickly down the path and back to his car next to the grit bin. It was a good thing that his ex-wife would not come to the door today.

25

Innes tucked his shirt into his trousers and buckled the belt and looked at himself in the mirror. He untucked his shirt from his trousers and straightened it and looked in the mirror.

Should I tuck my shirt in or not, he shouted. Alice was in the bathroom.

Tuck it in, she shouted back. It's smarter.

The telephone in the hallway rang and Innes picked it up. The line was silent and then something clicked and the familiar recording kicked in: This call originates from a Scottish prison, the voice said. It will be logged and monitored and maybe recorded. If you do not wish to accept this call, please hang up.

Innes waited and after a few seconds there was a new audible background. Voices and echoes and bustle. He pressed the receiver into his ear.

A man's voice spoke: Hello? Alice, is that you darling?

I think you've got the wrong number, said Innes.

Is this not the number for an Alice Green? She's a teacher. I was given this number for her.

She's not here.

But is it the right number?

You've got the wrong number. Do not call back here again or I'll report you.

Innes hung up and looked at the phone. His hand was shaking. He picked the handset up again and held it to his ear but there was only the empty dial tone buzzing out of it. He had never met Alice's father but she had told him enough about the man. Innes feared what would happen to Alice's mental state if she found out he had traced her now to this place where the world was supposed to be peaceful. In his pocket was a little foil of pills and Innes ate two of them standing in the hallway then looked at his face in the mirror.

Innes had made a reservation for dinner at Marini's, a restaurant about an hour's drive away. Marini's had the best food on the peninsula but they only had a few tables and Innes had heard that you always had to book ahead. He had not been there with Alice before.

Innes tucked his shirt back into his trousers and put on a blazer. He went into the kitchen and swallowed a couple of painkillers with a glass of water. He was eating a lot of painkillers at the moment.

Need to leave in five minutes, he shouted.

I'm coming, I'm coming.

When Alice came out the bathroom she smelled of perfume and her legs were fake tanned and she wore a teal dress. There were curls in her blonde hair.

Well?

You look beautiful.

Are you sure?

Absolutely stunning.

Thank you.

Are you ready then?

I haven't done my nails yet. She held her fingers up to show him the pale, bitten tips of her fingers. But I'll do them in the car.

Innes drove. They bumped down the potholed driveway and turned left at the Shore Road and were soon out of the village and the sky was darkening already and there were flecks of purple and navy blue hovering in the late summer sky above the mountains across the loch. They drove through the glen with steep banks of heather on both sides looking out the windows to try and catch a sight of any deer grazing there, then turned onto a single-track road which rose in a steep zigzag. Innes flicked his headlights on and stayed in second gear but it was quiet on the roads and while Alice painted her nails they listened to a CD of American grunge music that reminded them of when they were teenagers.

How's school been this week?

Really good.

I feel like I've hardly seen you. With these collegiate meetings and parents' nights.

I know. It's been hectic.

Are you enjoying it though?

The children are great. Really nice kids.

How's that girl Jessie doing? From your senior class.

She's doing fine. I feel sorry for her. You know her Grandpa's dying?

She told me. She goes to see him after she's finished cleaning at the hotel.

Do you really think it's a good idea to have her working there? She's too young.

It's cash in hand.

Then you should give her more time off.

I've offered. She wants the money. She'd come in every day if I let her.

Maybe she fancies you.

Very funny.

Maybe you fancy her.

Why would you even say that?

I'm kidding.

They reached a long flat stretch of road and Innes could see it was clear and smooth so he accelerated and moved up through the gears. Mum was on the phone the other day, he said. She thinks I should appeal against my dismissal. Have the case looked at again. Mum says it's not out of the question that I could go back to the teaching.

Your mum's an idiot.

Innes nodded and pushed his tongue out between his top and bottom teeth and bit down.

When they arrived at Marini's the dining room was busy and the air smelled of garlic and candlewax.

I've got a booking, said Innes, for eight o'clock. The waiter was an overweight man in a white shirt with a name badge that said Luca. He spoke in a Scottish accent with little flourishes of Italian dialect.

Luca ran a fat finger down the list of bookings and back up to the top.

I phoned during the week, said Innes. Table for two. For eight o'clock.

I'll find you something my friend, said Luca. Give me a minute. He walked quickly to the back of the restaurant.

I phoned them, said Innes. I knew it would be busy.

It'll be alright, said Alice.

What if they don't have a table for us, he said. What'll we eat?

Luca returned, smiling, with menus under his arm. We have a table, he announced. You are very lucky. He wagged his finger at them from side to side.

That's why I phoned, said Innes, and Alice nipped the back of his arm.

Their table was in the back corner of the dining room. It was dark and away from the windows and behind one of the chairs was the door to the toilets.

Here we go, said Luca, pulling out a chair for Alice.

Is this okay? asked Innes.

It's fine, she replied. It'll be fine.

Some drinks?

Innes raised his eyes to Alice. Prosecco?

Prosecco.

A bottle of prosecco, please.

Good choice, my friend, said Luca, and he left them at the table with the leather menus.

It's nice in here, said Alice. Good to see there is a nice restaurant nearby that we can go to.

Yes. Innes reached his hands across the table and Alice reached out and they held hands. Now we can relax, he said. With someone to cook for us and clean up after us and we don't have to worry about the school or that bloody hotel for a night.

Just a couple of country bumpkins, said Alice. Out for dinner.

Innes laughed. Yes. I suppose we are. He looked around. Can you imagine if this place tried to open up in Glasgow? Or Edinburgh?

It wouldn't last a month. It's so old fashioned. Look at these wine glasses. Jesus Christ, they're like something my gran would have in her house.

The food looks good though.

The food does look good.

Luca brought the prosecco and poured them both a glass, leaving the bottle on the table.

Well, said Innes, holding his glass up and out. Here's to us. To a new life, and happiness, and getting back to a bit of normality.

Yes, said Alice. Here's to us, just a couple of country bumpkins.

Cheers.

Cheers. They clinked glasses and Innes sipped the prosecco and Alice drank a good third of hers in one.

Innes fished in his pocket for some painkillers and ate two of them with his wine.

What's wrong, Alice asked.

Sore head.

When the starters came the bottle was half drunk. Innes had his in small nervous sips, topping up his glass any time there was more than a thumb's width free space. Alice left hers alone for longer and then drank the bubbles in long, greedy tilts of the head.

What about this missing persons thing? asked Innes, smearing a chunk of grey pâté onto some bread. That Young Bobby guy. What have you heard about it?

Everyone thinks he's just done a runner, said Alice, touching a napkin to her mouth to mop up her minestrone. His father's a maniac. An absolute gangster. Everyone knows it.

What about that journalist friend of yours?

Valentine?

Aye.

He's hardly a friend of mine.

He must know something about it.

I don't think so.

I bet he does.

Do you want me to find out?

No. I'm just curious. It's quite a scandal isn't it? Quite mental. For something like that to happen in a place this place.

Something like what? The guy's obviously just laying low somewhere. Why do you need to overdramatise everything? As if he's been abducted or something.

They finished the prosecco and ordered a bottle of pinot noir to drink with their main course. They swirled the wine around in the glasses and dipped in their noses and took deep breaths.

Smells lovely, Innes muttered.

Yes, said Alice. They drank and pinched their lips and looked up to the corners of the room as they swallowed.

Very nice, said Innes.

Delicious, said Alice. She took another mouthful of wine then rearranged the cutlery in front of her. Luca put the plates of hot food down with a clunk on the tablecloth and offered them both a grinding of black pepper.

When Luca was gone, Alice said: Still no sign of that cat.

What cat? Innes blew on a forkful of spaghetti.

The missing cat. My pupil's missing cat. I told you about this.

Yes. That's right. I saw the posters.

It's been a couple of months now, said Alice. She cracked a mussel shell and scooped out the flesh with her fingers then sucked the grease off them. It's not looking good.

A month? It'll be long gone. A fox'll have taken it. Or mashed under a lorry.

Do you have to be so disgusting? I feel bad for that poor wee boy. You should've seen his face.

Not a bad thing. To get used to disappointment at that age. Life's not all biscuits and cheese.

He's just a child.

He'll get over it.

You have no empathy, do you? Maybe it's a good thing you're not a teacher anymore.

Innes clattered his fork down and stared at her but her face was obscured by the wine glass and when she put it down she smiled at him. Oh shut up. I'm kidding. Get a sense of humour.

Right.

You've not been yourself lately.

There is something on my mind.

Luca came over when the plates were cleared and when he picked up Innes's dish his elbow knocked the red wine and it bounced on the table and poured onto Innes's white shirt.

Innes scraped his chair back to try and avoid it but the wine was already staining his shirt and the crotch of his trousers and dripping onto the floor. Oh, he shouted. Oh, you absolute idiot. Look at the state of this! He stood up and rubbed at the wine stain with his napkin. Thanks a lot, he shouted. Oh thank you very much.

I am so sorry, let me get you a cloth. Luca hurried away.

Innes looked at Alice with wide eyes and she laughed. She held her own wine and swirled it and laughed.

What are you laughing at?

I'm sorry, she laughed, I can't help it. She drank her wine and made eye contact with the woman at the next table and smiled at her.

Luca came back quickly with a clean dishcloth and Alice took it from him. I'll get it, she said. Thank you. Could you get us the bill?

Alice got up and used the dishcloth to dab at the stain on Innes's shirt and trousers. She leaned in and kissed him. Look at the state of you, she said. I think we'll have to get you home and out of these wet clothes.

Really?

Really. Will you take care of the bill? I'm going to the bathroom.

She went through the door and into a cubicle. In her handbag there was a little plastic bag and she took this out and balanced a little white powder on her fingernail and snorted it up her left nostril. She dropped her underwear and urinated loudly. Then got up and went back into the restaurant without wiping herself or flushing the toilet or washing her hands.

Innes was already standing near the door. His shirt stained. He had buttoned his blazer to try and cover it.

Alice ran her fingers through the back of Innes's hair. That was lovely, she said. We'll come back here.

A bit stressful at the end.

It was lovely. Are you okay to drive?

I only had two glasses, he smiled.

Make sure you drive home slowly then, she said, with her arm linked in his.

26

When she walked over to the complex it was still light, the low sun glancing off the water and then back off the windows so that Jessie squinted all the way. And then it dropped and the wind felt instantly colder and the shadows stretched out long on the path.

Jessie was thinking about her mother, who had not been outside the house for many months now. If her mother knew that Galloway had been in the village, had been in her street, she would be furious. He only ever came to this side of the loch in uniform these days. Not even then, if he could help it. When they divorced the village had decided that he was the one to be outcast. Lifelong friendships abandoned just like that. Her mother's exile was more self-inflicted and now they were both absent from the girl's life.

When she came to the security door at Grandpa's block it was hanging open. A burst lock and the thing was swaying a little on its hinges. She pushed it open. Some leaves and dirt had blown into the hallway and spoiled the carpet, which was usually bright and clean.

The residents liked to keep their hallways neat with planted flowers in pots and framed watercolours and sideboards with vases or ceramic ornaments. But today the carpet was soiled and the flowerpots had been knocked aside and there was a smashed vase with its thick base turned upright again and shards of glass scattered around it. It was cold in the hallway. This door had been lying open for a while.

Jessie turned the corner to the staircase leading to Grandpa's flat and almost stood on a man's outstretched arm. He was lying blocking the hallway at the bottom of the staircase. A man with a skinny face and sick, grey skin. His clothes were dirty and old with frayed hems at his sleeves and trousers. On his feet were brown, torn trainers but no socks.

Jessie thought he might be dead but she watched his chest for a moment and saw he was breathing. Asleep, he was fast asleep, a drugged, toxic sleep. His head cradled against the bottom step of the staircase as though it were a pillow.

Jessie kicked him on the shin.

Excuse me, she said loudly, and kicked him again. You can't sleep here. The man mumbled and turned his body away from her, cradling his knees in his arms.

She bent down closer. The smell of damp from his faded raincoat. His face was lined with deep creases around his eyes.

Excuse me, she shouted into his face. Wake up! You can't sleep here! And she reached out and gripped his chin and used it to shake his head from side to side.

The man's heavy eyes blinked open, squint and bloodshot. He looked at her sideways then closed his eyes and rolled his head away.

Right, she said. Dropped her schoolbag and squatted and grabbed the man under both armpits. You need to get out of here. People live here.

He growled as she pulled at him but she took the strain on her thighs and straightened her knees and got him up and leaning against the wall.

113

Can you hear me? she said.

His eyes were flickering open and his mouth gaped to show brown speckled teeth. Hot sour breath as he gasped.

Come on, she kicked his shin again. This is where old folk live. My grandpa lives here. You need to get out.

The man opened his mouth and yawned. A thin string of spit fell from his lip and down his front. He was thin and bony underneath the raincoat. It was warm in his armpits where Jessie's hands held him.

We're going this way, she said, and manhandled him off the wall and put her arm under his ribs. His feet tripped and dragged on the carpet but he managed a facsimile of a walk.

No, he wailed. No, don't.

But he had no physical strength and she easily marched him down the hallway towards the door that still lay open.

Outside in the fresh air he recoiled and tried to shield his eyes from the dim light and wailed again.

I'm fine, he wailed, and his eyes were opened but unfocused.

What have you been taking? Jessie said. What a state to get yourself into. A grown man like you should know better. You junkie!

Even when Jessie was little the idea of drugs being used in Cullrothes was a fantasy. But you heard things about people and it seemed the village was catching up with the rest of the world.

The gardens outside the block were tended neatly and Jessie dropped the man onto a bench there facing the water. He fell slowly onto his side and pulled his knees up and hugged them. She pulled his collar up around his neck and left him to his deep, poisoned sleep.

In Grandpa's flat Jessie kicked off her shoes and sat on the couch with her legs tucked up under her.

You'll never believe it, she said. Some man broke into the hall downstairs. He was out of his face on drink or drugs or something.

But Grandpa didn't seem to be listening properly. Did you hear the news? he whispered.

What news?

I'm off. Pzzt. He shaped his hands like an archer firing an arrow from a bow.

To where?

The hospice, he said.

This was a couple of miles out of the village, west on the A871 in the direction of the lighthouse.

Already?

Grandpa pointed to his forehead where there was a small bruise and friction marks. I had a wee fall. In the kitchen.

Are you sore?

He shook his head. No, no. Just my pride, he laughed. It's the doctor's orders, so.

Just got to do what you're told.

As always.

Jessie got up and started tidying some old newspapers and envelopes from the side table. She picked a tissue from a box and touched it to her eyes with her back turned so Grandpa wouldn't see she was crying. Are you still struggling to swallow?

I can take a little porridge.

Are you okay with liquids?

Oh yes.

How about I make us a cup of tea?

That would be lovely.

Okay. She gathered a handful of papers for the bin.

She leaned over him to take away a dirty plate. Grandpa reached out and touched her on the arm. Either you're getting taller, he said, or I'm getting smaller.

Maybe it's a bit of both.

They sat there, the two of them, and drank the hot, milky tea. Grandpa looked around the room with his wet eyes and rubbed at his nose with a tissue. Jessie slipped her hand down the back of the couch between the cushions and pulled out a handful of lost change. She handed the coins over to him. He waved them away and looked out the window.

Keep it. What am I going to be buying with that? he said.

27

Into the house came Jessie from the rain where she kicked her wet shoes to the corner under the stairs and hung her school blazer over a radiator to dry. She opened the living room door and lowered her hand for the dog to sniff but he did not appear. She went into the living room and looked around the corner under the coffee table where he sometimes slept but he was not there. She stood at the bottom of the stairs and called out Murphy! in a low voice in case he had somehow got up there. But he did not appear, and she looked for him in the living room, under the coffee table, again.

Then she heard the distant barking. Frantic and repeated. Jessie opened the back door in the kitchen and Murphy hurried in, head bowed, dripping wet, his paws leaving thick puddles of rainwater on the floor.

In the kitchen there was the detritus of Jessie's mother's raid on the cupboards. An empty plastic cup with dried-out noodles and a dirty fork. Crumbs from toast spread across the worktop. The milk was out the fridge with its lid off and when Jessie sniffed it the stuff was beginning to go sour. There was a half-finished cup of tea with the teabag still floating in the dark brown liquid and in there also were cigarette butts and black ash clogging up the sides.

Jessie knew her mother had come down and let the dog out the back and gone to bed without letting him back in. This would have been hours ago. Murphy bumped his head between her knees and she bent down and held his sodden face in her hands and ran her hands along his ribcage and felt how cold he was, and the dog stuck out his tongue and trembled.

Look at the state of you, said Jessie. Did that bad woman leave you outside? Did that bad woman lock you out?

She took a dish towel from the drawer and ran it over Murphy's coat but there was too much water and the smell of wet dog was growing stronger. Mixing with the smell from the dried-out noodles and the clogging cigarette ash and the sour milk.

Right, she said. Right.

Jessie walked the dog up the stairs and held on to his collar. His wet tail bounced off the wall leaving streaks on the paint. He was not accustomed to being up here. Sniffing at the corners and staring at the closed bedroom doors. She pushed him into the bathroom and locked the door and turned on the hot water in the bath.

Jessie sat on the toilet seat while the tub filled up. Murphy stood staring at her, his tail in constant movement, excitement at seeing this strange room at long last.

What is it? she whispered, and his ears twitched.

What is it? she said again, and he cocked his head to the side.

She leaned over and turned the cold tap on now so that the bath did not fill up too hot.

Who's a good boy? Did that bad woman lock you out? Who's a good boy? She reached under him and unclipped his collar and he tried to grab it with his mouth so she hid it on the windowsill.

The bath water was warm and a quarter of the way up the tub. Come on then, she said, and patted the edge of the bath. Murphy looked at her. Up, she said. He raised onto his hind legs and placed his front paws on the rim. Up, she said. Come on. Get in.

But he didn't seem to understand so she grabbed his rear end and helped him over the bath's edge and into the water where he walked in tight circles, his pink tongue hanging, licking at the steam.

Jessie rubbed shampoo into the dog's coat and then turned on the shower head. Murphy ducked away from the water but she held him under it and rinsed the soap from his coat. When she had finished he stood there and shook himself violently and soaked Jessie' school uniform. Stop it, she laughed loud. Stop it!

She put a towel on the floor and Murphy jumped out. She was towelling his ears dry when the door handle turned on the locked door.

I need in there, shouted her mother. I need into the bathroom. What are you doing in there?

Nothing, said Jessie quickly. I'm not doing anything, I'll be quick as I can.

Why is this door locked? I need in now.

I'll let you know when I'm done.

But her mother started kicking and slapping at the door. What are you doing in there! Let me in right now, you goddamned little whore!

Just a minute!

My house, my bathroom. If I tell you to get out then you better do it. I am your mother!

Fine! Jessie opened the door. Her mother was standing in her dressing gown. Red in the face. Mouth hanging open and hair straggled greasy down the side of her face. Murphy slipped past them both and ran down the stairs, still wet.

You had that dog up here?

He was freezing. You left him out in the garden all day.

You had that dog in my bath?

He was freezing cold, he was shivering. I had to warm him up.

He's just a dog.

He's my dog.

Maybe he can look after you then. Maybe you don't need me anymore.

I just wanted to warm him up.

If you ever bring him up here again, said her mother, I'll give him away. Do you understand me? I'll take him to the vet and have him put down. I'll feed him rat poison. I'll drag him out down to the water and drown him.

Get out of my way.

But Jessie's mother stood in the doorway, blocking her path.

Let me out. Jessie pushed past her mother and started down the stairs.

You're just going to leave the bathroom like this are you? In this mess! You've got dirt all over the sides of the bath.

Jessie got to the bottom of the stairs and slammed the living room door shut. She could still make out her mother's voice shouting at her.

I'll clean it then, shall I? I'll clean up after you and that disgusting animal. That's fine. Leave it to me. Just you leave it to me.

Jessie clicked on the television and looked at her mobile phone. It had a signal for a change but it was weak. She typed a text message to her dad: *Not every day you get a missing persons case, is it?*

He replied quickly: *What's that?*

Young Bobby going missing. I'm guessing you're having to get involved.

I did hear about it. But nothing official for us to look at yet.

I got your note. What were you at the house for?

But then her signal cut out, and no more messages from her dad came through.

28

Donald pulled over at a farm gate on the way up to the Distillery and killed the engine. He ran his long fingernails across his bald head and scratched behind his ears then dug the heels of his hands into his eyes and rubbed them.

In the mirror his face looked worn. Lines around his eyes. Dark bags under them with blue and purple like he was bruised. He licked his lips. They were chapped and dry with spots of blood where they'd been picked at. Sleeping had become hard. Constantly thinking about the Distillery's cash arrears and what could be done about it. Those letters from his accountant. The phone calls from the solicitor. Constantly thinking about his missing boy and his heartbroken wife.

He wound down the window in the driver's door. The morning air poured in. Donald clenched his fists to his chest and pushed his forehead into the steering wheel until it hurt.

There was a hip flask in the glove compartment and he unscrewed its lid. It was early in the morning. The grass in the field was still wet with condensation. The birds sounded sleepy with long, low squawks. The hip flask's grooves rested coldly on Donald's bottom lip and he drank half of its contents in one pour, the whisky drowning his tongue, little glugs as he tipped it back.

He swallowed and sat there breathing. The back of his skull began to tingle and the tremors in his hands seemed to subside. He gripped the steering wheel and twisted it left and then right. Through the open window he heard the tyres crunching against the gravel. He pushed hard against the steering wheel with both hands and felt a pop in his spine. Another touch of whisky took his mind off it again.

The road was still quiet at this time and Donald pulled out into the empty lane. He kept his window wound down even when spots of rain began hitting the windscreen, splashing his forearm.

29

Nearing the end of a busy, wet day on the Corran Ferry. Brian guided the last of the cars on board and signalled to the tower. The thrusters began to pound under the water's surface. Brian signalled to Craig with a thumb's up and the tall boy pulled the lever to lift up the ramp. The iron surface scratched and then pulled away from the rotting concrete slipway. The alarm sounded loud above their heads and a couple of seagulls hung lazy in the sky.

Okay, shouted Brian over the noise of the water and the engine. You do the fares this time. See if you can get them all in before we get to the other side.

Craig nodded and quickly tapped on the window of the first car. A foreign registration plate. A foreign driver.

It's four pounds, said Craig.

The driver leaned out and handed the exact money over in pound coins. Craig gave him a ticket from a little book of stubs.

I want to visit the lighthouse, said the driver. Do you know what way to go?

When you get off the ferry, said Craig, you turn left and follow that road all the way round the coast.

To the left?

Yes. Craig pointed with his hand held out flat. Follow the A871 west and then you'll get to the village. It's called Cullrothes. You want to drive through the village –

Straight through the village?

Straight through. Then take a right turn at the sign for the lighthouse. Follow the road and it takes you all the way there.

Is it far?

It'll take a couple of hours.

Thank you.

Hope you have a good time.

Craig lifted his head. The ferry was more than halfway towards the other side. He turned. Brian was moving swiftly between the cars, handing out tickets and taking money, his feet never stopping, conversations short and sharp.

Tourist, shouted Craig. Wanted to know how to get to the lighthouse.

There's signs on the road isn't there?

I thought he needed help.

Tourist information up the road. Get maps there.

The ferry's engine sputtered out and it was silent as they floated towards the pier.

On you go son, said Brian. Aye, aye, aye.

Craig pulled the lever and the alarm sounded as the ramp lowered to let the cars off. Brian stood to the side and let Craig manage them coming off. The tourist drove past with his window down and waved at Craig as he went.

At the end of the day's final journey, Craig and Brian stood side by side looking down into the dark water. The ferry anchored in the middle of the loch overnight and they would be taking an inflatable wee RIB back to the shore once the captain had finished his checks.

How'd you enjoy your first month on the ferry, then? asked Brian.

I think I liked it.

You get into the rhythm of it. The busy mornings with folk coming and going. The afternoons quieter. Then the rush at teatime again. Every day more or less the same. It comes and goes.

Like waves.

Aye, I suppose.

And you've done this for thirty-six years?

So far.

Do you not get bored of it?

Bored of this? He looked down at the rolling water and around at the mountains and the loch and smiled out of the corner of his mouth at it. The purple heather and the bottle green forest in the distance. No no no. Something wrong with you if you get bored of this. Fancy coming over for dinner tonight?

What you having?

Got a couple of venison steaks in the freezer.

Sounds good. Craig turned to lean on a handrail, yawning.

You tired, son?

Aye.

Aye. You'll get used to it. Looks like that's us.

The captain was finished his checks for the night and the three of them got into the RIB, which sat low enough in the water to reach down and touch the loch, with the ferry left anchored in the dark until the morning service started again.

30

Moodie stood alone in the Cullrothes warehouse, a giant hangar full of barrels with millions of litres of whisky. Ageing, colouring, leaching the flavour from the wood. Moodie liked this space. It was always cool, no matter how hot the sun was outside. Always dark too, with a few narrow windows admitting only sharp slices of light. The ground was just compacted dirt. Smooth, uneven and ancient.

He dropped to the floor with his palms in the dirt and pushed himself up twenty times so his arms would look pumped.

Just after midnight, the drivers appeared. They'd come around the long way, circling the A871 that clung to the loch's edge round the peninsula rather than crossing the water on the ferry. Both drivers had thick stubble and hanging skin beneath their eyes. One of them wore a hat but the other's head was shaved.

The man in the hat took off his rucksack and opened the drawstring and held it for Moodie to see inside. There were clear plastic wallets filled with banknotes.

From underneath the table Moodie lifted an identical rucksack. It was dark green, with scuffs around the bottom. He opened the drawstring and offered the man in the hat a long look inside. There were dozens of plastic bags, zip-locked, filled with powder and pills and buds.

Moodie and the man exchanged rucksacks.

Will you need us next month? asked the man in the hat.

I'll make a call. Are you staying the night? The rooms are made up.

The two drivers looked at one another. Maybe a few hours only, said the man in the hat. Leave before the sun comes up.

Moodie had a key in his pocket and he gave it to the man. Same cottage as usual. Drop the key through the letterbox when you're leaving.

Thanks.

Oh, said Moodie. Try to leave the place a bit cleaner than you did last time. The towels were filthy. We had to throw them out.

The drivers nodded and avoided eye contact and left the warehouse from the same door they'd come in. Moodie trusted they'd be gone before daylight, on the long winding road back around the loch to the mainland. The ferry was too static to risk travelling on. The ferry was dangerous.

He pulled the plastic wallets from the bag and stacked them on the table to count the notes. These were not fresh prints from the bank, but notes picked up by dealers on streets all over the country. Wherever there was boredom and poverty you could make money. Places like Kilmarnock and Dingwall and Arbroath. What else were the people going to spend their wages on? It was not unusual to find a few torn notes. Some fakes. Even some American dollars slipped in from time to time.

He settled on a folding chair and drank half a measure of whisky and counted the notes out in piles of one hundred. Soon they spread across the table. The shy blue of five-pound notes. The tan of tens. The hot pink of twenties and a couple of scarlet fifties. One of these was a fake. He held the note up to the bulb of a lamp. A good fake. Someone knew what they were doing.

He re-packaged the bundles into the plastic wallets and placed these in the rucksack. Donald would want to re-count them in the morning.

Lately Moodie had been speaking with an American investor who wanted to buy the Distillery. Take everything from Donald including the hotel and the manse and the cottages. He didn't know the guy's name but it was clear that he was serious. Something was coming. Donald wasn't going to give the place up without a scrap. Something was coming but Moodie didn't know what or when yet.

He put the fake fifty in his pocket. Something to spend in the pub.

He got up and took a slow stroll around the silent whisky barrels. His eyes savoured the curves of the wood. The tightness of the steel. That subtle perfume as the whisky transformed and coloured and evaporated into the night sky, forever lost to the stars.

31

The mid-morning ferry was quieter than at peak times and would often travel with only a couple of cars on board. A grey day with a sky the colour of coins.

Brian and Craig waved the cars up the ramp and quickly collected the fares before the vessel was halfway across the loch. When you got here you could look north, up to where the water narrowed and splintered off into outlets and streams and rivers at the mainland. And you could look south, to where the loch gradually filled out until the horizon was just flat blackness.

There were some metal benches up on the deck and a tired little sheltered area but Innes chose to stand. He leaned his hands on the railing and stared down into the water foaming and rushing underneath. When the ferry touched on the other side, he nodded at Brian and got off without speaking to either of them.

The bookies was a dark little room up at the bad end of the high street next to the charity shop and an empty unit. Red plastic lettering outside and the windows all covered with polythene signs. Innes opened the empty door and there was nobody else there. Some games machines blinking and chirping in the corner. Formica shelves with empty coupons and dispensers with the half-sized biros. In a high corner there was a television showing horse-racing and the commentary was ringing around the room.

Behind the glass counter there was a middle-aged woman with a thick brown perm. Innes had Young Bobby's green slip in his hand already.

Do I give this to you? he asked.

What is it?

I've got some winnings to pick up. Lucky guess.

Let me see.

He put the slip down on the metal counter and she pulled it through to her. Picked it up and examined it in the light. She looked away from the slip to Innes and then back again. Then said: Are you wanting a cheque?

Can you do it in cash?

Aye. Wait there. She went through a door behind the counter and it closed softly behind her. The horse-racing commentary still echoing up in the corner. Innes watched it for a moment. Two horses clear out in the lead from the others. As they took a fence, one of the horses clipped its hind legs and staggered and the jockey was thrown to the ground. He covered his head and his face while the other horses landed around him. The riderless horse tore forwards, inching into the lead. Head up, hooves pounding, looking strong and sad at the same time.

The woman returned from the back office with a tray of notes and an envelope. Innes watched as she counted them out, placing the clean sheets on top of one another, her hands fast and efficient. When she got to the end she looked at Innes. He nodded. So she put the money in an envelope and passed it to him through the glass counter.

Anything else, son?

No thanks.

Don't spend it all at once.

32

Margo waited outside the shop until someone else was coming out so she wouldn't cause the bell to ring when she entered. Her hair was tied up to hide the grease and the grey that she hadn't got around to dyeing. She had on a thick coat and old shoes. Kept her eyes down and turned away so that the shelving hid her from the counter.

She carried a basket and she sat this at her feet and began adding cans of food. Yellow macaroni. Thick brown beef stew. A four-pack of beans.

Margo, said the shopkeeper brightly. She had left the counter and stood in front of the doorway. I thought I saw you coming in just now.

Hello, Sheila.

Sheila took a step forward and touched the sleeve of Margo's raincoat. And how are you?

I'm coping.

It can't be easy.

It's not.

You'll let me know if there's anything I can do?

Sure. Thank you for saying that.

Sheila was a fat woman with pink cheeks and white hair.

She looked down at the basket on the floor with the cans of food. She looked at Margo's tired face and the raw, bitten skin around her fingernails.

This isn't what you're buying to eat for yourself, is it?

It's just a few things for the cupboard.

Oh, Margo.

It's fine. It's convenient.

I'll tell you what. I'll come up to the house tomorrow with some home-made meals. You can put them in the freezer for when you can't be bothered cooking.

Oh, no, I couldn't ask you to do that.

It's not a bother. It must be hell! Cooking would be the last thing on my mind if my boy was missing.

Margo swallowed and shuffled her feet.

How long has it been? Since he's been gone.

It's a month now.

Christ. It's a sin. That's what I'll do then, I'll bring some food over. So you and Donald make sure you're looking after yourselves What do you like?

I really don't mind.

I can do a casserole. A pie. Maybe a curry. Does Donald eat curry? And soup, I can do you a big pan of soup.

I really don't know, Sheila. Thank you, anything would do.

That's what I'll do then, smiled the shopkeeper. She looked down at the cans. Well, I'll let you get on. You'll still want some of these for the cupboard. For emergencies.

Yes.

Young Bobby used to come in here often, said Sheila, looking behind her but there was nobody else in the shop. Most days. Came in for his fags, his drink. Newspapers, that kinds of thing.

Margo nodded.

The thing is, said Sheila, he never seemed to have any cash

on him. Fivers and tenners here and there but never enough for what he was buying, do you know? Always said he'd left his wallet in the office or something like that.

What is he like?

So obviously what am I going to do? He's your boy, I've known him all his life. I was running up a tab for him. Pay me when you've got the money, son, that's what I used to say.

I'll make sure he does pay you back, said Margo. Every penny. When he finally turns up.

It is quite a big tab. And I don't know how long it'll be before then. Will he even have any money? She held out her hands and shook her head.

Okay, said Margo. I hear what you're saying. I can pay it up just now.

Oh, thank you, smiled Sheila. I really am certain that he'll be back soon, you know. Try not to let it get you down. You shouldn't worry about it.

Shouldn't I? asked Margo. She turned back to the shelf and put three cans of chicken soup into her shopping basket.

33

On a morning of mist and low cloud Brian, who had been a ferryman his whole working life, stood quietly side by the side with his son as the slow passage neared its end at the mainland. The first ferry of the morning coming from Cullrothes was always full of cars. Normally they would have to leave a small queue of folks at the slipway as well, who would have to wait another fifteen minutes before the ferry could come back for them. It was a morning like that.

The pair stood side by side and gazed into the fog. The ferry was full of regulars. The same cars every morning and they all had season tickets. This was an easy journey. They knew most of the cars by sight and there was no need to go around issuing stubs or calculating change.

It's getting thicker, said Craig.

Aye, said Brian. Aye, aye.

In unison they looked up to the cockpit where the captain was. The ferry was navigated in a little control room at the end of a short bridge.

She'll be fine, said Craig.

Oh God, aye, said Brian. The ferry service had been cancelled for high winds before but never for fog. This was a quiet channel and the vessel made the return trip so regularly the crew could do it blindfolded.

At the mainland Craig lowered the ramp and Brian guided the cars out one at a time. The drivers nodded and lifted their hands from their steering wheels in recognition of the simple act. There was a long queue of cars on this side too, and one pedestrian. A short man in a red jacket, with a baseball cap which he wore backwards and a heavy backpack.

What's the fare? he shouted to Craig as he began to conduct the cars onto the ferry.

No charge, said the ferryman. Go sit inside.

The man in the red jacket gave a thumbs up and went into the little waiting area, with its pamphlets for tourists and the seats with torn upholstery.

When the cars were again loaded and the drivers had shown their tickets, the boy stood with his dad in their habitual spots and they squinted their eyes at the fog.

Easing off, said Craig.

Not yet, said Brian.

Some thick fog, said a voice behind them. They turned and there was the little man in the red jacket. An American accent. A clean-shaved, smooth, handsome little face. With a triangle of hair just beneath his lower lip. You get a lot of fog like this around here?

Depends, said Brian. Different times of year.

Wait an hour or two, said Craig. The sun'll burn it off. Like it was never here at all.

Beautiful place, said the American, looking around. When you can see it, I mean.

Aye.

Aye.

The ferrymen looked around themselves, unimpressed.

You two are related, right? You look alike. And you work together too?

Most days.

Man, you must get along fine. I'd kill my old man if I had to spend so much time with him.

Well, said Brian.

It can tempting, said Craig.

I'll bet. You must want to throw each other over the side sometimes! The American was laughing and the ferrymen both laughed, all three of them looking over the side, at the black waves rebounding off the ferry's hull.

Well I'm just visiting, said the American. Hoping to get a little work. I don't suppose you need a new hand on board here?

Brian shook his head. Nothing going on the ferries.

You heard of any vacancies nearby? I don't mind hard work.

What can you do?

A little bit of this, a little bit of that.

The ferry was pulling close to the shore. Craig stepped to the control panel to start bringing down the ramp. You could try the tourist information stall, he said. Or the shop. Sheila that works there usually knows what's going. Maybe something at the hotel. Or the Distillery.

You guys making whisky over here?

Oh aye. They take plenty of casual workers over the summer. You'll find something.

Thank you both, said the American. He pulled his baseball cap around so the peak faced forwards now. That's good to know.

The ramp was lowering, the alarm sounding at the same time, and the car engines were starting up.

Cheerio then, said Craig.

Sure there's no charge for the trip?

No charge for pedestrians.

At least take a tip, said the American. He folded a fifty-pound note and jammed it into Craig's breast pocket while the ferryman shook his head.

Away, he said, take that back. You're off your head.

But the American was already walking off, head down, one hand in his pocket and the other waving. You hang on to it, he shouted back.

Craig fumbled off a glove and got the money from his pocket but he was needed now, the cars were inching forwards all at the same time and the wee American already was fading into the fog as he walked off the ramp and up to the road at the shore, and Brian his dad was staring at him, and Craig faced the cars and held his hand out so one knew to wait and he looked at another and waved it forwards towards the ramp. Come on then, he shouted at it, locking eyes with the driver. Come on, come on, yeah, yeah, yeah.

34

When Alice swung her head from side to side there was a lag in her vision and she blinked hard a few times to try and clear it. She was lying back on the couch and when she lifted her knees and crunched her stomach she came forwards slowly until she could lean over the coffee table.

I will roll us another one, she said, reaching for the cigarette papers, and the pouch of tobacco, and the bag of green buds.

Innes was lying back on the couch with his hands over his face. He grunted.

Can you empty this? She passed him the ash tray that was full of dead roaches.

Does it need emptied?

It's disgusting.

Innes levered himself out of the couch and stood quite still for a moment before going to the kitchen.

Why don't you make us some tea while you're in there?

She rolled a joint then picked at a ragged toenail while she waited. She could hear Innes banging in the kitchen with mugs and spoons. The kettle boiling. The fridge door.

Alice felt a tight burst in her chest. Innes! she shouted. Are the doors locked?

Yes.

Can you check them?

I locked them.

Can you just check again?

She heard him trying the door handle at the kitchen door and then at the front door down at the end of the hallway. All the curtains were closed even though it was the middle of the afternoon. Alice didn't want anyone from the school dropping by and being able to look in the window to see them smoking joints.

Innes came back with two teas and a packet of biscuits.

Alice sparked the joint and took three big draws and passed the thing to him.

I haven't had this much to smoke for years, he said.

Isn't it great?

I feel a bit mushed up.

Me too. It's just what we needed.

It is good.

I can get more. We can do this once a month. It can be our thing.

Where did you get it?

From Valentine.

He just gave it to you?

I bought it.

Where did he get it?

From a guy in the village. I don't know. She took the joint back and smoked it and looked at Innes's pink eyes.

He's the one that did the story about you in the paper?

Yes. About the missing cat. Did I tell you what we're going to do for it now?

No.

We're going to get Father Jaine up to the school. With all

the children. Including Derek obviously, it was his cat. And the priest is going to give a memorial service. Isn't that cute?

Do we know the cat's definitely dead, then?

Alice sipped her tea and picked up a biscuit and held it close to her mouth. Do you want to know a secret? she asked before taking a bite.

Go on then. Innes put a whole biscuit in his mouth.

I killed it. About a month ago. I was driving home and it ran out into the road and kind of froze right in the middle of the lane. I was heading straight for it and I pulled the wheel to the left to try and miss it and the stupid thing went the same direction. Right under the tyre. Dead. Just like that. She snapped her fingers then ate half her biscuit.

Innes stared at her. You're kidding?

Nope.

What about the posters? The piece in the paper?

I was just having a laugh.

You're completely insane. You've gone completely insane.

I know, she smiled. It is quite crazy isn't it?

They were both laughing now. Innes picked up the joint from the ashtray and lit it again and puffed it and passed it to Alice. He doubled over on the couch and laughed and his face went red with it. He started coughing as he laughed with his chest rattling.

They never found its body because I threw it in the loch, shouted Alice.

You never! You never! I can't believe it. Innes shook his head and wiped tears from the corner of his eyes. This is the most messed up thing I've ever heard. He started trying to get his breath back.

It just happened. I didn't plan it. Then after the thing was dead it just grew arms and legs.

When were you going to tell me?

I hadn't planned that either. I didn't know if I could tell. It's good to share with someone though. I've been keeping it all bottled up. Alice folded her arms across her chest and trembled and mimicked being a bottle about to explode.

I can't believe it, said Innes, calm again now. You killed that cat.

After this memorial that'll be it all over. Forgotten about. It's given me a buzz. I'm going to miss having a terrible secret. Have you ever heard anything like it?

Do you want to hear something worse?

What could be worse?

Innes squeezed his nostrils and blew out sharply. I might have a secret of my own, he said. That I think is a bit worse.

Alice folded her legs underneath her body and swivelled on the couch to face Innes directly. Go on then, she said, and took a long drink of her tea.

It's about that Young Bobby guy.

Uh-huh.

He was in the hotel bar the night he went missing.

Uh-huh.

He was drunk and he was being really threatening towards me. Really aggressive.

You never told me that. Alice stretch a leg out and put her foot reassuringly on Innes's thigh.

He was saying things to me about my job, he was talking about me getting struck off from being a teacher. Being really horrible about lots of things. I felt bullied.

I never met him, but I heard he could be like that.

Innes looked to the closed curtains and then he got up and opened them and put his head in the gap and looked outside. Then he closed them tight again and sat on the coffee table putting his hand on Alice's knee.

He poured a drink over me and it went all down my shirt.

I was angry and I pushed him. Not very hard but I think he caught his foot and tripped. He fell over. There was this big stag's head on the wall and when he fell he twisted and he ended up landing on the antler. It hit him in the throat. It punctured the skin and went into his throat. And I couldn't do anything to help.

This was coming through deep, gasping breaths. Alice felt her chest and her temples hammering with the blood in them.

Innes looked up and their eyes met. I couldn't do anything to help because he was bleeding so much. And then it didn't take very long from there. He was dead quick. But I didn't mean it. I didn't mean it.

Are you serious? Is this true?

Innes ruffled his hair and nodded.

So you're a murderer now?

He balled his hands together and his face fell apart and he started to cry like a child. Alice sat on the coffee table next to him and put her hands behind his back and pulled his head into her chest. There there, she said. It's alright. Everything's going to be alright.

Alice's skin grew wet as Innes cried on her.

Can we go outside, he asked. I need some air.

Let's go and stand at the door.

She put her arm around his shoulders and they unlocked the door and stood on the threshold feeling the cool air around their bare feet. It was getting towards evening and the sun going down made it look as though the sky was on fire.

I can't believe you're being so nice about this, said Innes. He thought now about the phone calls from Alice's father and the stories he'd heard about that man and the things he'd done. Maybe this was normal to her.

I wish you told me sooner, she said.

I didn't think I could.

143

So where is he? What did you do with it?

I buried it.

Where?

I don't know if I should tell you. I want to protect you.

Is it buried good?

I think it's good.

You poor boy. You poor, poor boy.

The sun was almost gone now, and the night was coming in, so Alice turned on the oven so she could heat a frozen pizza to satisfy their hunger.

35

In the sacristy the priest changed out of his corduroys and hung his blue cotton shirt on a rail that ran along the wall. It was a compact room the school had given him, with a crucifix mounted on the wall, and a picture of Mary framed on the back of the door. But there were no windows. He suspected it had originally been used as a stationery cupboard.

He pulled his robes over his head, knocking his spectacles down his long nose, and adjusted himself. Looking into the mirror as he fed the white collar into position and secured it there. It was a silly thing, to come up to the school for this. There was fluff sticking to the robes when he looked down to examine them. He had a lint roller in his bag and he took this and rubbed it all over himself to clear it.

The children were sitting waiting on the low wooden benches in the school hall when he entered. A dark room with high windows and the faded template of a basketball court on the flooring. Their teacher stood and snapped her fingers at the pupils and they stood as well, turning their heads over their shoulders to look at him as he clasped his hands and walked slowly to the lunch table at the front. He motioned for them to be seated once again. As the children sat, one of the boys on the front bench, Derek, began to cry. Strong, wet cries that poured from his nose and changed the whole shape of his face. This was the little boy whose cat had gone missing and was now presumed dead. Of course it was dead. The girl sitting next to Derek handed the boy a tissue and put her arm around his shoulder.

Father Jaine had never officiated at a memorial for a cat before.

Well, children, he began. This is a sad day. A terribly sad day in the village of Cullrothes. We have gathered here today to say farewell. Farewell to a loving family member. A friend.

The priest spoke slowly and deliberately, with twitches of his head as he met the children's eyes with his. The grieving boy jammed his fists into his eye sockets and howled.

A beautiful creature, said the priest. And one of God's finest creations. We are here today to say goodbye, yes. But also to say thank you. Thank you for the good times. Thank you for your companionship.

Then the priest stopped and looked at the floor and then he looked at Miss Green in her nice purple dress sitting there on the benches with the children.

He spoke quietly: Sorry, remind me of the cat's name?

Hercules, said the girl at the front. The one with her arm around the sobbing boy. I have a picture of him here.

The girl stood and walked the few short feet to the priest, holding carefully onto a creased photograph.

Thank you, said Father Jaine. He looked at the photograph then turned and balanced it on the table next to him, so that the cat's portrait faced out towards the mourners.

Hercules was so much more than just a cat. I, in fact, often saw him on my way to and from the wee shop, where I sometimes go to buy my chocolate. And whenever I saw lovely Hercules I couldn't help but feel happy. Indeed, there were days when he would jump up on the wall as I was walking past, and he would stand there and let me pet him. And he would purr, boys and girls, he would purr. And sometimes that was enough to take me from a bad mood and put me into a good mood.

The children sat staring now, mesmerised by the priest's voice. Father Jaine went on: And in a way, in a very real way, Jesus is a little like Hercules. Isn't he, boys and girls? We do not always see or feel Jesus. But we know he is always there. And when we need Jesus, when we are in a bad mood, or are sad, or feel angry, he can help us to feel better. Jesus does not let us pet him. Jesus does not purr. But if we allow Jesus into our hearts and into our minds, then he can help us to understand ourselves, just a little bit better.

Is Hercules with Jesus now? asked one of the children near the back.

Yes, said the priest. Hercules will be in heaven now. And Jesus is also in heaven.

Will Jesus pet Hercules? asked Derek, who had looked up suddenly and his red-swollen eyes were wide and desperate.

I am sure, said the priest, that if Jesus does meet Hercules up in heaven, he will pet him.

Derek sat up, nodded, and blew the last of his snot into the tissue. The girl next to him whispered something, and Derek nodded again. He breathed out a strong breath of air and nodded to himself a final time.

Well, shouted Miss Green, clapping her hands together and jumping up. That was a lovely service, wasn't it? Children, I think we should thank Father for coming all the way here and giving up his afternoon so that he could say those beautiful words about Hercules.

The pupils applauded politely.

You don't have to clap, smiled the priest. And you are very

welcome. But if anyone wants to thank me properly, tell your parents to bring some chocolates along to the church with them on Sunday. I only like the expensive ones.

The children sniggered and looked at one another, unsure of whether or not he was joking.

None of your cheap rubbish, the priest concluded, clasping his hands. I only eat reputable brands.

36

Donald clutched the toilet bowl with both arms wrapped around it. His breathing was thick, stomach muscles tensing with the threat of another attack. He half turned onto his side and felt his cheeks warm and wet. He was crying. A grown man lying on the bathroom floor crying.

But his knees felt good. The ache in his shoulder had gone.

The textured wall to his left was dashed with his vomit. It was leaking down the paper and pooling around the skirting board and settling on the linoleum.

Donald, shouted Margo from upstairs. Donald, are you alright?

He groaned.

Did I hear you throwing up? she shouted. Voice getting closer. Have you been sick?

He turned and looked into the water and spat out the taste of bile and flushed the toilet.

Are you in there? Getting closer. He put his hands flat on the linoleum and pushed his body up into a sitting position, his head resting on the towel rack, numb and happy.

Oh my god, she said. Standing in the doorway now, in her

pyjamas, looking at him and then at the wall. You've thrown up all over the wall, Donald.

I didn't mean to, he tried to say.

She stepped carefully into the bathroom and examined the stain.

This won't come out. We'll have to re-paper it.

It's fine, he tried to say.

You're absolutely wasted aren't you? Drunk out of your mind.

I'm fine, he tried to say.

It stinks in here. It stinks of whisky. How much have you had?

Donald tried to stand up but his wet hands slipped and he fell back onto his backside and his head flopped against the floor.

Wait a minute, he tried to say. Let me explain. I am fine.

And he did feel fine. But by the time he'd righted himself to demonstrate it, Margo was gone.

37

The junior class had a test this Tuesday morning and they'd had all weekend to revise. Alice arrived at school early and sat at her desk combing her hair and putting on a little foundation and mascara. It had been a cold, uncomfortable night and it was still brisk so she wore a skirt with thick tights and her feet in warm boots crossed underneath her desk.

When it was nearly time for the morning bell Alice tied her hair up and slipped on her shoes and went to the photocopier with the master copy of the test.

The headteacher was already there running off copies of a fundraising flyer.

Good morning Alice, she said.

Good morning, Mrs Hughes.

I won't be long.

Thanks.

Just running off some flyers for the ceilidh. You're coming to the ceilidh?

Oh yes, said Alice, we'll be there.

Good. It's a real family event. The headteacher wore a smart dark blazer and she was from a different village on the mainland and her accent was subtly different from the locals on

151

certain words. You're feeling okay after our little chat? About the complaint.

It's completely out of my mind.

Good. I felt terrible having to bring it up like that. The things we have to deal with in this job. But you've put it behind you now. Good. Have you got a busy day ahead of you?

Very. I'm just copying these questions for the juniors, said Alice. I'm giving them a test first thing this morning.

A test? Mrs Hughes tilted her head to the side to see the copy in Alice's hand. What would you need to be testing them on? It's very early in the term to be giving out tests.

Alice's nostrils flared. It's just a progress check. To see if they've been paying attention in class.

Surely you would know if they are paying attention in class?

Yes. But I want to see if they have gaps in their knowledge.

And the best way to see if there are gaps in their knowledge is by setting a test?

The photocopier ran out the last of the ceilidh notices and the headteacher gathered them and tapped the edges down to straighten the pile.

Remember what I said about our aspirations for these children. About pushing them and nourishing them. Come to my office on Friday afternoon. It would be good to catch up again. See how you feel it's going.

That would be good, said Alice, I will look forward to it. She slipped her master copy into the feed and punched in the details and watched the hot paper run out.

When the children arrived they sat at individual desks arranged in rows with the papers already laid out and got their pencil cases from their bags and wrote their names at the top of the answer sheet.

Okay, said Alice. This morning we're going to sit the comprehension test that I told you about last week. Did everyone remember to revise?

Most of the children nodded.

Did anyone forget?

A little laughter and some of the children pointed at a boy with curly hair called Rowan.

Well, you'll just have to do your best. You have one hour to finish. There is a passage to read on one sheet – she held up the master copy as an example – and questions on the other. Read the passage carefully then answer the questions. Okay?

Some of the children nodded.

Okay. Get started. Go.

While the children worked Alice walked around and read their answers over their shoulders. She stopped at Rowan's desk and reminded him to write his name at the top of the answer sheet. She smiled at a little girl called Mandy and told her that her answers looked good. She got to the front and watched them all working quietly for a moment.

Class, she shouted. Remember to pay attention to how many marks each question is worth. This will tell you how much detail we're looking for.

Alice sat at her desk and looked at her diary. A little love heart drawn in the corner of today's page that acted as a reminder, or maybe it was more like an omen. She felt the low-level anxiety that she had started to enjoy since the affair started. In her handbag there was a pair of stockings and good heels. Innes was working late locking up at the hotel so tonight was a love heart night and the journalist Valentine liked her legs in stockings.

Miss, said a girl called Rebecca. I'm finished.

Alice looked at her watch. There's still half an hour left, Rebecca. The other pupils were still working.

Rebecca licked her lips and looked at her answers and then at the questions.

I've done them all.

Alice stood up. Did you leave any out?

No.

You must have rushed them. Take ten minutes to check over your answers. Remember that a three-mark question needs a more detailed answer than a one-mark question.

Rebecca picked up her pencil and went back to her paper.

Alice looked in her handbag to make sure that her little make-up tote was there.

Miss, said Rebecca, I've checked them.

You're sure you don't want to add any more?

No. They're fine. I'm sure.

A couple of boys near the back of the room began muttering.

Boys, said Alice, focus. Get back to it! Class, you still have twenty-five minutes left. There is no need to rush.

Miss, said Rebecca, shall I hand this in? She held the papers out.

I'll get them in a minute.

Alice took a ball of Blu Tack from her drawer and ripped off a crumb off the putty. She rubbed it between her fingers and stretched it out into a narrow string and the balled it up again.

Rebecca went into her schoolbag and got out a fantasy novel and started reading. A couple of girls were watching Rebecca instead of doing their tests.

I said to focus, Alice shouted. Just because Rebecca has finished early does not mean that you are!

Alice got up and walked to the back of the room between the desks. She rubbed the Blu Tack between her thumb and her fingertips.

154

I'll take that now, she said when she got to Rebecca's desk. Thanks.

You just read your book and relax for the next twenty minutes.

Okay.

Alice picked up Rebecca's test paper and dropped the warm dot of Blu Tack into Rebecca's thick dark hair, right near the crown. She went back to the teacher's desk and lined up Rebecca's paper next to the marking instructions. Watching the girl carefully, but she was only interested in reading her book so far.

Oh, said Rebecca. Oh, oh!

It had only taken five minutes. Alice felt a delicious wave of energy rush through her and she half-stood at her desk. A few children looked up from their tests.

Oh, what, what? The girl was delicately picking at her scalp with her fingers, her eyes screwed up and cheeks already turning red.

Alice took a deep breath and said: What is it now, Rebecca?

The girl stood up, twisting at a small handful of hair.

Sit down, shouted Alice. Boys and girls, get back to doing your tests! Rebecca, you do not have permission to leave your seat.

But Rebecca got up anyway and walked with quick steps to the front of the room where Alice was leaning forward in her chair with her toes clenched in her shoes.

Miss, the girl whispered. There's something sticky stuck in my hair.

What is it?

I think someone's put chewing gum in it, the child moaned. There were tears gathering in her eyes and the knuckles on her clenched fist were white.

Let me see, said Alice. She stood up and the girl bent down

and Alice could see the perfect blue dot in there, mashing a good thick pile of hair together right at the crown where the follicles began.

Oh dear, she said.

What is it? Is it gum?

Alice gently moved Rebecca's hands away from the clump and pressed the Blu Tack even more firmly into the girl's crown.

Everybody stop! she yelled. Stop what you are doing. Eyes on me.

The children looked up but one or two kept on writing quickly to finish their sentences.

I said to stop, shouted Alice again. Her voice was strong and well projected and she could see the fear already in some of the little children's faces.

Who has done this? She pointed at Rebecca. Who has put gum in Rebecca's hair?

Rebecca was sitting on the floor now, holding her head in her hands, crying loudly.

Well I think it's disgusting, shouted Alice, that someone would do this to one of their classmates. What do we say in the school prayer every morning? To have kindness and understanding! To be responsible and to help others! Just because Rebecca is different from the rest of you – just because she is *cleverer* than you – is no reason to do something so despicable.

The children were silent.

Who did this?

Nobody answered.

She looked at Rowan, who sat at the desk directly behind Rebecca. Was it you?

No, no.

Who was it then? If it wasn't you then you must have seen it. You are sitting right there.

I don't know, miss.

I take a very dim view of bullying, said Alice. That is not something I would expect in this school. We are supposed to be like family to one another. You have known each other for years. Since you were little babies. Your parents know each other. I am disgusted. And I know that Mrs Hughes will be disgusted, too.

Alice stared at the children one by one until their eyes fell downwards. Come here, Rebecca, she said more quietly. Rebecca moved closer. Her hair was messed and stood up and away from her scalp. The Blu Tack was stretched thin and had gathered in a good rope of hairs.

Stand still, said Alice. She took a pair of scissors from her drawer and stood behind the girl. She began to cry more loudly, standing there facing her classmates, who all stared back. The pupils all watched as Alice lifted the stuck fistful of hair and opened the scissors and snipped quickly and loudly at the base near the girl's scalp.

Rebecca yelped and the girls in the class muttered and gasped.

Alice held her hand out in front of Rebecca. A pile of the girl's hair and the Blu Tack congealing it together. Rebecca put her hands to her mouth and wept.

Go to the bathroom, said Alice, and wash your face. And here. She handed Rebecca the hair. Flush that down the toilet for me while you're there.

Rebecca took the hair and ran from the room and the door slammed behind her.

Alice sat at her desk and smiled at the children. Mrs Hughes will be hearing about this, she said. Now, come on. There's still ten minutes until the bell. Get these tests finished.

While the children worked, Alice looked at Rebecca's answers. They were clear and concise and showed good insight. Alice gave Rebecca full marks and drew a smiley face at the bottom of the answer sheet.

38

After school Alice went to the bathroom and put on some fresh make-up and combed a spritz of perfume through her hair. She locked herself in a cubicle and changed her underwear and sprayed a little perfume around herself.

She drove in her flat shoes away from the village, away along the winding single-track roads towards Valentine's house. The journalist had his own place surrounded by empty land and from up there you could see no other civilised habitat. Only endless sheets of heather and the distant mountains and the massive sky. She took the corners slowly and drove with her eyes scanning the ditch alongside the road in case a sheep or a wild goat should appear. There were signs dotted along the road that said Beware of Sheep although she thought that really it was the sheep who should be scared.

Valentine's house was a long flat cottage with high windows that looked out over the peninsula. It faced away from the water inland, so that the views were of the mountains and the heather. She parked at the side of his house and put on her high heels. Got out the car and straightened her skirt and left her schoolbag on the passenger's seat.

Valentine was drinking a glass of white wine and he poured

159

one for her and they clinked glasses and kissed hello. Alice let the cold wine coat her tongue before swallowing it. The journalist lit a cigarette and took a drag and then passed it to her and she smoked it while he lit one of his own.

Come and sit here, he said, and pulled her down to him on the leather couch. She sat there and he tucked her hair behind her ear and rested his warm hand on the back of her neck.

Mmm, she said, that's nice. What a day I've had.

Really? He took her hand and kissed her fingers.

I had a chat with the headteacher. Is it just me or is she a bitch?

Hughes? Total bitch.

Now I need to go to this damn ceilidh. Are you going to it?

Valentine finished his wine and put the glass down. Oh, I'll be there. Never miss a ceilidh. He starting undoing the buttons on Alice's blouse.

I haven't even finished my wine yet, she said.

Down it, he said.

She finished the rest of the wine in one long slow motion while he unbuttoned the rest of her blouse. She put down the glass and hitched up her skirt and straddled him on the couch. There was a long ornamental broadsword mounted on the wall.

I've never been to a ceilidh, she said.

You'll like it. We can dance together. I've got a new guy who's going to get me a few pills for it. Some American guy who's just turned up but he's got good stuff for a good price. Undercutting everyone else. You want anything like that?

Alice touched the collar on Valentine's shirt and felt the pulse at his neck beating hot and fast and dragged her fingers across his stubbled throat.

No. I'll take some more weed though. I'll need to bring Innes to the ceilidh.

Fine. I'd like to meet him finally.

That's strange, she said. What a strange thing to say.

You're strange, he said, and pulled her down to him and her hair draped across his shoulders and the cold early winter light filtered in through the curtains onto them. It would not be dark for a little while yet.

Later, Alice drove home with the windows rolled all the way down. She stopped in a dark passing place on the single-track road and changed back into her normal underwear and tied her hair up and checked that her make-up was tidy.

In her handbag was her school planner and she opened this and marked another page in the following week in the corner with a love heart. She coloured in the shape in so it was a solid block and drew a cartoon arrow firing through the middle of it. That at least was something now to look forward to.

She smoked a cigarette halfway down then flicked it with her fingernail out the open window into the ditch by the side of the road and it arced brightly before landing in the wet grass. She drove fast back to the village, leaning into the corners, with her full beam headlights on so she would get a good look at any lambs that might wander onto the road in front of her.

39

Jessie was round now at Grandpa's flat. The room with his chair and the television and his single bed was hot. The storage heaters pumping out low, constant warmth. The window wedged open with an old cassette tape to let in a little air.

What else will you need? asked Jessie. She was kneeling on the floor with Grandpa's green leather suitcase opened in front of her. There was in here already his underwear, pyjamas, jumpers. A photo album with pictures of his wife and his son when they were all much younger.

Grandpa shook his head. What I don't know, he said, is how long I'll be away. They haven't told me. How am I meant to know what I'm going to need?

I don't think you're coming back, Grandpa.

We don't know that do we?

I can always come by and pick up anything else that you forget to pack.

Aye. So you could.

So what else do you think you'll need to start off with? For the first few days anyway.

Grandpa squeezed his windpipe between two fingers and huffed up some air. Well, he said, I'll need socks.

I've packed them already.

Good. He pointed one finger in the air. Shoes!

Well, said Jessie, I've packed your good slippers. The ones you got last Christmas.

He frowned. I wouldn't be able to wear them outside.

I don't think you're going to be going outside, Grandpa.

I like to go for a walk.

When was the last time you went out for a walk?

He shrugged his shoulders.

But I'll put in some boots anyway. You might get a burst of energy one day.

Aye. Do that.

Okay. What else?

Something to read.

What about this? She took down a Sinatra biography from his shelf.

Aye.

Okay. Jessie packed this and then opened Grandpa's wardrobe and pushed the clothes hangers along the pole. How many jackets have you got in here?

Oh, I've got plenty of jackets.

We'll need to get rid of some of these. The charity shop will take them.

I might want to wear them again.

They're going.

Okay, okay. He held his hands up in mock surrender. All this packing is making me thirsty. How about a wee goldie?

Your throat feeling okay?

I think it's feeling good enough.

Jessie twisted the cork from a half-empty whisky bottle and poured them two measures into a couple of glasses that were still dirty from the last time.

Well, said Grandpa, sniffing the caramel notes at the top of the drink. Here's to your good health.

Cheers, said Jessie, staring at Grandpa's hands for a moment while her eyes stung. Then drinking.

They drank together happily and quietly for a time. Then Grandpa shifted in his armchair.

I wish, he whispered, I could take that clock in with me. He pointed at the wooden clock mounted on the wall, which would chime every half an hour. It had been there for as long as Jessie could remember.

Why?

I don't know if I'll be able to sleep without it. He mimicked the motion of the pendulum with his hand. The ticking. The chiming. It's always been there.

When did you get it?

Oh, he said. I couldn't tell you. Your granny picked it up in some department store in Inverness – he closed his eyes – must be fifty years ago.

I don't know how you can sleep with it in the house, said Jessie. It's so loud.

You get used to it. I don't even hear it anymore. He laughed. Funny how your brain can blank these things out.

Maybe it's just your brain going blank in your old age.

Grandpa laughed and pointed at her. That too. That's true.

Jessie kneeled beside the suitcase again. Right. Is there anything else you're going to need? Remember the hospice will have bedding, towels, toiletries, television. What else is there? She looked around.

Grandpa followed her gaze with his own. How, he said, am I supposed to know? Everything that I need is here. I've had these things my whole life. How can it go into just one suitcase?

You don't use all this stuff, Grandpa.

That's not the point. It's mine. My stuff. I should be the one to decide what I'm going to keep and what I need and what I'm getting rid of.

Jessie held up an old jacket from the wardrobe. What about this? she said. It's got tears all along the lining. It's filthy. She put her hand in one of the pockets and pulled out a little slip of paper. This is a receipt for a magazine from 1989. Is that the last time you wore this?

Grandpa glared and shrugged. Probably, he said.

So, she said. We can throw this one out, can't we?

That one? Oh yes. I never liked that one anyway.

When the suitcase was packed and Grandpa was dressed in his good coat and a new hat for the occasion, they switched off all the sockets in the flat at the wall. The family photographs were still there and the armchair and the clock, set to chime every half an hour. Grandpa looked around and backed into the hallway and locked the door.

Will I take the key? asked Jessie. In case you need anything else brought into you.

Aye, said Grandpa. I'm not going to need it.

They left the complex slowly. Jessie carried the suitcase. Grandpa stopped at every other resident's flat door on the way out and knocked quietly. Some of the residents stayed indoors but some answered him. Small, white-haired little people with bushy eyebrows and thick spectacles. Jessie standing a respectful couple of steps away from these conversations.

That's me away, he would say to one of them.

Oh Lord, said a neighbour. That you away already?

That's me away now, he would say to another one. Time to go.

Och. Good luck to you. And they would shake hands or put their hands on each other's shoulders and touch their lips to one another's cheeks.

That's me away, he would say again to the next one. Time's up. And open his hands out, a little shake of the head.

Right enough, son. I'll be seeing you.

No, you'll not.

Oh, yes I will.

In this slow and polite way he said goodbye to his home and his neighbours and his life there. A car from the hospice was waiting outside and after a while the driver leaned gently on the horn to hurry things along.

40

It was a dark morning when Moodie dug out his hiking boots and packed a rucksack with some waterproofs and a flask of hot coffee and a quarter bottle of whisky and some sandwiches wrapped in tinfoil.

He walked for an hour east along the Shore Road in the direction of the ferry then lifted his leg over a wire fence and off the road. There was a hiking trail cutting through a field from years of erosion that led up and away into the mountains with thick dark forest on one side and nothing but heather and bush on the other.

This was a walk Moodie knew from childhood. He would come up here on Saturdays with his father and walk silently up into the mountains together, stopping halfway to eat bananas and drink milky tea from a plastic flask. Sometimes Donald came too, the two schoolboys lagging behind and complaining about the blisters on their feet.

One time they came up in the middle of a cold February, when there was frost and snow lying even down as far as the village. By the time they were halfway up the mountainside the temperature was below zero and the boys' breath condensed in front of their faces. When they stopped to eat their bananas and share the plastic cup of warm tea, Donald dropped his rucksack to the ground and kicked at a stump.

I want to go back, he said. It's too cold.

The worst part's over, said Moodie's father. If you stay moving you'll stay warm enough.

I'm going back.

No. We're going up together.

You can't stop me.

Moodie's father worked as a maltman at the Distillery and Donald's father was his boss. He chewed the banana slowly and stared at the boy who flopped down cross-legged. Donald, he finally said. You're not a wee boy anymore. Don't act like a wee boy.

You can't call me that.

When you come up here into the mountains with me, you're under my care. Everyone in the village knows you're under my care. You will not leave my sight, son. None of that down there matters when we're up here.

Donald began to speak again but got cut off.

It can be dangerous up here in this type of weather. You could slip and break your neck. Get your little trousers tangled up in barbed wire climbing a fence. Your daddy won't be able to help you up here. The mountain doesn't care who your daddy is and neither do I.

Let's just keep going, said Moodie.

Donald stood up.

Come on. I'll race you to the top.

They began climbing again, the two boys scrambling in front and Moodie's father following up behind. Once, when Donald turned around to gaze up at the brilliant blue sky, they caught eyes. The man gave the boy a wink but it was not returned.

Moodie and Donald reached the summit alone. It was flat

ground up here and the snow lay in thick drifts. The boys added a rock to the cairn and stood back and admired the icy plateau.

I dare you to walk on that, said Donald. He was pointing at a shallow pool with a thick black layer of ice on the surface. The blue sky and the clouds reflected in it.

Think it'll hold?

Definitely. Go on. I dare you.

I don't think it will. The boys stood closer to the pool and reached out their boots to tap at the ice. It crunched and squeaked with the light pressure.

Do it, said Donald.

I'm not sure.

I'm telling you, go for it. Go for it.

Moodie looked at his friend and back down the mountain towards his father. The blue jacket was coming slowly towards them. Taking his time. Enjoying the walk. Letting the boys be boys.

Moodie peered down at the ice and then felt Donald's hands on his shoulder blades and he was thrust forwards onto the pool's surface. His right foot slid forward and his body jerked to stay upright. The ice held but groaned loudly and Moodie brought his left leg down sharply to gain better balance and the surface ice easily gave way. Moodie felt his foot and ankle and shin freeze as the limb slid down. Then the ice beneath his right foot popped and both his knees were under, his thighs, his hips, as he groped and scratched at the ice on each side with his gloved hands. Moodie found his voice and roared, the ice water hitting his chest and his ribcage like a punch to the throat. Then there were hands under his armpits, and he was clear of it, the shards cracking and crumbling all around him as he rose out and there was the hard ground underneath him again.

Jesus Christ, shouted Moodie's father. What are you playing at in there? You're soaking.

I told him the ice would break! This was Donald's voice, high and distant. I said it, I knew it would break, I told him not to go onto it!

Moodie would eventually get down the mountain that day and dry off and warm up but he had despised Donald ever since. Donald had just never been smart enough to figure it out.

Moodie reached the summit again. It had become a mild grey day, with a low cloud settling on the mountains. The visibility was poor and it had been a tricky climb. He sat on a rock and ate his sandwiches and waited. Moodie hated being late for meetings so he was used to being early and didn't mind it being up here on his own. A hawk flew overhead and dipped down to head height for a better look and then disappeared once again into the mist.

He could hear the American coming before he saw him. A short man with broad shoulders and bright activewear. Bought specifically for the hike. A backwards baseball cap and wraparound sunshades.

You're Moodie? asked the man.

I am.

Thank you meeting me. Apologies for the venue. We want to keep our presence low key for now.

That's okay.

The American took off his gloves and they shook hands. He introduced himself: Johnny Coca-Cola. Not my real name.

Whatever you say.

Moodie opened his rucksack and gave the American two glass tumblers to hold. He went to the rock pool, the same one he'd fallen into as a boy, and reached down to pick out two pebbles. They were bone cold. He dropped them heavily into the tumblers where they clacked then he poured over a thick swirl of whisky from his hip flask onto the pebbles.

This is how we treat new friends around here, he explained. He took one of the glasses from the American and held it outwards. Slainte.

They clinked glasses.

Johnny Coca-Cola took a sip then whistled. He offered Moodie a bag from his pocket that was filled with white powder and said: I come bearing gifts.

Moodie looked at the bag and slugged down half his whisky then shook his head.

What can you tell me about Donald Fleck? I hear he's the straw that stirs the drink around here.

This is about the takeover then, said Moodie. How fast are things moving? The sooner the better.

The two men stood up on the mountaintop and drank a few more drams and their conversation was picked up by the gales and whisked into the sky and that was it away.

41

Grandpa woke up slowly. His face hurt from lying so still and his arm had gone numb under him. He released it and lifted it up above his head and dangled it down the side of the bed and then rested it outside the covers until the blood was moving in his veins again. His eyelids were sticking together and his mouth was so dry it ached.

He blinked hard and when his arm felt better he levered himself up on his pillow and scanned the tray in front of him for a drink.

A newspaper rustled and Grandpa looked to the armchair on his left and the man put down the paper. Grandpa stared. A small man in a black shirt. Tanned face with lines that creased his temples and a bald head.

Hello Grandpa, said Donald. Grandpa was the oldest man in the village and so everyone just called him Grandpa.

The old man still stared. His mouth opened and closed silently.

It's Donald. Junior. From the Distillery.

Grandpa closed his eyes and nodded and smile and patted the quilt. Donald, he said, so it is. I didn't recognise you.

It's been a long time.

You're getting to be some age now, aren't you son?

You're not looking too great yourself.

Aye, Grandpa pointed at him. I'll give you that. I'll give you that. He struggled to sit further up and again looked about the tray and the bedside table.

Do you need something?

Some water, Grandpa whispered.

I can manage that. Donald filled up a plastic cup from the sink in the corner of the room. He emptied the water down the drain and filled it up again, repeating until the tepid water ran cold.

Grandpa took the cup in both hands and took a long mouthful, a little of it running down his chin and onto his t-shirt. He swilled the water around with his tongue then swallowed and put the cup down.

Grandpa pointed at the newspaper on Donald's knee. I've been reading about your boy, he said. Missing.

That's right.

Where do you suppose he is?

The police think he's shacked up somewhere with a girl.

Grandpa laughed and nodded his head. Could be, he whispered. Doesn't sound too like too bad a thing now, does it?

Donald blew out his cheeks. But I'm no buying it. If he's over on the mainland, someone's seen him going on the way. The boys on the ferry say he never crossed. I asked them myself. Which means he's still here somewhere. Which means that someone's hiding him.

Why would he hide?

That's what I need to find out. But enough about that wee arsehole. I've come to see you, haven't I? I heard what was going on. How are you feeling?

I'm getting by.

It's in your throat.

Aye. Grandpa touched his windpipe with two fingers. In there somewhere.

Is it sore?

Sore in the mornings. But I'm on the morphine.

That's good stuff.

It is.

If you need anything while you're in here, all you need to do is ask. You know where I am.

There's nothing. When you get to this stage your demands are fairly simple.

Donald unbuttoned the cuffs on his shirtsleeves and rolled them up to his elbows. He cleared his throat before he spoke: You've still got the shares in the Distillery, of course.

Right enough. Ten percent of it.

You're not thinking of selling them?

That was the plan. I wouldn't bother now. They'll get passed on I suppose.

To your son?

It'll all go to him. Not that there's much of it.

I need you to do me a favour.

What can I do?

I need you to give me those shares back. I need control of the place. For security.

Why would you worry about that?

There's a bigger picture. We're not as sound as we used to be. I need control.

You've got control.

I need more.

You want to buy them back?

No. I want you to give them back.

I paid your father fair and square for them.

I know you did.

You can make me an offer. Or make my son an offer once I'm gone. But I paid good money at a time when your father needed it. Saved him from bankruptcy.

What can I say to change your mind?

I'm dying here. Give me a bit of peace.

Okay. You can't blame me for trying. I'll go and get myself a coffee. Want one?

On you go. I'm fine.

Donald left Grandpa's room and went out into the communal area where there was a kitchen with a microwave and a kettle and a fridge. He put a five-pound note in the collection jar and made himself an instant coffee.

Grandpa was asleep when Donald got back to the room. Donald sat in the armchair and picked up the newspaper again. When he finished the bitter coffee he stood and straightened the armchair so it was parallel to the bed. He folded the newspaper and sat it on Grandpa's bedside table. He put one arm on the bedrail and leaned over and looked into the old man's sleeping face for a minute.

Right, he said finally. I'll be seeing you, Grandpa.

42

The queue of cars for the morning ferry curled up round the road. These were tourists in campervans and commuters travelling across the water for work and delivery drivers with loads of mail or timber or livestock. The loch was at its narrowest here, connecting the ports at Corran on the mainland with Ardgour on the peninsula, and the ferry took less than seven minutes when the crosswind was good.

Galloway sat in his unmarked Passat with his policeman's hat on the passenger seat. The white shirt and black tie of the Northern Constabulary. He had left early this morning but was still near the back of the queue, a snaking line of red lights in front of him. There was an early morning haar clinging onto the air, and the ferry was taking its time in the cold sea fog.

The ferry arrived and an alarm wailed as the ramp lowered. The cars came off slowly, inching from the corrugated metal surface to the slick concrete. One of the ferrymen stood there with his hands out blocking the queue until all the cars were off. Then he stepped slightly to the side and waved. He had seen the police car. Galloway flipped his indicator and slipped from the queue. He drove quickly past the waiting cars and nodded at the ferryman – Brian or Craig, he could not tell the difference between the two tall men in their hi-vis in this mist – and eased up the ramp.

Galloway parked towards the front of the ferry. He would be first off at the other side. The ferrymen wore heavy raincoats and hoods tied up around their faces. They waved each car forwards and shepherded them into position on the platform, only inches apart. When the ferry was full, the alarm sounded again and the ramp pulled up and the ferrymen squeezed between the cars, taking payment and stamping tickets.

The ferry lurched forwards onto the water, untethered from the shore. The waves today were thick and slow, and the platform swayed smoothly from side to side.

The knock came on Galloway's window. He unwound it.

Morning Brian, he said, recognising the ferryman's scarred nose. I don't actually have any tickets left so –

Fine, fine, fine, said Brian, in his quick, high voice. No charge when you're on duty, boss.

Thanks. Busy this morning.

Aye, said Brian, looking back at the packed cars and looking forwards across the rolling waves and looking back at the Corran port just visible in the haar. Tourists like to come across early, don't they?

So long as I get off before them, laughed Galloway.

Aye, aye, aye, said the ferryman. Will be. Are you over about the Young Bobby thing? The boy's been missing over a month. Must be nearer two months now.

I heard about it.

What's taken so long to get it investigated?

There's a timeline for these things. Reports, paperwork. It's all in hand.

His father's not heard a peep.

Not like him, is it? Usually out and about.

He is, he is. Mother's worried sick.

He'll turn up somewhere, said Galloway. Even if I have to dredge the loch to find him.

Aye, aye, aye, laughed Brian. He slapped his hand on the top of the car. Cheerio now.

Cheerio now, said Galloway. He rolled up the car window and the ferryman disappeared somewhere behind him.

After the ferry there was still a forty-minute drive to Cullrothes. This was a smooth road that had been resurfaced to replace the chipped old track where the farmers used to walk their cows. Along the way there would be sheep to avoid. The wide gates leading to farmhouses popped up on the left and the right every half mile or so. Once the ferry port of Ardgour had left the rear-view mirror there was no reminder of the mainland. You might as well be on some far-flung island.

First off the ferry so Galloway had the road to himself. He went through the glen at a good speed and glanced to the left where the herds of deer were usually grazing. Big muscled stags and lithe does and shadowy fauns. At this time of the year they were far enough off, but when it grew colder and the roads got gritted for the ice the deer would come down the hills to lick off the salt and there were always a few incidents then. Always a few shattered windscreens and a few lumps of venison for the freezer once the beast had been slaughtered and skinned.

When Galloway got to the village he dropped gears and drove slowly along the Shore Road past the hotel and the shop and the church. The village was as quiet as he always imagined it. He had become used to the quiet when he lived here but now it seemed like a forced peacefulness.

He turned and drove uphill towards Donald's manse and the man was standing there on the driveway dressed well and holding a mug of coffee. He waved sharply to Galloway and pointed down the side of the house so Galloway took the car round the corner and parked out of sight of the road.

Morning, Donald, he said, and left his hat in the car.

Come in. Margo's waiting. She's made breakfast.

The three of them sat at the long dark dining table and Margo passed out plates. In the middle was a pot of coffee and a pot of tea and a plate of toast and the jams and marmalades and some butter.

I hear my girl's working for you at the hotel now, said Galloway. After school's done. Thanks for taking her on. It's good for her.

She's a good girl, said Margo. Reliable.

Donald took a slice of toast from the plate and buttered it then spread jam over the top and put it on his wife's plate. He held out the rack of toast and Galloway took a slice.

How's your father? asked Margo. We saw him at Sandy's funeral. But he didn't stay. He looked like he was struggling. Donald's been up at the hospice to say hello.

I was, said Donald. He's as tough as a two-pound steak.

He's not doing so good, said Galloway. Getting old. He poured himself a coffee. I'll pop in to see him later.

Margo nibbled at her toast then scraped a little of the jam off onto the plate. Well, she said. You'll pass on our best wishes. But first you're going to find our boy for us.

Galloway opened a small notebook and started writing with a black pen. Tell me what you know, he said.

We know he was in the bar at the hotel, said Margo. Last we know of anyone seeing him. Old Jim spoke to him. And Innes said the same. He's the new guy we've hired to manage the place.

Was Young Bobby drunk?

What do you think? said Donald.

Galloway stopped writing and looked up.

Yes, said Margo. They say he was drunk.

And what do you think?

I think he was probably making a damn fool of himself again.

Donald?

He'll have a few, aye. There was a game on. He'd have been watching the game. Never misses the football.

Does he support a particular team?

Whichever mob he's bet on usually.

Do you think he'll have had a bet on the game the night he went missing?

Most likely, aye, I would say so. A bad waste of good money.

I can check in with the bookies. See if they remember anything. Galloway stopped writing. He stood up and wiped the crumbs from his mouth then spoke: I want you both to stop worrying about this. He'll turn up when he's ready. And I'll look for him as if it was my own son. You'll get the entire might of the Northern Constabulary behind you. I can promise you that.

Donald walked Galloway back out to his car and the two men stood looking at the distant crags.

When I went to see your dad, said Donald, the subject of his shares in the Distillery came up.

Aye. I always forget about those.

He put money into the business in the eighties. There was a whisky reservoir at the time. We were sitting on barrels and barrels of the stuff with nowhere to ship it. In the end we had to get creative.

He was very happy to contribute, said Galloway. To preserve the heritage of the village. That's how he put it to me.

I need those shares back, said Donald. If you want the heritage to remain preserved, I need them back.

Have you asked him?

I'm asking you.

They're not mine to sell.

They will be soon.

The policeman arched his neck and put his arms behind his back and stretched. Then said: They're worth quite a lot of money in today's market. You could make me an offer?

Donald reached under his chin and rubbed at the coarse hair growing there. This is a bad look for me, he said. This thing with Young Bobby. The Distillery's haemorrhaging money. I don't like losing control of things.

Some things are outwith our control.

Here's what I'll do. Here's something I can control. You find our boy and bring him back here, alive mind you, I want him alive, and I'll buy those shares back off you and your old man at face value. Full market rate.

There's always the chance –

If you can't find him, if you don't bring him back here safely in one piece, I will consider you entirely to blame. Not the Northern Constabulary, not the authorities. You.

Donald, I am going to make every effort –

You'll be a dead man, said Donald. If you don't bring that boy back to his mother, you're a dead man.

43

Johnny Coca-Cola sat in the Distillery car park on a low wall smoking a Marlboro. He was wearing his waterproof jacket and he pushed the blonde curls out of his eyes and pulled on a baseball cap. There was a bike shelter and well-maintained planted areas and some Japanese tourists whose eyes flicked between a map and the white Distillery buildings and the road.

He had used the payphone in the village earlier to call the reception and book himself a place on the one o'clock guided tour. But he was early so he sat here smoking and admiring the flower beds and tugging at the zip on his coat.

He enjoyed the smell from the Distillery. It reminded him of joints of ham, slow cooked and then flaking apart. He finished his Marlboro and mashed it underfoot and sat enjoying the Distillery's meaty perfume.

At five minutes to one Johnny Coca-Cola went through the doors and looked around the gift shop at the bottles of rare Cullrothes and novelty boxes and whiskies from other distilleries, from Speyside and Islay and Campbelltown.

A girl with blonde hair and a navy blue staff uniform came over.

Can I help you with anything?

Her name badge said: Olive.

I'm here for the tour. I phoned yesterday.

Olive waited until a few more tourists, Japanese and Italian, had joined them and then she clapped her hands and they all gathered around her.

Olive told them about the history of the Cullrothes Distillery. About how it had survived bankruptcy scares when there were whisky reservoirs and nobody to sell it to. About how it had survived thanks to the generosity of the villagers and anonymous backers. About the difference between peated and unpeated malt. About the importance of the river that had come down from the mountains and which streamed round the back of the village and round the hotel before finally joining the loch.

Then they were through to the hopper, the machine roaring as it milled the malt down. The Japanese tourists chatted among themselves and the Italian backpackers asked a few questions in broken English. Johnny Coca-Cola listened politely to Olive, and adjusted his baseball cap.

Then, as if suddenly remembering, he said: Can we take pictures?

Of course, you can.

He had a little disposable camera in his pocket and he took the thing out and pointed it at the hopper and clicked the button and then wound the spool on with his thumb.

Olive led the group through the next door. It's going to be warm in here, she said. Remember this is a working distillery and we are distilling today. Treat it as you would a factory.

The group congregated on a small square of textured iron and looked up and around at the brass machines in the room.

It is very warm in here, repeated Olive. If anyone starts to feel a little too hot, please let me know. We don't want anyone fainting!

Johnny Coca-Cola and the Italians laughed. The Japanese group were taking pictures of one another with the equipment in the background.

We call this room the mash house, said Olive. And this drum is called the mash tun. She pointed to a huge, copper dome which funnelled down from the ceiling and had a small window bolted onto it. This is where the malted grains go, she explained. In here we soak them in hot water. Mix and drain. Then repeat. The malt goes in here in one state and is transformed into something else. The mash tun gives us two things. One is a hot, sweet liquid which will eventually become malt whisky. The remainder, the dried-out husks, the wort. We sell this for cattle feed.

She was in full flow with the narrative, swinging her arms and mimicking the whisky's journey, face red and smiling.

Excuse me, cut in Johnny Coca-Cola. I'm not feeling great. I'm too warm in here.

Would you like some fresh air?

I'd like to use a bathroom.

Go back the way you came. First left. There's a bathroom there. The signs says Staff Only, but it's fine for you to use it.

Thanks.

We'll wait for you here.

No, he waved. It's fine I'll find my way through. I don't want to hold you up.

Johnny Coca-Cola went back the way they had come and through the doors and into the bathroom. He took off his cap and his jacket and underneath he wore a navy blue polo shirt, just like the one Olive had on.

He left the bathroom and went through another door marked: No Entry.

He was in a long, low-lit corridor with offices leading off from both sides. He went into the first one and used his disposable camera to photograph the signs sticking on the noticeboard. He opened the drawers in an unlocked filing cabinet and pulled out folders and took shots of everything page he could get his hands on, going quickly, flicking through the sheets and winding the camera on after every click.

Soon the camera stuck at the end of the film. Johnny Coca-Cola stored this in his pocket and pulled out a new camera.

The other doors in the corridor were locked. He tried all the handles, entering rooms and moving through them with expert speed.

When the second camera's film ended, he went back to the bathroom and zipped up his jacket and pulled the hat down on his head again.

Olive and the group were still waiting for him in the mash house.

Are you okay, she asked?

Yeah. I just had to splash my face with some water.

Can I get you anything? she asked.

Are there samples at the end of the tour?

Yes.

Well, smiled Johnny Coca-Cola. I'll wait for that then.

At the end of the tour Johnny Coca-Cola sipped some sample whiskies with the rest of the group and laughed and smiled as they all made faces at the different flavours and strengths. He bought a map of the different distilleries of Scotland and a little book for tasting notes. When they got outside, he stood with the Italian backpackers for a little while, chatting by the roadside, a nice couple of students with long hair from Milan. He arranged to meet them later in the hotel, where he would be happy to sell them the bag of weed they were asking about.

44

It was afternoon when Galloway got to the hotel bar. The little room was hot from the fire. The sweet smell of stale sticky beer. A couple of old men sat around the table with half pints of beer and measures of whisky. They saw the policeman come in and looked at him in silence then fell back to their hushed conversation.

Galloway took a good look at Innes standing behind the bar. A skinny boy with ginger hair in a clean white shirt. This was tucked into black denims that clung neatly to his legs. A two-week beard that wasn't taking to his face properly. The barman looked up sharply and his red mouth opened when he saw the uniform.

Afternoon, said Galloway, placing his hat on the bar. I'll take a shandy.

Innes poured half a pint of lager and topped it up with lemonade from the draught gun. What else can I get you?

Nothing.

Galloway handed over a banknote and Innes waved it off.

Is there anything else I can do for you then?

You know Robert Fleck? Gets called Young Bobby by most people around here.

Yes. His father owns this hotel.

You probably know that Young Bobby's been reported missing?

Innes nodded. Poured himself a short glass of lemonade and said: It's terrible.

Why would you say that? asked Galloway, making a note in his pad.

Nobody's heard from him. Could be anywhere.

Could be. We know he's not here. Why would being away from here be terrible?

I didn't mean that. I'm sure he's okay. I just mean it's terrible for his mother and his father. The not knowing.

Galloway took a sip of his shandy. Got any nuts?

Sure. Innes tore some dry roasted peanuts from a strip and gave them to the policeman.

When was the last time you saw Young Bobby?

He was in here, one night a few weeks ago. Maybe a month ago. I think it was a Tuesday. We'd been showing the football.

He on his own?

Yes. Came in late and left when I locked up.

Was he drunk?

He was drinking.

Did he say where he was going when he left?

Not to me.

If you think of anything, you call me. Galloway put a card with his name and number on the bar.

I don't see what else I can tell you.

Could be anything. Names, places, any details that come back to you. Okay?

Okay, I will. Innes took the card and shrugged as though the whole thing was a waste of effort.

Right then. Galloway poured himself a fistful of peanuts and threw them into his mouth. He turned and looked around the pub. The fireplace. The old rug. The photographs on the walls. It had been a long time since he'd been in. He even recognised one of the old men drinking at the table. An old neighbour of his. Hello Joe, he called out.

Joe nodded at him quickly and then looked down at his drink.

Right then, said Galloway, finishing the peanuts and folding up the empty packet. Thanks for lunch.

Actually, said Innes, he was talking about a girl. I don't know if that could have anything to do with it? Over on the mainland. Some girl he'd met. Now that I think about it, I do remember that.

Do you have her name? Where she lived?

He didn't say. Just told me he'd met this girl and he was in love with her or something.

In love?

That's what he said.

That does sound like Bobby Fleck, said Galloway. The rascal.

That's all I know. But sounds to me like he'll be a long way from here by now. If it really is love.

Sounds about right, said Galloway. He's famous for it. No doubt he'll turn up in a few weeks on the back of a tractor. Skint. Heartbroken.

Innes laughed.

He's not a bad lad. Thick as a plate of mince, but not a bad bone in his body. Not like his father that way.

Innes raised his eyebrows and smiled.

I hear you've hired my daughter to work here after school, said Galloway.

You're Jessie's dad?

I am. I live over in town across the water. Me and her mum are divorced.

She's doing a good job. We're very happy with her.

That's good to hear. But I want you to do me a favour.

Aye?

Let her go. Make up some excuse for it. I don't want her working for Donald anymore.

She doesn't really deal with Donald.

I don't care. She needs to focus on her schoolwork and I don't want her to owe him anything. So make up whatever you want but get rid of her.

You sure?

I'm sure.

I'll sort something out.

Much appreciated. Cheerio for now.

Cheerio then. If there's anything else I can do.

I know where you are.

45

Johnny Coca-Cola stood a little down the road from the school gates and watched the buses and cars and taxis. The buses filled up quickly when the bell rang, children throwing their school bags under the seats and kneeling up to shout to each other as the drivers pulled slowly away. The cars and taxis collected children in ones and twos, parents hugging them quickly before starting the engine. The vehicles were gone in minutes. The remaining children lived close enough to walk home and they meandered down the road away from the school in small groups and in pairs and a few just walking on their own.

The American sat on a low stone wall and unfolded a tourist map. He held this out in front of him, tracking a line here and there with his finger, as though checking for landmarks. The school was pitched up a slope and from here you got a good view of the loch with the mountains behind it and the sky that was already growing darker with touches of mint and peach.

A teenage boy broke away from his group and stopped just before he reached Johnny Coca-Cola. His name was Harry Duncan, and he was in some of Jessie's senior classes. A tall nice-looking boy with a spiky haircut.

Are you the guy they're talking about? Harry asked.

Johnny Coca-Cola stared at the boy. He exhaled loudly from his nostrils. That's not what you're supposed to say, he said quietly.

This gave Harry confidence and he asked: Are you lost, traveller?

Johnny Coca-Cola smiled and stood up. Very lost, he said. Come and take a look at this for me, will you?

The boy came and stood next to Johnny Coca-Cola and held the map with one hand while Johnny Coca-Cola held on to the other side. What's the best way to get home, asked Johnny Coca-Cola. In his free hand was a bag filled with green buds and in the boy's free hand there was the money and they quickly, seamlessly, exchanged them.

I don't know, laughed the boy.

Never mind, said Johnny Coca-Cola, and he sat back down. His face settled to a peaceful expression once more and he watched the trees moving in the wind across the road. He crossed his legs and coughed gently and waved his hand as though Harry was an unwanted pigeon. He went back to his pals and the boys marched away together, arms touching, talking in whispers, giggling as if they could not believe their luck.

A moment later Jessie came down the hill from the school on her own, that heavy bag straining on her collarbone. Getting dark already and her needing to get to work. It was a short walk down from the school to the hotel. She walked quickly, on the pavement and then weaving onto the road to avoid a group of slow pupils and then back onto the pavement again.

She stopped short when she saw Johnny Coca-Cola sitting there. Baseball cap, red rain jacket, the tourist map.

Slowly, Johnny Coca-Cola uncurled his leg and stood up and opened the map, examining it.

Hello, said Jessie.

Johnny Coca-Cola looked up from the map. Tilted his head slightly to the side.

Are you lost, traveller? she asked.

Very, beamed Johnny Coca-Cola. Come and help me out. He angled the map towards her and she stepped in closer. Johnny Coca-Cola could smell her body. A little shampoo, a little sweat.

What do you suppose, he said, the best way to get home is? He held the map in his left hand and dropped his right hand to his side and kept his fist closed around the packet.

Jessie looked at the map and then down at Johnny Coca-Cola's fist. He heard her swallow.

I don't have a clue, she said. Couldn't tell you. Sorry.

She walked quickly away down the hill towards the hotel and Johnny Coca-Cola grinned and dropped back down into the wall and put the plastic bag back into his pocket. Halfway down the road she stopped and looked back at him.

46

On a quiet night in the hotel bar there was a football game playing on the screen and the men in there were watching it, barely paying attention, barely drinking, barely talking. Old Jim with his one leg sat at the bar, half doing his crossword and half watching the game. A European game on a midweek night. The volume turned up loud so the old men could hear it and when they did speak to one another their voices were loud and hoarse.

Some player, him, said Mick.

Eh?

Some player, that boy.

Italian?

Portuguese.

Oh, Portuguese.

He's an internationalist.

Is he?

He's some player.

Innes loaded a couple of empty pint glasses into the dishwasher and closed it. He had been growing a beard for two weeks and his face was raw and itchy under his chin. The skin there was dry and when he scratched it flakes of skin clung to his fingertips. Alice said that the beard gave his face some shape.

He had open in front of him a catalogue from a jeweller's on the mainland. It was open on a page with diamond engagement rings and each one came with a little description and a modelled photograph. He flipped through them looking at the prices before looking at the rings. He couldn't remember if he was supposed to spend a week's or a month's worth of wages on the ring. Either way, he was going to need a credit card. But if they looked at his past income they'd turn it down. Maybe he could get the money someplace else.

He picked the last couple of painkillers from the packet and threw the empty foil in the bin. As he poured himself a glass of lemonade to take them with, he noticed how badly his hand was shaking.

The door opened and the men all looked up to see who was joining them and a woman wearing pyjamas walked into the pub. Her pyjamas were well worn and faded. Baggy tartan trousers with a drawstring dangling from the waistband. A light pink vest with straps and a unicorn printed across the chest. With no bra underneath.

Shut the door then, shouted one of the old men above the noise of the football commentary. You're letting the cold in.

The woman turned and closed the door gently then she came up to the bar. She held her arms around herself with her hands hugging her shoulders.

Are you alright? asked Innes.

Yes, she said. She looked down and moved a bar stool out a little and got up onto it.

Can I get you something?

She looked over his shoulder to the gantry and pursed her lips together and made a small noise in the back of her throat. A glass of chardonnay.

A glass of chardonnay?

Please.

Anything else?

No.

Innes raised his eyebrows at Old Jim and opened a miniature bottle of white wine and poured it out into a small fat-stemmed glass. He put it on a beermat in front of the woman.

Well, she said, and took a sip.

Innes left the bar to collect some dirty glasses from the tables. Who is that? he asked.

I do recognise her, said Mick. I have seen her about. Can't mind who she is though.

They turned and looked at the woman sitting there in her pyjamas. The skin on her back was loose and pale and they could see from here dark hair growing under her armpits.

I'm going to have to phone the police, said Innes.

Don't be daft, son. Woman's just looking for a drink and a bit of company like the rest of us.

She needs help.

There's no point phoning the police. Be the middle of the night before they got here. What are they going to do, anyway? Bring her a dressing gown?

The old men laughed at that and turned their eyes back to the television and the football game.

What are you, said Old Jim, some kind of grass? What are you talking about phoning the police here for?

Innes rubbed his hairy chin and sat on the stool next to the woman. I've got a jacket in the back office, he said. Would you like to wear it? Are you not cold?

Oh no, she said. It's nice to feel the heat from the fire on my arms.

How did you get here?

I walked.

Do you live nearby?

Yes. Close by. Very close.

I haven't seen you in here before.

I've not been in here for a long time. She tipped the glass and poured the last trickle of wine down her throat and shoogled the empty glass at Innes. Could I have another?

No problem.

Innes made the drink and put it down in front of her. I forgot to charge you for the last one, he said. So that's eight pounds forty for the two of them.

Oh, she said. I forgot my handbag. She picked up the wine and took a sip from it and held it in her hand.

You don't have any money on you?

Do I look like I have any money on me? She gestured at her unicorn vest as though proving her point then turned away and looked at the screen.

You can't just come in here and order drinks without any money.

What are you going to do? she asked. Call the police on me? There was a little smile on her lips.

I should do that, yes.

Good luck with that. I hope you don't mind waiting. You'll be waiting a while on those useless arseholes.

The woman turned to Old Jim and touched her hair. What have you got there?

It's just my crossword.

Do you need a hand?

He said nothing but she got off the stool and stood next to him, very close, so that her bare arm touched him. She peered down at the crossword. Hmmm, she sighed.

I never finish these things anyway, he said, and folded the newspaper up. Just helps to pass the time. He took a drink of his beer and held eyes with Innes over the rim of the glass.

We all need something to help pass the time, she said. Don't we?

Nice to keep busy, aye. He took another longer drink.

What do you do to keep busy?

I just come in here, get my messages in the shop, try to keep the garden tidy.

The woman turned so that her back was against the bar and with her elbows touching it on either side of her.

Sounds very boring, she said.

Maybe I like it boring.

Maybe you don't know what you like.

The woman's wine was finished again and she turned and put the glass down and winked at Innes.

Want to buy me a drink? she asked Old Jim. I promise I won't be boring for you.

Come on, said Innes. I think that's enough.

The man can buy me a drink if he wants to. Can't you?

I would indeed, Old Jim said, but I need to get myself home. To my nice boring home and my nice boring wife. The old man finished his beer and levered himself off the stool and limped over to the door.

Thanks a lot, she shouted at him. Thanks a bloody lot. You bloody cripple!

I'm going to have to ask you to leave, said Innes.

I want another wine.

You don't have any money.

Take it out of my daughter's next payslip.

What?

You've got my daughter working here, don't you?

Jessie?

Spends all her time here and comes in so late I hardly see her. You should be ashamed of yourself. Taking advantage of a young girl like that. I bet it's all under the table isn't it. I should be phoning the police on you!

You're Jessie's mum?

So?

I'm calling her. Innes went into the back office and opened a filing cabinet. He found the folder and got Jessie's details. He came back into the bar to use the telephone. All the old men were turned away from the football match, staring at the bar. The till drawer was lying open and all the banknotes were gone. Innes looked at the empty stool then around the room but the woman was gone and he rushed to the window and saw her in her pink pyjamas running across the road and down to the edge of the loch. Banknotes scooped up in her arms and fluttering up into the air all around her.

47

Alice sat at the end of the bed and brushed her blonde hair and shook out the loose strands onto Valentine's bedroom carpet.

Did you always want to be a journalist? she asked.

No. He was lying on the bed with his hands behind his head. Wanted to be a pilot.

What happened to that? Scared of heights?

Scared of crashing.

He shoogled up the bed and tucked himself in behind her with his legs either side and took the hairbrush from her and started to gently run it down the hair lying across her shoulders.

How did you get into it, though?

My dad was a journalist, so I fell into it.

Is he retired now?

Yes.

Is he a nice man?

He is. Did you always want to be a teacher?

I think I always thought I wanted to be a teacher. The idea of it was always there.

And does it meet your expectations?

Not yet. I thought it would be more fulfilling.

You don't find it fulfilling?

I keep thinking there's something missing from it. Maybe it's me. Maybe I've not found the right school yet.

Did your parents teach?

No. Mum died when I was a wee girl.

I didn't know. Sorry. He put his arms around her bare stomach and linked them but she reached down and pulled his fingers apart.

And I never really knew Dad. He's in prison.

What for?

You like asking questions, don't you?

I'm a journalist. It's my job.

Alice had a bobble on her wrist and she pulled her hair up into a ponytail and secured it high. There was a mirror at the end of the bed and her eyes met Valentine's in its reflection.

You don't have to tell me, he said. I shouldn't have asked.

Alice looked at the corner of the room and said: He killed her. Dad killed Mum.

You're joking.

Why would I joke about that? She stood up and turned to him.

I just can't believe it. That's horrible, Alice. It's horrible.

Do you want to know how it happened?

Only if you want to talk about it.

It doesn't bother me to talk about it.

You can talk about it if you want to.

She pulled on her underwear, pale skin against dark lace. I don't want to talk about it, she said. Dad used to want to talk to me about it. Can you believe that? Anywhere I went he would find me and want to have this big conversation about what happened and how and where and why. Try to explain himself. But I think he's given up on it now.

Can I make you a coffee?

No. I want to go home now.

Okay. I'll get up.

You're fine. Stay where you are. Alice reached down and tickled Valentine's bare foot then got her clothes back on and left.

48

The girl sat in the armchair with her long brown hair pushed back from her face. She was taking a wet wipe from her bag and had started to remove her make-up when the old man in the bed woke up. He woke up slowly, with a flicker of his eyelid, then a curling of his fingers, then an upwards shuffle into a sitting position.

Hello Grandpa, said the girl. The wet wipe was stained black with make-up and her face looked new and clean. How are you feeling today?

He stared hard for a second and then smiled. He reached both hands towards her and she reached back. They each squeezed one another's fingers. Hello Jessie, he whispered.

How are you feeling today? she asked again. She pinched the crumpled wipe and dropped it into her bag.

Fine, fine, said Grandpa. He was actually her Grandpa, even though everybody who knew him called him that as well. Everybody's Grandpa.

She leaned forward to hear him better. Feeling any pain?

He shrugged his shoulders.

Are you still getting the morphine?

Aye, he nodded, and mimicked a needle, the injection going into the wrinkled skin above his left elbow.

But you're doing okay? I like this new room they've put you in. It's some place, isn't it. Like a hotel room.

His eyes turned up and he appraised the room, the standing floor lamps, the cushioned sofa, the heavy curtains, the television on the wall.

I think this place is even bigger than your flat, isn't it?

He lifted both hands up to the room and nodded. All this space, he whispered.

49

Moodie rapped the cottage door with his knuckles and waited. Tweed hat pulled down low over his brow. It was a dark night and nearby the sound of an owl like a metronome.

Innes opened the door carefully. Peeking round the edge to see who it was and then trying to slam it shut again. Moodie's boot blocking the way.

What the hell do you think you're doing? said Moodie.

You can't come in, shouted Innes. Get your foot out of there.

Moodie put his shoulder into the door and eased it open. Innes's resistance giving way when he realised he could not hold off the bigger man. He was wearing a white t-shirt with tartan pyjamas and his slippers were in the shape of furry rabbits.

What exactly is wrong with you? snapped Moodie.

Nothing, nothing, said Innes. No, I just got scared.

Scared? Why are you so jumpy?

I'm not. I'm just tired. I'm fine.

Moodie took off his coat and crossed his arms across his chest so Innes could see how thick they were. Sit down, he said to the boy. We need to talk.

Innes pulled out a chair from the kitchen table and took a seat. He put his skinny elbows out on it and cradled his head.

I heard you had a bit of a problem in the pub the other night. A bit of money went missing.

I got some of it back. It was scattered all over the beach but I got some of it.

Not all of it?

No.

Most of it?

No.

This is a problem for us. For you.

Is it?

Can you deal with it?

I can pay it back. Make up the difference.

Good. What else?

What else do you want?

You need to do something about it.

Like what?

You tell me.

What about the girl?

Sounds like a good place to start. Donald's happy to let you deal with this one. Don't arse it up. Get the money back and make sure nobody else gets any ideas about bumping us off again.

Okay.

Moodie looked around the small kitchen. Dishes soaking in a greasy sink. A stack of empty bottles next to the bin. The hob needed cleaned.

Nice place, he said.

You want a coffee or something?

Moodie laughed, stood up, and left.

50

Innes was standing there behind the bar one night drying glasses with a tea towel. The bar was quiet but there were a couple of tourists in drinking dark beer and a table of old guys playing dominoes. They huddled over the table in their oatmeal cardigans and their hats all still on their heads.

Soft rain ran down the window, smudging the view outside. The tourists laughed suddenly and loudly, red faces and big open mouths. The radio playing quietly in the background. A song about lost love.

One of the old men broke away from the dominoes and came to the bar.

Three half 'n' halfs, he said.

Innes lined up the three beer glasses and the three whisky glasses. I'll bring them over to you, he said. But the old man stayed where he was.

He leaned into the bar and glanced back at the table before speaking. You heard about this American takeover business?

Innes shook his head. Hasn't been mentioned to me.

Supposedly, said the old man, some rich American tycoon is going to take over the Distillery in a buyout. The whole thing. Land, buildings, stock.

I can't see Donald going for that, said Innes. He levelled the foaming heads off the beers with a straw.

He's not going to have a say in it. Not with the money that's being talked about. That means the hotel will probably be bought out too.

Donald's a wealthy man. Doesn't look to me like he needs the money.

Ach, said the old man. He's rich for this place. But he's no millionaire. This guy that's coming in, supposedly he goes about in helicopters. A real Mr Big Time. Apparently Donald's got wind of it and he's about as nervous as a hoor in church.

That right? Innes poured out the whiskies, letting the measuring cup overflow before tipping it in.

He's buying it all up. Building a golf course down near the lighthouse. Even wants the manse. Wants Donald's own house to stay in when he visits. Going to turn us into a tartan shortbread village for rich Yankees to visit.

Innes took the man's money and got his change from the till.

Keep your ears peeled, the old man said. You hear anything you let us know. We're the lifeblood of this place, aren't we?

I will, Innes said.

He rolled up his sleeves and leaned forwards on the bar. The veins in his forearms and hands and wrists popped up the pale skin. In his pocket was a little bottle of pills. He threw three into his mouth and swallowed them dry.

Two of the tourists came to the bar now. They ordered more dark beer.

Can you help us? one of them asked. A thick-necked young guy in hillwalking gear. A European accent. German or Dutch. We heard we could meet with someone here to do a little deal.

What sort of deal? asked Innes.

What kind of deal? Are you a cop? he replied, laughing. Just a little deal, he continued. We were told that a man here could sort this out for us.

Innes put the drinks down. The frothing beer the colour of charcoal. Sorry, he said. I don't know any guys like that.

He took the money for the beer and the tourists went to their table muttering. The low sun was beginning to crack through the clouds and hit the window but it was too late in the day to do any damage.

A bee swung in from the open bathroom door and hovered in front of the bar before landing. It interested itself in a sticky drop of beer that was left puddling there. Innes watched it. A fat bee, well out of season now here in November. Innes rolled up a newspaper but the bee took flight. It buzzed near his head. He ducked and stepped to the side. Swung the paper through the air but missed and the bee disappeared. It had landed somewhere amongst the optics and the bottles.

Innes stood still and waited for the bee to move again. After a moment he heard it buzz and it flew up and to the side over the top of him. He turned and it had landed again on the bar, next to the spill of beer. Innes brought the newspaper down with a nasty slap and missed. The bee buzzed slowly up and away from him and back towards the bathroom, almost appearing to look back at him over its shoulder as it went.

Unlucky, wee man, shouted one of the old dominoes players.

Aye, shouted another. You'll get him next time.

And the old men roared with laughter.

The door opened soon after and Jessie came in, still wearing her school clothes. Grey blazer with blue and yellow trim. Sky blue blouse with a striped tie. Black tights and black shoes with a heavy weekend bag full of ring binders gripped over her shoulder. Too young to be working behind the bar serving drinks yet, but they let her do the cleaning. It was cash in hand and she needed the money.

Hiya. She smiled, dropping the bag and hanging her blazer over the back of a chair. She quickly took the empties from the tourists and the old men and wiped down their tables and replaced their soggy beermats.

Here she is, said one of the old men. Here comes trouble.

Jessie went into the bathrooms with a cloth and bottle of bleach and Innes followed her.

How's it going? he said.

Fine. I want to get done quickly today. Try and get away a wee bit early if I can.

No bother. He stood watching as she sprayed disinfectant on the surfaces and then rolled up her sleeves. Your dad came in here earlier.

Dad? What did he want?

He was asking about Young Bobby going missing.

Right.

I didn't know your dad was police.

Yeah. I barely see him anymore though.

Has he spoken to you about Young Bobby?

I haven't spoken to him about it.

Innes nodded and put his hands in his pockets then took them out again and folded his arms. I don't like him coming in here during the day. We had customers in. It's bad for business. Him coming in wearing that uniform. Sends the wrong kind of message.

What are you telling me for?

I'm just saying.

Nothing I can do about it. Now, do you mind? Jessie untucked her blouse from her skirt and stepped into the cubicle. I'm bursting for a piss.

Spoken to your mum lately?

Not much.

She came in here.

I heard about that.

You heard what she did?

It's nothing to do with me.

It is though, isn't it?

My mum's got issues. I can't control her. I don't even know what she was doing out. She doesn't go out.

I don't care. I don't want this kind of thing around my business.

She'll not be back.

You'll not be back either. I'm letting you go.

Are you serious?

Dead serious.

Do you want me to at least do tonight?

No.

Jessie looked at the cloth and the bleach in her hand and dropped her shoulders. I really need the money, she said.

You're more hassle than you're worth, said Innes. On you go. He left the bathroom and walked over the bar's tiled floor to the door and opened it and went outside and dry swallowed another couple of pills and looked up at the bright clear sky. The weather here changed so quickly.

51

Innes stirred the rice and poured in another half cup of chicken stock and had himself a drink of red wine. He was wearing his good trousers and a white shirt and he'd shaved his face smooth so the beard was gone whether Alice liked it or not.

When the liquid in the pot evaporated he poured in another ladle of stock and stirred the rice and left it simmering. He had cleared the piles of envelopes and old newspapers and the fruit bowl from the dining table. He wiped its surface with a wet cloth and laid out the knives and forks so the place settings were opposite one another. He folded red napkins and placed them between the cutlery. An empty Chianti bottle sat in the centre of the table with a long white tapered candle jammed in it. He would light the candle later.

He stepped back to the cooker and adjusted the flame under the stove and stirred the rice and poured in another ladle of stock. The liquid burst and fizzled as it hit the bottom of the pan.

Innes tapped his pocket with his right hand once more. The box was still there.

When the stock evaporated this time Innes switched the gas

to its lowest setting and poured in more stock and stirred. He went down the short corridor and into the bedroom.

There was a candle lit on either side of the bed, and a fresh bouquet of wildflowers in a vase on the window ledge. The bedding was clean and freshly changed. The candles were scented with lavender.

He went into the bathroom and switched on the light and stared at himself in the mirror. Leaned in more closely to get a look at a spot forming in the groove between his nose and his cheek. Picked at it with a fingernail until the yellow head was replaced with a prick of blood. Straightened his shoulders and adjusted how the collar of his shirt was sitting. Fixed the way his shirt tucked into his belt. Ran a hand through his hair. Saw specks of grey which were not there before. Smiled at himself, teeth clenched, the skin around his eyes wrinkling in on itself.

Looking good, he said to his reflection.

In the kitchen, the rice was catching the bottom of the pan. Innes snatched it up and poured in some stock and stirred it with the spoon. He felt the grains sticking and congealing at the base of the pot. Little burnt flecks mixed in with the creaminess of the rice. Innes ground in some salt and black pepper and stirred. Finished his red wine and poured himself another glass without putting it down.

When the stock had been fed to the rice, he stirred in a fistful of cheese and mixed it in and put the lid on the pan. The kitchen smelled of garlic and olive oil. Innes sat at the dining table and lit the long candle and waited for Alice to arrive.

The headlights from Alice's car shone through the kitchen window as she pulled up. The cottage was at the top of a long drive with no visible neighbours. Innes finished his wine and put the glass in the sink and prepared two champagne flutes.

He'd been keeping the bottle in the freezer. When Alice came into the cottage through the kitchen door he was pouring two glasses.

What's all this? she asked.

A surprise dinner, said Innes. Here you go. He handed her a glass of champagne.

Alice looked at it bubbling in the glass. Let me get my coat off at least, she said, and put the flute down on the table. I wasn't expecting this. I've actually got work to do.

I've made us a meal, said Innes, rubbing the back of his neck. Surely work can wait.

He put his arms around her and kissed her mouth but she wriggled away.

No, she said, I'm all sweaty. You've just sprung this on me.

Right, said Innes. Can't you see that I'm trying to do something nice?

It is nice. Let me get changed. Alice went to the bedroom and Innes looked in the pot at the risotto and stirred it. He sat at the table. The champagne tasted good.

When Alice came back she had changed into a dress and tied her hair up and was barefoot. Innes stood and handed her the glass of champagne again.

Cheers, he said.

Cheers. They touched glasses and kissed before drinking.

Smells nice, said Alice.

Do you like what I've done with the bedroom?

Alice laughed.

Are you hungry?

Sure. Alice finished her champagne and poured herself another. Innes piled the risotto into bowls and brought them to the table.

Did you burn it?

I don't think so.

It looks burnt.

Does it taste okay?

She scraped a little rice off the fork with her teeth. Yes, it tastes okay.

Do you remember how scared we were when we first moved up here?

I know. Couldn't even find it on a map.

And look at us now. I'm managing the hotel. You're the best teacher in the village. Haven't we done well?

It's a good start, said Alice. But you're not going to want to be a hotel manager for the rest of your life, are you?

I suppose not.

It's not exactly challenging, is it?

It is hard work.

Hard work for a stupid person, said Alice. She used her fingers to push the rice onto her fork.

How's your dinner?

It's good.

Good.

When they had finished eating, Innes took the dirty plates to the sink and Alice lit a cigarette and smoked it in long drags, letting the ash grow long at the tip before flicking it off.

How are you feeling? asked Innes.

Okay.

Can I get you anything else? Some chocolate?

No thanks.

Okay.

Why are you being weird?

I'm not being weird.

You are being weird.

Stop saying I'm being weird.

Stop being weird, then. Why are you standing there like that?

Innes was standing next to Alice's chair at the dining table and when she stubbed out her cigarette in the ashtray, he lowered himself onto one knee.

I never thought I would be so lucky as to meet a woman like you, he said. You make me so happy and you have been through so much for me already. I don't think anybody else would have moved their whole life away for me like you did. I am so pleased that you did. I love you and I want to marry you.

He had the box in his hand and he opened it and took out the ring and held it out.

Alice swivelled in her chair and covered her mouth. Tears in the corners of her eyes.

You're doing this here, she whispered. In this horrible little cottage with dirty dishes in the sink and me with my hair tied up? I don't even have any shoes on.

Innes shifted on his knee. You don't need to have shoes on, he smiled. I love your toes.

Have you asked my dad's permission? Have you even spoken to him?

Your dad? I didn't think you would want him involved. After what he did. He's scum.

You never think, she shouted. He is my dad. Of course I want him involved.

Have you heard from him?

That doesn't matter. You think you're better than him. Do you think I don't remember what you told me? That thing we never talk about? What you did that night?

Innes said nothing and Alice stared and he looked away.

You are a killer. Murdering scum. Just like him. You think I want to marry someone like that? Someone just like my dad? Then she was up and pushing past him and into the bedroom. The door slammed shut. Innes stood up and put the ring back in its box and closed it quietly.

Alice had stubbed her cigarette in the ashtray before finishing it. Innes picked up the dirty filter and lit it off the candle and took two big drags before burning his lip.

52

Donald took the dirty plates into the kitchen and turned on the hot tap. Squeezed some washing up liquid into the sink. Rinsed the bacon grease and leftover sauce from the plates.

The radio was playing quietly. Christmas hymns, children's voices in harmony. Bells tinkling in the background.

I'll do these, said Margo, touching Donald's waist from behind.

He stepped to the side and she dipped her hands into the hot water. Could you turn the oven on?

Donald turned the dial around and the old oven gasped into life.

Why don't you go into the living room and light the fire? I'll peel the potatoes and put the turkey in the oven then I'll join you.

Donald left her in the kitchen humming under her breath to the children's choir on the radio. Church bells.

The living room was a long, wide space with wooden flooring and a thick rug. Oil paintings on the walls. A cabinet with good decanters and crystal glasses. Donald kneeled in front of the mantel and built the fire. Torn newspapers, dried twigs, thick slabs of chopped timber.

He struck a match and the newspaper crinkled under its bright orange flame. Blew on the blackening newsprint. Got up and poured himself a drink. Cullrothes 25-year-old. Heard Margo singing now in a sweet high tone in the kitchen.

The living room was transformed for Christmas. An eight-foot balsam fir wrapped in electric lights and weighed down with baubles. A highland dancer. A ceramic thistle. Plastic stars.

The whisky was good. Caramel and black pepper on his tongue.

The mantel above the fire which they normally kept clear was covered now in cards. Difficult cards which meant two things. Messages of hope and good cheer and longing and condolences.

Margo came through from the kitchen. Still wearing her apron. It was red with snowflakes down the front. Isn't it looking nice in here, she said. Very festive.

She sat next to him on the couch and tutted at his measure of whisky but she had in her hand a flute of champagne mixed with orange juice.

Well, she said, happy Christmas.

Happy Christmas, he said, and they touched their glasses together.

That tree, she said, looking around. Does that tree look squint to you?

Donald focused with one eye and looked at the tree.

It looks fine.

It looks squint. Will you fix it?

I didn't want to put the damn thing up to begin with this year.

Well I did, she said. Just because.

I'll fix it. Donald stood up and grabbed the tree by its trunk near the top. The needles bent and pierced the top layer of skin on his palm. Left or right?

Left a bit.

Donald moved it left.

Back a bit.

He moved it back.

Perfect, she said.

He let go and looked at the tree and thought it stood just the same as it had to begin with.

He sat back on the couch. The music had stopped and the radio was playing a religious sermon but the preacher's voice was muffled.

When is the service today? asked Margo.

Midday, said Donald.

I think we should go. Don't you think we should go? It'll do us good.

He held her hand and smiled but did not reply.

The church doors were open and Father Jaine stood smiling on the steps when Margo and Donald arrived in the black Range Rover.

Hello, shouted the priest, waving. Hello! I was so hoping you would make it. Donald stood back a few steps and took a nip from a hip flask while Margo and the priest embraced and exchanged words. Then Donald stepped up. They shook hands. Father Jaine looked into his eyes. It's good of you to come. How are you today?

Fine.

Must be hard.

Aye, well.

Donald and Margo took a pew near the aisle and kept their gloves on to keep out the chill.

There were some prayers and some hymns and then Father Jaine looked up from the altar and sighed and brought his hands together. Brothers and sisters, he began. We find ourselves in strange territory this year. We are joyous and thankful for everything that we have. But we know that in Cullrothes this year has not been without its challenges. As we gather today we must recognise the sorrow that has fallen upon our village these past few months. The friends that we have lost. The friends that we still search for. And the friends that we know, sadly, we will soon lose.

Margo squeezed down on Donald's hand and he felt her body shake as she sobbed.

As we come together to celebrate the birth of Jesus, we must put our faith in God's plan. Yes, my friends, we must have faith. Faith in the Lord's justice. Faith that good things will happen to the good people among us. And faith that those who stray from the Lord's path will be met with hardship. With obstacles. And with suffering. But we also know, do we not, that repentance is central to the idea of faith. We know that when we stray from the path, we can return to it. When we lose sight of the message, it will echo until we learn to listen. When we feel that something is missing, it is not impossible for us once again to be made whole.

Margo released Donald's hand and she was out of the pew before he could react. He turned and watched her march with quick steps up the aisle, her head down. Out the church doors and into the street with everyone watching. Once she was gone, their eyes turned towards him.

Donald stood slowly and straightened his coat. He nodded to the priest and followed his wife up the aisle but before he got to the doors he stopped. Turned to face everyone gathered for Christmas mass.

Someone here knows what happened to my boy, said Donald. Whoever it is, you know who you are. Take my advice. Leave. Pack up your things and sell your house and move far away from here. Because when I find out who has done this to that poor woman I will bring you back here. I will drag your beaten body up to that altar and I will slit your throat. Okay? Okay.

And he left before anyone could say a word in reply.

The turkey sat wrapped in foil while its juices rested. The flesh tightening and congealing. The meat coagulating away from the animal's bones.

Donald watched as Margo set the table for their meal. Place mats, cutlery, glasses. Napkins and Christmas crackers. Candles flickering across the room. Bread sauce and cranberry sauce and gravy served in separate little bowls. Donald and Margo's places set opposite one another, and a third table setting between them just in case Young Bobby wandered in.

You're wasting your time, growled Donald, again.

If he walks in this door, and I haven't done it –

He won't.

You don't know that. What harm is it doing? If it makes me happy?

Donald sighed and tore the cork from a wine bottle with a screw.

In the hospice the care staff wore coloured paper hats and Christmas music played from a big stereo in the communal area. All the patients who were able to had been helped into armchairs and they sat in a circle while the others stayed in their bedrooms with the doors open. Grandpa drank sweet whisky liqueur and opened a present from his son. It was a photobook with pictures of Galloway as a boy and Jessie as a baby and there were old holiday snaps from Spain and the Outer Hebrides.

Happy Christmas, said one of the nurses. Can I get you another one of those?

Grandpa tipped the remained of the whisky liqueur into his mouth and held the empty glass out to her. I think you can, he said. Oh yes, I think you can.

Up the long drive in the damp rented cottage Innes and Alice sat side by side on the couch watching the television. Innes rubbed his swollen belly and stroked Alice's hair. They had agreed to put the argument about the engagement behind them since it was Christmas, and were watching a film. It was not long before she fell asleep.

Innes pulled a blanket over her and made sure the phone was unplugged from the wall before he swallowed a couple of good painkillers with his wine. He wasn't going to ask her again.

Donald halved a sprout and ran it through some gravy on his plate. I was thinking, he said.

Yes?

About this Young Bobby situation. If the boy's decided he wants to start up somewhere new or have a fresh go of things, we need to do the same.

How can we do that?

He's not a child anymore, Margo. He's made a grown-up, adult decision to remove himself from here and do his own thing. God knows why but that's what he's done. I don't think it's good for us to go on like this. Like we're mourning a death. Setting a place for him at the table for Christmas dinner.

He is my boy. How can you pretend nothing is wrong?

We didn't run out on him. If he was missing us he would be in touch. Christ, it's not hard in this day and age to pick up the telephone is it?

Margo pushed a slice of turkey around her plate.

I don't see what alternative there is.

It's almost New Year. Let's give it that long. If we don't hear from him, or there's no word from Galloway –

Have you spoken to Galloway recently?

I'll phone him tomorrow. Donald stretched his leg and heard a crunching somewhere in the kneecap. But if we don't hear by New Year we need to do something. Do you realise how weak this whole thing makes us look?

I don't care about how it makes us look.

I do. Once people think you're weak you're in trouble. We're not far off losing it all. You've seen the overdraft? The loan statements? We're in deep.

How deep?

We've got to do something.

What about the hotel? asked Margo. You could get rid of the hotel. Free up some capital.

Do you have any idea how long it would take to find a buyer?

Don't be silly, said Margo. I'm not talking about selling it.

What then?

It's insured, isn't it? Why don't you burn it? Burn it to the ground.

53

There was a ceilidh every New Year's Eve in Cullrothes. You were expected to attend. The ticket prices kept the village hall maintained all year round so without the ceilidh there would be no hall. And if the hall closed there could be no ceilidh.

So the venue was the same every year. And the band was, too. And they would play the same songs. They'd have the same amount of beers and whiskies give or take a few depending on how early they'd started on the drink. The songs were the same each time and so therefore were the dances. The Gay Gordons with its wild swings and sweaty circles. The Dashing White Sergeant with its careful footwork. Here was the village hall decked out again with the white tablecloths and tartan table runners and thistles with heads as thick as lightbulbs in glass jars.

Alice and Innes were together at the bar. Ordering a glass of beer for him and a prosecco for her. Alice asked for an ashtray and lit a menthol cigarette and leaned so that her lower back rested on the ridge of the bar and she looked out across the small hall and blew a cloud of smoke up. She kept a little of it in her lungs and let that slip from her nostrils.

You look lovely tonight, said Innes.

Thank you, she smiled.

It's good to be out. To be away from the hotel.

Yes.

How's your drink?

She took a sip and scowled. It's flat. Not a fresh bottle.

Innes gulped a mouthful of beer. The glass trembling in his hand. He was pale with dark bags under his eyes and had lost weight so that his wristbones strained under the skin.

The first dance was still on. The whole village and the surrounding farms seemed to be here. Everyone bouncing around the tight dance floor on their toes with the pipes and the drums. That sense of anticipation and tension. Already the hall smelled of sweat, whisky and perfume. Already the ceiling was becoming obscured with the streams of cigarette smoke. Already there was a queue at the toilets.

Want to dance? asked Innes.

Alice swallowed more wine and said: Not just now. She had made eye contact across the room with Valentine and he was coming over to them in his kilt with his waistcoat and white shirt unbuttoned to the collarbone.

He wrapped his arms around her waist and kissed her on both cheeks and let his mouth linger near her ear. You look good enough to eat, he shouted over the music.

Alice smiled and removed his hands from her waist and put her hand on Innes's sleeve. This is Innes, she shouted over the music. Honey, this is Grant. He writes for the Courier.

Innes said hello and shook hands with Valentine.

You're the manager at the hotel, said Valentine. I've seen you there. Let me buy you two a drink. As a welcome to your first ceilidh in the village. Same again is it?

Valentine ordered a double whisky with no ice for himself. A beer for Innes. And another glass of prosecco for Alice. When he got this he picked up the flute and tapped the side of the glass with his fingernail and stared at the lifeless yellow liquid.

This is flat, he said. Can you open a fresh bottle?

The barman poured the old drink away and made a new one.

The three of them clinked glasses and said cheers. The band stopped playing and the dancers stopped whirling and they fell into each other's arms, red and exhausted, and another song started and a new crowd formed to dance the next one.

I need to nip to the bathroom, said Valentine.

When the dancing had pounded for two hours the band took a break and went outside to cool in the fresh air. A long table at the back of the hall was covered with a cloth and a squad of old women from the village proudly appeared from the kitchen carrying heavily laden silver platters. Hot sausage rolls with seasoned pork meat wrapped in flaking buttery pastry. Crumbling oatcakes piled high with creme fraiche and violently pink smoked salmon. Haggis pakora, crispy and fried in a red spiced batter with lemon wedges and half crescents of onions. A dish of steaming stovies, corned beef mixed with buttery mashed potatoes. White triangle sandwiches with smoked ham and mustard.

The people mingled around the buffet. Innes hung back and found himself a damp spot on the bar to lean his elbow on. He ordered another beer and squinted across the hall. Looking for Alice. She was wearing a green dress and he focused on the colour, trying to recognise its shade in the crowd of kilts and ballgowns, but his vision was too blurred. Only a few drinks was enough now to get to his head with the medication he was taking. He turned and leaned his forearms on the bar top and rested his head there, closed his eyes, enjoyed the darkness he created for a moment.

Alice was outside the village hall with Valentine. He had her pushed up against the wall round the back of the hall where there was no light. Just the two of them and the muffled shouts from the hall. Just the smell of dirt and leaves from the trees that hung over them. Valentine hiked his hands underneath her skirt.

Are you feeling okay, she asked, and pulled her head back. But she could not make out his face.

Yes.

You're hot. She touched his cheek. You're burning up.

It's just the dancing. No air in there.

They kissed again and again he reached under her skirt and grabbed her thighs.

That's enough now, she said. I need to go back in.

Don't.

What are you on?

Nothing.

You're off your face.

Valentine laughed: I am not! And wiped a trickle of sweat from his forehead.

Why are you chewing at your mouth like that then?

Valentine stretched his mouth and rubbed his jawbone and smiled at Alice. He tried to pull her towards him again but her hand was balled into a fist at his chest.

I need to go back in. You stay out here. Get some air.

They needed people to stay sober and work at the ceilidh clearing tables and washing glasses and this was the first year Jessie was considered old enough to do it. She had on a white blouse but it was not as white as it used to be. A black skirt and black tights and the same flat black shoes that she wore to school. She was carrying a tray of dirty glasses to the kitchen when she walked past Innes leaning against the back wall and he held his hand out and pointed at her.

It's wee Jessie, he said.

Hello there, she said.

Happy New Year. Hey. Hey. Happy New Year.

It's not midnight yet, but happy New Year when it comes.

Do you want to dance?

I'm working.

Come here. Come here until I tell you something,

Jessie gave a tight smile and stepped closer to him and she was holding the tray of glasses between them.

You're still at school.

Yes.

I used to be a teacher. Did you know that?

I heard that.

I liked being a teacher. It's a good job, you know. Innes pushed back against the wall and staggered a little closer to Jessie so she inched backwards on the balls of her feet. Some people think it's a last resort but it's a good job.

I'm sure it's good managing the hotel too, she said.

Oh, it's good. Being the boss. But let's not talk all work. Are we having that dance?

I can't.

You don't like me? Is that it?

I never said that. I really need to get back to work –

But Innes grabbed her by the shoulders and the glasses rattled against each other. Know what I think? he said. I think nobody around here likes me. That's the truth isn't it? Village full of creeps and weirdos and none of them can be bothered with me.

I don't know.

I'll never fit in. But that's okay. Because I know something you don't know.

Do you? Jessie was trying to make eye contact with other people over Innes's shoulder for help.

The big secret. The big scandal. That Young Bobby guy everyone's always going on about.

What's it got to do with him?

Go and ask him. Everyone misses him so much. Go and ask him. Go and dig him up from that hole I put him in. Go and see how deep down he is.

What are you saying? Jessie stared at Innes and he still gripped her by the shoulders. He could feel her soft skin through the blouse and as she opened her lips again he slapped his hands down on the tray so all the empty glasses shattered on the floor with shards tinkling all around them and then there was silence in the room as everyone turned to see what had happened.

Back in the hall Alice's headteacher was waiting for her in the doorway. Hello, smiled Alice.

Hello, said Mrs Hughes. I'm afraid you'll need to take your gentleman friend home now.

Home?

He's made a bit of a scene. Smashed a whole tray of glasses. Poor man can barely stand up.

Alice looked over and there was Innes. He was pale and his shirt was stained damp. Somebody was holding on to his elbow and trying to get him to drink a glass of water.

A shame you couldn't have stayed, frowned Mrs Hughes. But that boy really has had quite enough for one night. Don't you think?

54

Grandpa sat up in bed with a good clean t-shirt on and his hair combed back from his face as it was growing longer then he normally wore it. His face was freshly shaved and the skin glowed pink where the razor had dragged. Jessie nudged him along with her backside so she could sit there on the bed next to him and held the old man's hand.

Happy birthday, Grandpa!

He sucked in a breath of air before speaking. Thank you.

Ninety-five, she said. How does it feel?

Tiring, said Grandpa, showing his little brown teeth as he smiled.

I got you a present, she said. Jessie lifted a large gift-wrapped box from the floor and placed it on the bed. It's not heavy, she said.

Grandpa shuffled his body upwards on his pillow and tore at the wrapping paper with his long fingernails. Underneath the colourful paper it was a plain cardboard box. It was folded shut but unsealed. He prised the flaps apart and from inside the box a huge golden balloon floated up in front of his face and then towards the ceiling, a curled ribbon dangling from it. The balloon bounced on the ceiling and twisted and settled.

Now all the nurses will know it's your birthday, said Jessie. You know what that means. Extra ice cream. Kisses on the cheek. Maybe a sponge bath.

He grabbed her hand in his strong one and shook his head with a little smile. Thank you very much.

You're very welcome.

Grandpa squinted his eyes and looked around the room. Where is Mark? he whispered.

Dad is here, she said. I saw his car outside. I think he must be speaking with the doctors. He'll be along in a minute.

Ah.

Have the doctors told you anything?

No.

Have you asked them?

I don't want to know. What else can they tell me?

They might know if the lump's still growing or not.

It's not the lump that's going to get me. He pointed at this throat. I can't eat. If you can't eat, you're snookered.

If you change your mind about it, you just need to ask.

Okay.

I've just remembered. I brought you another present. From the machine outside.

Jessie reached into her schoolbag and got two cold cans and put them on Grandpa's tray.

Freezing cold Irn Brus, said Jessie. But these ones are ice cream flavoured. Can you believe that?

Ice cream?

Ice cream.

Grandpa stared at the can with his mouth open. He picked it up with his sore hand and turned it around and looked at the ingredients and mouthed the word silently again. Ice cream.

One for you and one for me, said Jessie. Since I'm not allowed to sneak any whisky in here for you.

Let's have a bash.

Jessie opened the cans and popped a straw through each ring pull. Grandpa picked up his ice cream Irn Bru and sucked at the straw. Jessie watched him for a second and then drank her own. She swallowed the cold sweet liquid. Grandpa swirled his around in his mouth and then spat it into the cardboard bowl like he did with most of his liquids now.

He replaced the can and sat back.

What do you think?

Wonderful. Wonderful.

The door opened then and Galloway came in, closing it softly behind him. He wore denims and dirty boots and a knitted jumper.

Sorry, he said. I had to wait ages to see the doctor. He put his hand on Jessie's shoulder and pulled her towards him for a hug but their bodies did not touch. He put his hand out to Grandpa and the two men shook hands. Galloway stood at the end of the bed. Well, he said. Happy birthday. He pointed at the balloon. This is a nice touch.

I brought it in, said Jessie. Did you not bring a present?

What can you buy the man who has everything?

Just a token present would have been nice.

I'll split the cost of the balloon with you. It can be from both of us. Galloway nodded at it. Then said: How are you feeling, Dad?

Not too bad.

Feeling okay?

Same as before.

That's good.

Aye.

And how about you, young lady? School going okay?

Oh yes. It's a joy to be so stressed about exams that I can barely sleep at night.

Galloway laughed. Well, stick in there. We've all been through it. He pulled the armchair from the corner of the room over next to Grandpa's bed and sat down. He put his hand on the bedsheets close to Grandpa's hand.

Well, whispered Grandpa, how is work?

Och. Too much to do. Never enough time.

Are you still looking for Young Bobby?

Not actively. He's still a missing person but there's not much we can do. He isn't here! I must have interviewed every villager and farmer in a twenty-mile radius. He'll turn up eventually.

Donald came in to visit, said Grandpa.

Did he?

And Jessie. Every day. He reached up and cupped his hand around the girl's warm neck.

She's some kid, said Galloway.

What did the doctor say? asked Jessie.

Galloway sat back and crossed his arms. No change, he said. They're still using morphine to numb the pain. Are you in pain?

A bit sore in the mornings.

And they're using steroids.

What are those for?

To stop the tumour from growing too quickly.

Sounds like they've got it under control.

It's not really a treatment, said Galloway. They're just delaying the death.

Grandpa lifted his can and sipped. They both watched him.

Have you spoken to Mum recently? Jessie asked her dad.

Me?

Aye, you.

No. Why would I speak to your mum?

Do you know how she's doing?

How is she doing?

Not very good.

Ah.

Maybe you could go and see her while you're over here.

Galloway looked at his watch. I need to catch the last ferry.

Of course you do.

But I will. Next time I'm over. Tell her I'm asking after her.

Galloway and Grandpa spoke about how life used to be in the village when they were younger until the old man started yawning and his eyes took on a glazed look. Jessie and Galloway understood that he was growing tired and got up to leave. It was taking less time for him to grow tired now. Grandpa's eyelids had drooped and his breathing was short. They did not want to wake him, or disturb the patients in the other rooms, so as they left they did not speak a word to one another.

55

The viewpoint up the Cat's Back looked over the whole of Cullrothes and the peninsula, across the loch and the distant mountains and eventually towards the darkness of the Atlantic, at the edge of which a pinprick of light shone intermittently from the lighthouse. It had been a winding single-track road to get here up the long ridge. The car park was surfaced with coarse gravel and there were potholes so large that Alice's car lurched and squealed before pulling up next to where Valentine was waiting.

He was sitting in the driver's seat with the engine off and he gave her a little salute with his fingers when she pulled up. The radio was on in his car. She could hear the low, muffled music through her window.

Alice turned the key to kill the engine and pulled down her sunshield. Her face in the mirror looked drawn. She picked at a couple of spots around her chin and pinched her cheeks and ruffled her fringe until it was sitting right.

She took off her flats and exchanged them for a pair of nude heels she kept in the passenger's footwell. Lifting her backside up from the car seat, she rolled up the waistband of her skirt a few times and unbuttoned her blouse so that her bra would show. A spray of perfume. And then she was ready.

Inside Valentine's car it was uncomfortably warm in comparison with the cold winter night. The smell of bodies. He kissed her then sat back and dipped his head towards the windscreen.

Happy New Year, he said.

Same to you.

What happened at the ceilidh? I saw you leave early.

Innes was hammered. I think someone slipped him something in his drink.

Unlikely. So what do you think? Not a bad view, is it.

She looked to the enormous vista where the sun's final light was dying.

It's beautiful, she said.

I've been coming up here since I was a boy, said Valentine. My friend got his first car and we'd come up here and smoke and stare up at the stars. He looked out the side window. Kids don't seem to come up the Cat's Back anymore.

What does the name mean?

Who knows, he said, and turned to her. Put his hand on her leg under her skirt. I think from a distance it's supposed to look like a cat lying down. I don't know where you have to go to get that perspective though.

Alice thought about Hercules and the cat's curled spine on the road. A nice little irony.

Valentine moved his hand further up her leg. No tights today?

Thought I'd do you a favour.

Trying to make things easy for me.

I thought you could do with a hand.

Valentine laughed.

The sun soon went down, and the stars slowly appeared as

the sky's hue changed. A strong wind buffeted Valentine's car and it rocked from side to side up there on the Cat's Back.

When he was finished, they kept their seats reclined and lay back, breathing. Holding hands. Listening to rock music and the wind outside. Alice nuzzled her face into the headrest and sighed.

Want a smoke?

Okay.

Valentine stuck two cigarettes in his mouth and lifted a lighter to them. He inhaled and both cigarettes caught and he drew in the taste and then gave one of them to Alice.

How gentlemanly.

I do my best.

It's too hot in this car.

The heating's broke. I can't turn it off.

Open a window. It's roasting in here.

He unwound the window slowly and the wind rushed in, cold on their skin, and it picked at the burning tips of their cigarettes, flecks of ash floating up and around them.

So how long do you see this lasting, he said.

You mean this song?

No.

The cigarette?

No.

Ah. You must be talking about our illicit affair.

If that's what you want to call it.

That's what it is.

Maybe from your point of view.

Alice smoked the cigarette and poked at the radio controls with her toe to turn the music up. I like this song.

They play it all the time.

Because it's excellent.

The music was loud and the wind still spun around their heads from the open window.

How long do you want it to last? she said.

I don't know.

Years?

He laughed.

I'm serious. Can you see us doing this for years to come?

Probably not.

What about one year?

I don't know.

A month? A week?

Well what do you think?

I honestly couldn't care less.

Charming.

She had finished her cigarette and she handed him the burning tip. He pursed it between his fingers and flicked it out the open window.

What about now? he said. What about just finishing it now?

That suits me okay.

We'll stay pals though.

Absolutely. Pals. Good, good pals.

Alice wriggled her underwear back on and started to do the buttons up on her blouse.

Did you have a good Christmas? he asked.

It was alright.

Did you hear from your dad at all?

Alice laughed. Why would you ask that?

I just wondered. Can they send cards from prison?

If they can, I didn't get one.

What about Christmas dinner? How many turkeys would be needed to feed a prison block?

You sound like you're making notes for a story.

It's not a bad idea.

Shut up.

It would be a good feature though.

Are you serious?

I could get you a decent fee.

Do you ever take a break?

The news never stops.

What kind of fee do you think it'd be worth? Just out of interest.

Five hundred, easy.

Slow down, big spender.

It's a local paper, what do you expect?

What's the most you would pay for a story? The maximum payment possible?

It would depend on the information.

Alice lit another cigarette and put her feet up on Valentine's steering wheel so her legs draped across him.

Are you on something again?

Just a couple of lines.

Why would you take a couple of lines to come and see me?

Thought it would make it more fun?

I'm not fun enough on my own? You need to be off your face.

Are you okay? he asked.

I'm brilliant, pal. Thanks for asking. I better get home. Got a pie to bake.

Valentine pulled at his trousers and zipped them. I'll drive ahead. So you know where you're going.

Alice snapped her seat back upright and hooked on her heels. She smiled at Valentine: You're such a good pal.

Come on. Enough of that.

She leaned towards him and kissed his cheek. Yes. Enough now. I think we've had quite enough haven't we? Do me a favour. Pack it in with the gear. It's not a good look on you.

I'll try.

I'll see you later.

She opened the door and skipped across to her own car. Valentine was still buckling his seatbelt when she reversed to the left, turned in the viewpoint, and disappeared back down the single-track road that led winding down to the village from the Cat's Back.

56

It was too warm under the covers to be comfortable but the air was baltic. Innes lay in his bed sweating with his feet and his face sticking out.

He was exhausted but could not sleep. The co-codamol had made him dopey but he could not sleep. The wine made his head spin and his empty stomach sore but still he could not sleep.

He heard Alice's car coming up the driveway. The engine being snipped. The kitchen door opening and slamming closed again. Her heavy handbag hitting the dining table.

Innes tucked the duvet between his thighs and rolled onto his side facing away from the door. Alice came into the bedroom and tiptoed across the carpet towards the bed. Her skirt hit the floor. Her blouse over the back of the chair. She slipped in beside him and her hand tucked underneath his arm.

Hmm, he said, and shifted. Her skin was freezing cold.

Hi, she said. Are you asleep?

What time is it? he mumbled.

I didn't mean to wake you. She pulled him round onto his back so that she could bring her face close to his.

Sorry for waking you, she said. I missed you.

Her breath smelled of smoke and mint.

You're so cold, he said.

You're nice and cosy, she said. And snuggled in more tightly to him rubbing her toes against his.

Get off, he mumbled, but she lifted her bare leg over him and straddled his waist.

So nice and warm, she said, and pressed her chest against his. Don't.

Wake up, she whispered. I need to tell you something.

What is it?

Wake up. Open your eyes.

What?

I shouldn't have said those things to you when you proposed to me. I was horrible about it. You are a good man. I don't know why I reacted like that. I think maybe I was scared.

Innes rubbed his eyes. Why? he asked.

Because of what happened with my mum and my dad. It's not really a postcard impression of marriage to have. But we're not like them. You're not like him. I've been thinking about it. About what happened. I wasn't fair to you.

It's okay.

Ask me again.

Really?

Yes.

Innes put his hands around Alice's neck. Here?

Yes!

Will you marry me?

Of course I will. Alice smiled and they kissed. Innes felt her mouth smiling against his as they kissed. He reached around her and threw the covers off her and rubbed her bare back with his hands. He reached down and felt her bare thighs with his hands. She wriggled against him.

We're engaged, she said.

We're engaged.

We're going to get married.

Innes laughed. Alice's hair fell down and tickled the skin on his cheek. We're going to get married. Can you believe it? Can you?

Aren't you forgetting something sweetie? She held out her hand and wiggled her fingers at him.

I am. Excuse me for a moment. Where are my manners? Innes leaned over into a drawer in the unit by his bedside and shuffled a few things to the side. He turned around again and opened the blue velvet box.

It's a princess cut in a platinum setting, he said. Just like the one you always wanted.

Alice put her hands to her mouth and her eyes were wide and beautiful. It's beautiful, she said.

Want to try it on?

Immediately.

Innes put the ring on her finger and pushed it roughly over the joints down to the knuckle and twisted it so the rock faced upwards.

It's absolutely massive, she said. How much did this cost?

That's not important.

How did you afford this? Innes, we don't have any savings. Where did you get the money?

I stole it, he said, and laughed. Now please, shut up and model that thing for me. Hold it up to the light. Let me see how it looks.

57

Jessie knocked on the classroom door and waited. Some of her classmates walked past on their way to the lunch hall but she kept her eyes down and away from them. She had no money for the lunch hall and hadn't brought any food to school with her.

Faintly she heard the teacher calling from behind the door and she opened it. Alice was sitting at her desk and the radio was playing music and the blinds were all open so that sunlight lit the room.

Jessie, hello. You've come to talk about your essay.

Hello, Miss Green.

I just read it this morning. I have some thoughts. Come and sit here. Close the door first.

Jessie closed the classroom door and dropped her heavy bag on the floor and scraped a chair across to Alice's desk.

First of all, it's very well written. I like how you use the symbolism of the snowflake. What did you mean when the character worried about melting?

Just, said Jessie, struggling to find the right expression. Just that she might melt and vanish.

She might die?

I suppose so.

I think you could play about with the structure of the story. It's very linear at the moment. The character does one thing, then the next, then the next. It might be good if you used some flashbacks. Go back to her childhood. Show us a happy memory. Show us a sad memory.

Jessie lifted a soggy tissue to her nose and blew hard. The wetness gathered in the tissue and clung to her nostrils.

It's quite a dark story. You've got this character who feels like she's going to melt.

Only if she's alone. If she can find other people like herself, other snowflakes, she'll be okay.

I got that as well.

The essay was on the desk and it was covered in red pen marks and comments and scribbles.

Most of this feedback is just questions and comments. You can make any changes you want but it's a good story. It'll get a good mark.

Thank you.

I am a bit concerned though, Jessie.

Why?

Well, you've given me a story which is about a character feeling isolated. This idea of vanishing, or melting, it really means dying, doesn't it.

Jessie shrugged her shoulders and snorted to clear her nose a little.

You can talk to me about this.

The girl felt her face grow hot and didn't know if it was going pale or blushing.

If I talk about this, it'll get worse, said Jessie. It'll be shared and passed on to the headteacher and then to my mum and it won't be mine anymore.

Anything you tell me, said Alice, sitting forwards now,

anything you choose to tell me will be treated in the strictest confidence. It won't get back to your parents. I won't mention it to the headteacher. Is the character in the story you? Are you the girl who's scared of melting?

She's not scared of melting. She *is* melting. She wants to melt sometimes.

Alice put one hand on Jessie's shoulder and squeezed. I know you have things going on at home. It can't be easy.

Jessie looked up into the teacher's face. She could feel the damp from her nose touching her lip and knew that her eyes were blazing and pink.

This is supposed to be the best time of my life, she said, and it's horrible. Everyone else here has it so easy. Why is it so hard for me?

Alice shuffled forwards and hugged Jessie with both arms around the girl. You are amazing, she said. Nobody else could do what you're doing. And the Christmas holidays are often the worst for feelings like these to bubble up. This isn't going to last forever, this feeling. It's going to go away and you'll feel better again.

When?

Soon.

She let go of the girl and passed her some tissues from a drawer and Jessie wiped her face and blew her nose again.

You need to do something that's just for you. Something you enjoy. Take this. She put a ten-pound note on top of Jessie's story and gave it to her.

No, I can't take that.

Take it. Buy yourself something, whatever helps you relax. Buy some cake, a magazine, some bubbles for the bath. Even get yourself some wine and cigarettes if that's what you want.

They both laughed, loud.

I know that's what works for me, said Alice.

Jessie nodded and folded the note and put it in her bag, along with the essay.

And you're not going to tell anyone about this?

It's our secret.

Congratulations on getting engaged at New Year. I heard about that.

Isn't it wonderful? Alice showed Jessie the ring and twisted her finger so it would sparkle in the light.

That is beautiful. You were at the ceilidh with your fiancé weren't you?

Yes. We popped in but we couldn't stay.

I was just working at it. I spoke to him. I spoke to Innes.

What about?

I think he was drunk. He wasn't making sense.

What did he say?

He was talking about Young Bobby going missing.

Alice nodded and leaned forward so her nose was close to Jessie's nose. That's been very hard for everyone, hasn't it? A hard situation to deal with. But I think when you're working at things like the ceilidh, at adult events, you need to think about what is appropriate and what is not. Is it appropriate for you to come to your teacher and talk about this?

I'm not sure.

You shouldn't even have been working at the ceilidh, should you? You're too young. I saw you pouring drinks. Did you get paid in cash? Are you declaring tax for it? You could get into a lot of trouble. You think this is a good idea to have a black mark against your name so young?

That's not what I want.

If you want people to keep things confidential than you have to keep things confidential too. Okay? On you go.

The girl stood and hoisted her bag onto her shoulder and

walked, shoulders slumped, to the classroom door and opened it.

Jessie?

Yes?

Give me a new draft of that story on Monday.

Jessie wiped her nose on the back of her blazer sleeve and nodded.

Okay.

Close the door behind you.

58

Johnny Coca-Cola watched the hotel from the Shore Road sitting on the kerb and smoking a Marlboro. The heavy rucksack sitting next to him. Baseball cap pulled over his eyes.

Soon a lorry came along the quiet narrow road, squeezing itself into the hotel's car park and reversing into position so the barrels and the bottles could be unloaded and rolled into the cellar. Johnny Coca-Cola watched the manager come out to meet the driver. A thin red-haired boy with a white shirt and skinny black trousers. Nervous as he spoke to the thick-necked driver.

The American mashed his cigarette under his foot and crossed the road and went into the bar when the manager's back was turned. There was a door with a sign on it saying Rooms, and he pushed this open and went into a cold dark corridor. It smelled of dust and damp. Through another thick door and then he was in the residential wing of the hotel, with yellow wallpaper and a wide hallway with numbered bedroom doors all along each side. Soft carpet so he made no noise. Johnny Coca-Cola reached the furthest point of the corridor and chose a room facing away from the loch. The window for this room would not be seen from the road.

Johnny Coca-Cola looked back down the empty hallway. He took a step back from the door and then lunged at it, the sole of his boot slamming flat into the wood at the point where the lock was. The old door swung open on its hinges with a bang. The jamb splintered and came free and fell onto the thick carpet. Johnny Coca-Cola stepped inside and closed the damaged door over behind him.

He glanced into the empty rooms and unzipped the side pocket of his rucksack. Here there was a screwdriver in a small case. Johnny Coca-Cola lifted the door jamb back into position and fixed it with small screws at the corners. He opened the door and used a rag to clean off his footprint where it had connected. There were small shards of splintered wood on the carpet in the hallway. He knelt and collected these in his palm and when he had them all he flushed them down the toilet.

The room was warm and dark, with the curtains drawn and the storage heaters slowly pumping out heat. There was a security restrictor on the window which it meant it could only open by about six inches, but he kept it shut. If it was opened even by a crack, someone might notice from outside. His room looked onto the car park and to the right was the beer garden with its tired picnic tables and the parasols all tied up for winter.

Johnny Coca-Cola took off his jacket and shoes and stored them in the hall cupboard. He stood still for a moment, listening to the pipes, to a boiler gurgling somewhere. On the side table he found a Bible and a glass ashtray branded with the hotel's logo.

He sat down in the armchair and flicked the television on with the remote control. He muted the sound and put on the subtitles and found an old cowboy movie. It was a comfortable armchair. Better than rough camping in the woods with a sheet of tarpaulin and a pillow made from leaves. The clock was ticking and the room's warmth was unrelenting and soon

Johnny Coca-Cola fell asleep with his mouth open and he did not snore.

When he woke it was mid-afternoon. There were noises bleeding into the room from the window. He looked through a slither in the curtains and could see two women in the car park. One of them was delivering a parcel. The other had been passing but stopped for conversation.

That's the weather turning now, one was saying.

Bad, is it?

Storms, they're saying. Coming in from over the water.

In the en suite, Johnny Coca-Cola ran the cold tap and drank from it and then he filled up the small portable kettle that came with the room. On a tray there was a small bowl of packaged shortbread and some teabags and some granulated coffee. He made a cup of black tea and ate all of the shortbread, dropping the packets to the floor. Standing in his socks in the hotel room. Staring at the scenic photographs on the wall of old stags and old mountains and old pipers.

There was a cordless telephone on the side unit. Johnny Coca-Cola picked it up and held it to the side of his face. Heard the dial tone buzz. He pushed a series of buttons, summoning the sequence from his memory. Then waited for someone to pick it up.

Yeah?

It's me, sir. It's Johnny.

Where you been?

Camping.

What about now?

Found myself a good spot. Safe and warm and secure.

How's business going?

Healthy. Got word around the school kids pretty fast. Lots of tourists over here. Europeans mostly on backpacking trips.

You got enough gear to keep you going?

Johnny Coca-Cola picked up his rucksack and emptied one of its zipped compartments onto the worn carpet. Dozens of small plastic bags filled with powder, pills and green buds.

Yes sir, he said. I've still got a healthy supply.

And what is your impression of Mr Fleck?

He's a small-time thug. Got everyone over here scared shitless.

Sell as much of that stuff as you can. Get it everywhere. I want him to know his territory is under threat.

Yes sir.

Call me in a week.

Yes sir.

That night, Johnny Coca-Cola folded his clothes over the armchair and got into the single bed. It was soft and sagged deep in the middle. The pillowcases smelled sour. The sharp little tips of duck feathers poked through and scratched the back of his neck. Still the clock ticked. The American woke almost every hour, startled by nothing, staring into the darkness of the room until his breathing settled again. Woken from thick, exhausted sleep unpunctuated by dreams.

59

Innes stood in the cold and dark kitchen with a handful of pills in his hand and the tap running then overflowing into an empty glass. The telephone in the hall was ringing again.

He threw the pills to the back of his tongue and briefly felt the bitter chalky coating. He turned off the tap and swallowed the water in two mouthfuls, arching his neck back to encourage the pills down. Wiped his mouth and put the empty glass into the sink. There still was that telephone in the hall ringing again.

Hello, he answered. The handset greasy in his palm.

It's me, hun, it's your mum.

Hello, he said.

I've been trying to get through all night.

Have you? I was at work.

You said you had tonight off.

I had to go in.

I don't like how many hours you're having to do.

It's fine.

Your voice sounds funny.

Funny how?

Are you drunk?

I've had a drink.

It's the middle of the week.

Yes.

Is Alice there?

She's working late. A parents' evening.

Make sure she's looking after you properly. Away up there. You've been through a lot.

I'm fine. How are you?

I'm excellent. I was phoning because I have some good news. I was speaking to this lawyer that I met –

Mum.

– and I was telling him about your situation. About how unfair the whole thing has been. And he thinks he might be able to help.

I don't want help.

I've got his telephone number to give you. He says you've to give him a call, any time during the day. Just explain it. He thinks he can help.

Mum.

I think he might be able to get you reinstated. Not in the same school, obviously, I said you wouldn't want that anyway, not after how they treated you. But get you back on the register. So you can teach again. You were so good at it. It suited you so well.

I wasn't that good.

You were the best. And I should know. I made you. Will you give him a phone?

Innes slid down the wall onto his backside and the long telephone cord draped across his shoulder.

No. Forget it. Enough.

Sorry?

I said no.

Are you okay, hun? What's happening?

But Innes had dropped the telephone receiver to the floor and rested his head backwards on the wall, passed out. His hand still gripping the receiver. Too many pills. And there was his mother's voice still, now and for the next twenty minutes. Hun? Are you there? Innes? Innes!

When he woke up it was still dark and the telephone handset was buzzing a muffled alarm. The blood was trapped in his legs and they tingled weakly. He rolled onto his hands and knees and pushed the phone out of the way and opened his mouth and felt the strain begin in his stomach.

He threw up, a hot wet stream of stomach acid. It splashed the carpet and rebounded onto the skirting boards and onto his hands and forearms and a little on the walls as well.

He stayed on the ground a little longer. Retching. Nothing more coming out. His stomach spasming and contracting. His throat squeezing tightly to eject the phantom liquid.

Finally it was over. He stood up and his head throbbed in his ears. He drank a glass of water in the kitchen. Slow and careful sips. In the kitchen there was still the empty box from the microwave hamburger and the plastic container he'd eaten it from. He binned these and washed his face and took another couple of pills from a bottle and swallowed them with a little water.

He sprayed the kitchen surfaces with bleach and wiped them down. He took the bleach and sprayed it all over the carpet where he had thrown up. It was mostly liquid. He used a fistful of kitchen paper to scoop up the solids and then scrubbed at the carpet with the rough side of a sponge. He sprayed more bleach and wiped the skirting board. The stained wallpaper. He binned the sponge and the kitchen paper and went now to the bedroom.

He turned on the light and Alice immediately rolled over and shielded her eyes from the bulb.

For God's sake, she shouted.

I didn't know you were in here.

Turn the light off. I'm trying to sleep.

He turned the light off and the room returned to blackness. Dropped his trousers to the floor and threw his shirt on top of them. He got into bed. Alice had her back to him. He tucked himself into her.

When did you get back?

Ages ago.

Why didn't you wake me up?

I tried to. What on earth were you doing blacked out like that in the hall?

I was just tired. How was your parents' night?

Just tired?

I'm not feeling very well.

Neither am I. I'm trying to sleep. I need to get to sleep.

Innes stroked her shoulder and lifted his leg on top of hers. Felt the warmth of her body. I'm sorry, he said.

Get off me.

Innes rolled onto his back and left her alone. One hand he left near her so that it touched her hair. His eyelids were heavy and the room was dark and peaceful.

Wake up, said Alice. Wake up, for Christ's sake.

What?

You're snoring.

Am I?

You've come in here, turned the lights on, woken me up, and now you're keeping me awake with your snoring.

Sorry. I can't help it.

What are you on?

What?

What have you taken? You're on something. I can't believe this. Is everyone in this damn village at it now?

No.

I know you're on something.

I had some drinks earlier.

You've thrown up all over the carpet. It'll be ruined. I had to walk around it. And they'll be taking that out of our deposit.

I've cleaned it.

You can't clean that. It's ruined.

It's cleaned.

I think you should go sleep on the couch.

No.

I have to get up for work in the morning. I need to sleep. Go and sleep on the couch. Please.

He didn't speak but got up and took a blanket from the wardrobe and went to the living room, feeling his way along the walls, his bare feet recoiling when they touched the cold and wet stain in the hall.

60

Jessie couldn't stand the thought of telling Grandpa she'd lost her job. He'd had enough disappointments recently. So she had an hour to fill between school ending and going to visit him. It was easier to lie. One Tuesday she was sitting on a low stone wall at the Shore Road looking out in the cold over the loch. A tree behind her with long bare branches. Grey clouds scudding across a grey sky.

The American she'd seen selling weed at the school came along the Shore Road and sat next to her. A nice face although his fingertips were black with dirt.

Hey, he said.

Hello.

Your father a policeman?

Yes.

Thought so. Thought I'd heard that right.

And who told you that?

Nobody told me. I'm just a good listener.

Jessie snorted and pulled her schoolbag closer between her legs and tucked it between her ankles.

What do you want to do after school?

I don't mind. Just get out of this place mainly. Go to college or university.

It's good to have ambitions.

You could get in a lot of trouble for what you're doing around here. Selling that stuff to schoolkids.

You haven't told your father, have you?

No.

Thank God. I'd be scared out of my mind.

Jessie looked at the American and he was laughing softly.

Listen, he said. You want a job? I could live without doing the school run every day.

Working for you?

Sure. You got sacked from your last job huh? I'll even take you on without seeing your resume. How about that?

Jessie licked her lips and blew into her cold clenched hands. What's the pay?

Let's say a fifty percent cut of whatever you move.

What if I get caught?

Don't get caught.

Can I think about it?

Nope.

No?

You already know you're gonna do it.

Do I really?

You just want to be wooed a little. Come on sugar. What do you say?

Jessie shrugged.

I've got all this stuff. Somebody's going to get rich off it. I'd prefer it was you.

Why me?

I like the idea of a cop's kid pushing gear for me.

You've got a sick sense of humour. Fine. Let me try it for a few days.

Johnny Coca-Cola opened his rucksack and gave Jessie a cardboard cereal box from it. She flicked open the torn lid and saw that it was full of neatly tied little bags. See if you can get this shifted in a week, he said. Then we'll know what you're made of. Okay partner?

Jessie pushed the hair from her forehead and rubbed the end of her pink nose and smiled at him. Okay, she said.

In at the hospice that night there was a Frank Sinatra documentary being shown on the BBC. Grandpa's television was turned up loud and the songs were connected by talking heads segments. There was footage of Sinatra on an old American chat show. He was wearing a tan suit with the collar unbuttoned.

Now that, said Grandpa, is what you call real style. He was sitting up straight in bed and his face was shining.

Did you ever go to see him in concert?

Aye. He played at a football stadium in Glasgow. He was older then. His voice wasn't as good. But he still had the style.

Jessie had kicked her shoes off and now she pulled her knees up to her chin and tucked her head into them.

Grandpa muted the television and whispered: What's the matter, toots?

I'm having a bad few weeks.

Hey. Look who you're talking to.

Jessie smiled. I'm sorry, I shouldn't complain.

You're right to. You can complain to me. I'm all ears.

I really don't think you want to hear about this.

I am your grandfather. Do as you're told.

I have kind of a bad secret. It's the worst thing and it's making me feel horrible.

Tell me.

I can't.

You can tell me. Who am I going to be gossiping to?

I heard something about Young Bobby going missing. And I don't think anybody else knows about it. I don't think Donald knows about it or the police. I'm scared to tell Dad.

Why?

In case he doesn't believe me.

What did you hear?

If I tell you this you can't tell him. You have to promise.

Grandpa pinched his thumb and his finger and mimicked a zip going across his lips. Jessie unfolded her legs and sat forward in the chair with her arms crossed over her chest.

So what I heard was that Young Bobby got killed. That he's dead. And his body's still in the village, buried behind the hotel somewhere.

Grandpa stared at her with his mouth open.

Do you know a guy called Innes Foley? He's new to the village. He's not from here.

Grandpa shook his head.

Well it was him. I think it was him that did it.

And you've told nobody else this?

Nobody.

Don't. Leave it with me. Okay?

Okay.

Grandpa unmuted the television and on the screen was footage of Sinatra, an old man in this clip with his black tie loosened, singing that he did it his way.

61

The priest picked a piece of lint from his new, black pullover. Straightened his collar in the mirror. Looked more closely at his face and squeezed an imperfection at the corner of his lip.

The sacristy at the hospice was small and bare. A room set aside for him to change and prepare for visiting the residents. He had hung a crucifix high on one wall and on the other was the mirror. Someone had left a mop and bucket in the corner since his last visit. He wheeled this outside and left it lying in the middle of the corridor.

Good morning, father, said Nurse Robyn. She had a gift bag and held it out to him. This is from Mrs Potter's family. For you. I'm afraid Mrs Potter passed over the weekend.

The priest took the bag and looked inside. A box of chocolates. He lifted out the box and examined the tasting card on the back. Can you put this in the staff room instead?

You don't want them?

I get chocolates every day of the week. I only keep the good ones. These – he held out the box – can be donated to your colleagues.

I'm sure the staff will take care of them, said the nurse. I'll leave you to your rounds.

Thank you. Is Mrs Potter's room still empty?

There's a new resident in there now. With throat cancer. He's strong.

I'll spend some time with him today.

The priest walked through the lobby. Rooms on all sides, with wide glass doors. Some had the curtains drawn but most were open. People sleeping in their beds, heads turned away from the door, bodies curled in on themselves. Others sat up, watching the television. There were visitors already in some of the rooms. Children playing with toys on the floor. Husbands and wives sitting pensive at the edge of the beds.

He went to the room where Mrs Potter had been before she died. The windows had been left open to get the smell of death out of the room. The equipment sterilised and the carpet cleaned and the bedsheets boiled. He could see a small white-haired man sitting up here in his bed. On the tray in front of him there was a box of tissues and a Daily Record and a can of Irn Bru.

The priest went in and closed the door behind him and stood at the end of the bed. Hello Grandpa, he said warmly. Has it come to this already?

Grandpa stared for a second at the priest through his reading glasses. What the hell do you think you're doing here?

Father Jaine laughed. It's good to see you too. It's been a long time. You stopped coming to mass.

Grandpa inhaled and dipped his head from side to side. Aye. After Mary died. It just wasn't for me. I like to go for a walk on a Sunday instead. Down by the water. A couple of times I stood outside the church. During mass. Everyone inside. But I couldn't go in.

You were always welcome.

Ah. Grandpa waved his hand downwards. Do you know?

He coughed and caught his breath. It's been eight years since Mary died?

Eight? Seems like longer somehow.

Aye. Feels like a lifetime.

The two of them shuffled. Grandpa in his bedsheets, Father Jaine in the armchair. Their breathing synchronised. The heating was on in the room and blades of sunlight shone in through the blinds so that the sweat began to dampen underneath the priest's collar.

So, whispered Grandpa. You going to get on with it?

With what?

The speech. The sales pitch. The story about how it's not too late to repent, ten Hail Marys, eternal life. Grandpa was leaning forwards from his pillow, smiling at the priest.

Sounds like you know it all better than I do.

The old man nodded. There was moisture at the corner of his eyes. When you get old, he said, you see everyone you know vanishing. Your whole world just goes away. Your family. Your friends. I look out that window and it's not my world anymore. That's all gone.

You've got your son, said the priest. And your granddaughter. She seems like a great girl.

She is. Wonderful. And that causes me great pain as well. She's going to have this whole life that I won't get to see. What jobs she gets. Where she lives. Who she gets married to. I won't even be here for her next birthday. And it's a very painful thing to know that.

She comes in to visit you here.

Aye, Grandpa shouted in his whispered voice. And that makes me feel awful too. This is no place for a girl like her. Having to come in here. She should be out there living. I don't want her to come in here because it makes me feel guilty. But

I want her to be here all the time. Because the thought of not seeing her. It breaks my heart.

You needn't feel guilty. She loves you. She wants to see you as much as she can.

Grandpa lifted a tissue from the box in front of him and wiped his face. He gripped the can of Irn Bru in his swollen hand and brought it to his mouth and sucked through the straw.

Can you eat?

Not anymore.

How about sucking on a toffee?

Oh I do think I could manage that.

Father Jaine had a foil packet of toffees in his pocket and he put one in his own mouth and gave another to Grandpa.

Grandpa sucked it and exhaled deeply and began tapping and slapping the bedsheet on either side of his legs, as though conducting a song, alternating with different fingers and rhythms.

See if I was to go to heaven now, he said, with a smile on his face. I'd be useless like this. An old man. Can't eat. Can barely walk the length of myself. What good would this old man's body be in heaven?

I'm not sure that's how it works.

See this, said Grandpa. He indicated to his own body as though it was an exhibit. See this thing, to be aware of your own death. It's no fun at all.

It can't be.

It doesn't just happen like that! Grandpa clapped his hands together. It's not sudden. There's no moment where you shift from living to dying. It just happens. It's just happening to you. It's fading away. Look at me. I'm just fading away.

Is there anything you'd like to confess?

Give me peace. What grotesque sins do you think I'm capable of now?

Something from your past, perhaps. Something you want to get off your chest.

Actually, said Grandpa. There is something. Something I heard. That I might want to run by you.

Something you've overheard?

Something I've been told.

See, it's quite a big thing. If it's true. But I'm no grass. I've never been one.

I understand.

You know that poor Fleck boy that's been missing these last few months?

Young Bobby.

Grandpa pointed at the priest and said: I hear he's buried in the garden behind the hotel.

Father Jaine rubbed his face and his skin grew pale. Who told you this?

What did I say? I'm no grass.

It can't be true.

It might not be.

Do you trust the person you heard this from?

With my life.

I can't believe it. Behind the hotel? So he's dead?

No, he's only hibernating for the winter. What do you think? Of course he's dead.

You need to tell the police about this. Your son will know what to do.

My son can bloody well do his job and work it out without any help from me.

This is horrible.

You were correct though. I feel much better having that off my chest.

Father Jaine steepled his hands together and nodded. Would you mind if I said a prayer for you?

Ach, on you go. Can't do any harm. And then bugger off out of here. You've got more folk to visit in here than just me today.

62

The card was in the pigeonhole in the staffroom that morning. Sitting there in a blush pink envelope with a Royal Mail stamp and her name and the school's address in careful handwriting. She looked at the front and the back of it.

Someone's birthday? asked one of her colleagues.

You should've told us. I'd have made a cake, said another.

No, said Alice. It's not my birthday. I don't know what this is.

Only one way to find out.

Alice felt them watch her as she slipped her finger into the envelope's seal and tore down its length. The card inside was cheap with a picture of some flowers and a generic message: Thinking of You. She opened the card and read the message inside:

To my daughter, I am sure this is where you are and I pray this card finds you there. Please get in touch if you have the time. It would mean an awful lot to me. I love you and miss you every day. From Dad.

Alice put the card back in the envelope then ripped it down the middle and dropped it into the paper bin.

What was it? her colleague asked.

Oh, she laughed. Just another note from my secret admirer!

What do you mean?

Nothing. It was literally nothing. She let the rest of her mail sit in the pigeonhole and left the staffroom, her fingernails furiously scratching at her scalp.

Alice held the book above her head with the spine bent back on itself. She had her senior class in for a double afternoon lesson. What is Macbeth saying here? she asked. His wife has just died and what is he saying? Who can tell us?

Jessie made eye contact with the teacher and held it.

Jessie? What is he saying?

Is he saying that it doesn't matter? I think he's saying that he doesn't care that she's dead.

I don't think it's quite that, said Alice. No. It's not that he doesn't care. Life's but a walking shadow, he says. We are all just shadows. Caught by the sun and then gone again. Life, he says, is a tale told by an idiot. *You* are that idiot. We are all that idiot. All these fine opinions that you currently have, all your passions and disagreements and love affairs. These are the sound and the fury that Shakespeare mentions, but nobody cares. In a hundred years' time, nobody will care about you or what you thought or why you did what you did. Why would they?

It was quiet in the classroom. The ticking clock. A boy at the back sniffling. The smell of ink.

Hands up if anyone has any pets. Cats, dogs, that kind of thing.

Most of the students raised their hands. Jessie was one of them.

They'll all be dead before long, said Alice smiling. All dead. Just dust. Hands up if anyone has any brothers or sisters. Little cousins.

Some of the students raised their hands. Jessie did not.

Alice looked around and smiled again. All dead. Who has grandparents still alive?

Jessie put her hand up and met Alice's gaze and held it.

All of your grandparents will die, sooner than you realise. Then I will die. Then you will all die. And nobody will care. It won't matter if you were a good person or a bad person. It won't matter if you were pretty or sporty or rich. In a hundred years' time nobody will even care if you got an A in your exams. And that is what Shakespeare is saying here. We are all getting our hour on the stage right now. This is it. This is all we get. And once this hour is up, we will be heard no more. We are all, then, just rehydrated dust.

But it does matter, said Jessie. It matters if we are good people.

How? Why?

Because. We are humans.

That's a very adolescent perspective to take on the matter. Don't you think?

What do you expect? I am an adolescent.

The teacher stared at the girl for a second and then smiled and said: Okay class, I have some questions for you to do. They are written up here on the board. Make a start on them just now and then finish them at home for the next time I see you.

Alice walked among the desks as the students began to copy down the heading from the board. She stopped at Jessie's desk and spoke quietly. Can you wait behind for a minute after class? I want to speak with you.

Jessie looked up.

You're not in trouble, don't worry.

The bell rang and Jessie packed her bag slowly to let everyone get ahead of her. She stood re-reading a poster on the wall until everyone else had left and it was just her with Alice.

The teacher folded her arms and leaned back against her desk and Jessie folded her arms and her heavy schoolbag bit into her shoulder.

I shouldn't have said that thing today, said Alice. I heard your grandfather isn't keeping well. I didn't mean to bring it up.

He's in the hospice.

How is he?

He's dying. He can't eat. Can barely talk.

Are you doing okay?

No. Jessie unfolded her arms and dropped her heavy schoolbag to the floor and linked her fingers together and cracked her knuckles one at a time.

I didn't think so. You've not been yourself in class recently. The last essay you wrote for me. It was good. But it wasn't the level we expect from you.

I rushed it.

You need to find the time.

I'm in school all day. I did have a job but I got sacked. Which means I'm skint. Then I'm either visiting Grandpa or sorting out the housework. Jessie put her hands behind her head. So, I don't see where I can find any more time.

You lost your job at the hotel?

Yes.

Maybe that's a good thing.

I don't see how.

Your exams this year are so important.

Are they? Jessie raised her eyebrows and nodded her head.

I'll tell you what I'll do, said Alice. I'll be in my room every lunchtime from now on. If you need somewhere to come and catch up with work, or catch up with revision, or sleep, or you just want somewhere to be quiet and relax, you can come here. And if you need any extra time for deadlines, you just let me know. You can have extensions. But you have to let me know.

Thank you. Jessie looked at her scuffed shoes. Can I go now? I'll be late.

Yes. On you go. No, in fact. Wait. There's one other thing. Yes?

I'm sorry for bringing it up.

What is it?

What age are you, Jessie? Sixteen? This isn't easy to bring up. But you need to start taking better care of your appearance.

What do you mean?

You're a good-looking girl but you're coming into school a mess. Your shirt's not been ironed. It has stains all down it. When you get home look at the back of your collar. It's turned brown with sweat. Alice looked down. You've got holes in your shoes. Holes. Like a tramp. What happens when it rains?

Jessie looked at the rip along the instep of her left foot.

What happens?

My foot gets wet.

Your foot gets wet. And your hair. It's full of grease, Jessie. Grease. How often do you wash it?

Depends.

I can smell you. Do you know that? When I walk past your desk I can actually smell your body. And if I can smell it, so can everyone else. What do you think the other kids are saying about you? What do you think the boys think of you?

Jessie squeezed her nose and pulled on her earlobe and walked towards the door.

Time to grow up, said Alice. Jessie was out of the room.

You're welcome! The teacher's voice echoed down the corridor, following Jessie as she rushed with the heavy schoolbag to her next lesson.

63

When Jessie visited, Grandpa was sitting up in the armchair, dressed in trousers and a collared t-shirt. The day's Daily Record was folded across his knees. When he saw her he smiled and clenched his fist and gave the air a little punch.

Hello Grandpa, said Jessie, look at you! She bent over towards him and kissed his old cheek and he cupped his hand behind her head and pulled her to him for a moment.

How are you? he whispered.

I'm a bit flat, she said. How are you today?

He held out his hand and wavered it in front of her face like a see-saw.

You're feeling okay? she asked again.

No bad, he managed. How was school?

Jessie blew out her cheeks and took off the blazer. It was light grey with yellow and blue trim. Horrible. Too much homework, she said. And my English teacher is turning out to be a right cow. She threw the blazer across the empty bed.

Grandpa scrunched up his face.

Can I get you anything?

How about an Irn Bru?

The girl got up and went to the mini fridge and took out an

Irn Bru. The fridge was full of cans. She opened it and popped in a straw and sat it on the table.

The old man slowly clutched it in his hand, raised the straw to his lips, and sucked. Jessie wiped a little spill that dripped onto his t-shirt. It looked too big for him. He was getting skinny now.

Grandpa put the can back down and swirled the juice around in his mouth, coating his tongue and his teeth with it, then picked up a cardboard bowl and spat the Irn Bru out.

Are you struggling to swallow today, Grandpa?

Aye, he whispered. Can't get it down.

You just like the taste of it then?

I do, he whispered. Oh, it's marvellous.

That's good.

You're not working tonight?

No. I don't work at the hotel anymore. They didn't need me anymore.

Grandpa tilted his head and patted the bed. Ach, he said.

So that's me back to being unemployed.

Tell you what, said Grandpa. How about I give you a lend of some money?

That's kind of you. But it's okay, honestly. I've been offered a new job already. A job that pays much better.

Doing what?

Sales. Door to door sales. Tablet, macaroons, that kind of thing. I'll bring you a free sample.

You make sure you do that, said Grandpa. That sounds like just the ticket.

64

The red Megane came up the driveway, jerking from side to side in the potholes. The car was streaked with mud along both its flanks. It crawled to a stop outside the house and Innes's mother got out, stretching her legs and bending her arms above her head. Dyed blonde hair. Good boots. Alice watched all of this from the kitchen window and sipped a cup of hot tea.

Innes ran out of the house to greet his mother, wearing his slippers with his jeans, and Alice watched as they grabbed each other and hugged and Innes's face was squashed in her hands. They stood there speaking quietly for a moment. Then Innes got a small suitcase from the boot of her car and they came towards the house. Alice poured her tea down the sink and began washing the dirty mug.

There she is!

Hello, Vonnie.

Come here sweetie, come here. Vonnie took Alice in her arms and squeezed. Alice kept her wet hands from touching the woman.

How are you?

I'm wonderful. I'm so happy for you both. Congratulations, it's the best news.

Thank you. We're very happy.

Innes came in carrying his mother's suitcase.

You can put that in our room, said Alice. I've made up the bed.

No, said Vonnie. I'll take the couch, I couldn't possibly take your room.

Yes, you will. I've put on fresh sheets and there's a towel in the bathroom for you. We'll take the couch. It folds down, it'll be fine.

Are you sure, sweetie?

I'm sure.

Vonnie squeezed Alice's hand in hers. Aren't you lovely? Isn't she lovely? I think I'll take a quick shower just now. Freshen up after the drive. And then – she pulled a bottle out from her handbag – some champagne! Oh we have a lot to talk about don't we. So many plans to make.

I'll put this in the fridge, said Alice.

Come on, said Innes. I'll put this in the room for you.

Alice poured three glasses of champagne while Vonnie showered. She gave Innes a packet of tealight candles. Go around and put these in the candle holders and light them, she said.

Innes checked his pockets then opened the cutlery drawer and closed it. Have you got a lighter?

No. Alice halved a couple of strawberries for the champagne.

Do you know where one is? asked Innes.

Jesus Christ, said Alice. Can you not figure out one little thing for yourself? She opened the cutlery drawer and looked through it then slammed it shut. She went into her handbag on the dining table and rummaged in there and pulled out a lighter. Here, she said.

Innes lit the candles and Alice topped up the champagne glasses. Then stood, waiting.

The three of them sat in the living room with their champagne.

I love your cottage, said Vonnie. Very cute. Very cosy.

We didn't have much choice for accommodation, said Innes. The village doesn't have many places to rent.

Now about this wedding. Do you think you'll have it way up here or back home?

I don't think we've thought that far ahead, said Innes.

I'm not having it here, said Alice.

Oh, laughed Vonnie. I like that. You tell him who's boss. I know it's a long way in the future, but I want to make a contribution. I want to pay for half of the wedding.

Mum –

I've got the money set aside and I want to do it and you can't say anything that'll change my mind.

That's really generous, said Alice. But we really can't accept.

Don't say no straight away, said Innes. Let's think about it.

What is there to think about? I don't want someone else to pay for it. I don't want parents involved in it. It's our wedding and I want us to do it on our own.

When are we going to be able to afford that?

Maybe if you find a proper job instead of working in a pub we'd have a bit more to put into savings.

Innes opened his mouth then closed it and drank from his glass.

Vonnie clasped her hands together and said: Please don't fight over this. I'm sorry to have mentioned it. It's too soon to talk about it.

It's very generous of you to offer, said Alice.

Yes, said Innes. Thank you. We'll think about it. Won't we? We will think about it.

65

Donald came into the hotel bar one early afternoon and stood waiting at the counter. The place was quiet with none of the day drinkers in yet and he made a neat pile out of the beermats, making sure their edges were straight and that they all faced up the right way.

Hello boss, said Innes. He had been putting some clean glasses back on the gantry.

You got ten minutes?

Sure.

Over here. Donald and Innes took a seat at a table in the corner from where they could see the door. We're going to host a fundraiser here next month.

Sounds good. Not in the village hall?

No. If you use the village hall the funds have to *go* to the village hall.

Where are these funds going then?

Back to me. Into the hotel. Into the Distillery. We need a bit of a boost. We're going to call it the Bobby Fleck Foundation or something like that.

What do you need me to do?

Organise a buffet. Get lots of the locals involved. Make sure the stockroom's full and we've got plenty of barrels in. I'll sort out a band and posters and get some tickets printed.

You're charging an entry fee?

How else are we going to make money from it? Get this place spruced up a bit. Get that stag's head replaced. Find a new one. I know a guy, I'll give you his number. How's the beer garden looking?

We won't be using that in February will we?

Aye. I'm going to hire big heaters for it. I want the place packed. Inside and out. The garden's a mess, is it?

I've not had a good look at it.

Have a look. I want the tables cleaned. The path weeded. I'm going to send Margo down next week to have a look at the flower baskets. You'll have it sorted for then?

Innes looked pale and beneath the table his legs twitched. He said: I really don't think the beer garden's going to be any good. It'll be too cold. It'll rain!

It's happening, said Donald. This place is going to be jumping. My boy's name's going on the ticket so it had better be full. Get it looking like the Garden of bloody Eden out there.

I'll do my best.

Now about that woman who dipped the till a wee while ago.

I got pretty much all of that money back.

That was bad for business.

I sacked her daughter.

That was a mistake. Made us look bitter. You shouldn't have done that either.

Moodie told me to!

You should've used your own initiative. You should've reasoned with him.

I thought it was what you wanted.

Here's what I want. I've found a way for you to make it up to me. You listening?

Yes.

After this fundraising party. This Bobby Fleck Foundation thing. When everyone's spent all their money on the tickets and on the booze and they're all away home. When it's just you wiping down the bar and bleaching the toilets. I want you to burn it.

Sorry?

Make sure it's empty and then burn the place to the ground. Make it look like an accident.

I can't believe I'm hearing this.

You heard nothing. Not from me.

I don't think I could.

Donald rubbed his chin and looked around again.

You can and you will. I'll make it worth your while.

In what way?

I'll make it worth your while. Okay? Okay.

When Donald was young he got on well with his mother, but was terrified of his father. A sober and religious man, Donald shared his name. People in the village had taken to calling them Big Donald and Wee Donald to distinguish them. Big Donald sat in the first pew every Sunday and although he ran the Distillery at a good profit he did not touch the stuff himself.

Wee Donald came home drunk after a ceilidh one night in the village. He was sixteen so it should not have seemed unlikely. He had even kissed a girl that night. She had been fixing her make-up at the side of the dance floor and she turned to him and showed him her face and asked if it looked okay.

Yes but there's something missing, he'd said.

What?

And then he had kissed her very gently. He had held her

hand in his. They had kissed for a long time and he'd hung his leg over hers on the bench and the music had swirled around them and their tongues tasted of whisky and when it was over her lipstick was barely visible at all.

So he had come home like that, drunk and pleased with himself and when he came home to the manse the front door banged against the wall and woke his father up. Big Donald came down the stairs wearing his dressing gown and carrying a leather belt.

What time do you call this?

Wee Donald looked at his wrist but couldn't make out the hands on his watch.

You're drunk.

I'm not too bad.

Look at you. Wee Donald was wearing the new kilt his mother had picked out for his sixteenth birthday. You think you're the big man now. Big Donald stepped towards his son, the belt wrapped around white knuckles.

You don't frighten me, the boy said.

Big Donald grabbed him by the waistcoat and opened the door and hurled him out into the garden. Do not speak to your father like that.

Maybe you should do a better job of being a father.

Big Donald unfurled the belt then and lashed at his son's bare cold legs. Wee Donald leapt back but lost his footing and in a moment he was curled up on the lawn, hugging his body tightly while his father whipped at him with the leather while his face smeared into the dry dirty grass. When the belt aimed at his shins, Wee Donald covered the wounds with his hands. When he thrashed at his hands, Wee Donald pulled them up and into his armpits.

When the beating stopped Big Donald got a bucket from the side of the house. He sat this upright in front of his son.

Take off that kilt. You don't deserve to wear it.

Mum gave it to me.

Big Donald pulled his hand back with the belt again.

Don't! Don't, cried Wee Donald. His legs and forearms were laced with red welts that raised drops of blood along their edges.

Take off the kilt.

Wee Donald knelt up and unfastened his sporran and the belt around his kilt. He unwrapped it from his thighs.

Big Donald snatched the kilt from his son and held it in his fist. Men wear kilts, he growled. Not boys.

He dropped the kilt and its sporran into the bucket and in his hand he had a gas lighter. He opened the lid and flicked the wheel and the flame humped up, blue and sideways in the wind.

No, shouted Wee Donald, getting to his feet, keeping his hands over his crotch. No, no, don't.

But the lighter was already falling through the night air, his father's fingers flicking it towards the bucket. The kilt did not catch fire straight away, but it smouldered, dark smoke forming like a cloud.

Wee Donald took a step towards the bucket and his father flicked the belt at his bare legs.

Don't make me whip your arse as well, he said.

The pair of them stood staring into the bucket and then the flames were there, starting to light up in the cylinder, a strange glow from the tartan, and the smoke was in their lungs and in their eyes but they watched it burn. Big Donald in his dressing gown, panting, eyes white. Wee Donald in shirt and waistcoat and socks, hands still cupped between his legs to stop his father from seeing. When the kilt began to blaze and the flames leapt up higher and higher, Old Donald sagged his shoulders and sighed.

Come in, then. I'll make us a cup of tea.

He turned back into the manse and the boy followed him slowly. Eyes down. Squeezing the worst of the whip's lashes with the palms of his hands. He could still taste the whisky and the lipstick from that girl's mouth.

66

Jessie sat on Grandpa's bed, her warm fingers intertwined with his cold dry ones. There was a game show playing on the television and the volume was turned up loud and Jessie was keeping scores between them.

Le Louvre, she said.

And the correct answer, said the television presenter, is *Le Louvre*.

Oh, said Grandpa.

I'm winning by three now.

Three?

You're in trouble, old man. This one's your question.

Grandpa listened to the television with his head cocked to the side. Raith Rovers, he said.

And the correct answer, said the television presenter, is Raith Rovers.

Well done, Jessie said.

It was a guess! He laughed and sat back on the thick pillows behind his neck.

The door opened and Galloway was there in his jeans and trainers and a t-shirt. Jessie muted the television and swallowed the last of her cup of tea.

I thought you were coming at three, she said.

I know, I know. Some weather out there. He cupped his hands together and blew into them.

Cold? asked Grandpa.

Freezing. He put his arms around the old man's shoulders and squeezed him and held his face very close. How are you feeling? Are you feeling okay?

Same as always, said Grandpa.

I've been here since three, said Jessie. Like we agreed.

Sorry, said Galloway. Traffic was murder.

You could try leaving earlier.

I said I was sorry.

I'm going to make more tea, said Jessie. Want a cup, Grandpa?

How about a coffee?

With pleasure. What about you?

Coffee would be good, said Galloway.

Jessie picked up some dirty mugs from the side table and closed the door behind her.

What's wrong with her?

Grandpa put his fingers to his throat and let out a long exhalation before speaking. She has got a lot on her shoulders.

I know she does.

Me in here. The state of her mother. Exams at school.

It's a lot.

Aye it is a lot.

I'll do better.

Not working today?

Day off.

Any sign of that missing boy?

None. If somebody wants to go missing it's very hard for us to do anything about it. They've just said they're setting up a foundation for him. Having a big shindig at the hotel to raise funds.

Grandpa picked up a paper napkin from the tray in front of him and wiped his eyes.

Galloway sat forward and spoke in a low voice. Do you want me to go to the post office and collect your pension again this week?

Might as well. It's not as though I'm going to be queuing up for it any time soon.

Dad, said Galloway. How much have you got in your bank account?

Why do you ask?

He rubbed his nose and looked over his shoulder towards the door but Jessie was not back with the coffees yet.

I've got a few payments coming off that I can't cover. Just one-off things. Need to put the car in the garage. My electricity bill's gone up. That kind of thing.

How much do you need?

Quite a bit.

There is money in my account, nodded Grandpa. He tapped his fingers on the bedsheet in a rhythm.

I just thought, since it's coming to me sooner or later anyway, I could take some of it now. For these bills. Really help me out.

I've been thinking, said Grandpa. About my will.

Yes?

I'm going to have a look at it. While I've still got the time.

You want to make some changes?

I want to leave half of it to you, said Grandpa.

Half of it?

The other half, said Grandpa, I want Jessie to have that. He put his hand on Galloway's and squeezed. You've got a good salary. You're a grown man. You've no need of it.

I do need it.

She needs it more. And she's here every other day to see me in this place. It's the right thing to do.

Galloway stood up and looked out the window at the little garden and ran his hand through his short hair.

He turned. This is my inheritance you're talking about.

And it's hers.

It's not right.

It's fair. You're still going to get half.

I should be getting it all.

Jessie came back from the kitchen with the hot drinks on a tray. Galloway stayed standing and Jessie gave him his coffee and sat next to Grandpa and put his mug on the bed tray.

What are we talking about? she said.

Your dad was telling me about his car.

What's wrong with it now?

Nothing, said Galloway. He blew on his coffee then took a sip and put it down. It needs to go into the garage. It's nothing.

Fascinating, said Jessie.

Actually, said Galloway, I have to go.

You just got here.

And now I've got to go.

We've been waiting for you all afternoon, said Jessie.

Don't stay on my account, said Grandpa.

I'm sorry. I just have to go. Galloway hugged Jessie loosely with his cheek close to hers and then reached down and took his father's hand and shook it formally.

I'll see you soon.

You'll pick up that pension for me?

Yes.

Good. Bring it in with you next time.

Galloway left and closed the door softly behind him.

Can you believe him? said Jessie. Can you believe him

leaving so quickly? Like he's got somewhere more important to be than here with his own father in the hospice and God knows how many more times—

Grandpa held his hand out.

Sorry, she said.

It's okay.

He frustrates me.

I know.

I can't help it.

Put the telly back on, said Grandpa.

She pushed the power button on the remote control and the television screen came on bright.

What's the score?

Three one to me.

Three one?

It's your question.

They sat side by side on the bed and sipped their hot drinks and watched the game show, laughing whether they got the questions right or wrong.

67

It was getting dark when Valentine left Alice's cottage but it was not late and he was not yet tired despite the visit. He had not showered afterwards and could still taste her and smell her on him. He walked down the lane with a field of sheep on his left and he sang to them in low, undulating tones so that they looked up and their ears pricked and some of them came towards the fence to be closer to him.

He thought about how Alice had taken her engagement ring off when they started to kiss. It had not been his idea to come over but she'd invited him over. Something about a story she'd heard and wanted to run by him. That had quickly fallen and then they were in bed again together.

He passed the field and walked a little around the loch's edge. What was left of the sun filtered dimly through some cloud and sparkled on the water. Valentine stopped and squatted and dipped his hands in the cold lapping water and rubbed them together. He cupped his hands and filled the hollow and splashed his face with it. He cupped his hands and filled the hollow and slurped it into his mouth and then spat it out.

Then Valentine dried his hands in his trouser pockets and walked quickly in a straight line to the Cullrothes Hotel.

It was warm inside the bar. Old Jim perched with his crossword. A group of women laughing. Pockets of men with their heads down looking into their glasses.

Innes was drying a glass behind the bar. I remember you, said Valentine.

From where?

We met at the ceilidh. You were with Alice.

Of course. You're the journalist.

I didn't see much of you that night. Did you leave early?

Alice had a headache.

Right. I'll have a Guinness.

Innes lifted a glass under the tap and pushed it up tight and at an angle. He pulled the handle down and the blackness trickled down the edge and pooled in a light brown froth.

I heard the pair of you are getting married. Congratulations. When's the wedding?

We're only just engaged. Not got as far as planning anything yet.

Will it be soon?

I don't think we're in any rush.

The American in his red jacket walked slowly past the bar and into the bathroom. Valentine turned and looked around the room. Busy tonight, he said.

It's not bad. Innes put the pint glass down on the bar. About two thirds full.

Actually, Valentine said, I need the bathroom. I'll be back.

In the gents there were two cubicles and a urinal trough running along one wall. One cubicle door was open and the other was closed. Valentine pushed it and it swung open.

Let me guess, said Valentine. You're lost again. Need directions.

Correct, said Johnny Coca-Cola.

Valentine opened his wallet but the American reached out

and closed it. Don't worry about that. He gave the journalist a bag of powder.

You don't want paid?

Not in cash.

What else, then?

Johnny Coca-Cola took off his baseball cap. He was balding and the skin on his forehead and around his crown was much paler than his face and neck. He took a step closer to Valentine. So that the two men's noses almost touched.

What else? he said. Just a little friendliness, that's all. Okay buddy? I need to know you're on my side.

Whose other side is there?

That's what I'm hoping you can tell me.

Without waiting for Valentine to answer, Johnny Coca-Cola slipped from the cubicle and was gone. The journalist laughed and weighed the bag in his hand and cut himself a quick line on top of the cistern.

The Guinness was waiting for him on the bar. Black, shining, with its cloudy head. Valentine opened his wallet.

No need, said Innes. That American guy paid for it.

He paid for this?

It's paid for.

Where is he?

He's gone.

Right. Valentine shook his head and handed over a ten-pound note. Well take this anyway, get yourself one. An engagement present! I'm dead happy for you guys. She's some girl. And you my friend are a very lucky man.

Innes took the money and pocketed it. Cheers very much. I'll have one at the end of my shift.

Valentine lifted the Guinness up and mouthed: Slainte. When he drank he left a dirty streak of foam sticking to his upper lip.

68

Father Jaine filled the kettle up with water and clicked it on. Looked out the kitchen window. Another grey day. The water in the loch like black leather with no sunlight bouncing from it. The mountains in the distance draped in low, ashy fog.

The doorbell rang and he quickly wiped his hands and went into the hall and answered it. A good-looking man with good teeth and a fresh cagoule.

Yes? said the priest.

Good afternoon, Father, said the man. An American accent.

Good afternoon.

I hope you don't mind my dropping by.

What can I do for you?

I'd like to talk with you.

Right.

I brought some cake, said the man, smiling. He held out a cardboard box.

Well, smiled Father Jaine. Say no more. Come in, come in.

The man stepped into the hallway and Father Jaine returned to the kitchen.

This way. Shoes off if you don't mind. It's a new carpet.

The man looked down at the floor and whistled

appreciatively. He kicked off his shoes and looked quickly around the walls and followed.

Tea? asked Father Jaine.

Do you have coffee?

Sure, coffee, I should've known. You're American?

Yes.

Where from?

Oh, the man smiled. All over.

It's a marvellous place. Our little corner of the world must seem very unimpressive to you.

No. It's beautiful.

Thank you, smiled the priest. It is beautiful. We like to think so.

Have you got a knife? To cut the cake.

In the top drawer.

The man opened the drawer and got a chef's knife and opened the box and cut two thick slices from the slab of sponge.

Carrot cake? My favourite.

Mine too. The man ran his thumb along the blade, collecting the icing, and sucked it off.

Father Jaine plated the slices and put everything on a tray. Let's sit in the living room.

After you.

They sat side by side on the old couch and sipped their drinks and broke off chunks of cake to eat with their fingers.

So, said Father Jaine. What brings you to my door today?

I wanted to run something past you.

Does it concern the church?

I came here to solicit your support on quite a sensitive matter.

That's going to depend on what the matter is.

Great cake, said the man, finishing off his slice.

It is.

Want another piece?

No thank you.

How long have you worked here in the village?

I came to Cullrothes in 1990, said the priest.

About fifteen years, then.

About that.

You're happy here?

Absolutely. It's a wonderful place. Great people.

That's not universally true though, is it Father?

What do you mean?

I mean that Cullrothes seems to me to be under the control of a tyrant. A bully. A liar. A criminal. A murderer. Call it what you want. I'm talking about Donald Fleck.

Father Jaine snorted. Come on now. That sounds a little bit far fetched.

I don't think it is, smiled the man. I'm going to get a little more cake. Want some?

No, not for me.

The man took both plates away. Father Jaine rubbed his stomach and burped quietly into his hand. The man came back with both plates again and there was another big piece of cake on each.

Oh I'm fine for cake, thank you though, said Father Jaine.

The man had brought the knife from the kitchen and he sat this on the coffee table in front of him with the handle within easy reach.

It's such a good cake. So moist. Have another piece. I insist.

Father Jaine said nothing, but he picked up the plate and bit off another mouthful of sponge. The man nodded and stuffed a fistful of cake into his own mouth.

So, he spat. As I was saying. This village is being run by rats. If I know it, you must know it. He took another oversized bite and the crumbs dropped down his collar and the buttercream shone greasy in his stubble.

Let me be clear, he said, wiping his lips. The Fleck family have got this place by the throat. They run everything. The hotel. The school. The shop. The newspaper. And I think they've got their grip round the church's throat as well.

That's quite an accusation to make.

You must know, said the man. You must. It's an international operation. This is the nerve centre. Every evil in the Highlands comes through here. Weed. Cocaine. Heroin. Every pill and powder you could think of. And now they're getting desperate. What's going to be next? Guns. Knives. Girls. Eat your cake.

Father Jaine ate the last of his slice, staring at the wall opposite. The man put his hand on the priest's knee.

I know you're scared. I won't ask but I must presume the Flecks look after you. A little extra money for maintenance. A little Christmas bonus. An envelope at every service.

They are part of my parish. I've always found them to be very holy people.

They're animals. Animals. But I said I needed your support. All I need is this. No opposition. Okay? Places like this are nervous of change. That's fine. But change is coming. I've got a good friend back home. He's asked me to come over here and run a little interference. Lobbying is what they call it in my country. My friend wants to come over here and buy out the Flecks. Return this place to family values and faith. And all we need from you, my friend, is neutrality. Oppose nothing. Your services on a Sunday, keep them just as they are. No propaganda. Can you do that?

I won't promise anything to you.

Think about it. Because change is coming, and I can make you a promise. Make me happy, and you'll be rewarded with more than just carrot cake. When the time comes there'll be carrot cake every day. Carrot cake coming out of your ears.

The priest said nothing.

Thank you for the coffee, Father, said the man. And thank you for your time. God bless you.

The man stood up and Father Jaine walked him to the doorway. The man bent and worked his feet back into his shoes.

I will not be bullied or bribed, said Father Jaine.

Who said anything about a bribe?

I just want to make myself clear.

There's a hell of a lot in this world worse than bribery, you know. Johnny Coca-Cola cocked his hands like pistols at the priest and took a pretend shot. Pow!

They stared at each other. Then the man smiled and turned down the path and the priest closed the door quickly and locked it from the inside.

69

Jessie joined the line of students in the corridor outside Miss Green's class. The teacher was standing in the doorway with her hands clasped in front of her. Her hair was tied up.

Line up please, she shouted, as more students arrived from the double doors at the end of the corridor.

We have a new seating plan today, she said. Some of the students groaned at this. Jessie turned and looked at them. When you go into the room, do not just sit down at your usual desk. I have placed a card with your name on it on the desk at which I would like you to sit. Everyone understand? Okay. On you go.

They shuffled into the classroom and walked around the desks looking for their name cards. Miss Green had shifted the desks and changed them from being laid out in groups of four to being in pairs, all facing the front. Jessie's name card was near the back of the class. She dumped her bag on the desk. Sitting next to her would be the boy called Harry. They had known one another for years but never been good friends.

Jessie got her folder out of her bag and took a long drink of water from her bottle. She sat and opened her notepad at a fresh page. Harry came into the class with a couple of boys at the back of the line. He had quiffed blonde hair and carried his school bag loose over one shoulder.

I think you're here, she said, as he looked at other desks.

Next to you?

She held up the card with his name on it and showed it to him. Looks like it. Sorry.

Suits me fine, he said, and flopped into the chair. I need someone brainy to copy anyway.

Miss Green stood at the front of the class and clapped her hands three times. The students still chatting and slowly unpacking their stuff. She clapped her hands three more times and shouted. Get yourselves settled! Come on, get your stuff out, we haven't got all day.

Jessie folded her arms and leaned back and waited for the teacher to begin the lesson.

Now, shouted Miss Green. You are sitting in very particular seats. And for a good reason. I have had a look at everyone's latest essays. It is clear to me that some of you are really finding your feet. Really getting a hang of the standards required. But for others, there are still too many mistakes being made. Not enough detail in your analysis. So you are sitting in pairs now so that you can help one another. If you are struggling, ask your shoulder partner for help. If you are confident that you know what to do, try to share your understanding with others.

Harry had been rustling in his schoolbag this whole time and he finally now pulled out a ragged sheet of lined paper and flattened this on the desk in front of him. He patted his pockets and peered into his bag again and then sighed.

He turned to Jessie and said: Got a pen I could borrow?

She gave him a black biro from her pencil case.

Miss Green had fallen into conversation with two students at the front of the class and it was not clear yet what the others should be doing. Jessie looked over her notes from the last lesson and checked her homework diary to see what deadlines were coming up.

Nice, said Harry, nodding at the dividers and the coloured notes in her folder. You like to be organised, I take it?

You could say that.

I'm rubbish at things like that. Being organised.

You seem to have a pretty good system. She nodded at the ratty sheet of paper on his desk.

Aye, he laughed. Preparation is key, as they say.

Jessie crossed her legs under the desk and took the lid from a highlighter and started using it to pick out lines from her previous day's notes. Harry lifted his arms above his head and there was a cracking noise from his spine.

What you doing? he asked.

Just going over this poem from yesterday.

Did she say we had to do that?

She hasn't told us what to do yet. I'm just revising.

He reached over and turned her notebook towards him so he could read it. Do you do this in every class?

Most days.

Harry whistled. That's crazy.

He sat back in the seat and began tapping his pen against the desk and spread his legs until his thigh pressed up against Jessie's.

Sorry, he said, and pulled his leg away.

It's fine, she said.

Don't want to annoy you.

It's not annoying me.

Aye?

Might as well be comfortable.

Harry spread his legs again until his right leg rested against Jessie's crossed thighs. He looked up to the corners of the room and at the posters Miss Green had put on the wall.

Jessie kept on highlighting her notes. Her cheeks felt pink and she was swaying her toes from side to side underneath the desk.

After school Jessie was walking with her head bowed into a smart hail-strewn breeze. Coming at her almost horizontally. Loud wind and the sound of the ice bouncing off the concrete.

Since she got sacked from the hotel she hadn't been able to buy any lunch from the school canteen and her stomach felt hollow. She still carried about some of the bags of weed that Johnny Coca-Cola had given her but hadn't sold any yet. She couldn't bear the thought of it or the consequences of getting caught. That would be it for her. Expelled from school, no exams, no qualifications, no university. Here she was, so close to escaping Cullrothes and these temptations were trying to pull her back in. As soon as she saw the American again she was going to give him his stuff back. But she had not seen him for some time now.

An arm touched her shoulder and she turned around and it was Harry from English class. His blonde hair was wet and sticking down on his forehead.

I was shouting your name, he said.

I couldn't hear you.

Can I talk to you?

What is it? I need to get to home.

Just for a minute.

He walked her by the elbow a dozen yards into the bus stop. The hail made a racket on the plastic covering but it was warm and dry compared to being out on the road.

Are you alright? asked Harry.

I'm fine. Why?

I just wanted to talk to you.

Well here I am.

He smiled and wiped the water from his forehead.

Do you need me to help with your homework or something?

What? Jesus, no. Nothing like that.

I didn't mean—

Do you know anywhere I could get some weed?

Of course I don't, said Jessie. She tightened her grip on her schoolbag.

I didn't think so. I just heard from a friend of a friend that you were the person to talk to.

You can tell your friend of a friend to shut their mouth and not start rumours about me.

Don't be angry.

How could I not be angry?

I actually wanted to ask you something else. Something different.

What?

Are you seeing anyone just now?

Me?

Aye.

Seeing anyone?

That's what I said.

No. I'm not seeing anybody right now.

Would you like to?

I don't know. She looked outside the bus stop. An old woman was coming up the road towards them, her head wrapped in plastic. I don't really know, Harry. Are you seeing anyone just now?

I would like to see more of you. Have a think about it. I'm pretty sure we would have a good time.

Alright. I have to get to home.

Aye, aye, no problem. I'll see you later.

They stood there looking at each other's faces pink from the cold and then Jessie leaned forwards and they kissed and she felt his cold nose press against hers, his cold lips and cheeks, the hot breath behind it all, and then it was over. The old woman ducked into the shelter of the bus stop and shook her coat and stamped her feet.

Oh, she said without looking up. Hell of a day out there. Hell of a day.

70

As it happened the fundraiser for the Bobby Fleck Foundation got a wet night. Rain coming in sideways and slapping the guests as they hurried in the doors. The hanging baskets in the beer garden burling around and all the men's kilt socks getting soaked before they were even inside.

The hotel bar was full and they'd cleared out the old function suite as well so there was space for more tables and chairs and a dance floor. It got warm fast with the sweat and condensation steaming off all the hot bodies.

Donald's bald head gleaming under the disco lights as he shook hands and kissed cheeks and put the envelopes with the people's money in his sporran. Moodie with his cuffs rolled up and his big forearms twitching away under the tattoos. Margo with her hair done nicely, and looking more like herself, everyone said. Looking more like herself now.

Alice wore a ballgown the colour of heather, with her hair tied up and quick to show everyone the engagement ring on her finger. Sharing a drink of champagne with Valentine, a touch of sweat running down by his ear and his jacket off over the back of a chair already. Whispering in Alice's ear and making notes in a pad for an article about the event.

Galloway with an evening off work, wearing a suit instead of a kilt, drinking a glass of lemonade and standing against the wall near the exit on his own. Nodding at people as they passed. Finding himself in conversation with the headteacher, Mrs Hughes, about the state of the roads and the speed drivers go at these days and the things that go through these young boys' minds.

Above the stage, a banner specially made for the night that said: Support the Bobby Fleck Foundation and next to these letters a big photograph of Bobby's face smiling and happy.

Innes kept busy. He had a couple of staff to serve at the bar and a couple of local girls to clean tables and plenty of volunteers from the village to do the food. Donald had found from somewhere a large gazebo for the beer garden so people could still go outside but it was gasping in the wind and nobody had been tempted beneath it.

The dancing came quick and fast. The band going just a little quicker than the people could organise their feet. Sheila the shopkeeper was thrown and skidded on her bare knees and got up again, swinging her body around a man's arm. Brian and Craig kept themselves neat and tucked their elbows in, clapping politely in time with the music as they watched the others. Margo found herself pulled up into the dancing, joining a group of three, holding hands with two men she didn't know and holding their hands as tight as she dared.

Halfway through the night the band took a break and huge queues gathered around the bar and Innes left the double doors open to let in some air. Somebody tinkled a spoon against a glass and Donald was at the front of the room with a microphone in his hand. Everyone shushed one another until the room was quiet enough for him to be heard.

First of all, he said. A big round of applause for the bar staff tonight!

Everyone whooped and cheered and banged their fists against the tables.

Second of all, I want to thank each and every one of you for coming. For raising money for the foundation we've put together. With this money we can increase the search for our boy and bring Young Bobby back home to Cullrothes.

Everyone whooped and cheered, but it was quieter this time.

Donald stood nodding, unsure whether to say anything more, and then put the microphone back down. He sat back down at the table next to Margo and Moodie.

All set? asked Margo.

All set.

You think he can pull this off? She was watching Innes in his skinny white shirt across the room.

He'll be fine.

You sure you're not wanting me to take care of it?

You're too close. We can't have any suspicions here. Let's drink up and make sure we're out of here early.

Soon Donald finished his wine and helped Margo into her coat. They said goodbye to everyone as they left, with Moodie walking behind, still carrying a whisky. When the music started up again and there was more dancing, the founders of the Robert Fleck Foundation were already on their way home.

Later in the wee hours of the morning when they had all gone home or at least out into the streets, Innes stood in the function suite looking around at the broken glass and the upturned tables and the remnants of food trampled into the carpet. For the first time Donald's plan began to sound like a good idea. A burning building did not need to be bleached or have its bins emptied or have its surfaces polished. So it was one less thing to worry about.

Innes took a final slow walk around the hotel's public spaces. The bar was a scene of carnage with broken chair legs, abandoned half-drunk pints of beer and squashed cigarette butts flicked into the corners. In the public bathroom Innes had to tiptoe around rancid puddles of urine. All the toilets were blocked and clogged with faeces-spattered tissue paper. Innes gagged and threw up a little in his mouth then swallowed it. In the kitchen the dirty dishes and the uneaten food had been piled in uneven towers along the stainless steel work surfaces. The plug in the sink was congealed with grease and the black bin was full, with scraps of food spilling out the sides.

The door which led to the hotel's bedrooms was still double locked. Innes tried the handle just in case some of the guests had snuck away from the party for a little privacy. But the padlock remained secure and the hotel was closed to residential guests between October and April. So the bedrooms were empty, there was no doubt about that, and Innes had nothing to worry about there.

When he was sure the place was empty, Innes sat on the bar dangling his legs over the edge and looked around. There was a new stag's head mounted on the wall now, a light-coloured brute with kind eyes and not nearly as many antlers as the one that got Young Bobby. He thought of how the blood had soaked itself into the mop that night.

There was no real plan for it, but underneath the bar was a pile of old newspapers and magazines and brochures that had never been tidied away, and Innes bunched this up in his arms and thrust it into the gantry tucked between and behind the litre bottles on the optics of white rum and vodka and blended whisky. He pumped the optics each a few time so that the alcohol came down and laced the dried-out paper and dribbled from the shelf onto the floor.

He lit one corner of newspaper with a match and stood back,

worried that the whole thing might catch and explode at the instant. But it did not. It went slow, with the flames taking their time across the edge of the newsprint and jumping to the brochures and puttering with excitement when it hit the booze. Spreading slow and the light from it casting shadows and a pineapple glow across the bar and up the walls. Black smoke beginning to gather and then the sound of it. Innes knew the fire had taken by the sound of it. It cracked and began a quiet roar. He picked up the briefcase with the takings from the till and backed away towards the door. One of the rum bottles split down the side and the fire was climbing the wooden gantry and that was probably enough, then. Innes had seen enough.

That night from all across the peninsula you could smell the burning ash from the old hotel and people miles around reported seeing the glow of the flames and miles inland the black smoke spewing from the blaze up, up into the sky.

71

Smoke slowly filled the room through the crack underneath the door and it sifted up gathering at the ceiling growing dense. There was a weak fire alarm whining in the hallway but Johnny Coca-Cola's head was full of bourbon and he had been smoking weed so he did not wake at the noise.

The coughing was what brought him around. He was lying coughing into the dark room and could not clear his throat. He rolled to his side and coughed into his pillow and that was a little better. He reached out and turned on the lamp on the bedside table and it clicked on but the room stayed dark with the bulb barely illuminating anything. He rolled over and pulled the covers over his head and managed to doze off again.

The next time he awoke it was the noise he found disturbing. Like something roaring out in the hallway. And the smell of smoke was stronger now. The lamp had gone out and he reached for it in the blackness of the smoke-filled room and clicked its switch but nothing happened. The electrics must have gone out.

He swung his legs out and collapsed onto the floor. The smoke filling his lungs now and hard to shake it. Hard to catch a breath. He crawled to the hotel room door and reached up for the padlock he'd installed. But it had a combination lock and he couldn't make sense using just his fingers of the jumbled numbers.

Grabbing the door handle for leverage, he managed to get to his feet, and turned to go back across the room and find a way out of the window, to break the security restrictor or smash the whole thing in. His rucksack was lying in the middle of the floor where it had been dropped and it caught his foot and tripped him and the American came down hard, his head splitting open on the wooden frame of the bed.

72

School had been back for a month, and Alice had her junior class working in groups to make posters. The students had chosen local landmarks to research and advertise. This way, Alice had explained, I can learn more about Cullrothes and the places where you all live. I haven't been here for long enough to know for myself.

It was a double lesson in the afternoon and the classroom was warm which made the children sleepy. They were quietly reading through tourist brochures and cutting out pictures and writing elaborate headings in bubble letters.

Remember, Alice called out from her desk, I want every group to include good images, clear information and some persuasive language.

This was a small class with quiet, obedient children. Most of them lived on farms somewhere in the countryside nearby. Some of the boys had the thick, red hands that came with outdoor work. Weekends were for things like lambing and mending boundaries. They were not good at handing in homework, so she had stopped giving them any. Some of the girls were at the age where they'd started wearing make-up and liked to read magazines about celebrities. Alice had come to school one day with green eye shadow on. The next morning, a small group of girls came in wearing a similar shade. When she tied her hair up in a high ponytail with a little red ribbon, the girls did the same.

Now a girl called Mhairi jumped up from her chair and screamed. Knocked glue sticks and felt tip pens to the floor. She grabbed another pupil by the shoulders and hid behind their back.

Alice shouted: What are you doing? Sit down.

The little girl screamed again and pointed to the corner of the room.

What is it? Alice yelled, standing up now. Sit down and be quiet! Stop it. Some of the other children had started screaming. I said stop it, Jesus Christ, that's quite enough.

I saw a mouse, said Mhairi quietly. Behind the bookcase. She pointed.

The rest of the class began to laugh and shout and Alice silenced them with three slow loud claps. They clapped back in unison.

Everyone sit down. I want to hear silence. Alice put her forefinger up to her lip in a shushing pose and stared at the children until they were all silenced. Mhairi, are you sure you saw something? She stood next to the little girl. Show me where.

It ran along the skirting board and then behind the bookcase, said the girl.

And it was definitely a mouse?

Definitely.

You haven't seen it come back out?

I don't think so.

You either have or you haven't.

I haven't.

Alice grabbed the edge of the bookcase with one hand low

down and one high up. She shunted the thing away from the wall and looked down to where there was a little tear in the carpet and the opening to a narrow tunnel between two bare floorboards.

Well children, she announced. It looks like we do indeed have a visitor.

The pupils spoke excitedly to one another.

Wouldn't it be great, said Alice, if we could catch this mouse ourselves? If we didn't have to get the janitor to help? Wouldn't that be an excellent class project? To catch the wee mouse?

The pupils agreed.

I want to make a deal with you, said Alice. I want this mouse to be our secret. Top secret. I need you to keep this from your parents. From other teachers. From friends in other classes. Can you do that? It'll be just for us. Nobody else.

Most of the pupils shouted in agreement.

Can I trust you?

In unison they cried out: Yes!

Here's what's going to happen. Over the weekend I'm going to buy a trap. Together, we're going to set the trap next to the bookcase. And with any luck, we'll catch it. We'll catch the wee mouse. Can anyone think of anything else we might need?

One boy put his hand up. A bit of cheese, he said.

Good idea. We'll bring in some cheese to tempt the mouse.

A shoe box, said a girl. To put the mouse in once we've caught it.

Good idea, said Alice. And then shall we release the mouse into the wild? Into the woods somewhere?

The children shouted: Yes!

And what are we not going to do?

Tell anyone about it, said one boy loudly.

Good. I am very excited about our new project. Now, let's

get back to our posters. Alice opened the window to let some air into the stuffy room and sat back at her desk and began chewing on the end of a pencil.

That afternoon after the bell had rung and the corridors hummed with the sound of hoovers and mops, Alice sat with a pad of paper and a pen and wrote a letter in her best handwriting:

Dear boys and girls, I cannot believe you finally caught me in your classroom today! I have been scuttling about around your shoes and into your schoolbags and stealing crumbs from your lunchboxes for months! It has been so much fun! And today I overheard your plan to try and catch me in your mousetrap. You do not scare me, boys and girls. You can try your best to catch me but you will fail! From your friend, Michael the Mouse.

Once the note was finished Alice took the pad to the copy room and fed the sheet into the photocopier. She adjusted the settings to that the A4 page would shrink and the printouts would be one eighth of the original's size.

Ever since she was a little girl herself, Alice always had a keen sense of justice. Crimes deserved punishment. When she was in the Girl Guides they'd taught them the passage in the Bible that talked about taking an eye for an eye. Alice had nodded along. It made good sense to her then and it did now. She had not forgiven the children who complained and made up lies about her swearing in class. But this would go some way to achieving justice. And it would be good.

Alice took the tiny letters back to her classroom and trimmed them into neat squares. She folded these and hid them in the plastic trays where the junior pupils kept their jotters and their textbooks, so that it would be a surprise in the morning.

It was already dark when Alice put on her coat and headed down the flight of stairs with her car keys in her hand. Before she could get out the door Patricia came out of the school reception with a slip of paper in her hand.

Goodnight Patricia, said Alice.

I've got a message for you here, said Patricia.

Who's it from?

It's come through from someone at a prison. You were teaching so I asked if I could take a message. I thought it was a prank call at first.

Alice bent and put her handbag on the floor between her feet.

I ended up speaking to someone, said Patricia. He said he was your dad. She held out the folded note and Alice took it from her.

You spoke to him?

I didn't know if you wanted to hear it or not.

Have you told the headteacher?

No, pet, I haven't told anybody else. This is a private thing. I just wrote down what he said.

Thank you. Alice picked up her handbag and put the note in there. When she got to her car she rolled down the front windows and lit a cigarette and took three long deep drags on it.

The note was written on pale yellow paper and Alice read it in Patricia's decorative handwriting: *Tell Alice that I tried to call and that I will keep calling until I get through.*

She held it in front of her and turned it over but the other side was blank and then when the cigarette was smoked down she gently pressed the burning tip into the message until there was a blackened hole and ash all over her tights.

A few days after Mhairi had spotted the mouse, Alice gathered the junior class around her desk at the front of the room. They pushed and prodded one another to get close to the front. The tall ones straining their necks to see better. The short ones huddling in, cramped. Some children ostracised at the back with nothing to look at but the back of their classmates' shirts.

Alice had a small plastic device on her desk. This, she announced, is the mouse trap. It was grey and had a serrated clamp laying open with a small balance in the middle. On the balance was a crumb of chocolate.

Does anyone want to guess what will happen if this little piece of chocolate is moved?

A blonde girl called Laura put her hand up. Will it snap shut? she asked.

Laura thinks it'll snap shut, said Alice. Any other guesses?

The children looked at one another and stared at the trap but there were no more suggestions.

Well Laura, why don't we find out? See if you are smarter than a mouse. Try to get the chocolate out.

Laura scrunched her forehead. Try to get the chocolate out?

Try to get the chocolate out. Go for it. Free chocolate.

Laura leaned in more closely to the trap and examined its smooth plastic sides and the little square of chocolate sitting in the middle of the teeth. She pinched her thumb and her forefinger together like a tweezer and lowered it towards the trap and then pulled back.

I don't think I can do it.

For God's sake, mocked Alice. You haven't even tried.

Laura looked around at her classmates. It'll snap shut on my hand, she reasoned. It'll hurt. I don't want to.

That's pathetic, said Alice. You mean you won't even try? What a little baby.

Laura looked down at her feet and some of the other children grinned and nudged one another and whispered it under their breath. Little baby.

Can you get it out, miss? asked a tall boy near the back.

Can I get it out? laughed Alice. Of course, I can. Watch closely.

They leaned in and she lowered her face to the trap. Alice pursed her lips and blew hard. The chocolate twitched and the trap snapped shut with the delicate movement, jumped into the air with a loud and clear crack, spun, and landed on the floor. The girls screamed and one boy swore. Alice pointed at them and laughed.

Everyone back in your seats, she said. Bunch of babies.

They sat and Alice opened the trap again, re-setting the chocolate. She carried it carefully over to the bookcase, which was still shifted a little away from the wall. She kneeled and placed the open trap next to the skirting board.

If I leave it here, she said loudly, we'll catch the mouse when it comes running out of its little hole, won't we? She stood up and wiped the dust from her hands.

Won't it hurt the mouse? asked Laura.

What?

That trap. If it snaps shut won't it hurt the mouse?

And?

Aren't we supposed to be catching it? Laura looked around at her classmates for support. And releasing it into the woods?

Okay. Say we catch it and then release it. What do you suppose will happen then? Will the mouse make a new home in the woods and stay there? Will it build itself a little mouse

317

house with a little mouse garden and drive a little mouse car? Or will it come back here? Will it find its way back in here and dig itself an even bigger hole. Maybe have babies. Suddenly the school's over-run with filthy mice. Running wild in the corridors and running up your skirt. Is that what you want?

Laura looked up at the ceiling.

Do you want the school to be infested with dirty baby mice, Laura?

No.

No. Well then. There's no point in releasing it is there?

Laura said nothing.

I didn't think so. Get back to your work.

73

Innes fell asleep with too much wine and too many painkillers in his system. Almost instantly the images began flashing through his mind again. Young Bobby's face, the grey tinge as it spread from the tip of his nose and across his face as the blood settled and stopped flowing. The soil at the bottom of the grave, with the worms and tiny ants crawling up Innes's wrists; digging out ancient rocks, clawing at them with his fingernails to dislodge them. The pool of blood glazing the tiled floor. The skin that settled on it after a while, like a vile custard.

These were his normal dreams now.

Soon he found himself in a bath with Alice. A hot bath where their pink flesh tangled and merged and became one. Where the steam clung to his eyelashes and the heat grew and grew.

The bath had no edges, no end, nothing to hold on to except one another. A white place with bright lights and brown, dirty water, water with floating sediment, with chunks of dead skin and locks of twisted hair that clung to his legs and his arms.

Alice was staring at him. She was kicking at him under the water. Alice was clawing at him and scratching him with her toenails underneath the water's surface and it was horrible.

And then he was strangling her. Innes had his hands around her throat and he was trying to shove her head beneath into the hot water but she was too strong and she kicked with her strong thighs so that he could not force her to the bottom. He struck her on the head with all his weight and all his strength but somehow by the time his hand reached her skull all the venom in the blow was gone and he just stroked her, just tickled her, just skiffed her forehead. So he drew his fist back again and lunged at her but his strikes were as weak as a kitten's.

Innes tightened his fists and his arms and Alice smiled at him with a sweet smile and then he realised. It came to him instantly. He realised that he was dreaming.

He was able to control the dream now. He knew he was dreaming and he carefully took hold of Alice's head. He stroked her temples and gripped the skull underneath there and pushed it under the water easily this time. Watched her mouth snap open and closed and the swift flow of air escaping. The silly bubbles breaking on the surface. He knew he was dreaming and this was not real so he pulled her from the water and held her by the hair in fistfuls and threw her head from side to side, hearing and feeling the strands ripping from the scalp, sticking wetly to his palms and between his fingers. He knew he was dreaming and then he was not. He was awake. In bed in the morning.

His stomach burned with shame and regret and guilt. He could have killed her. He rolled to his side and put a hand out and Alice was there, sleeping in the bed next to him, her breathing steady and gentle. He stroked the hair on her head and it was dry and clean and smooth. She clicked her lips together when he touched her and sighed in her sleep. He lay back and took deep breaths. He could feel the sweat running from his hairline down past his ears, circling his neck.

74

The telephone rang when Jessie was in the kitchen making a hot chocolate, and she ran to pick it up before it disturbed her mother. Murphy lying there on the rug with his big tail thumping against the floor.

It was unusual for the telephone to ring at this time of night. She answered quietly: Hello?

Hi, can I speak to Jessie?

She instantly recognised Harry's voice and felt a trickle of excitement in her spine. She wetted her top lip before continuing: Speaking.

It's Harry from school. What are you up to?

What am I up to? It's ten o'clock.

Is it? I'm sorry. Is it a bad time?

A bad time for what?

For a chat.

You phoned for a chat?

Harry laughed at this. That was the plan, yes. Are you available for a chat?

I'm available.

So what are you up to?

I'm making a hot chocolate.

Right now?

Right now. She took the cordless handset with her and went back to the kitchen and added the chocolate powder to her hot milk and then stirred it in with a slug of whisky from the cupboard.

Sounds good.

It is. Hang on. Jessie put her hand over the receiver and listened carefully.

There was her mother's voice coming from upstairs. Shouting inaudibly from her bedroom. Jessie went to the bottom of the stairs, still holding the telephone handset muted against her palm.

Were you calling on me? she shouted.

Her mother sounded irritated. Yelling: Did I hear the phone ringing?

Yes.

Who the hell is phoning at this time of night?

It's someone for me.

And just who is phoning to speak to you? Do they have any idea how late it is?

It's someone from school. He's in my class.

It's a boy?

Yes, it's a boy.

What exactly does a boy want to be speaking to you about?

Homework.

There was silence from upstairs.

Do you want a hot chocolate?

You can speak to him for five minutes and then I want you up here and in your room.

Jessie closed the living room door and took her palm away from the handset. She held it to her cheek and could hear Harry breathing on the other end of the line.

Sorry, she said. I'm back. Mum was harassing me about something.

About what?

About the fact that a boy's phoning the house for me.

I bet it happens all the time.

It doesn't.

I don't believe you. So what are you doing now?

I'm just sitting on the couch. With my dog. Having my hot chocolate.

That sounds nice. I wish I could be there with you.

You do?

Yes. It'd be good to hang out some time. Watch a film together, share some popcorn.

And here I thought you were only interested in getting me to do your homework.

You think I'm only interested in you for your brains? I'm much more shallow than that.

What do you mean?

I think you know what I mean.

I really don't.

I mean that I think you're hot. I like you.

Jessie held the receiver so close to her cheek she was sure Harry would hear her pulse through it. She held it there close to her cheek and listened to his mouth move silently.

Did you hear what I said? he checked.

I heard it.

What do you think?

I think you need your head checked if you think I'm hot.

Maybe other people don't see it. But I do. You've got really good looking over the last year or two.

But I was ugly before that?

I never said that, Harry laughed. I don't think any of us could claim to have been supermodels in primary school.

You always had a nice smile, she said.

Jessie, came her mother's voice from upstairs. Jessie! Get off that phone now. You've had plenty of time.

We're still talking about the homework due for tomorrow, yelled Jessie. She mashed the handset tightly against the palm of her hand again.

Get that boy off my phone line. He's blocking it up! What if other people need to get through?

Who? Nobody ever phones us here.

Get off that phone. I will not say it again!

Jessie had finished her hot chocolate and anyway wanted to go to bed to replay the conversation with Harry over and over in her head. She uncovered the receiver again and whispered: Hey. I need to get to bed.

Okay. Sweet dreams.

You too.

I'll talk to you another time?

Yes.

75

Midnight, and Donald lay in a hot bath trying to stop the muscles spasming in his back. The painkillers had not worked and the drink had not worked and the hot water was not working.

The fire had destroyed the hotel completely. It burned all night and it was hours before the fire brigade was able to get enough machines over to temper it. The bar was gone and the function suite was gone and the rooms were gone. Just blackened carbon where the furniture and the door frames used to be. The whole structure held up by old stone foundations that were too precarious to allow anyone to enter. The police had cordoned the site off with tape and then soon a team from the council had come with chipboard and built a quick barrier all around it.

The insurance claim was going smoothly. They'd made plenty of money at the fundraiser for the Bobby Fleck Foundation. You could say it had been a success.

Donald pulled the plug and let some of the tepid water down the drain before filling the bathtub up again with scorching water from the tap.

Margo was snoring. Loud, rasping breaths that echoed around the bedroom. Before getting into bed she had taken sleeping pills with a bottle of good red wine. Donald lay on his side, head cradled in his palm, watching her. Her face looked younger and fresher than it did during the day. He reached over with his free hand and moved a twirl of hair away from her face. Margo was hot. Sweat on her forehead and down the sides of her nose.

With his spare hand Donald reached over and pinched his wife's nostrils together gently. The snoring stopped. It was silent without the sound of her breathing. Then she snorted a loud breath back into her lungs and rolled onto her side, with her back turned towards him.

It was in his sleep that Donald's father died. On a cold winter's night around twenty years before this. In old age Big Donald had grown tired of all the things that had consumed his younger self. He had not gone out hunting stag in years. Let his membership at the golf club expire. By this time he had left the running of the Distillery to his son. And his customary pew was occupied by other knees on a Sunday. Religion had lost its appeal just as the old man would seem to have most need of it.

Wee Donald had come to the family manse one night to talk about new distribution suppliers for the Distillery. A contract with a trucking company that could get the stuff out wider and faster. The downstairs rooms were empty and when Donald shouted on his father there was no answer. He climbed the staircase slowly. Then he could hear breathing and grunting and he had rushed up taking two steps at a time expecting the worst.

The landing at the top led on to bedrooms on both sides with the bathroom straight ahead. The bathroom door was open. Big Donald stood there in the bright harsh lighting with his back to his son and his trousers and underwear down around his ankles. He was standing urinating into the toilet. His breathing was ragged and he gasped every time another splash of urine hit the toilet water. From behind, Wee Donald could see between his father's legs the bright red spurts of his bloody piss.

The old man's hearing was not so good anymore, so Wee Donald went back downstairs. His father never knew what he had seen. But it was the next year before Wee Donald heard his father was attending regular appointments with the doctor over in town, taking the ferry in the morning for long appointments with specialists. He knew, by then, that it would be too late.

When it happened, it went quickly. Big Donald's visits to the hospital on the mainland were brief and unproductive. Within weeks, he was confined to bed with a catheter sticking out of him and a nurse visiting every few days.

Don't let anybody else in here, he said.

I won't.

I don't want anybody else sticking their nose in my business.

I won't let anyone in.

I don't like that nurse.

She has to come. It won't be for long, anyway.

A cold night at the back end of winter, Donald sitting at his father's bedside. Smoking a cigar. The old man was sleeping. Donald had been reading over the will. Had been making some changes to the inheritance specifications for the Distillery. He had power of attorney now.

Big Donald's breathing was harsh, rattling in his throat, and his hands and fingers were growing cold to the touch.

The nurse had been just that day. She had not been able to bring any more morphine for the pain even though the old man needed it. It had been a bank holiday and there was a problem at the warehouse and the transport had not turned up. There was no morphine coming for another day or two. Maybe he could sleep through it. She would be back as soon as she could.

The night wore on. Frost grew on the window. Big Donald began to moan in his sleep. Little, uncomfortable moans. He moved his thinning body under the sheets, from side to side. Held his arms around his torso and opened his lips and moaned. His eyes stayed shut.

After a little while Wee Donald got up and went downstairs and stood at the back door with a cigarette and a glass of whisky. The cold night air stole the smoke from the cigarette and pulled it away and out of the house. It curled up towards the sky and into the night. By the time he finished his cigarette the whisky had turned ice cold and it was tasteless and smooth in his mouth.

He could hear his father more clearly now. Rasping and howling now. There were bangs and bumps now, as though the old man was trying to get up and falling back onto the bed.

Wee Donald took the staircase slowly. He left his dirty shoes at the back door and went up slowly in his socks. The numbness of the cold whisky in his throat. He rubbed his face. The stink from the cigarette filter in his nose.

When he went into the room, his father was still lying where Wee Donald had left him. The old man looked up and they caught each other in a long glance. It was like looking into the eyes of an old stag through a rifle's sight. Big Donald's chest filled with air and he opened his mouth to show his rotten yellow teeth and then his son was on him, a pillow over those judging eyes and crushing his nose and corking the groan that was about to come. He smothered his thin, dying father quickly, and neither of them made a sound about it.

When it was finished Donald wondered if he had made the

right decision. He wondered if his father would have approved, given half a chance to do so.

76

Grandpa woke at four in the morning and rolled onto his side. The curtains were parted and he could see out to the spotlit lawn and the textured flowers and the ink-coloured sky.

He stretched his legs and heard cracks in his knees but no pain. He sat up slowly and felt the gas bubble and settle in his belly but there was no pain there either. He spread his palms on the mattress and stood up unaided and cleared his throat and he felt good this morning. He felt young. He opened the curtains wide and took off his pyjamas and got dressed in a jumper and a pair of trousers and his good slippers that he got not last Christmas but the one before.

The hospice was quiet. The staff made hourly checks but unless an alarm sounded they left the patients alone to sleep or die. Grandpa padded quietly down the corridor and opened the security door and then he was out into the fresh morning air. He walked to the end of the pathway and pushed the gate open. It was heavy and cold but his hand felt strong as it pushed against the iron. He closed the gate behind him and stepped out onto the road.

The hospice was a little way out of the village of Cullrothes, with no houses nearby. The road was quiet. There would be no traffic here until closer to eight o'clock when the ferry started. Grandpa stood in the middle of the two lanes and arched his back to look upwards. He stared at the stars and wondered how many times in his life he had allowed himself to really look at them like this. He closed his eyes and tried to reconstruct the map of stars on his eyelids. His opened his eyes and stared up some more.

Eventually he crossed to the other side of the road. Bent low and held firmly on to a rock as he eased himself down from the verge and onto the banks of the loch, where the ground was carpeted with pebbles and shingle and rocks and pieces of broken seashell and, here and there, tiny, scuttling crabs. When was the last time he had come down this close to the water?

Grandpa bent at the waist, carefully, slowly, and picked a handful of slim circular stones and put these in his pocket. He put his arms out for balance and shuffled down to where the water was coming in, foaming silvery on the pebbles. He took a cold thin stone in his right hand and cradled it in his forefinger and spun it towards the waves where it bounced up once then plopped below the surface. He took another stone and tried again, then another, then another, until his pocket was empty. He stood with clenched fists and stared at the spot where the stones had disappeared and thought to himself that this was the last time he would ever skim stones in the loch. And tried to remember when it had first happened.

Grandpa walked along the beach a little and found a nice flat groove in a rock that he could sit on. He sat down here, facing the loch. Soon he found himself watching the sun as it rose directly in front of him. The colour of burnt pineapple creeping up and up. It was the same sun rising over the same water as there had always been. Although the water was not the same, was it? This wave breaking now, a little in front of him, was made up of droplets that must have travelled the world

331

an infinite number of times. These drops had evaporated into clouds and formed into rainstorms all across the world. And now here they were, breaking in a perfect arc of white foam in front of a dying old man just as the sun began to warm his face and then they would be gone, these drops, and who knew when they would be back here again in this place.

And here on this cold piece of rock with the sun glowing on his wrinkled skin, Grandpa fell asleep. The loch unfurled across the pebbles towards his slippers and the morning warmed with a bright low sun and he was dreamless, with his mouth hanging open, his hands cradled between his legs, the wind picking up the thin hair on his head. When he woke it was three hours later and his mouth was dry and the water was lapping at his good slippers.

When he stood up this time, every bone in his legs ached and his chest felt tight. A sick old man again. He bent over and took deep breaths and when he touched his face the skin stung under his fingertips. His toes were numb and when he climbed back up to the roadside the cars tore past so fast that it took some time before he felt safe to cross between their flashing colours.

He crossed the road, holding his hands out to stall any approaching cars, keeping his face forwards. He did not want to die in his slippers on the Shore Road here this morning.

The gate to the hospice was heavy, and he had to lean his whole upper body against it before it swung open. He limped up the path. There was a bench halfway and he stopped here, catching his breath again. Then he was up and moving and finally at the door.

Grandpa, shouted Jessie. She was standing at the reception desk in her school uniform, her face pale and worried. Grandpa! There you are. She rushed to him and he put his arms around her warm waist and they held each other.

Where the hell have you been? she whispered. They said you went missing.

I went for a little walk.

Look at the state of you. Your face. You're all sunburnt.

He touched his cheek. It felt raw and cold.

I went to watch the sun come up.

And did it?

I made sure of it.

Come on. Back to your room. Jessie linked arms with Grandpa and they walked slowly. It was dark in here after so much sun and sky. Grandpa's wet slippers squelched on the tiled floor.

Are your feet wet? asked Jessie, looking down. Then: Are those your *good* slippers? Oh for God's sake, Grandpa. What are you like?

It was the last time Grandpa watched the sun rise with his own eyes, and the last time he went skimming stones.

77

There were three of them in the little boat. Donald, Moodie and Father Jaine. A nice invitation it had been to the priest. A childhood hobby in need of resuscitation. Good to see the land from the water for a change.

You sure you won't try a cast of your own, Father?

No thank you. I'll leave the fish where God intended. But this beer, he held up the glass bottle, I shall happily see that this beer gets sunk.

It was a clear day of late winter with blue skies and a low, cold sun that reflected in blinding shards off the loch. A keen wind skimmed the waves and clung to the men's bare faces. Father Jaine wore a padded jacket for insulation.

Moodie was standing at the front of the boat, silently watching the water, his fishing line drifting side to side. He had a cap pulled down low over his forehead and smoked a pipe, the smoke drifting off into the spray with each puff.

Have another beer, said Donald. He was sitting with a cool box between his legs. The priest tilted his head back and finished his beer and Donald opened two more, groaning with pain as he bent down, and they clinked them together.

How is everything in the church? Any more problems with the roof?

Dry as a bone, thanks to you.

The cottage okay?

Fantastic.

Good. You'll let me know if there's anything else we can do for you.

You know me. As long as I have peace in my heart and a well-stocked fridge, I'm happy.

Moodie and I used to come out here fishing when we were boys, said Donald. I was useless. Never caught a thing. Didn't have the patience for it. But Moodie, he was prolific. Pulled in all sorts of beasts. We used to throw most of them over the side. Watch them splash and wriggle away down. Donald drank more beer. But every now and then we'd take a big one home and skin it and gut it and cook it over the fire.

There was an easy silence as the men enjoyed the air and the cold and the feeling off the waves beneath them.

I've been meaning to ask, said the priest. What is happening with the search for Young Bobby? Have there been any developments on the poor man?

Donald leaned forward and spoke quietly. We now think he's on the mainland. Shacked up with a floozy. He'll come back when she gets fed up of him. Or when he needs some money.

Has he been in touch at all? Has anyone reported seeing him?

Nothing.

So he could still be around here, for all we know.

No. Not here. And if I could speak to him, I'd tell him to steer well clear. His mother's sick with nerves. When he does turn up, he's going to regret it. I'll bite his nose off.

The priest finished another bottle of beer and then spoke in a calm, slow voice: I think you need to at least be cognisant of the possibility that he isn't coming home. Or that he might not be able to. People go missing all the time. People suffer accidents all the time. Turn up in different places. Up mountains. Car wrecks. In bodies of water. You and Margo should at least be preparing for something.

Inspiring words, said Donald. You can always trust a man of God to lower the mood. Here. Another beer might shut you up for a minute.

Father Jaine laughed and accepted another beer and drank greedily. The wind had dropped a little and the sun seemed to shine harder now as the morning peaked and they were well away from the coast by now, well out there on the loch.

I think, said the priest, I'd better take my jersey off. Getting a little warm under here.

He stood up and planted his feet and took off his jacket and then his jersey. The boat drifted a little to one side and swayed and the priest's knees wobbled for a second, but then he was right again. He sat down. Too many of these. He picked up his bottle. Losing my balance.

You had a visitor to the parish cottage recently, said Moodie, speaking for the first time. An American.

Yes, yes, I did. Nice man. Travelling through, I think. Going island hopping.

What did he want from you?

Just a little hospitality. Conversation. We had a coffee and some cake. Very nice man.

Nothing else?

What is this? laughed the priest. Getting an interrogation here. He pointed at Moodie over his shoulder and spoke to Donald. I think your big pal's getting a bit big for his boots.

Answer the questions, said Donald.

The priest opened and closed his mouth. Are you being serious right now?

Answer my friend's questions.

Okay, yes. The man came to the door. He just turned up. He was very polite, even brought a cake with him. I made a coffee, we chatted, and then he left. A normal day in my line of work, really. He turned and smiled at Moodie's wide back.

You chatted?

We did.

What about?

He was telling me about where he grew up, and his impressions of the village.

How much did he know about the village?

The priest put his beer down between his feet and half turned so that he could see Moodie and Donald.

I'll be honest, he did say a few things that I thought were strange. About how the village was being controlled. About how changes were coming. He wanted me to promise that I wouldn't oppose any changes. I mean, really.

How much did he pay you?

Pay me? Nothing, nothing, no money changed hands.

How much did he promise you?

The priest stood up, gripping the bench between his knees for support.

I am a priest, may I remind you. I am not to be bought or sold or bullied by anybody. I am a man of God and God only can induce me to behave one way or another. I am really quite offended by this.

If you want to know what I think, said Donald. I think you've been bought. I think these Americans have waved their dollars at you and you've taken a bite already. You think I don't know what's happening around here? You think I don't know what people are saying about me?

It's all in your imagination, smiled the priest.

Look, shouted Donald. Look, it's a dolphin! He was leaning to the starboard and pointing over the edge of the boat, laughing at the waves.

The priest turned awkwardly and stood at the side of the boat peering across into the water. Where? he asked. I don't see it! Where did it go?

From behind, Moodie reached around the priest's waist with a thick iron chain and wrapped it twice round the fat little tummy. He tried to scratch at Moodie's face with his fingers but already he was tumbling forwards, Donald's boot shoving into his lower back, knees banging painfully against the boat's edge as he lunged towards the water with his arms spread out wide and the beer bottle still held tight in his hand.

Father Jaine hit the waves with his mouth open, in the middle of an unfinished protest, and the water rushed quickly into his lungs. The coldness of the water shocked his core and the heavy chain dragged him down into the darkness. The priest kicked and grabbed at the water around him as though he might find something he could clutch onto.

Donald and Moodie sat watching the red shape of the priest disappear further and further into the loch. It was quick and quite beautiful to watch once the bubbles stopped breaking the surface. Then it was blissful silence again, after the shouting. The land was so far off that only faint smudges of colour could be seen. The yellow of the sand. The purple of the heather on the distant mountains. The white of the low Distillery buildings.

How's your back feeling? asked Moodie.

It's killing me, said Donald. We need to find that wee American arsehole. Where the hell is he?

Don't look at me.

Moodie's fishing line suddenly went taut and started jerking under the strain of something tugging at it.

Quick, shouted Donald, pointing. That'll be the Father. Reel him back in! And both men laughed hard, wiping tears from their eyes.

78

A strange dark day when the sun barely filtered through the clouds, and Jessie went to the hospice to visit Grandpa again. Out of all the residents he had been there the longest now. She took with her two cappuccinos. Tidied up the room. Tissues and old newspapers and half-empty cans of Coca-Cola. She opened the blinds to let in the Sunday afternoon. Grandpa sipped his coffee and swirled it around his tongue and spat it out. He pressed his emergency button and an alarm sounded in the room.

What is it, asked Jessie, what's wrong?

I need the toilet, he whispered.

I can help.

No, he whispered.

You've lost more weight, she told him.

Have I?

You're looking skinny. Who knew the Irn Bru diet would work so well?

He threw his head back and laughed.

A nurse came and pulled the curtain around Grandpa's bed and Jessie went to the kitchen for a cup of tea. When she came back, Grandpa was sitting up in bed. Daily Record folded in his lap. His hair had been wetted and combed smoothly back.

Grandpa, she said, don't you look handsome!

Well, he whispered, and ran his hand carefully through the thick white hair. You never know who you might meet.

When Jessie was a wee girl, Grandpa had told her about an adventure he'd gone on as a boy. He'd packed his tent and taken his bike and cycled all across Scotland, not returning home to his mother's house for weeks. It was summer time, and he'd slept in bothies or camped in farmers' fields, eating food cooked over fires, buying bread and milk and anything else he could find at the farms. He cycled east and north, following the Caledonian Canal, up to the Highlands. This was before the war, when he was still a boy.

79

I do wish you hadn't drowned the priest, said Margo. She was kneeling in the garden wearing gloves with compost dotted up her arms. Was that really necessary?

Donald was sitting on the bench that looked out onto the loch with a big glass of whisky in his hands. The pain in his back tolerable just now while he sat still so he did not plan on moving. He did not answer his wife's question.

Don't you think we've got enough on our plate? First Sandy, and now the hotel fire and the debts and Young Bobby. Isn't that enough already? It makes me feel so sad.

Don't you have a diary you can write this in? asked Donald.

A village needs a church. A church needs a priest! A man of God. You've messed with the natural order of things.

If God is so upset about it, he'll let me know.

You spoke to the insurance company about the claim?

I spoke to them.

And?

And it's all being processed. They're going to want to investigate it a little. Speak to someone at the fire station. But it'll be fine.

Moodie came walking up the long garden path wearing a

black coat and dirty boots. Donald and Margo watched him come up the hill at his slow pace.

Here's Moodie, she said.

Aye.

Did you know he was coming?

I did.

What for?

Donald ignored his wife's question again and stood up from the bench, gritting his teeth as his back seized up and then loosened a little.

Moodie unbuttoned his jacket and waited until he was within spitting distance before he looked up at them and spoke: Afternoon, Margo. Pots are looking nice.

They will be if we ever get the weather for it.

Moodie nodded at Donald too and waited.

You know that wee American guy who's been punting his gear all over the place? said Donald.

Johnny Coca-Cola.

That's his name?

That's what he calls himself.

I'm fed up seeing him skulking about smoking those fancy cigarettes of his.

It's Marlboro. He smokes Marlboros.

Donald snorted and took a glug of whisky and shook his head. Then said: Time to bring the wee fella in. It turns out it was him that started the fire at the hotel. I got a tip-off.

From who?

From someone who saw him doing it. Find him and bring him in.

What's the plan?

Let's start with the kneecaps and see how we get on. This is our village. Our slab of land. And he's overspent his welcome.

I'll find him, said Moodie. He buttoned his jacket back up.

Shouldn't be too hard. You seem to know all about him. Has he made pals with you or something?

I've not even spoken to the boy.

Did he slip you a wee taster bag of something? A bit of a freebie?

Moodie smiled as though it was a funny thought and shook his head.

Go on then. Bring him in.

Moodie headed back down the long garden path away from the manse and Donald fell heavily back onto the bench spilling a splash of whisky over his knuckles. Margo was still planting her flowers.

Moodie's lying to you, she said.

I know.

That's not like him.

It's not his style usually.

Do you trust him?

I don't think I trust anyone anymore.

Good. Neither do I. What do you think? She presented her potted flowers to Donald, neatly arranged with bright colours and the compost tightly packed around the stems.

They're looking good, he said. They'll be looking good by the time the summer comes.

80

Alice came into school early and helped herself to coffee from one of her colleague's jars. Free-poured a heavy measure into someone else's mug and filled it with hot water from the kettle. Found a new two-litre bottle of milk in the fridge and added a splash to her coffee before pouring the rest of the fresh milk down the sink and binning the bottle.

Someone had left apples on a plate in the middle of the staff table. She picked these up one by one and wet her tongue and licked them while she drank the hot coffee.

The corridors were dark and cold. Smelling of bleach. She turned the lights on as she passed the switches on the walls. The chairs were stacked on the desks in the dark classrooms and the place smelled of light disinfectant.

She had a key to her own classroom, and she sang lightly as she went in and switched on the lights and sat at her desk. Give me joy in my heart, keep me singing. Give me joy in my heart I pray.

She swallowed more hot coffee and opened her planner and checked her lessons for the day. There was no love heart for Valentine in the corner of the page.

Give me joy in my heart, keep me singing. Keep me singing for the break of day.

There had not been a love heart for Valentine for a while now and she missed drawing them and colouring them in and getting dressed up for him.

She got up and took the chairs down from the desks, clattering them to the floor. She stopped after three and looked to the corner where the squint bookcase was, where the trap was laid, and sucked in air through her teeth. The fat backside of a brown mouse hung twitching from the trap.

Sing hosanna, she continued. Sing hosanna, sing hosanna to the king of kings.

She stepped slowly and quietly toward the mouse. It was still alive. Its back legs kicked weakly at the floor as it tried to stand upright. Its entire upper half was clamped in the trap, head, neck, front legs.

Sing hosanna, sing hosanna, sing hosanna to the king.

She squatted down. The mouse had moved about half a foot across the vinyl floor from where the trap was set. It had been here for a while, struggling and wriggling blindly. She reached out and flicked its backside with her middle finger.

The mouse tried to jump and twist, but the thing's movement was limited. It stopped dead still.

Give me peace in my heart, keep me loving. Give me peace in my heart, I pray.

She took another long sip of coffee.

Give me peace in my heart, keep me loving. Keep me loving till the break of day.

She left the coffee on her desk and turned out the classroom light and locked the door behind her. It did not appear as though any of her colleagues were around yet anyway. The janitor's base was along the corridor, near the back end of the school. Tam had been the janitor for years. His base was a mess of tools, broken equipment, old materials and filing cabinets full of unfiled papers. Alice went in and quickly found a metal bucket that was rusted but sturdy. She picked this up. Threw in a trowel. Found a claw-head hammer and put this in. Found a little length of coarse rope and some masking tape and garden shears. She put all of these in the bucket and turned the light off again and hurried back to the classroom and the mouse that was waiting there.

Alice had no classes timetabled for the morning so she spent her non-contact lessons marking jotters with encouraging comments and glittery stickers and she made a wall display with some colourful examples of pupils' work and she photocopied her worksheets for the week ahead. She'd placed the bucket upturned over the mouse so she wouldn't be distracted by it but couldn't help checking every now and then to see if the little bugger was still going.

At morning interval, she sat in the staffroom and listened to the complaints about the missing milk. The cleaners were getting the blame. Alice nodded her agreement. Someone vowed to draw up a warning sign to fix on the fridge. She watched Iain, the technical teacher, wrap his thick lips around an apple from the fruit bowl and take a bite, the fruit's flesh and juice speckled on his chin. She acquiesced to put another pound into the communal coffee fund as it was running low. She didn't have the money on her. She'd bring it in tomorrow. She made herself a strong coffee with twice as many granules as was necessary.

After break she had the junior class so she left the staffroom before the bell had rung to be there early to greet them at the door. Her knees felt weak as she walked and the thick vein at the side of her neck was pulsing.

Line up please, she called out as they arrived. Line up. Single file. I said, line up! Listen to me when I speak to you. Single file.

She admitted the pupils and watched their faces as they entered. Her throat felt dry. All the desks were pushed back towards the walls so that in the middle of the room there was an open space. This was where she had dragged the upturned bucket to, and there it was.

Take a seat somewhere around the sides, she said softly. Yes, drop your bags on the floor. No, you don't need any pencils or jotters out just now. Just sit down somewhere. Just sit down.

You two. She pointed at two boys. You're not sitting together today. Move.

But why?

Because I'm telling you to, that's why.

Once the class were sitting Alice stood with her legs spread either side of the bucket. Well, boys and girls, she said, we have a guest in class today. Would anybody like to guess who our special visitor might be?

Lots of the pupils put their hands up. Yes, Sadie?

Sadie had bright eyes and a little mole on her chin. Did we catch the mouse? she asked.

Yes! shouted Alice. That's it. We got the mouse! Give yourselves a round of applause.

The children clapped and high-fived and shouted out: Yes, woohoo, yay!

You should be very proud of yourselves, said Alice. I know that I am proud of you.

Can we see it? shouted the boy Rowan. Can we let it run about?

Be patient, smiled Alice. We're all going to see it. But first, who can remind me how a mouse trap works? Remember, we talked about this in class already.

Some of the children sat quietly and some of them put

their hands up in the air and then down again and some of the children put their hands straight up and kept them there, straining towards the ceiling.

Yes, Lauren?

Lauren was a little blonde-haired girl with thick black glasses and pink cheeks. She spoke with clarity and confidence: You put in some cheese and the mouse eats it and then the trap closes and locks the mouse in.

Close, said Alice. But not quite. You were right about the cheese, although it doesn't *have* to be cheese. Chocolate works as well. Can you imagine that? A mouse eating chocolate? A mouse eating an Easter egg? Wouldn't that be funny!

The children laughed.

Alice looked at Sophie, a clever girl with long hair that ran all the way down her back. Sophie, what do you know about it?

Is the cheese or the chocolate or whatever on a kind of weight? asked Sophie. And the weight flips when the mouse takes it.

Excellent. Well done. So, we've set out a treat. We'll call this the bait. The mouse takes the bait. This makes the weight shift. Now what?

Orla was a quiet girl with freckles, but she put her hand up now, slowly.

Yes, Orla?

Does the weight make the cage door close? To trap in the mouse?

Yes – you're very nearly right! I'll tell you what actually happens. The bait is set in the middle of the trap, and the trap is like two strong jaws. Can you imagine that? With jagged teeth, just like a shark's. Imagine you were lying with your mouth wide open. And I balanced a piece of chocolate on your tongue. You would wait like this, until a wee mouse came along to steal the chocolate. And what would you do when the chocolate was moved, just a tiny bit? You would snap your teeth shut, as fast as you can! Let me see you trying that.

Many of the children tilted their heads back and opened their mouths skyward then closed their front teeth sharply down on one another, with rapid little clicks. But some of the children were staring quietly now at the bucket.

Who can tell me what might happen now to the mouse?

I'd bite its head off, shouted Rowan, laughing, and the children around him laughed, and Alice allowed herself to laugh at this as well.

Almost, she smiled, and bent over and picked up the bucket and revealed to the children the closed trap, the plastic teeth digging into the brown fur, the fat little backside sticking up, and the hind legs still moving, still trying to walk, to get itself home.

Oh my God, shouted Rowan. Look at it. It's been cut in half.

Alice's toes had curled painfully and she felt like a current passed through her. Be quiet everyone, she said, but the rest of the class was silent already. She leaned backwards against a desk and let her fingers grip the cold wooden edge of it. Now she looked around at the children's faces.

Sophie sat back and made a face and folded her legs and arms over. Orla grew pale and she covered her mouth with her hands. Sadie very quickly went red and started to cry, looking around at her classmates and at the windows where you could see the blue sky outside.

So, said Alice. Here it is. Our wee visitor. Look what you've done to him. Look at him still fighting. So brave.

How did we do this? asked Sadie.

Of course you did, said Alice. Everyone here agreed to do it. We were to trap the mouse. That's what everyone said.

I thought we would release it, said Laura. Into the woods.

It would only have come back, said Alice. That's not really a solution, is it? Let it out so that it can find its way back here in a day's time? Mice are very clever animals, you know.

Is it going to die? asked Orla, speaking through the gaps in her fingers.

Alice sighed. It's probably got a broken back, she said. A broken neck. She touched her own neck on both sides to demonstrate where the injuries would be. Its head's been crushed. It's probably blind and brain damaged now. But look at its little legs. It's a fat mouse. There's a lot of life still in it, isn't there?

It's in pain, said Rowan. It's hurt.

So what should we do?

Rowan shrugged, staring down at the mouse, which was only moving itself in blind circles.

Put it out of its misery, said Sadie.

Aye, said Rowan. He was standing up now. Kill it. We have to. He looked round at the rest of the children and pointed at the thing. Look at it. It's not going to get better. Kill it now, make it quick and painless.

Well done Rowan, said Alice. You're handling this very maturely. I am impressed. Now, I want to send you on a mission. Who else wants to go on a mission with Rowan? Sophie, how about you?

Sophie stood up.

I want you both to take this bucket to the drinking fountain and fill it up. About halfway. Then bring it back here. One of you carry it and the other one open the doors. Alright?

Rowan took charge of the bucket and left the classroom without a word and Sophie followed him. Alice sat on one of the vacated chairs among the pupils. How does it make you all feel? she asked.

Sad, said Orla.

But we didn't want the mouse in here, did we?

No.

Do you remember how scary that was?

Yes.

So something had to be done about it?

Yes.

Would you have preferred to have the janitor come in and take care of this overnight? Without knowing what had happened? What would we have learned then?

The children were quiet. There was no good answer to this. Sadie had started to cry again and she was rubbing the snot on her sleeve. The mouse kept on waggling its fat backside at them as it tried to shake off the trap and make a run for freedom.

Rowan and Sophie came back with the bucket. Half full of cold water. They carried it between them by its metal handles and struggled with the weight of it.

Thank you both, said Alice. Pop it down here. They put the bucket on the floor and returned silently to their seats but Rowan stayed standing, out of the way, moving his weight from one foot to the other.

I want you all to remember this, said Alice. This is an important lesson about consequences. In life, everything that you do has consequences. Every decision that we make leads to something. When this mouse decided to sneak in here and make his little mouse home behind my bookcase, that action had consequences. When you all decided that you wanted to catch the mouse and get rid of it, that action also had consequences. Do you understand me yet? Why I had to do this? Do you?

She picked up the mouse trap up by the plastic casing so that the mouse's rear end dangled from it. The fur was matted and greasy. This mouse – she held it out – is what will happen to you if you do not make good decisions. Life will crush you. It will trap you. And you will sink.

She held the trap above the bucket and released it. The mouse fell and splashed quietly into the water, its eyes already dull, its face and body flattened by the trap like plasticine, its hind legs still cycling around. It kicked itself around the perimeter of the bucket, half-paralysed, in a slow circle.

Who wants to come and see? smiled Alice. It's nearly over.

Only a handful of pupils ventured near the bucket. They leaned over and looked in as though leaning over a cliff edge then retreated to their seats.

Sadie, said Alice. For Christ's sake, go and wash your face.

Sadie was red and hot from crying so much. She ran from the classroom and slammed the door behind her.

Finally the mouse stopped kicking and twitching and floated in a slow circle.

Well, boys and girls, said Alice. I think our little visitor has moved on to the next life. Shall we stand? And say the school prayer together? That would be nice. Come on then. On your feet everyone. Hands together. Who wants to lead us in prayer?

Mary our mother, said Rowan, crossing himself. And then they all spoke in unison: Guide everyone at Cullrothes School with your kindness and understanding. Teach us to be responsible and to always help others. Lead us when we are lost, and comfort us when we are lonely. Amen.

Well, said Alice. What do you say we break up for lunch a little early today? I'm starving.

81

Jessie had to tidy the kitchen before she could light the candles. There was a dirty plate with a smear of thick dried ketchup that she rinsed in the sink. There was a glass that had been used for milk and it was smeared up the sides. She sprayed the worktop with bleach and wiped clean the toast crumbs and flecks of butter and dead cigarette butts that were left there.

The cake was in a cardboard box and she burst the tape open with a pair of scissors. She dropped the candles into the soft icing in a random pattern and lit them. The lighter's flame burning her thumb.

Jessie carried the cake in two hands to the bottom of the stairs. Murphy padded out from the dark living room and looked at her. Mouth open. Tongue out. She nudged him back through the door with her leg and pulled the door shut, hooking her toes around the edge of it.

Upstairs the hall light was on and her mother's bedroom door was closed.

Happy birthday to you, she sang as she climbed the stairs.

Happy birthday to you, as she reached the landing.

Happy birthday dear Mum, as she reached her mother's

bedroom door. She balanced the cake plate in her palm and opened the door with her free hand.

Happy birthday to you!

The curtains were drawn over the window and her mother's room smelled sour, of vinegar. Jessie stepped over dirty clothes and found a space with her backside on the bed.

Happy birthday, she said. Look. I've got you a cake. Are you going to blow out the candles?

Her mother lay on her side with her face turned away. The candles' orange glow crept up the wallpaper and made faces out of the floral pattern.

Mum? The wax is dripping.

But her mother said nothing so Jessie blew out the candles herself and put the cake down on the bedside table and lay down on the bed. She put one arm around her mother and her face rested on the pillow at the back of the woman's neck where she could smell smoke and sweat.

They both lay like this until their breathing synchronised.

How are you feeling today? asked Jessie.

Exhausted.

Have you been sleeping?

Can't sleep.

What about some fresh air?

I don't want to go out.

They both lay in the same position until Jessie's mother turned around and faced her daughter.

How was school? she asked.

Stressful.

What was stressful about it?

Just the usual. Too much work to do.

Did you see Grandpa tonight?

No. I came home to see you.

Do you think he's okay?

He's as good as he can be.

I should go and see him.

He would love that! Jessie sat up. We can go together at the weekend. Take him something to cheer him up.

This weekend?

Yes. Why not? It's not as if he has unlimited time.

Yes, okay. The woman sat up. Let's go together at the weekend. It'll be great to see him. Better than moping about here all day.

Jessie hugged her knees and wriggled her toes until she heard a little crack.

Now what's this about a cake?

Oh now you're interested?

Now I'm interested. I'm starving. Haven't eaten all day.

Do you want me to re-light the candles so you can blow them out?

No, I'm not a child, she laughed.

Jessie picked up the cake and held it under her mother's face so she could see the icing. A champagne bottle and a bouquet of flowers in fondant icing.

Did you bring plates?

Napkins.

Jessie used a butter knife to cut thick slabs of the birthday cake. They took slices from the edges to get more icing. The cake had two layers and in the middle there was jam and buttercream.

Jessie and her mother ate their cake with their fingers in the bed and dropped crumbs into the sheets.

It's a bit dry, said Jessie.

No, it's delicious.

It's good but the sponge is a bit dry. I should have home-baked one for you.

I don't need a fuss made for me.

Do you want another bit?

Yes.

They ate more of the cake and then Jessie's mother lay back on the bed and rubbed her stomach. I feel sick now, she laughed.

I could eat cake for dinner every night, said Jessie.

Not me. It's too sweet.

I think I'll take Murphy out for a walk. Do you want to come?

Where are you going?

I usually walk down to the shore and along the coast then double back. You should come. It'll be good for you.

What does that mean?

It'll be good for you to get out. It's a nice night.

I think it'll be too cold.

It isn't.

I don't feel well.

You look okay to me.

No, it's that cake. I've eaten too much of that bloody cake. She rubbed her stomach and burped under her breath.

Let's go out. It's late. There's nobody about. Nobody will even see you.

What does that mean? You're embarrassed to be seen with me?

No. I just mean you don't have to worry about what you're wearing or your hair. Nobody's going to see you.

Charming. This is a nice way to speak to your mother. And on my birthday too.

Jessie's mother curled back down on her side and turned her face away.

Please come out. It'll be nice.

I don't feel well. You've upset me.

I didn't mean to upset you. I wanted to have a nice time. I got you a cake.

You bought a cake. Didn't even make it yourself.

Jessie stood up and brushed the crumbs from her skirt. Why do you have to be like this? Why does everything have to be so hard? Why can't you just be normal?

You think this is my fault? You think this is how I want things to be?

Can you turn around so we can talk?

Go away.

Mum.

Leave me alone. Take your crappy cake downstairs. Away you go with that hideous dog. You prefer spending time with him anyway.

Mum!

Don't pretend you care about me. You care more about your Grandpa than you do about me. Go and spend the night with him. See if I care.

I didn't mean to upset you again.

Jessie grabbed the duvet and tugged it away.

Get out, shouted her mother. Get out of my room. I don't want you here.

This is just typical. Why do you have to ruin everything? I try to do something nice and you ruin it. Do you even care that you got me fired from the hotel? They fired me because of you.

Maybe I was doing you a favour.

You could do me a favour by pissing off out of my life.

This is my house! You get out. You know what I think? It's a real shame you weren't working in that hotel when it burned down. A real shame. That's what I think.

Jessie wiped down her wet cheeks and picked up the cake

plate and left the room where her mother lay in the dark with the cake crumbs scattered around the sheets.

82

The knock on the cottage door was loud and the wood rattled. Innes thought of police and warrants. Perhaps they had found the body, Young Bobby's rotten, worm-bitten body buried behind the hotel, and here they were now to relieve him of his freedom.

The knocking sounded again as he pulled up his trousers sitting on the edge of the bed. His hair was still mussed up from sleep and his mouth tasted bad and he put on a baggy t-shirt along with his jeans and went to answer the door barefoot.

The morning sun was bright in his eyes after the darkness of the curtained bedroom and Innes squinted into it and shielded his face with his hand as he undid the chain and opened the door.

The journalist Valentine was there. Standing on the path outside the house.

Thank God you're here, said Valentine. Something has happened! You have to come with me. Now.

Innes looked down at his bare feet and at the shoes left lying in the hall but Valentine grabbed him by the arm and pulled him into the garden.

The cold concrete of the pavement like ice on his feet.

Rough as well. He opened his mouth to yell but then there were strong hands gripping at his arms and he was thrown forwards. His feet leaving the ground completely as they held him by the armpits and Valentine's face smiling before a hood or a sack consumed his head and it was darkness and a string was being tightened and fastened around his neck and his hands were pinched together behind him and they too were tied. Then he heard Valentine whooping and jumping and there were hands tickling him around the ribs, jamming into his bones, and the bodies on each side were moving, carrying Innes barefoot and barely awake away from the cottage and down the garden path. It could only have taken three seconds from him opening the door to being taken like this and he began to roar underneath the hood and kick his legs out at the desperate air beneath.

The men took him down the garden path and they were laughing and talking to one another in low voices. Ignoring Innes when he spoke.

What is this? Where are we going?

Then he thought of Young Bobby's glazed eyes as the moisture in them had begun to dry out and he stopped kicking his legs. Why ask questions which would not be answered.

They lifted him up higher at what would have been the bottom of the garden path and he fell heavily onto rough wooden boards. He could feel the cold grain and the heads of screws digging into him. The surface bounced a little under his weight and it was clear that he was in the flat bed of a truck. He sat up and tried to move but his tied hands were anchored down to something behind him and he could only sit on his backside with his legs splayed out and his bare feet shown to the world. The engine started and some of the men there went into the truck and it felt like some others were sitting up in the back with him in the flat bad.

Why are you doing this? Innes shouted into the black fabric of the hood.

It's only just begun, said one of the disembodied voices. Innes felt like he recognised it somehow.

It's only just begun, said another voice, following a kind of tuneless tune, and then they were all at it, in a poor imitation of a choir, laughing and poking Innes in the ribs again.

The truck drove quickly and Innes mapped out the first couple of turns in his head. But with the winding roads and the uneven surface he was falling from side to side with each corner. Soon he had lost track of their route and could not tell if they were moving east, towards the ferry and the mainland, or west, in the direction of the lighthouse and the endless forests and the Atlantic Ocean.

Valentine, shouted Innes. Valentine are you still there? What is going on?

Only mocking laughter and more fingers in the ribs. Then a fierce pain in his foot as something like electricity touched there. He jerked away and felt a burning spot on his cold bare skin.

Give the boy a break, said one voice.

How? They did a lot worse when I got done.

Aye but it's his first one.

Better make it a good one.

They drove on a winding road for more time. Soon the sun came up and Innes felt the warmth on his toes and specks of light came through the fabric hood to his face and it grew hot and stuffy under there.

Someone put their hand on Innes's shoulder and he could make out a man's silhouette through the hood. You doing okay? the voice asked.

Innes recognised it.

Valentine, he said. Is that you? What's happening?

It's a blackening.

What's that?

You'll find out. You're a lucky boy, you know that? With Alice.

I don't feel so lucky just now.

You breathing okay under there?

It's hot.

We'll be there soon.

Where?

You'll see.

Soon the truck turned to the left and the terrain became rougher. The pickup jerked from side to side and Innes fell heavily backwards and hurt his arms tied at the elbows. The sound of gravel and dirt underneath the tyres. Under the fabric of the hood he sensed a darkening; the sunlight was gone. It was colder in the air now. Birds singing.

The truck stopped and Innes felt the engine cease. The men got up and he could feel them standing over him. They jumped out the back and landed heavily. The truck rocked up and down as the weight of them dissipated.

The hood came off. Although they were under the shade of forest trees Innes felt blinded by the sudden light. He was sitting up in the back of the truck and they had parked up in a clearing. Thick old trees with dry bark all around. Compacted dry dust with potholes on the ground. Green from the trees diminishing into dark shadows behind. Then he saw the men. Six of them in black jeans and black t-shirts and black masks covering their heads and their faces with only their eyes showing. He had a minute to look at them. The one who took the hood off had his back to him. That was Valentine. He recognised the shape of the man's waist.

One of the masked men had a bottle of whisky in his hand and he stepped forwards and held it over Innes's head.

Open up, he said.

I don't want to, said Innes. I haven't even had breakfast yet.

The man turned to the others and they all laughed. Then he poured the whisky over Innes, nipping his eyes, the stink in his nostrils. Innes opened his mouth to gasp and the man gripped his jaw and poured glugs of it down. Innes spat and gasped and shook his head from side to side trying to get rid of the stuff.

Open up, said the man again. He had wrinkles around his blue eyes and a fat belly under the black t-shirt. Innes opened his mouth a little and the man poured the whisky in. It filled his mouth then overflowed and ran down his chin and he spat it down his chest.

The man slapped Innes's face a few times. Good boy, he said, and took a suck from the bottle himself. He had emptied half a litre of it over and into Innes. Who's got the bucket?

The fat man backed off and another came forward in his black mask, a thick-chested man with big hands, and a metal bucket filled with black liquid. It shone purple and red as the surface of it shifted from side to side.

Wait, said Innes, to the man. Wait, shouted Innes, to the rest of the men standing a few feet behind, holding cans of beer.

Fresh pig's blood, said the man. Slaughtered the poor thing just yesterday. Especially for you, darling.

No, I don't want this, no, screamed Innes. He was scrabbling at the truck bed with his bare feet but his hands were still tied and staked and there was nowhere to go but sideways. The man poured the blood over the back of his head and it was cold and thick and smelled of rusting metal.

Stop, cried Innes. Stop!

The man with Valentine's waist came over and knelt close to Innes. He wiped the pig's blood from his eyes. He whispered: The more you complain, the worse they're going to be.

What's happening?

It's a blackening. It's a surprise. Happens to everyone before they get married.

We haven't even set a date yet.

Aye, well. That's the surprise.

Highland games, roared one of the men in the crowd. Innes looked over. The man had a thick chest and tattoos up his forearms. It must be Moodie from the Distillery. Valentine put a chain with a clamp around Innes's ankle and unfastened his arms. The chain was about ten metres long and heavy.

You're going to want to get up and move around for this one, said the journalist.

The man with the tattooed arms had cradled in his arms a long tree trunk, sawed flat at each end. He held it straight upwards supported by his shoulder and his neck. Three other men had hoisted tree trunks up and they all stood in a row.

Valentine stood to attention and announced in a mocking tone: Let the caber tossing world championships commence!

Moodie bent and took a short run and then straightened his back and lifted the tree trunk up into the air, aiming straight at Innes. It twisted as it rose and fell and Innes ducked to the side while the trunk thundered into the dry ground next to him.

For God's sake, he shouted, but already the other three had taken their short runs and launched their trunks towards him. He barely had time to react before the giant slabs of wood battered into the ground, just missing him, and then one of them bounced awkwardly and caught him flush in the face. Innes staggered back and tripped and heard a fleshy pop in his nose as it burst.

Oh ho, shouted one of the men. Direct hit!

And the rest of them laughed.

We have a winner, declared Valentine, and the men slapped each other's backsides and drank some more whisky from the bottle and bent over laughing.

Next up is the Scottish country dancing, roared one of the men. Innes struggled to his feet, still chained at the ankle. Valentine had in his hands a huge broadsword and a traditional targe. He handed the decorative shield to Innes. Straighten your forearm and hold it close to you, he said. And jump when you have to.

One of the men in the crowd had inflated a set of bagpipes and he began to pick out a tune, something low and melancholy and horrible. Valentine held the broadsword out in front of him and circled on his toes. It was the length of a man as thick as a cleaver.

As the pipes picked up, Valentine lunged at Innes, who threw the targe out to meet the blow and felt it shudder in his collarbone. He almost tripped over his chain and crouched under the shield while Valentine brought the blade crashing down again.

Get up, you wee lassie, laughed the journalist. On your feet!

Innes made it upright again and prepared for another strike at the targe but this time Valentine went low, bringing the sword out and round in a low arc. Dance! he yelled, and Innes skipped his feet up, barely missing the blade as it cut through the air beneath him.

Oh ho, shouted one of the men watching from the trees.

Yee ha, shouted another, and the pipes changed to something much more upbeat and jolly.

Can you not dance better than that? hissed Valentine, circling again. No wonder your woman likes it better with me. No wonder she keeps coming back to me for it.

Innes knew what he meant. He had known in his heart for a while that Alice was sleeping with the journalist. He loosened his grip on the targe and threw it at Valentine. It caught him heavily on the shoulder and bounced away.

Dance, laughed Valentine again, with the pipes now

piercing the air like some sort of ghoul. He swung the broadsword out low and wide as he had done before and brought it whistling through the air. Innes lifted his feet to skip out of its way again but felt the chain tangle and catch and his leg was still there when the blade arrived and it sliced clean through his standing limb just below the kneecap.

Innes collapsed and reached down to where his leg had been and stared in horror at the severed part with the chain still fastened around the ankle. Valentine dropped his broadsword and took a step towards the fallen man and then stopped still. He covered his mouth with his hands and shouted: I didn't mean it. Sorry. I didn't mean it!

The bagpipes continued for a few more seconds, and then ceased, just the quietening drone of them lingering in the air.

83

Murphy stood on the pebbled shore barking at Jessie in a high pitch. The sky was grey and the dark loch barely moving today. Murphy barked and pawed at the pebbles with his forelegs and looked up at Jessie.

Will you stop it, she said. She bent and picked up the wet tennis ball and threw it down the coast. Murphy turned and tore after it, his heavy paws pounding and kicking up the shingle.

She watched his golden fur shifting, tight muscles moving beneath the skin, and then he had the ball in his mouth, and he was running back towards her, and his ears were bouncing, and the ball was at her feet again and Murphy began to bark.

Will you stop barking, she said, and as she bent to pick up the ball she swung at him and clipped him on the nose and he snorted and took a step back and barked again until she released the ball over his head up the beach. Jessie watched him and wiped the drool from her hand on her trouser leg.

Murphy plucked up the ball and ran in a circle and lay down.

Above the calm loch, gulls were hovering and swooping down towards the water. A dark shape broke the surface and it might've been a seal.

Hey, said a voice. Jessie turned. It was a girl from school, a girl from the year below. They didn't know each other well. The girl worked in the Distillery at weekends. Her name was Olive. She had on a black parka jacket and her cheeks were pink.

Hi, said Jessie.

Can I ask you something?

Okay.

Here came Murphy with the ball in his mouth and he dropped it, heavy with saliva, to the stones. He reached his nose out to Olive and sniffed her sleeve and she opened her hand and he licked her finger then looked at Jessie and started to bark.

For God's sake, she said, and bent and threw the ball hard as she could.

Olive watched the dog run. Is it a boy or a girl?

Boy.

What's his name?

Murphy.

I've always wanted a dog. How old is he?

Six. You can borrow him if you like.

The dog was back and Jessie scooped the ball out of his mouth before he could bark and she threw it away then wiped her hand again on her trousers.

Do you sit next to Harry Duncan in English?

Jessie thought about the boy's blonde messy hair and his cold lips in the bus stop.

Yes.

Olive exhaled through her nostrils and looked out to the water. Has he asked you out?

Why? Jessie felt a rush of heat in her chest.

Please just tell me if he has.

No, he hasn't asked me out.

Murphy was back, shaking from side to side, a string of drool hanging from his mouth. Jessie took the ball and pitched it up and punted it with her right foot, bouncing far down the beach.

Well, do you think he wants to ask you out?

I've no idea.

Because he actually goes out with me. So if he wants to go out with you then I need to know about it. That's something I think I should know about.

Jessie felt spit pooling on her tongue and swallowed it quickly. You and Harry go out together?

Yes but nobody knows. He said he didn't want me to tell anyone. That it was a secret. Nobody else's business. Olive hugged her arms around herself and rubbed at her nose.

How long have you been going out?

Murphy was back and he dropped the ball and barked at Jessie. She turned to him. No, she screamed. Bad dog, no. Get! She pointed down the beach and he looked behind him but didn't move. His tail began to wag.

Six months, said Olive.

It's been a secret for six months?

I go over to his house. We don't go out out. Just spend time in his room.

I lied to you. I don't know why. I was embarrassed. He did ask me out.

Olive stared. The dark hair was tangled in strands across her face and her lips looked dry and chapped.

So what did you say?

I didn't say I would. I never agreed to it.

I can't believe he's done this to me.

I'm sorry.

This is why he wanted me to keep the whole thing a secret.

So he could do this. Go behind my back and make me look like an idiot. What else did he say?

He kissed me. We kissed. I didn't know you were going out with him. I wouldn't have done it if I knew.

Olive's face stretched and her eyes creased closed then. She started to cry like a child. Mouth open and tears running down her skin and deep gasps.

I'm sorry, said Jessie, and she put her arms out to hug the girl.

But Olive pushed her hands away. Her breath coming in short gasps.

You should dump him.

So that you can have him all to yourself?

No. I'm going to tell him to get lost as well. We should both dump him.

Will you?

Yes.

Do you promise? Do you promise you're not just saying this and that you're going to be going out with him in a week's time?

I promise.

Olive turned and covered her face with her little hands and walked back up the beach towards the road.

Wait, Jessie shouted, but her voice was carried off on the wind. She felt a warm touch at her knee and looked down. The tennis ball perfectly equidistant between her two feet. She caught the keen look in Murphy's eye, and the dog began to bark again.

84

A mild afternoon, and Alice was clearing out her classroom after a day of lessons. The pile of unmarked jotters on her desk where the children had written stories. A plastic folder stuffed with poetry analysis that she was supposed to score. Then she had reports to write and then she had to fill in her termly personal evaluation log.

She had unbuttoned the top of her blouse and rolled up her sleeves but still the heat from the early summer afternoon was too much. So she also had the windows open full although it was unclear how much of the breeze was making its way in. The room had a smell of bodies from all the children that had come and gone throughout the day.

She had to stay until five o'clock because one of the directors of education from the local authority was coming to have a meeting with her and the headteacher about her professional conduct. There had been more complaints. About how she dressed and the language she used but mainly about the mouse. She had told them the children were lying about the whole thing.

As she moved around the classroom adjusting the desks so that their edges lined up neatly and the chairs were properly tucked in she became aware of another smell in the room. A faint burning. Not close, not near. Something in the air that she could barely identify.

In front of her floated a flake of something, and for a moment she thought it was snow. It moved like snow. Coming through the open windows there were more and more of these flakes, some fine like dust, others thicker and more substantial. The smell of burning hung heavily in the classroom now.

Alice looked out the windows and she could see up to the distant hills from here, half a mile up from the village. The hills which were no more than rolling miles of marsh and bogs and heather, with little relics of stone dykes and ancient fenceposts.

She could see now that the hills were on fire. Miles of horizon carried the brilliant blaze of the fire and above this the sky was filled with black, thick, moving clouds of smoke. It burled up from the burning heather and curled in the sky as it cooled and then it was floating down across towards the village of Cullrothes in that gentle summer breeze, bringing a blizzard of burnt ash to float and settle down.

Mrs Hughes had told Alice she should invite her union representative to join them for the meeting. But Alice had chosen not to. She didn't want this to get out any further than it needed to. Last week a lawyer had managed to get through to her on the telephone with the news that her father was getting out of prison. He was getting early release for good behaviour. There would be parole conditions which included not contacting his daughter but the lawyer wanted to let Alice know for full disclosure. He was getting out and Alice knew he would want to come and find her.

The heather burned and the flames seemed to get bolder and higher. Alice watched it from her classroom and she left the window open. Allowing the soot and burnt ash in. It settled on her blouse and on her bare arms. In her hair and upon her face. On the neat school desks and on the unmarked jotters and poetry papers that she had set aside. She opened her mouth and let the bitter little flakes land and dissolve on her tongue.

In the morning the air was clouded and misty with the fumes and the smoke from the burning heather. Brian and Craig met at the red postbox to walk down the Shore Road together. They stood in their fluorescent vests and looked away towards the hills.

Hasn't stopped all night, said Brian.

Is it still going?

Aye it's still going.

That's no right.

It's just going to keep on spreading. Brian looked up at the cloudless sky. No sign of rain.

They reckon it'll come at the weekend.

Brian kicked a pebble from the pathway on to the road. It might come at the weekend, he conceded. Aye, aye, aye.

They stood looking for a while longer at the long thin ridge of burning heather up on the hills, at how the flames descended at times and then reached skywards again, always pumping out that black thick smoke.

Fire service'll have to deal with it, said Craig finally.

There's only two chances the firemen have got wi putting that out, said Brian. Fat chance and no chance.

That's an old one, Dad.

The old ones are the best ones. You'll figure that out one day.

By the way, I meant to talk to you about something.

On you go.

I've been offered another job. Working with BT doing repairs on their masts and phone lines.

Like an engineer?

A trainee engineer.

But you don't know how to fix any of those things.

That's what the training will be for. It's better hours and more money and I can work my way up. I'll be able to spend more time at home. Me and Gillian, we're thinking about starting a family. Trying to have a baby.

That's good, son.

I don't want you to feel like I'm leaving you in the lurch here with the ferry. I'll work my notice.

Fine, fine, fine. Don't worry about it.

I'll speak to the skipper today.

Aye, aye, aye.

This has been good though. It's been good to spend this time with you. Feels like we got a chance to get to know each other again as grown-ups.

Brian nodded and looked up. There were gulls circling above their heads and one of them dropped a mussel it had picked up from the rocks. The shell came hurtling down out of the sky and cracked hard on the top of Craig's head.

Ah ya bandit, he shouted, and gripped his scalp with both hands.

What a shot that was, laughed Brian. He pointed at his son and looked up at the gull still circling and bent over laughing until his belly hurt.

Craig picked up the mussel, which had not broken, and threw it back at the gull. But the bird was too high and the mussel fell uselessly into the water.

The two men stood smiling and looking back towards the skyline that was filled with smoke.

You coming? Brian asked.

85

Jessie stood at the window looking through the glass at the torrential rain bouncing off the road. She zipped up her jacket and lifted the hood although she knew it was not waterproof. When she opened the door and stepped outside the fierce wind and the water it carried hit her face and caught in her throat so that she gasped then jammed her hands in her pockets and walked quickly down the garden and gasped again when she got to the gate.

Harry's house was out of the village, an old farm building with a neat garden and it took Jessie half an hour to walk there in the unrelenting rain. Before she was halfway there her shoes had filled with cold water and the jacket was letting in the rain up and down its seams. She felt it soaking into her vest and through to her skin. Her jeans were soaked, sticking to her legs and heavy.

She pressed the doorbell and waited. Through the frosted glass there was light. A figure stood at some distance and looked at her through the distorted glass and then there were voices shouting. A door slammed shut. Finally a woman answered.

Is Harry in?

He's in his room.

I'd like to speak to him.

Yes, said the woman, yes. Come in. She opened the door wider and Jessie took a step in and stood dripping water into the carpet.

Harry, shouted the woman. Harry! There's someone here for you.

Who is it? The boy's voice was distant.

It's a girl. Someone from school. Will you come down here! Jessie smiled and wiped the rainwater from her nose.

Oh, you're drenched. Can I hang your jacket up?

I'm not staying.

Oh. Terrible weather isn't it.

Yes.

Have you been out walking in that for long?

I walked from the village.

Oh. The woman looked over Jessie's shoulder to the closed door. It's supposed to be like this all night.

There were loud footsteps on the staircase.

Well, here he is.

Yes.

I'll leave you to it.

Thank you.

Can I get you a tea?

No thanks. I'm not staying.

Right. Maybe I should drive you home?

That's very kind, but no thanks.

Well. Okay, then.

Harry reached the bottom of the stairs and when he saw Jessie he stopped where he was. He had on light grey jogging trousers and white sports socks with dirty soles. A baggy black t-shirt and his hair was greasy and flat on his head.

Jessie, he said. What are you doing here?

She's here to see you, said the woman.

Can you leave us alone?

I thought I'd get you both a glass of orange juice.

Just leave us alone.

The woman raised her hands in defeat and smiled at Jessie and went through to the kitchen.

Are you wanting to come upstairs, babe? asked Harry.

No.

It could be fun.

Definitely not.

Harry stepped forward and brushed the wet hair from her face and looked at her up and down.

You're soaked through. Come upstairs. I'll get you a towel.

I don't want to go upstairs.

Hey, said Harry. He touched her underneath the chin and lifted her face to look up at him. Come here.

He bent to kiss her but she kept her lips shut and he moved his lips against her mouth for a moment and then stopped.

Get off, she said quietly.

But I'm excited to see you. I'm happy you're here.

This isn't a social visit.

What is it then?

Olive came to see me.

Who's Olive? He stepped back and crossed his arms across his chest and tensed his eyebrows together.

Olive's your girlfriend, Harry.

I don't have a girlfriend. Who told you that? She's not my girlfriend. If you mean Olive McGhee. She's a liar. I wouldn't even go near her.

Stop it, said Jessie.

Stop what? This is stupid.

How is it?

I can't believe this. Is this why you came to see me?

I came here to tell you to stay away from me. Sit somewhere else in class. Don't phone me again. Forget you even know my number.

Harry ran his hands through his dirty hair and his face was turning pink. Fine, he said. No bother to me. I don't even like you that much anyway. I don't even know what I was thinking trying to get with a tink like you.

Jessie smiled at this. Fine, she said. That suits me just fine.

Right, said Harry. He pulled at the seams of his t-shirt and looked over Jessie's shoulder through the frosted glass where they could hear the rain still hitting the ground. Well I suppose you better go then.

In a minute. But I just wanted to say. That girl, Olive. She's a nice person. She told me how you treat her. Like she's a dirty secret. Start behaving properly, Harry. How would your mum feel if she knew how you treated girls? Would that make her proud? Would she put up with it?

Whatever you say. Just go.

I think you're pathetic, said Jessie. A pathetic wee boy.

She opened the door and left the warmth of the house. The cold struck her again with fresh rainwater leaking into her shoes and across her shoulders. She heard the door closing hard behind her and she looked up at the sky, the impenetrable blackness, with the raindrops coming out of nowhere and landing on her eyeballs and she blinked these away and the rainwater ran down her cheeks and she licked at it and began the long walk home again.

86

A beautiful sunset turning the sky the colour of marmalade and watermelons with some low dark charcoal clouds. Up at the Cat's Back it might have been another planet. Moodie took a slow walk around the boundary of the gravelled car park with his hands in his pockets and ate a banana and threw the skin away into the gorse. He had walked up here from the village and it had not taken him as long as he'd thought.

Moodie had found out about Young Bobby's body from Galloway. Galloway didn't say who had told him but it was a personal matter for now. Not part of the police investigation into the boy's disappearance, although that investigation had tailed off after Christmas. Galloway thought that Donald deserved to find out about it from a friend.

Young Bobby had never been someone Moodie warmed to, although he had known him since he was a baby. A good baby he had been, too. Smiling and chipper. Moodie remembered going over to the manse one night when Margo had gone out to visit friends. He looked after the baby with Donald. The boy was only about six months old. Fine dark hair on his head and chubby legs. He had been screaming for something and when Donald went to warm up the bottle of milk in the kitchen

Moodie had taken the baby under the armpits and held him up above his head. The crying stopped. Then Moodie shoogled the baby up and down and bounced his feet on the bed. A smile. Then Moodie flopped the baby down onto the bed and kissed his tummy, nipping at his ribs softly with his teeth and pursing his lips on the skin around the belly button. Bobby had grabbed at Moodie's hair with his two hands and he had laughed, a deep instinctive chuckle. He had been a good baby. But as he grew up Moodie never warmed to him. A spoiled boy who turned into a bully.

Donald's black Range Rover appeared over the crest of the hill and turned into the car park and crunched over the gravel and stopped at the best viewpoint. There was a sign put up here for tourists to show them what they were looking at down below – what direction was the lighthouse and the names of the mountains to the north and the south.

The door opened and closed and Donald was standing there looking unsteady. His face and head were usually kept smoothly shaven but they had grown stubbled and his eyes had dark rings around them. When he stepped closer, Moodie noticed that he was limping.

What's this all about, asked Donald. What have you dragged me up here for?

I heard something you need to know about.

Could you not have phoned me?

I wanted to tell you this face to face in private.

Go on then.

Your son's dead. He was killed in a fight and he's buried behind the hotel. I don't know who did it yet.

Donald put his hands in his pockets and then took them out again and used them to cover his face and rub at his eyes. He turned away from Moodie and then back to him. When he spoke his voice was low and tired: Where are you getting this from?

Galloway.

Galloway's found him?

He only found out about it. He hasn't been to see if the body's there. The gates are locked and the grounds are still boarded up.

So it might not be true?

It might not be true.

Donald walked halfway back to his car and then changed his mind. What about the American? he said. I told you I wanted you to bring him in.

He's gone.

Gone where?

No idea.

Well thank God you're on the case, Robert. Thank God I've got you as my right-hand man. Just a bunch of rumours and innuendo and big fat nothings with you, isn't it?

Take it down a notch, said Moodie.

You don't tell me what to do, you useless big fuck.

Moodie put his hands behind his back and lifted his chin up and said: You got something you want to say to me?

Aye. See this? Us? We're done. You're out. Hear me? Finished?

That's fine. But I hate to tell you this. But you're the one who's finished.

What are you on about?

You lost your son and you lost respect and soon you're going to lose your business. Lose your home. And if she's got any sense you're going to lose your wife as well. But maybe the Americans will let you keep her.

Donald came up to Moodie and stuck his forehead right

under the bigger man's chin. What do you know about the Americans?

Get out of my face.

Tell me what you're talking about with these bloody Americans.

Get out of my face right now.

Are you in on this?

Moodie smiled and his tongue snaked from between his lips and he spat in Donald's face.

Donald reached up and tried to grab Moodie in a headlock but Moodie was too big. He easily threw Donald over his shoulder and when Donald landed heavy on the gravel Moodie kicked him hard between the legs. Donald whined and reached down and so his face was unprotected and Moodie punted it, kicking up a cloud of gravel and embedding little shards of the grit into Donald's cheeks and eyes. He lay there coughing and spluttering out blood from his mouth.

Moodie looked the short distance to the edge of the viewpoint and gave consideration to throwing Donald from it down onto the rocks. He gave consideration to killing Donald there.

But instead Moodie picked up his rucksack and disappeared over a fence into the gorse. It was much darker now and the sky was clouding over but he knew the way down. He had gone down this way before.

87

Olive slammed the car door and started the engine and wept. The tears hot on her cheeks. Wiping her nose on the back of her hand. Her chest rising shallowly and heaving as she gasped for breath. Feeling her lips split as her head hung forward and then wrenched backwards. Hearing her own voice loud, pathetic, the tone in her throat like an animal's. The settling breath as her cheeks dried. Blowing the wetness from her nose and touching the tissue to the corners of her eyes. Tying her hair back out of her hot face and looking ahead and starting to drive.

She drove slowly and turned left at the end of the road. As she switched gear from first to second the engine thumped and stalled and her clavicles snapped against the seatbelt. The car behind her sounded its horn then pulled out and drove past her very fast and swerved back into the lane. She turned the engine off and then back on again, and used first gear to pull away for a second time.

Olive drove carefully round the winding roads towards the village and Shona's Cafe. The road was quiet and she drove in third gear and then tried fourth. After a while she turned the radio on and sang loudly along with the music and banged the heels of her palms against the steering wheel.

She drove fast into the car park at the cafe and hit the brakes hard. The car rocked forwards and then back. Her face was dry now and the blood pulsed in her ears. She pulled up the handbrake and turned down the radio. Sat there in the seat with the engine running and looked out the window. Shona's Café had wide tall windows on two sides so that diners could look across the water. It was lit with warm lamps and even from here you could smell the cooking. Olive could see Harry sitting at a table near the window with his mother.

She got out from the car and picked up the jumper from the passenger seat. It was a jumper he had left behind in her bedroom. She remembered him with his red face saying how it was too hot in there. How he'd pulled it over his head and his shirt had ridden up with it and she'd seen his bare stomach. He had left it with her. To remind her of him, he said. She had sniffed this jumper and held it close to her on the pillow in her bed at night. Here now in the car park looking at him through the café window she sniffed the jumper again and the smell did still remind her of him.

The café door was heavy and Olive pushed against it with her shoulder and the warmth and the smell of the place hit her. It smelled of good Sunday dinners and there was the Gaelic radio station bubbling in the background and big chalkboards hung on the walls with details of the day's special dishes.

Shona was an elderly woman who had owned the café since almost anybody in the village could remember. She had a kind smile and always greeted each customer as they arrived. She was wiping down a table and she called over to Olive: Sitting in or taking away?

I'm joining them, said Olive, pointing.

I'll come and get your order in a minute, dear.

Harry saw that Olive had arrived and he said something to his mother and she got up from her chair. She squinted and looked at Olive.

Hello Olive. Did you get a lift here? Where's your mum?

She dropped me off. She's coming back later.

Won't all this be easier once you two start driving for yourselves?

Yes.

I keep nagging at Harry to sort out his provisional licence. But you know what he's like.

Yes.

Are you okay? You look upset.

I'm fine, thanks.

I'll be sitting over there. No rush. Harry's mother waved a paperback book in Olive's face and smiled. I'm desperate to finish this tonight.

Good luck.

Harry's mother asked Shona to bring her a coffee and she took a table at the other side of the café to give the young couple some privacy.

Olive looked at Harry sitting there. He had ordered each of them a milkshake and he was wearing a denim shirt and his hair was damp as though he'd showered and not bothered to dry it. His arms were crossed.

Olive, he said. Did you drive here? I think I saw you parking the car.

I only came here to give you this back. She threw the boy's jumper at him.

What's that? No, I said you could hang on to it.

I don't want it anymore.

Why don't you sit down? We can talk about this.

I know what you've done, she said. Her voice sounded calm and controlled but her fingernails were digging painfully into

386

the palms of her hands. I know that you're lying to me. I know why you've wanted to keep me a secret all this time. It's done. We're done.

There was a middle-aged couple sitting at the table next to them eating pink steaks and sharing a bottle of wine. It was clear that they could hear what Olive was saying and they stared at one another tactfully, chewing.

Olive, said Harry. He uncrossed his arms and put his hands flat out on the table and leaned back in his chair. When he spoke his voice was low and soft. What's this all about? What's happened? Sit down. Talk to me. I bought us milkshakes.

I don't want to sit down. I don't want to talk to you. I'm not going to be your dirty little secret anymore. You can't tell me what to do.

You were never a secret.

I was so.

Come here. Let's talk about this.

You're a loser, she said. And I'm going to make sure everyone knows how big a loser you are.

Olive turned and walked out the café towards the car without looking back. It was a yellow Fiat her father had bought for her older sister to learn in. The tears were springing from her eyes again so she did not look back even when he called her name. She heard no footsteps following her. He banged his hands against the café window but she was unlocking the car door. Her hand holding the keys shook as she found the lock.

Fine, shouted Harry from the doorway. His mother was standing behind him with her hand on his shoulder and in the café Shona was watching with her hands on her hips. Fine, be like that. You silly wee tart. I never even liked you anyway. No wonder I kept you a secret. His voice was high and it caught in the air and floated up and away from her, carrying into the night. Good luck finding someone else who'll put up with you, Olive! Because there's nobody roundabouts here who will! Nobody.

He was still shouting all of these things when she slumped into the driver's seat and pulled the door closed. His voice was muffled now but she still heard its shrill tone. When the engine started it drowned his voice out even more but it was still there. And when she pulled down the driveway, it followed her. It followed her out onto the road, round a bend, and another, as she accelerated and checked her mirrors then remembered to turn her headlights on. She could still hear Harry's awful voice in her head even out there.

The circuit of Olive's driving lessons had never ventured far out of the village. She was used to driving at 30mph along the Shore Road towards the ferry then doubling back. Watching out for other cars and people walking on the road where the path disappeared. But the traffic was quiet at this time of night. She followed the road towards the Cat's Back and sat at 50mph with her full beam lights on and no other cars passed her and she wound the window down an inch and let the night air dry her face and cool her skin.

She parked at the beauty spot at the Cat's Back and got out of the car and sat at a picnic table looking out over the Atlantic Ocean. The mountain dropped steeply down from here and when she had been a little girl one of the local men had jumped from here.

She heard that he did not die straight away but was still alive when they picked him up in a helicopter and still alive when they flew him to the hospital on the mainland. She heard that they held his body and his organs and intestines together with tight bandaging and that he would die if they ever loosened it. His insides would just flop out. She had not questioned it then as she was just a little girl. This was the first time she had thought about it for years and she had never questioned it. But now it seemed obvious that the story was made up. She knew the man had died eventually and that he had never come home or got out of the hospital again after jumping from the Cat's Back.

It began to get cold and she wandered back to the car. She wondered where to drive to now. Now that she was out it seemed that she might as well keep going. Here she was at the westernmost point. Maybe she should drive east now, towards the ferry, towards the mainland, and then she could say she had driven the width of this slab of land that was her home.

There was one other car parked up at the other end. A black Range Rover with its engine off. Olive walked towards it avoiding the waterlogged potholes to see if there was anyone there. She did not know why she did this.

Then just out of her eyeline she heard groaning. A man's groaning. She walked around the Range Rover and saw him there with filth all over his face and blood dried around his nostrils. Lying on his side wheezing and grogging into the gravel.

Are you okay? she whispered.

The man's eyes popped wide and he snarled at her and started scrabbling at the ground with his fingernails to pull himself up.

Olive took a step back and leaned over to get a better look at him. Do you need help? she asked.

He made it onto his knees and he reached out and grabbed her by the ankle. Where's Moodie? he hissed. Moodie!

Olive kicked at the man's wrist but his grip was tight so she lifted her boot into his throat instead. He fell back coughing and hissing with his hands around his neck and he stumbled upright onto his feet and staggered towards her.

Olive ran to her car and managed to get the key turned quick and the engine rattled. The doors locked automatically and the man clawed at her window as she found gear and pushed her feet down so that the old car lurched back onto the road.

88

Moodie made quick progress through the gorse and the heather down the slopes towards the Shore Road. He knew the route by memory and the sound of the wildlife scuttling around him was comforting. There was the rustle of mice as his footsteps disturbed them. There was the pulsing wingbeat of an owl somewhere in the sky to his left. There in the distance was the noise perhaps of two stags duelling, their antlers rubbing up against one another like old wooden swords. It was still light and the rain was coming and going but Moodie had everything he needed on his back.

The time had come to leave the place of his birth. Johnny Coca-Cola's disappearance had spooked him and Donald's spiralling paranoia was a warning. Moodie was headed for the mainland where he could book into a bed and breakfast, relax for a few days, and try to get in touch with his American contacts. The Distillery takeover was now a certainty. Donald was running at a loss and no longer had the confidence of the locals.

He reached the Shore Road and crossed it and passed into the cover of the forest. He could follow the tracks in here that wound between the trees as far as the ferry, which he would not be travelling on. It was a long hike around the loch that would take until the next day but he needed to stay unseen and unheard.

89

Spitting out blood and dirt Donald climbed into the Range Rover and started the engine. He reversed and turned in the car park at the Cat's Back and accelerated back into the road without indicating or switching on his headlights. His breath coming in short, sore little gasps and the palms of his hands leaving drops of blood on the steering wheel.

He moved up through the gears fast and took the corners hard. Thinking of his boy. Thinking if it was true. He had to find out. Flying down the road on his right-hand side there was a young fawn the colour of shortbread hopping off the road into the ditch just as he screamed past, its black eyes twisted backwards to watch the car go past. For a split second he almost swerved to hit it.

The roads were winding and soon up ahead he saw the red brake lights of a yellow Fiat, taking it easy round one bend and then another. Donald bore down fast on the car and then had to touch his own brakes, groaning as his shoulders took the tension. He flashed his lights and held his fist against the horn but the road was a single track here and he could not get past without the Fiat pulling over.

The road straightened out and Donald pushed down into the

accelerator, almost lifting himself out of his seat, until he was so close to the Fiat he could no longer see the licence plate over his bonnet. The yellow Fiat did begin to speed up on this straight road and as the driver in front accelerated so did he. He could see the head in the mirror turning over its shoulder. It must be the girl from the car park. But he had no thoughts for her. He only needed to find out if this was true what Moodie had said about Young Bobby.

There was another bend coming up and here the road widened just enough for him to pass. Donald knew the road fine. He switched on his fog lights and sustained them and hit the horn again in short blasts to tell the girl to get out his way. He saw the yellow Fiat swerve a little on the tarmac. The red brake lights that were so close they lit up the inside of his own car. Then the road widened and he swung to the right, feeling his tyres mounting the grassy bank at the side of the road, and he accelerated.

The gap between the cars was narrow enough as Donald passed that he could almost have reached over with his hand and touched the girl's shoulder if he had wanted to.

He pulled back in front of the yellow Fiat just in time to miss scraping alongside an ancient farmer's wall with white blobs of sheep on the other side. The Range Rover rocked from side to side as he steadied himself and straightened the wheel and let the engine open up so he could tear forwards. He glanced in his rear-view mirror but the yellow Fiat's headlights were not there. He tried his wing mirror and saw the car was airborne, twisting as it fell like a gymnast struggling for the perfect landing. He heard the crash as the Fiat landed but by then he had lost sight of it and his foot twitched at the brake pedal but no more than that.

90

Jessie spoke to one of the nurses outside in the hallway before she went into Grandpa's room.

Back again? asked the nurse.

Starting to feel like I live here, said Jessie.

Join the club.

How is he?

He's comfortable.

Has he been awake?

Not for a few days.

What are you doing about it?

This is normal.

Is this just what's going to happen?

It's different for everyone. But it's normal for them to sleep more and more and not wake very often.

Can I wake him?

You can try.

But he's comfortable?

He's comfortable.

You don't think he's in any pain.

We can't tell.

But what do you think?

I don't think he's in any pain.

At least that's something.

To be honest. At this stage. It's everything.

When Jessie went into Grandpa's room it was dark but she could see his silhouette lying in the bed and he turned his head to look at her. He saw it was her and he inched his weight backwards and upwards until he was sitting up a little.

She clicked on the floor lamp. Grandpa raised his hand to shield his eyes. It had been a long time since his hair was cut and his fingernails were long with pointed white tips.

You're awake, she said brightly.

He kept his hand up to shield his face from the light and stared at her.

She walked closer to him and then sat down. Made eye contact with the tiny old man.

Oh, he said then. Jessie, good God it's nice to see you.

I can't believe you're awake.

Grandpa shrugged his shoulders as though it were of no consequence.

How are you feeling?

He shrugged again, and Jessie could not read the look he intended on his face.

I'll get you some water, she said.

Oh, he whispered. Oh yes please.

She gave him the paper cup and he held it carefully and she helped to guide the hand to his lips. He drank a little and swirled it around in his mouth and then looked around, eyes moving across everything.

What do you need?

He pointed to his mouth and she realised he wanted to spit the water out. She held up one of the paper buckets they kept in his room and he dribbled neatly into it through pursed lips.

Grandpa's face was as pale as pearls and the skin under his eyes was dark.

The nurse said you haven't been awake for a few days.

What day is it?

Sunday.

He raised his eyebrows.

Do you know what month it is?

No idea, he smiled, and then laughed, and then reached out his hand towards her and squeezed.

Can I ask you a favour? Jessie asked.

No harm in asking, he whispered.

I got this letter. It's from one of my university choices. St Andrews. I'm too nervous to open it myself.

That's a long way away.

That's the idea.

Grandpa nodded and held out his hand for the envelope. Jessie handed it to him. With her name typed on the front and the university crest stamped across the seal in navy ink. She watched Grandpa struggle with his dumb hands to open the envelope but knew he would not want help so she sat with her chin resting in her hands and the sound of a shrill ringing in her ears.

Finally the old man had torn the envelope and he picked out the letter and unfolded it. Squinted at it and looked around. Jessie handed him his glasses and he put these on then licked his thumb and stared at the typed correspondence with his mouth open a little.

What does it say?

He made a point of reading to the bottom and following the line with his forefinger and then going back to the top and taking a deep breath.

Grandpa!

They're making you an offer, he said. A conditional offer, it says here.

What conditions?

They want three Higher qualifications at grade A.

Three As?

Can you manage that?

Yes. Yes I think I can get that, Jessie said. I can't believe it.

St Andrews University, said Grandpa. That is a real university. I am so proud of you.

I'm not there yet. Don't jinx it.

How are you going to afford it?

I don't know yet. I'll have to apply for a student loan. There are bursaries available as well for people like me. Because Mum doesn't work it counts as a low-income background. Then when I get there I'll try to get a job in a shop or a pub maybe to keep myself going.

That doesn't sound easy, Grandpa said.

When is anything ever easy?

Grandpa sat in his bed looking at the letter, turning it over in his hands and re-reading the words and even mouthing some of them.

It says here the course starts in September, he said.

That's right.

I won't be around then to help.

That's not your fault.

I would like to help. Can you do me a favour?

Yes.

Ask one of the nurses to bring me the telephone. Then I want you to go and make yourself a coffee and sit outside for twenty minutes and let all of this sink in. Will you do that?

Okay.

With the telephone, Grandpa called his lawyer on the mainland. He had used the same guy for years and called him

398

at home. He gave instructions for his lawyer to sell Grandpa's shares in the Cullrothes Distillery at market value and then transfer the funds directly into his granddaughter Jessie Galloway's bank account. It was worth fifty thousand pounds once the lawyer had taken his fee and the money was in Jessie's account by the time Grandpa said thank you and God bless you and goodbye my old friend.

Grandpa was almost sleeping again when Jessie came back into the room. It had been an unusually stimulating evening for him by now.

He told Jessie what he had done and she cried and cried and hugged the old man.

No loans, no bursaries, no pish jobs, Grandpa said to her. I want you to do this the right way. Get the best out of it that you can.

I will, Jessie promised. I've got my camera in my bag. Do you think we could take a picture as a memento?

Okay, said Grandpa.

You don't mind?

I don't mind, said Grandpa. Jessie opened her bag and reached in to find her camera and as she did so Grandpa added: If that's what you want to do.

Jessie held up the camera and looked through its lens to make sure the composition was right. She set a ten-second timer and placed the camera on a shelf opposite the bed. Then she sat next to Grandpa and between them they held up the university's acceptance letter so that this was visible too. Grandpa's white hair stood on end messily from his head, and his eyes were only really half-open, and he smiled a false, unreal smile. The skin around his neck was loose and his t-shirt hung in folds from his shoulders. But he held the letter out and smiled for the camera, and it was the first time that he had been awake for some days. Afterwards Jessie took some more pictures of Grandpa on his own. She got some pictures of this fading old man but also the embodiment of bravery, such bravery.

They spoke about accommodation and travel arrangements and what Grandpa remembered of the beach at St Andrews from when he had holidayed in a caravan there in his youth, and then he began to rub at his eyes. Jessie kissed his face and told him that she'd be back to see him soon. It looked to her as if he was sleeping again before she'd even buttoned up her coat.

91

Onto his knees where the wet mud saturated his trousers and let the cold water coat the pale skin underneath. With his palm first turning aside the dead wet leaves and bits of torn tree bark and small stones at the surface of the grave. Then cupping his hands, making them shovels, and gripping at the compacted grains and sludge as he levered it to the side and made first a dent and then a divot and soon a small growing ditch. Breath coming hard and cold out of his body. A face that quickly was red and hot. His nose was wet and he wiped at it with his sleeve.

The months of rain and then cold over the winter had made the earth dense and stubborn.

Donald dislodged a good bit of jagged stone, and he gripped this thing in his fists and used it to chisel at the earth, chunks of mud spitting up out of the growing hole and hitting him in the stomach and the chest and the face. It was good, the ground was shifting as he stabbed at it, and he shuffled back away on his knees to start chipping away at the edges. Then his jagged piece of stone hit a bigger unseen stone, and it burst in his hands with a quiet dull crack. Donald shouted to himself and dropped the tool. He clutched his hands to his chest and rolled back onto his backside and looked at his hands which were black with mud and bleeding now, where the broken stone had entered the ragged skin.

Donald clenched his fists to stop the bleeding and get some sensitivity back into his frozen hands. There was a good high moon and he could see how the dirt mixed with his blood and he wondered if maybe it would infect him. But he didn't think so. There was something clean and pure in the way this mud felt.

It took a long time to dig down but finally Donald's cracked and crippled hands touched with the familiar texture of clothing. He looked into the grave he had dug out but could not make out any colours. He pulled at the cloth and began to clear the dirt away from around it and then something happened that was like a bath being unplugged, and his son's arm lifted from the earth and he could hold its solid girth in his hands.

Finally the boy's body came free. It was heavy and rigid and blackened. Donald touched the boy's chest. He wiped the filth away from the boy's eyes and mouth and cheeks. It was him and it still looked enough like him. But a poor model, an imperfect replica. And when the digging was over Donald just sobbed and roared about the whole thing, with his body so cold now that it might as well have no longer been there to support him.

92

Galloway drove quickly although he knew the girl would still be dead when he got there. Her car had come off the road and flipped and driven through an old stone wall into a farmer's field where there was grazing sheep. She must not have been wearing a seatbelt because her body had been spat through the windscreen and bounced and minced itself across the rough concrete. The farmer had phoned it in. No point sending the ambulance. He had looked at the girl and that was enough to know. Seen enough dead animals to recognise the signs. And now these sheep were wandering all over the place.

Galloway drove with the window wound down even though it was cold and wet. His hands felt numb and he gripped the steering wheel hard as he took the corners.

There were sheep on the road as far as half a mile away from the farm. They stood staring at him from the muddy verge. They gathered in twos and threes as though this would protect them from the car. Galloway dropped into second gear and flashed his fog lights and touched his horn but some of the animals still stood obstinately in the road, and these ones he steered towards and budged them roughly out of the way with the car's bumper.

The farmer was at the side of the road now with his collie. The dog sat, looking bored, waiting for the call or the whistle which would tell him which deeply ingrained instructions to carry through. The farmer had a thick length of rope across his shoulder and his trousers were slick with mud up to the kneecaps.

That you here, he said to Galloway. Took your sweet time about it.

Ferry's off, said Galloway. What'd you want me to do, fly over the water?

Seen all these buggers? said the farmer. He kicked at a sheep's legs as it began wandering onto the road. I'm going to be out here all night. It'll take all night to get them back in.

That's bad luck for you isn't it, said Galloway.

And that wall's not going to fix itself, is it? continued the farmer. Wait till you see it. Ruins. Just ruins.

Galloway started inching the car forwards again. It's a sore one to take, he said. Where's the girl?

Just up the way. I put a sheet over her.

Did you?

Aye, well. She looked so little.

Galloway drove on, and now the sheep seemed a little more respectful of his passing, standing to the side and bending their heads down to the grass.

When he got to the girl she was as stiff and cold as a piece of meat from the freezer. A smear of blood and ragged flesh trailing the road where she'd hit. He took the sheet away. It was an old bedsheet with a light pink floral pattern. Now stained the colour of rust. She was face down on the road and from above she looked okay. She looked okay. Dark hair covered most of the abrasions and you couldn't see the horror of her face. Her arms were spread out in front, as though she had put up her hands to try and soften the landing.

Galloway left her and found the car nearby where it had battered through the farmer's wall and into the field. It lay on its back and there was a long furrow dug into the soil where it had landed and bounced. He had a torch and he switched this on and looked at the car, crushed like a fistful of foil. The wall's stones were piled and spread around it. Then he swept the light onto the road's surface and examined the tyre marks scorched black on the concrete. He stood at the corner and looked up and down at where the girl had driven from, back up the road where she had been conscious and freely travelled upon, to this spot where something catastrophic had fallen upon her, to the road ahead in the direction she had intended.

He went back to the girl's body and rolled her from her front onto her back. She moved easily, being so stiff and so light now. He may as well have been moving a doll. He shone the light down at the awful ruined body and the terrible things that had happened to her face. Quickly and quietly he threw up into the ditch at the opposite side of the road.

Later when the dark started to turn and the morning light was blending in, the farmer came with some boards of wood to block up the breach in his wall. Galloway had already put away the tape measure and the camera and written up his report of the accident. The farmer's sheep were back in the field, herded through an iron gate half a mile up the road, although some had vanished into the forest, and at least one had taken a bad fall among some rocks near the beach and now lay bleating with its front legs broken and the tide coming in around it.

Still here, he asked Galloway.

Need to wait. They'll come and get her once the ferry's running.

I could wait for them.

No thanks. I need to take care of her.

The girl lay there still underneath the patterned bedsheet. A crow was circling the body, and it swooped down now and then, close to the blood that lay congealed on the road, not yet brave enough to land so close to the men to pick at the bits of meat.

It is a shame, said the farmer, as though only just accepting this now. He lined up a fence post and hit it on the top with a fat hammer to push it into the soil.

Do you recognise her? said Galloway.

Thought I did. But it was dark when I saw her. He lined up another fence post and drove this one into the ground, level with the first.

I need to get her off the road, said Galloway. In case anybody's out early.

Should I help?

We just need to lay her down by the side there.

So Galloway tucked the bedsheet properly underneath the dead girl's shoulders and underneath her ankles. He took one end and the farmer took the other, each man bent quite low and with bent knees so that she barely cleared the concrete. They placed her down gently as if she were only asleep and they meant not to wake her.

Once the body was out of the way, Galloway sat in his car with the engine running and the heating on. Watched the farmer quickly nail some boards parallel to the ground between the two fenceposts so there was a temporary replacement for the wall. Then watched as the crow finally summoned the courage to come down. The black thing lifted its feet carefully and pecked at the bits of blood and skin the girl had left on the concrete; the car windows were closed but Galloway could still hear its beak clicking and scraping on the surface.

93

Alice got so seriously into yoga that she was considering putting on a weekly class in the village hall for the locals to come to. She was passionate and wanted to share her practice with others. Having this time off work was good. She had started journaling again. Given up smoking, even though Innes was no longer there to police her. Her skin was looking clear and she felt sharp and young.

They were calling it full suspension pending an investigation into her professional conduct. She was still getting her full salary and the teaching union had provided a lawyer to talk things over. Eventually there would be a hearing at the General Teaching Council's headquarters in Edinburgh. Alice looked forward to the day out.

Innes was refusing to see her. He said that the engagement was over. His hospital ward only allowed a pre-approved list of visitors in each day and he had omitted her name from it. But Alice wasn't worried. He could not avoid her forever. And she knew that once she got a chance to see him – once *he* got a chance to see *her* – that this silly break-up thing would be off and they could start planning their wedding over again.

She was in the kitchen of their little bungalow making

scones. The school was having a bake sale and Alice was determined to remain part of the community. Patricia had agreed to come and pick up the scones and deliver them to the gym hall; Alice was forbidden from entering the premises or having any contact with the children for now.

The scone mixture was crumbling between her fingertips, like fine sand, sticking and glueing beneath her fingernails. The telephone rang and she had to wash up before she got to it.

Yes? she said.

Can I speak with Alice Green?

This is she.

My name is Caitlin Moore. I'm your father's probation officer.

Okay.

I'm calling to inform you of your father's imminent release from Her Majesty's custody.

Alice picked at the drying scone crumbs on her apron. Okay, she said again.

As a direct family member I wanted to alert you to the reality that your father may try to contact you once he is released.

How?

Well, he might write to you or try to find your telephone number. He could even try to visit you in person. I want you to feel safe if this happens. Your father has served his sentence and our experts are confident that his rehabilitation means there is no risk to you or others.

That's good.

But if he does reach out, you should know that I am here to support any re-connections. Can I give you my telephone number?

Of course.

Do you have a pen and paper handy?

I do.

The probation officer recited her telephone number and Alice pretended to write it down all the while making affirmative noises and examining the dough stuck to her wrist.

Did you get that okay?

Perfectly, lied Alice. What did you say your name was again?

Caitlin Moore.

Caitlin Moore, said Alice slowly, as if she was writing this down too.

If you need anything at all, you can call. Your father is being released at the end of the month.

Thank you, Caitlin. I really appreciate it.

Alice hung up the telephone and went back to her scone mixture. She crumbed it between her fingers and cracked two eggs into a bowl of milk. She whisked these together and poured the mixture into the dry ingredients. Before combining it all, she stared out the window at the long grass and weedy driveway, and let a long dribble of spit fall from her mouth into the mixing bowl.

94

Days in the Southern General hospital in Glasgow were as slow as coastal erosion. There was a rhythm to the day that took some getting used to. The nervous excitement of the doctor's rounds. The chaos that came with lunchtime. The desperate longing for company and the anticlimax that each visitor brought with them.

Innes had a small rotation of visitors that came each day. His mother, who could barely conceal her delight that he was going to be moving back in with her. His sister, who seemed to treat the thing as some kind of biblical consequence that he'd had coming for years. A couple of friends from school who sat and stared at the stump of his leg and shook their heads and spoke about football players or video games as if these were the most important things in the world.

It was over with Alice. Innes wondered what kind of relationship he had been in for this to be a better alternative to marrying her. Valentine was welcome to her now. He had not spoken to her and he would not ever again. Any time he felt lonely the void at the end of his leg was enough to shake off the desire to call her. She didn't even know what had happened out there in the woods. He hoped she never found out. Every night Innes had nightmares about Young Bobby and the fire at the hotel, and he never wanted to see anyone or anything from that village again.

In the bed opposite Innes was a funny Glaswegian man called Paddy. He'd already had one leg amputated a year or two ago and he was in now to get his other one done. They were going to do it in a couple of days. It was clots caused by smoking. Paddy loved to smoke. He would light up and smoke a fag right in the ward if they'd let him – that's what he'd say to anyone who listened, as if his defiance was something to be admired. Sometimes Innes's mother would let Paddy use her as a crutch and she would help him to hop down the ward and into the lifts and out to the courtyard at the exit doors so he could light up and smoke his fags down there in peace.

Alice had phoned the hospital a few times until Innes asked the nurses if they had a way of blocking her number. Now nobody phoned for him and that seemed okay. He could live with it.

95

A grey day and the sky marbled with black streaks along the edges of the clouds and the sun was trying to burn through. Margo woke up on her own at midday. Donald's side of the bed was cold and his pillows still neat. She leaned over and looked to see if he was on the floor but no. She could not believe the time and had not slept for this long in months.

She put on her slippers and went downstairs to make coffee for herself. Through the frosted windows of the wide front door was a flashing blue light. She looked quickly into the kitchen and the living room to see if her husband was there before she opened the door to see what was going on.

Donald's Range Rover was parked in the middle of the lawn, its tyres leaving ugly scars in the well-kept green grass. Its front wheels were turned at an angle giving the impression that Donald had not been in control when he stopped here. Looking down the driveway there were plant pots and garden gnomes knocked over and cracked. A police van and several cars and an ambulance filled up the rest of the drive and were mounted up on the grass next to the Range Rover. Police officers surrounded the car and stood about speaking into their radios and writing in notepads.

What is it? said Margo, walking to the lawn. Her slippers suddenly soaked through with the ground still so wet.

Please stay there, said a young police officer. He held out his hand.

But Margo kept on walking.

Please ma'am, said the young officer.

But she ignored him again.

Donald was sitting up in the driver's seat of the Range Rover. His face was scarred and bruised and his head lolled to the side. He was utterly wasted and there were bottles of whisky and bags of powder sitting on the dashboard.

Next to him, strapped carefully into the passenger seat, was Young Bobby's corpse. His face was still quite recognisable although obviously the colour was gone from it. But it was him, it was her son, and he had somehow come home like this.

Donald was taken away in the police car and Young Bobby's body got zipped up in the back of the ambulance. A female officer stayed behind with Margo and talked to her in a soothing voice. About how Donald was being arrested under suspicion for murder and perverting the course of justice. For insurance fraud and arson. For dangerous driving and manslaughter.

Margo was upset about all of this until the officer told her about Olive. About how that wee girl had been run off the road and Donald hadn't even stopped to check her pulse. After that it was like someone had flipped a switch in her head and she took to letting the officer's consoling words wash over her while she looked out at the lawn and tried to work out how the hell she could ever get the spoiled grass to grow nice again.

413

96

He got there late at night as they were locking the front door and almost didn't let him in, but Galloway said he was here to see Grandpa and the nurses looked at one another and said it would be okay. The staff in the hospice made up a bed for Galloway on the couch in Grandpa's room.

Do you think I need to stay? he asked.

I think it would be a good idea for you to stay, said the nurse in charge.

Grandpa was asleep and Galloway made himself comfortable on the sofa bed. There was a floor-to-ceiling curtain that he could pull over to separate himself from his father but he left it open so that he could see the old man's face if he propped himself up on the cushions.

He wondered how Donald's arrest would affect his position. Northern Constabulary knew that Donald was his source but they did not know the full extent of it. How Galloway accepted bribes and turned a blind eye to the lorry loads of drugs that went pumping through the warehouse and out into the countryside. The violence and the abuse that he had helped Donald to facilitate.

Galloway fell asleep with his neck to the side and when he

woke at some time in the middle of the night it was aching. He twisted his head from side to side to loosen it and got up to pour himself a glass of water at the sink. He took a sip and looked over at Grandpa. The old man was not breathing. He was lying with his mouth open and his eyes closed. His chest was still.

Galloway stepped slowly closer to him and picked up his father's hand. The skin was still warm but there was no pulse there, no longer any life in the old body.

97

The ferry rocked across the water on this hot June day with big fat waves lapping at the side and of caravans and cars with European licence plates and the upper deck packed with walkers and cyclists and a spaniel that barked and tried to chase down the seagulls swooping up and down above the vessel.

Brian was working the morning shift with a new guy called Abel. A middle-aged former accountant who had lost his job for embezzling money and had a nervous stutter when he spoke. Abel had done a few shifts and was learning the procedures quickly. Brian thought he would do fine.

The ferry reached the port at the mainland and the two men waved off the trucks and the motorhomes and the fish delivery van.

Imagine if they came over in a limousine, said Abel. What would that look like?

Aye, that would be something, said Brian.

The stories of the Distillery takeover had been popular in the village and all across the peninsula for the past week. Since Donald's arrest distilling had stopped and the gates had been locked up. The newspapers were full of stories about administrators and creditors and assets. Everyone within a

416

forty-mile radius had been compelled to quickly become familiar with the language of insolvency to be able to keep up meaningfully in any conversation.

The famous story was that an unnamed American investor was going to arrive any day and complete a buyout. How or when he would arrive was open to conjecture.

Imagine trying to get a limousine parked up on here, said Abel. He shook his head at the idea of it. Where would it fit?

We'd make it fit, said Brian. He stared down the loch to where it widened and at some unspecified point became the ocean.

Or helicopter, said Abel. If he comes on helicopter we'll miss it. He would fly over from the west wouldn't he?

Aye, said Brian. Aye, aye, aye.

The last of the vehicles was off and Brian stepped onto the concrete slipway in his yellow hi-vis jacket and opened his arms and started waving the first car in the queue forwards. Come on then fine, he shouted into the air. Fine, fine, fine!

98

It was an old toilet and had been leaking ever since they moved into the bungalow. Innes had made a couple of phone calls at first to the landlord to see about getting it fixed but nothing had come of those. The problem was that it kept running after it was flushed. If you used the toilet before bed it would keep running for an hour or more afterwards. Alice was on her knees with her arms in the cistern up to the elbows seeing if she could fix it herself. She found a loose bolt and was tightening it by hand.

It would be good to get the toilet working properly. Already she had re-sealed the leaking doorframe and cleaned years of grease out of the oven and shampooed the carpets. The bungalow was looking good. The spare bedding was washed and ready for when Innes came back. Alice was ready to commit herself to nursing him back to health. She fancied herself as a good nurse.

She tried the toilet again. It flushed and cleared out the bowl and filled itself back up. She watched the rubber valve floating back to the top of the cistern and when it got there the water stopped running. It worked. Alice dried the water from her arms on her denims and took a look around the bleached bathroom and wiped a streak of dust from the top of the mirror with her finger.

Alice's father had not yet been in touch although she supposed he would probably have been released by now. She had not heard from him; however, in a way she could feel his presence closing in on her. One of these days a letter was going to fall through the door with his handwriting on it. The telephone would ring and she would hear his breath. Or the ferry would depart the mainland with a stranger for a passenger and he would board the bus at the port and it would bring him to her along the winding Shore Road. One of these days.

There was a knock at the back door. Valentine had come to visit. He was looking skinny and someone had given him a bad haircut. His shirt was creased around the bottom and it was clear he'd been wearing it tucked into his trousers earlier but now had pulled it out.

You, she said.

Got a minute?

I've got all day. She stepped to the side and he took off his shoes at the door and came through.

How's Innes? asked the journalist.

He's great. Just having to spend some time at home taking care of things for his mum. She's not doing great. I think he'll be back up here next week.

Alice twisted the engagement ring on her finger so the diamond was facing outwards.

Really?

Yes.

He's okay?

He's fabulous.

Valentine shook his head and reached into his satchel for a notebook.

What's the scoop today then? smiled Alice. They were

sitting on opposite sides of the room and she crossed her legs and leaned her elbows on her knee. Got a hot story?

I wanted to ask you about your suspension from the school, said Valentine. Get your side of things. We think we could run a human interest story about it. Include background information about your dad and your mum maybe. Try to soften your reputation a little bit.

What do you mean?

You must realise that everyone around here thinks you're insane.

Do they?

Yes. Haven't you heard that?

I don't talk to anyone.

I thought this could be a good opportunity to try to, I don't know, clear your name a little. Talk about how you made mistakes but you're a good person and you've learned from them.

The Highland Council made me sign an NDA, said Alice. I can't talk about it.

Our lawyers will look at that. That's not for us to worry about.

Alice got up and walked to the window and looked out. She'd cut the grass in the long garden and it was fresh and rich, the colour of limes.

I don't even know what I'd say, she said. And sat next to Valentine.

Just let me ask some questions and we'll see where we end up, he said. And shifted on the couch a little away from her.

See where we end up? That sounds fun.

I didn't mean it like that.

What do you mean it like?

Stop it. Move your hand away.

You used to like when my hand was here.

I said to stop.

When did you get so boring?

Alice stood up and pulled her top over her head and unbuttoned her denims and unpeeled them from her legs. She put her hands on her hips.

Valentine closed his notebook and took his satchel and left. Alice stood at the door and watched him walk down the driveway. She thought about shouting after him, about telling him he was useless and had never made her happy and that she was pregnant with his child and that she would kill him. But in the end she said nothing.

Back in the clean bungalow Alice walked from room to room without getting dressed. She stopped in the bathroom and clicked on the light and looked at her face in the mirror, her beautiful young face that was only going to get wrinkles and grow ugly and become old. This was the face she was stuck with now.

99

Soon there was a heatwave across the peninsula, moving up from the south, with long hot days and cloudless skies.

The loch began to smell around the edges, like drains and sewage. When the sun lowered the midges came out in swarms and gathered near the street lights and hovered above the gorse and the heather. The flowers in the villagers' gardens grew strong and bright and gladdened anyone who passed by.

There was a big funeral at the church presided over by a temporary priest who was covering until they found a proper replacement. An old man had died. So to commemorate his life lots of other old men and women came and shook hands and looked at one another while a Frank Sinatra song played on the stereo and they buried him where he'd asked to be buried.

At the edge of the water a young woman walked with a blonde-haired dog. It chased its stick and kicked up the sand and ran up to a crowd of strangers eating sandwiches by the loch until the woman shouted for it to stop. Eventually the dog tired and found some shade under a tree and turned in a circle before it lay down there to rest.

Two young boys were splashing about in the loch with the freezing water up to their waists. They had an inflatable ball and bounced it back and forward between them, gasping when the water splashed their ribs, their bared skin growing pinker and pinker as the afternoon went on.

And before long they would all go home. To their mothers and their fathers and their dinners and their beds. But not just yet. There was still time left in the day to play a little longer.

Acknowledgements

Writing a book has been my ambition since I was a wee boy. In 2011, I was posted to Ardnamurchan, in the West Highlands of Scotland, to work as an English teacher. It is a beautiful and sometimes bleak place. A few years later, I went to a whisky-tasting event run by the Tomatin Distillery, having always been fond of a nip. In some strange way, these events interlocked in my mind to inspire this story.

Thanks to Elaine Gillespie, who is the proudest and most caring mum. To Graham Gillespie, whose early encouragements and discussions allowed his firstborn to take this writing thing seriously. To my grandparents Mary, Jimmy, Tommy and Helen – thank you for nurturing my passions. To the boys from Glenrothes and Stirling for good company and friendship, through school and beyond.

I am grateful for lessons learned during sessions with the Glasgow Writers' Group, the University of Glasgow's Creative Writing staff, and the G2 Writers. Particular cheers are due to Bob McDevitt, George Craig and Alex Cox, for their smart advice and counsel. David Irvine, Bryan Laing, Barry Crookston and Mark Dalloway are Police Scotland's finest, and formed a knowledgeable sounding board. Any slips in procedure are mine alone.

This career as an English teacher can be all-consuming, and the offer to publish *The Mash House* came as I was losing sight of my ambition to write. Thanks are due to Xander Cansell, Anna Simpson, Andrew Chapman, Robert Leventhley, and everyone at Unbound for their hard work and cheer. Also to my editor, Russel McLean, for providing clarity and kindness with that messy first draft. I am thankful for the contribution of Laura Barbour, who brought the landscape of Cullrothes to life.

I have been fortunate to work alongside inspirational figures, whose mentorship has meant a lot: Laura Murphy, Patrick Scanlan, Andy Mimnagh, Raymond Soltysek, Robert Getty, Emma Corr, and many others. To my hard-working colleagues, wonderful students and the parents at Fernhill School – thank you for making ours the best wee school in Scotland.

As always, I owe everything to my brilliant wife, Chloe, and our wonderful daughter, Sofia; you motivate and inspire me more than you can know.

Finally, I am grateful to each reader, supporter and pledger who helped make this book a reality. Thank you for making this dream come true. I raise a glass. Here's to you.

Patrons

Unbound is the world's first crowdfunding publisher, established in 2011.

We believe that wonderful things can happen when you clear a path for people who share a passion. That's why we've built a platform that brings together readers and authors to crowdfund books they believe in – and give fresh ideas that don't fit the traditional mould the chance they deserve.

This book is in your hands because readers made it possible. Everyone who pledged their support is listed at the front of the book and below. Join them by visiting unbound.com and supporting a book today.

Diane Adam
Victoria Addams
Eli Allison
Karen Anderson
Julie Bale
Nicola Balkind
Gráinne Ballantyne
Laura Barbour

Alison Barclay
Damian Barr
Elise Barr
Kitty Barrett
Zena Barrie
Fathima Bashir
Alan Bell
Brenda Bell

Jonathan Bell
Terry Bergin
Alan Bissett
Fiona Bowie
Nikki Boyd
Alistair Braidwood
Nick Brooks
Gavin Broom
Dan Brotzel, Martin Jenkins & Alex Woolf
Emmie Brown
Karen Brown
Bekah Bundy
Maria Burns
Sadie Burns
J C
Margaret Callaghan
Sandy Cameron
Cheryl Campbell
Jillian Campbell
Margaret Campbell
Neil Cannon
Steve Cannon
Kit Cardinal
Deborah Carmichael
Piaras Carney
Mary Carrera
Jacqui Castle
Samina Chaudhry
Catriona Child
Jamie Chipperfield
Sue Clark
Johnny Comelately
Morag Connor
Susan Conroy
Brian Cook
Jude Cook
Robert Cox
Andrea Currie
Lynne Davidson
Bethany Davis
Clare Deans
Glenn Dietz
Samuel Dodson
Mark Donaldson
Georgia-May Drennan

Gerry Duggan
Gill Dunkley
Robert Eardley
Nicola Elliott
Gavin Emerson
Carol Farrelly
Dean Friedman
Laura Fyfe
Lynn Genevieve
Robert Getty
Alan Gibson
Elaine Gillespie
Ross Gillespie
Tom Gillespie
Lee Gillies
Brendan Gisby
Rodge Glass
Robbie Gorman
Josephine Greenland
Lisa Hamilton
Kathleen Harley
Linda Harris
Sylvia Hehir
Henry Hepburn
Blair & Laura Hopcroft
Philip Hopcroft
Morag Hughes
Zoe Hughes
Gareth Hunter
Bettina Hutchins
Colin Hutton
Nasim Marie Jafry
Jamie
Wendy Keiller
Marie Kelly
Sarah Kelly
Patricia Kennedy
Jacqueline Kiani
Dan Kieran
Shelley Kilgour
Patrick Kincaid
Lillian Kirk
Mit Lahiri
Diane Larkin
Andrew Leask
Pascal Lehner

428

Rebecca Lenagh-Snow
Chris Limb
Jacqueline MacDonald
Fiona Mhairi MacKenzie
Katie Mackenzie
Lynsey May
Heather McArthur
Lynn McCann
Suzanne McClafferty
Imogen McFadden
Mrs Mcfadyen
Ilona McGowan
Carol McGregor
Susie McIvor
Sophie McNaughton
Sean Medeiros
Orla Millar
Sheila Millar
John Mitchinson
Linda Mooney
Eve Moore
Fiona Morrison
Bernard Mournain
Maureen Moyes
Duncan Muir
Kenneth Myklebust
Carlo Navato
Frank Newall
Peter Newman
Michele Noble
Kirsty Nolan
Terry O'Neill
Catherine Ogston
Sheena Oo
Cameron Palmer
Alli Parrett
Iain Banzai Paton
Tracy Patrick
Simon Patterson
Mitchell Penman
Katherine Petersen
Kenny Pieper
Justin Pollard
Ben Potter
Sobia Quazi
Nicky Quint

Louise Rae
Shona Renicks
Gail Richardson
Maureen Robertson
Sandra Robertson
Andrew Ross
Peter Ross
Ross Sayers
Patrick Scanlan
Kevin Scott
Erin Sinclair
Lauren Sinclair
Ian Skewis
Jordan Slaven
Peter Sleight
Daniella Smith
India Smith
Lynsey Smith
Elissa Soave
Rebecca Spiers
Liz Stark
Nicola Stevenson
Eilidh Stirling
Orlaith Stirling
Simon Sylvester
Alison Tausney
Helen Taylor
Maisie Taylor
Christine Telford
Scott Tweddle
Alison Ure
Jonathan Walker
Michelle Walton
Tom Ward
Mia Hannah Watson
Andy Way
Jo Whitby
Elaine Wilders
Allan Wilson
Campbell Wilson
Derek Wilson
Helen Wilson
Karen Wilson
Phil Wilson
Henry Wright
Rachael Yates

429